COMPOSER OF THE CALM HORIZON

ESCAPE TO A NEW WORLD

COMPOSER OF THE CALM HORIZON:

ESCAPE TO A NEW WORLD

BY
AL ROMANO

This book is a work of fiction. The names, characters and events in this book are the products of the author's imagination or are used fictitiously. Any similarity to real persons living or dead is coincidental and not intended by the author.

COMPOSER OF THE CALM HORIZON: ESCAPE TO A NEW WORLD

ISBN: 9781093457155

Contents

PROLOGUE

The Karin'ga lies down in her own pool of blood, abandoned to die in one of the many forests of the Novaverse, with her arm torn right from her socket and a big chunk of meat missing from her neck. Her hair becomes soaked red and her objective beauty obscured by the crimson liquid that stains her face.

Next to her dying body a purple smoke quickly appears and disappears in the blink of an eye. The Doamar'ga finally arrives, responding to the distress call he received from the area. He looks down and he is shocked at the sight of what he now witnesses. He knows what has happened, but he doesn't want to believe it, even though the knowledge of such cannot be denied.

He crouches down to receive a final whisper that she might emit from her nearly destroyed vocal chords, hoping for a sign that she can still be saved. But it is evident from the sight of her mutilated being that she is seconds away from departing from this realm. But just as he feels the disappointment in himself, she violently coughs out the blood from her throat with whatever life she has left in her. With enough power to make her voice heard one last time, she utters naught but one name:

Sima Brak!

CHAPTER I

THE ONLY ONE THAT CAN KEEP THE THREADS AWAY

As I sit shirtless in my own personal bathroom like an Indian, I stare at the matchbox that's right beside my feet. I contemplate whether I should summon her or not.

Her ability to help me has gotten weaker over the years, and I don't think my life is getting any easier. I push through life in hopes that I will one day see the light, because the harder it becomes to subsist here, the more I just want to leave. Knowing how much I need this help, I reluctantly realize that I need her more than ever, even though that logic pretty much applies to every day of my godforsaken life.

I take the matchbox and pull a match out of it. I stare at the match and the box three seconds longer than I usually do, as I sigh and fill my mind with doubt over this session. Nevertheless, I go with it.

I light up the match. The gentle fire at the tip of it glows with such magnificence as it slowly burns down the rest of the match. Alas, the match's fire must be put out prematurely as I swing it through the air.

And as the smoke emits and fills the bathroom, one might wonder how one match can release so much smoke. I don't, because I already know the answer.

The smoke continues to fill the bathroom slowly and surely, until all there is left to breathe is nothing but it, and the sight of all is obscured by none other than it. I endure, for I know that very shortly she will appear.

And as the fumes slowly fill my lungs, choking me, poisoning me, the smoke collects right in the middle of the bathroom, right in front of me. As I stare at it from below, it takes the appearance of a ball. The ball quickly shifts its appearance to that of a figure. A womanly figure, might I say. Of course, this is no surprise to me. I also know that she won't settle for just appearing gently before my eyes, as she has this urge to come out with a bang.

The smoke violently disperses in all directions, rebounding against the walls and getting in my eyes. The mild sensation of hotness doesn't even bother me as I rub my eyes to relieve me of the pain. Faster than expected, I am back to being able to use them. The smoke around me has nearly dissipated, but the main attraction of this whole event is the lady in the middle.

The conjurer of the faucet! Standing as tall as the bathroom itself, her powers of cleansing the mind are only rivaled by her unusual appearance. With a long black skirt covering her legs, made from metallic silk as the bladed edge of it touches the surface of the bathroom. An equally black vest made from the same material, with a diamond-shaped hole in the middle of it, shows her cleavage. Her attire, seemingly made from darkness, would be an ironic choice of clothing considering her snow-white skin and slim physique which made her look like a porcelain doll. But the most intricate feature of all was that crest on her head, or is it really a crown? Shaped like a rotting rose that was deprived of its beauty, it too was pitch black; its three bladed points, wide and sharp, were crudely bent upwards, waiting for an innocent bird to sit on the tip, only to get impaled. It's a shame she has to wear such unnerving head gear, as it completely distracts viewers from her remarkable, unusually beautiful face which, weirdly enough, had no prominent features, because she just looks like a silky smooth statue. Did I mention she floats? So she isn't actually as tall as the room, but it sure seems like it.

"Hello, Neph." She says in a gentle, motherly voice. "What will it be today?"

"The usual," I tell her in a disgruntled but nonchalant kind of way.

As the deal for today's session has been established, I stand up and go to lie down inside the bathtub. I lean my head backwards and hold my torso against the surface of the tub with my elbows, for it is necessary for the process.

She hovers above me. And as I look her in the eyes and mentally prepare myself for what's coming ahead, she moves her hands around in front of my face. Her movements are so enigmatic yet so pleasant to watch at the same time, as if she were playing with smoke, making it move in different directions and giving it shape. Yet there is no smoke and I already know what she's doing, for I have seen this several times already.

I can feel something cold sitting on my forehead. The smell of rust fills my nasal cavity as what I'm feeling now becomes heavier with every second. Barely seeing what it is with my peripheral vision as it's just above my eyes, I can see grey particles moving inwards and outwards from their gathering point which is my forehead. Slowly but surely, they start to fly around violently, with more particles joining in. They become even heavier as they collect at one point, but the heavier they become the less they appear. Of course, I shouldn't be surprised as to what's forming on my forehead, yet each time it amazes me anew.

And as the particles slowly stop their appearance from out of nowhere, a faucet materializes on my forehead, directed outwards so as to not wet the front of my body.

Continuing with her enigmatic hand movements, the faucet's handle seemingly turns by itself as a nasty creak echoes off the ceramic walls of the bathroom, something which hasn't happened in the previous sessions. As it slowly turns and creaks, I await the pleasant sensation that will come ahead.

I start to hear the flow of water as the upper portion of my back feels a cold wetness. The cold sensation continues all the way down to my feet as my pants get soaked. I bring my hand in front of me, and as I see lavender water dripping down my wrist, I am reminded that it's not water coming out of the faucet, but the pressurized anguishes of my mentality given liquid form, as the conjurer would call it.

As the tub continues to fill, all but my head is completely submerged in this liquid as I feel a relaxation surging through my body. I feel like I'm receiving a scalp massage from the hands of a goddess, as my nerves tingle throughout my body and the hardships of my life physically squeeze out of all the pores. I feel like I'm floating, only to next roll around in the air as my arms and legs are slowly rendered into nothingness, until the only feeling that remains is that I do not exist. Now, whatever I am is no more; all concepts of positive and negative become obsolete, for I am a higher being that only exists in the minds of nihilists. A divine sensation I enjoy so much, no matter how often I do it.

Before I even know it, I am back to myself, upside down in a field of nothing, hanging by chains constricted around my feet as their base on the ceiling is just about to crumble due to my weight. The faucet is still on my forehead, endlessly releasing the lavender waters of my mind as the stream falls down to nowhere. It doesn't seem like it is about to end soon, as the feeling of relaxation continues to move within me.

And as I continue to enjoy this, the conjurer materializes out of nowhere right in front of me. She continues to enigmatically move her hands in front of me.

"Close your eyes," she gently orders me.

I do as she says.

Phosphenes rapidly change in shape and design as I continue to feel the relaxation surging through me. Black spots and white waves slowly become concrete images of wonderful worlds filled with magic and mystery. I wonder what I will see this time.

"What do you see, Neph?" she gently asks me.

I take my time to answer her, for the images still need to form before I can clearly see what they are.

"I see . . . ," I tell her, unsure of what I see, "a desert."

"And what happens in the desert?" she asks me.

I take my time to answer her once more.

"I . . . ," I struggle to reply. "I'm jumping really high. I can even touch the clouds."

"Now . . . ," she asks me. "What do you see in the desert?"

"I can see . . . a mountain of sand . . . and an oasis. Wait! It's not a mountain. It's a . . . a building?"

"A building? What would a building be doing in a desert?"

"It looks like a skyscraper. It's not even finished, and there seems to be several construction workers."

"Do you see anything else?"

"The unfinished building is now gone. I now see a . . . hotel? I'm still in the desert, but it seems to be a fancy hotel."

"Go into the hotel. Now . . . what do you see?"

"I'm at the courtyard. There seems to be a large buffet, and some nice jazz music. A lot of people are out here, and they are dressed really . . . fancy. Wait! I'm now inside the hotel . . . in a ballroom."

"What do you see in the ballroom?"

"I see . . . a lot of people dancing. But there seems to be a . . . there seems to be . . . one girl that isn't dancing. She's standing by herself at the corner."

"What does she look like?"

And at that moment, my mouth was completely robbed of words as I couldn't find them to tell the conjurer what I see. I am captivated by how incredibly beautiful this girl is. With her ocean-blue eyes and her smooth black hair reaching all the way to her lower back, it wouldn't be her blue gown that would catch the attention of her would-be dancing partner. She is prettier than a thousand auroras exploding in the night; more beautiful than the most sparkling gem forged under the best conditions of the earth's crust; a girl so beautiful, that if you put her in a field of butterflies, they would all revert back to caterpillars out of shame.

"She is . . . ," I struggle to find the words to tell the conjurer, "incredibly beautiful. Like . . . beyond words."

"I see." She tells me gently, supposedly intrigued. "Approach her."

And as the conjurer commands, I do so.

I slowly approach the girl. By the time I made it halfway, she seemed to notice that I was making my way towards her. She smiles at me with her beautiful white teeth as I continue to be captivated by her beauty. I, on the other hand, can't tell how I'm responding to her, as I can only feel myself moving and nothing else.

Surprisingly, she reaches her hand out to me, supposedly desiring to dance. I, too, reach out to her, but I can only feel my hand stretching out, as it is nowhere to be seen. But before I could hold her hand, the sight of everything around me starts to distort.

"Rrrghh," I grunt.

"What's the matter, Neph?" the conjurer asks me gently, not even for a moment panicking.

"I'm losing it." I tell her nervously.

The imaginative world that I'm in slowly falls apart as it continues to distort and slowly disappear.

"Hold it together, Neph." The conjurer tells me calmly. "You can do it."

But no matter how strong her words seem, and how much she encourages me, I can't muster the strength to pull myself together. With this realization, the world around continues to crumble.

"I . . . CAN'T!" I exclaim nervously as I continue to fail.

"You can do it, Neph." She continues to encourage me. "I know you can."

Despite her words filled with motherly benevolence, I can't fix this world. I can't fix this vision of pleasantness and enchantment as it continues to fall apart beyond recognition.

Yet despite the inevitable, I am unwilling to just yield and leave this wonderful place. I am suddenly fueled with the desire to save, as I can feel myself clenching my jaw and grinding my teeth as the veins on my forehead pump with blood. The world around me vibrates with psychedelic colors as it somehow manages to fix the cracks on the floor and the dancers reappear once more, only to revert to its destructive state immediately afterwards.

But the more energy I exert, the more I am left without to save this world; I realize that despite my strength, I can't do anything. I give it one last shot.

"AAAAAAAAAAAAAAAAAAHHHHHHHHHH!" I shout as I release every bit of strength I have left to save this paradise.

But it was of no avail, as I find myself once more in my own personal bathroom, lying down on the ceramic floor with arms spread apart as I stare at the light bulb in the middle of the ceiling, helpless to bring back what I couldn't. I am dry again, the faucet on my forehead is gone and the conjurer is nowhere to be seen. Of course, despite my frustration, this comes as no surprise to me, as this the end of every session.

And as I continue to stare at the ceiling like some kind of dolt, I wonder how long I will need these sessions. I know full well that they will be needed for as long as I stay in this prison. The prison that keeps me in chains to this miserable life that I so desperately try to escape from, contaminated by the same ignorant society that condemns me for no logical reason. And even though I know that I will need them still, I just hope it will end very soon.

And just as my vision gets blurry and I slowly fall asleep, I can hear the wind blowing in my ear, as if it's trying to tell me something.

"I'm sorry, Neph." The voice of the conjurer gently makes itself heard. "I promise . . . I will get you out of here . . . in time."

CHAPTER II

YET ANOTHER DAY . . . WHERE I HOPE THE NEXT ONE WILL BE BETTER THAN THE LAST

The conjurer of the faucet: she is the only one that can keep the threads away. The tar-black threads that seemingly materialize out of nowhere; moving, twirling and swirling in random directions like a thin snake slithering through the air. Each one is a messenger of doom, as everything falls apart when they appear so that they can be formed, rendering everything to nothingness, while only they stay. Because of this, the conjurer just spontaneously appeared one day in front of me, offering her services to me. She is able to show me worlds within worlds that change dynamically over and over, without the horrors of ever witnessing the threads. I can't exactly recall when they first came to me and showed themselves in front of my eyes. Not that it matters anyway, since I would have to deal with them eventually. And although at first it was tough, over the years, they became substantially easier to handle. Nevertheless, I can't find myself being able to accept them, as they represent the worst of me.

Of course, one might ask: how come I've never told anyone about this? And what? Have them lock me up in some padded room? Classify me as a whackjob; take away all my hopes and all that I have worked for? Not a chance. Society is foul enough as it is even without the threads. They say that shrinks are here to protect you. Truth is, they're here to protect others from you, as all the actions they take create gaps in society, locking away the chosen ones while allowing the weak ones to thrive and reproduce, creating even more inferior offspring. It's a shame, considering all those who have a unique power never get to express it, seemingly because they were deemed incapable of being part of society. I can't imagine who would be ignorant enough to desire to be part of this corrupt society, other than everyone. I don't plan to let them do that to me. Besides, it's not insanity if nobody knows about it.

But . . . horrendous feelings aside, it's time to get the day started. Not that there's much to do but whatever.

I know that it's a Sunday. So naturally, no school. I get up from lying down on the floor to sitting on it. I rub my eyes with my index finger and thumb, as I prepare myself for whatever I'm planning today, and I can't imagine there isn't much. Other than a date, of course.

I hear a distinctive growl coming from the entrance to the bathroom. It's Grasshead, who just woke up alongside me, waddling his way towards me with eyes partially closed.

"Morning, boy," I calmly tell him.

About Grasshead: I'm not sure how to describe him, but this guy ain't no dog. I think it would be easy to start with the fact that he's too big to be one, being three feet eight inches at the shoulder and twenty-three feet long, with a giant iguana-like tail to boot, a muscular body and dinosaur-like reptilian legs with sharp claws. I would like to say the body reminds me of that of a tiger, but the chest area is rather broad to be one. But what I find really eye-catching about Grasshead are the features that contributed to his name: the head and the fur. He has a big head, definitely not one that looks like it fits on his body. I'd have to say that it's about the size of a car engine, which is fitting considering that every time he opens his mouth he looks like he's about to crunch down on one, with a mouth full of giant teeth and vicious fangs. And of course, there's the fur, which just looks like grass, but feels nothing like it.

What is he? I have no idea. He comes in an unusual package: sort of the body of a tiger, a tail of a giant iguana, the legs of a raptor, the behavior of a dog, mountable like a horse and a dragonesque appearance. I just call him a monster-dog-thing for short. I think that term more or less sums up what he's all about.

But man, he and I go way back, and that's only relative because we've been together for four years. I remember when I first saw him, and it was an unpleasant sight to behold. He was being tortured in the woods by this local bully, a sadistic one too. Being battered and whacked with a stick over and over, the poor creature tried to free himself from the rope that tied him to a tree, but his legs couldn't even bear to hold up his body anymore after all that beating. At first I just witnessed, contemplating whether it's the right thing to interfere or not. The bully, the name of which I do not know, didn't even care about what he was beating—the creature looked like nothing ever seen before—and he enjoyed every moment the stick in his hand laid down upon the creature's skin. I was just about to walk away, but then I remembered what my life is about: Never abandon a friend. Even though the creature I knew was far from my friend, I could not stand the sight of a poor defenseless creature slowly dying at the hands of filth predestined to suffer for an eternity in the afterlife. I knew what the right action was, so I charged over there.

As I threw the kid down to the ground and beat his face in senselessly, for a moment I forgot what I was doing as the rage within me consumed me, and then I remembered I'm here to save someone, not hurt someone. I get up from the kid and he runs away with his face all red and nose all bleeding as I free the creature, releasing him from his torment.

Of course, I couldn't just leave him there by himself, so I decided to take him with me. Seeing that I don't have the desire or the patience to explain to my poor excuse of a family what I brought in, I just had to sneak him in. Surprisingly, it worked, and he's been hiding in my room since then. Of course, nobody ever comes to my room so it's not that hard keeping him a secret. I should probably mention that back then he was the size of a cat. Yeah, back then he was so small that when I snuck him out to take him for walks in the forest, he was riding on my back. Eventually, he became so big I was the one riding on his back!

Truth is, the memories of Grasshead are the only good memories I'd had in a while, and everything else is garbage. But I have to stop reminiscing and get this day started.

I get up from the floor as my body is still partially numb and my eyes half closed. Looking in the mirror, I can't help but notice that there are two things that haven't gone away, and I can't imagine they'll be leaving any time soon. Two key features that make up both my face and personality.

The first, the more prominent feature—actually THREE key features when you think about it, but I constitute them as one since they come in a package—is the three scars on my face, collectively referred to as the trifecta. First, there's the straight clean one that starts from between my eyebrows and ends just left of my left nostril, known as "the clean." Then, there's the crescent-shaped one on my right temple, with the horns pointing away from the eye, known as "the crescent." Finally, there's the cross-shaped one on my left cheek, known as "the cross." Don't ask me why I gave them names.

I rub the scars gently, each at its own turn; starting with the clean, going on to the crescent, and finally finishing it with the cross. I sigh as I try to forget their existence and pretend they're not there. But alas, they're still on my face, making me look like a murderer.

Weirdly enough, the scars don't appear in the conjurer's sessions. I would prefer not to think about it every time I look at them, but it's inevitable for me to remember all the hardships I've been through and the climactically serious ones that caused them in the first place. Tough life, but I have to push through, as I know that one day I will find myself in a better place. A place not ruled by this ignorant society. Hopefully, once I reach that place, I might just think that these scars paid off. But until then, I am bound to suffer endlessly at the hands of the filth that contaminates this world.

Of course, the scars are my more melancholic features, as looking at them all the time reminds me of nothing but pain. The more uplifting feature is the one I supposedly control, yet don't at the same time: the eternal frown.

The frown that just sits there on my forehead and seemingly refuses to leave. Waves of muscles and skin on the forehead and eyebrows bent downwards. It shows regardless of what expression I have on my face at the time, be it smiling or smirking or whatever, even though I'm more likely to smirk than smile, as it is not really representative of my inner state. Out of the two key features, this one doesn't bother me as much as the other one, as it is more subtle.

But what the two have in common is where they came from and where they end up: anger. A history of struggles that slowly built within me, growing and manifesting until it exploded outwards in physical form. Unfortunately, this was unavoidable, although I wish it had been. My life could've been a lot better without all this anger. Hopefully, one day . . . I can get rid of all of it.

But . . . I better put aside all that melancholy, as I have plans for today, and I plan to get on them right now.

I go back to my room and open my closet. I take out a random shirt, socks, a pair of jeans and a hoodie. I don't even bother to look at what color they are, but I'm pretty sure the socks are white, as it's only natural. One thing I do give my attention to is the fact that I don't zip up my hoodie, as I like it that way, and anyone who doesn't like it can get bent.

Following this, I walk down the stairs, telling Grasshead to stay behind to wait for whenever I come back. After all, I wouldn't want to cause a commotion in the house.

Reaching the first floor of the house, I look to my left and see my two younger step-sisters, Katie and Stephanie, sitting in the living room, eating cereal and watching something on TV. I couldn't care less what they are watching. To my right, I see a man who is my dad in name only, already prepared for work, sitting in the kitchen with a mug of coffee in one hand, while the other hand flips the pages of the newspaper. His name is James, by the way.

I go to the kitchen, grab myself a carton of milk, a bowl, a spoon, and then sit down to have a bowl of some random cereal.

As I chomp down on the cereal, bit after bit, with each scoop of the spoon digging into the bowl's contents, my dad glares at me with cold eyes as he simultaneously flips one page of the newspaper that he's reading. And after that trade of stares that we had one to the other, with equally cold eyes, he returns to looking back at the newspaper, but not before taking a loud sip of his coffee.

"Morning," he says.

"Morning," I reply.

"So uh . . . got any plans today?"

"Not much. I got a date with this girl at eight."

"Oh really? What's her name?"

"Kim."

"That's nice. Is she pretty?"

"She's okay, I guess. What about you? Why are you going to work? It's Sunday."

"Working on a project. Deadline is in about a month."

"Cool," I remark sarcastically in a nonchalant fashion.

We have a pretty dysfunctional relationship, he and I. Every day he looks at me with that disappointed look in his eyes, constantly wondering why I exist, endlessly blaming me for the death of my mother, Claudia. The contempt in his eyes hits so strong that it feels like he wants to tell me that I in fact murdered her. But the truth is I had just been born that moment, so there's no possible way I could've done it, at least not intentionally. But to him it wasn't just death from childbirth, but a baby born with a knife in his hand that crawled up his own mother just to stab her in the heart. But no matter the facts, and the reality that such scenarios could never happen, he could never accept me; he's constantly rejecting me, and in return, he receives the same amount of rejection.

I don't know what he felt for my mother, but I definitely know what he feels for me, and I definitely know what I feel for him. Supposedly, his feelings for her were strong enough to commit to her and keep me around. Unfortunately, this commitment only comes in the form of lending money and all the necessities that parents have to take, and it's the not the "I love you" kind of lending money, but the "take this and get out of my face" kind. Kind of sucks for me as I don't have a loving father to be with or a father figure to look up to. Even worse, he gives more love to my damn stepsisters, and they're not even his real children. But all that doesn't matter, as I will leave this place one day and never come back. I know it.

Speaking of stepsisters, my relationship with the other part of the family isn't too good either. Heck . . . I might even say far from that. Katie and Stephanie, the two stepsisters that I'm talking about, are only seven and nine. Naturally, they would care for the things that concern them, and I'm definitely not part of that package. More so, they wouldn't even bat an eye if I died. I'm sure I wouldn't either. I might even be happy about it. The same goes for their mother, Jessica, who would rather tend to her own children, naturally, and leave me to her husband, which is not saying much because he doesn't actually do anything with me.

Basically, everyone only cares for what benefits them in the end. Such is this cruel, ugly society.

But as I continue to complain about the mountain of bullshit that forms this society, the day passes by. And as it goes by, the time comes for me to meet Kim without me even noticing, as whatever I was doing until then distracted me.

Naturally, I walk to the place where we're supposed to meet and sooner rather than later, I arrive at the park.

Kind of an unorthodox place for a date, but I prefer a place with fewer people and eyes for me to be stared at with. Usually, people would prefer a restaurant or maybe even a movie for a date; there's a fancy Asian restaurant a few blocks from here too. I actually considered going there, since I really like chow mein; but once again, I prefer somewhere more quiet where I can focus on what's important without the atmosphere becoming too tense; where others can have a normal meal without concern that I might burn the place down. After all, nobody wants to mess with "the fire kid."

I don't think I should have a problem with this one. Seeing that the time is eight p.m., there aren't too many people and dusk is approaching so there's still a bit of light. I can see a mom with her two children by the slides, and there's a guy walking his dog by the trees. They've all got their cautious eyes on me, but seeing as there aren't too many people right now, I don't think there should be much of a problem, just as long they keep their distance. At least the heap of pigeons by the bench don't really seem to mind my presence.

I can see that she's a bit late, as it is already six minutes past our meeting time. Maybe next time I won't come so early.

But just I start to ponder that, I see her in the distance, walking slowly towards me and I feel I am required to wait for her to arrive. My impatience gets the better of me because it seems like forever until she'll reach me. It's as if she's a comet flying a path between celestial bodies that are separated light years from each other, and I'm the planet that's just gazing at her, waiting millennia for her to crash land onto my surface.

Finally she arrives and her beauty becomes more and more apparent. Being the pessimist that I am, brought on me by the society that contaminates this world, I merely smirk back at her. As she finally stands in front of me, we greet each other with a hug and a kiss on the cheek, as it's supposed to be.

Looking aside for a second, I see some people still looking, only this time their expression had more disgust in it than fear or concern for the worst. Nonetheless, I bring my attention back to Kim.

"Don't mind them," she tells me calmly.

"Believe me," I start to tell her, "I don't mind them as much as they mind me."

"Well, you're a force to be reckoned with, after all," she tells me wittily with a smile.

"Aren't you afraid?" I sarcastically ask her.

"Why? Are you gonna burn me?" she says, keeping with the witty attitude.

"I might."

She giggles as she tries to keep herself from smiling, although she can't help but show her white teeth. I smirk in response, as that is the most I can do to show the small amount of joy I feel toward her. It's directed at her personally, as I can hardly feel any positive feelings nowadays.

"Shall we start walking?" I ask her in a supposedly gentlemanly kind of way.

She says nothing, as her expression alone indicates that she approves. And with that, we start walking.

"Y'know . . . ," I start to say, "not many people would wanna hang out with me, let alone go on a date with me. You kinda surprised me with that. It means a lot to me."

"Yeah? Well, I don't believe in stereotypes," she says with utter certainty.

"Y'know, stereotypes don't just come out from nowhere," I tell her. "Every stigma has a story. Even if that story is complete bullshit."

"Maybe. But most of them aren't true."

"Aren't they?"

"What are you saying? That you did burn down that building?"

"Is that the implication? I'm sorry. I just meant to say that most urban legends are told by stupid people. Stories invented by stupid people FOR stupid people."

"Well . . . we think alike."

"I guess," I say, mildly sad considering where the conversation is going.

A slight silence occurred between us, mostly because of me, as the thought of this whole "burning down the building" thing keeps getting to me over and over. This is my bane, as it's what caused people to distance themselves from me in the first place. It's saddening, but I keep reminding myself of what my goal is, and that goal is to get the hell out of this place and start anew. And it will happen.

"C'mon," she suddenly says, cheerfully too. "Don't let it get to your head. You're famous!"

"Infamous, actually. Heh," I sarcastically say.

Once more, silence occurs, and again it comes from me. I'm starting to feel that I might bomb this date, as these feelings of anger keep coming over me. I need to be better than this.

"Where were you when it happened?" she asks me, although a bit hesitant.

"When what happened?" I ask her, confused as I'm deep in my own thoughts.

"The fire."

"Oh, that. Well . . . truth is . . . I can't really remember. Probably because I inhaled too much carbon monoxide. That's what the black smoke is called, right? The one emitted by fires."

"So you were there when it happened?"

"I guess I was. Maybe that's why everyone attributes the events to me. That and they couldn't find anyone else."

"Hmm. But I can't believe that everyone heard of it really fast."

"Well when you're living in a small town, word spreads like fire."

With that pun, she just starts laughing. Of course, she calms down rather fast. I just smirk, naturally; although I couldn't say that she noticed it considering that she was really enjoying that joke. It just came out the top of my head.

"You're cool, you know that?" she tells me.

"Wish everyone thought that way," I say sarcastically.

"Don't worry. I'm sure everything will work out in the end."

"Hopefully," I say, sarcastic once more.

I'm not even paying attention to where we are going as I was way into our conversation. I know this park like the back of my hand so I can instinctively find myself in a specific place I want to be. I've never had the opportunity to talk to someone while walking here, so I guess it's kind of a different feeling. Right now, I find myself by a bunch of trees on the outskirts of the park.

"You like it here?" I ask her.

"The park?" she asks me in return.

"Yeah, y'know, walking around the park and shit. I mean, most people would rather go to restaurants or something like that."

"Well, I guess you didn't take me to one because you can't afford it," she jokingly says.

"Not just that. Heh. It's also quiet here. I like it; I find it enjoyable. Just thought maybe you'd find it . . . uh . . . unusual."

"Nah. It's 'kay. It's always nice to try out something new."

"Wish I could say that for everything," I sarcastically say.

Our conversation grinds to a halt as I think about Kim. She's not like all the other girls, let alone all the other people. I want to express that to her.

"You're . . . very nice," I tell her hesitantly.

"Thanks . . . I guess," she tells me, also hesitantly.

"What? Not many people tell you that?"

"Well . . . no, actually. I don't get that a lot from my friends."

"At least you have friends. Most people just take me for shit, y'know."

She says nothing in return, but remains completely silent. I guess I might've hit a weak spot or something.

"The world needs more people like you," I continue to tell her. "Who knows, maybe then it would have less shit in it."

"Hmm," she says cautiously. "Maybe."

I don't understand what I just did. I can't imagine that what I just said can be that bad. She's probably used to just being different with everyone else so that her friends don't really have the opportunity to compliment her in that way.

"Hey, don't feel too bad right now." I try to cheer her up. "Look at what you get from this. You stood next to me, and you get to live the tale. You shoulda been crispy by now."

With that, she starts laughing, putting a smile on her face once more. At that moment, I know I did the right thing. And seeing her smile once more, it made me feel like I'm not the bad guy that people make of me. I could say that it made me feel . . . a tad better about myself and by extension, my life. But . . . I'll need more than a happy girl to compensate for all the wrongs that inhabit my life. A lot more than that, since what I need right now is an overhaul.

I realize at that moment that I'm avoiding what's important right now: the date. I need to remind myself to lean less towards the anger when it calls for it. I'll have to go on more dates to work on that.

Regardless, I have an idea that will make this date more enjoyable . . . assuming Kim doesn't have high standards for recreation, of course.

"How 'bout we go feed the pigeons?" I tell her. "I have some bread crumbs with me."

"Sure. Why not?" she tells me happily.

We head over to the pigeons from wherever we were at the park. Naturally, they were gathering by the bench, as that is the spot where they usually get to eat whatever people are throwing at them. I suppose they've realized that already.

So with a sack of bread crumbs in one hand, I take some with the other hand and spread it over the pigeons. The crumbs haven't even landed on the ground and they already jump up to catch with their small beaks, swirling together over it, fighting each other over who will get the most bites like a bunch of piranhas on a heron.

"Look at them," I tell Kim as I stare at the pigeons with such fascination. "The bread hasn't even hit the ground, and they're already jumping in the air to catch it. They couldn't wait half a second longer."

"And look how they're fighting over it," Kim remarks in curiosity.

"I don't think they're actually fighting over it. I don't think they're even aware that their friends also want some. I think they just realize that its food and they jump on it."

I feel a bit of joy hanging out with Kim and feeding the pigeons. I don't get a lot of opportunities like this. Better savor it while it lasts, because while I'll always have the pigeons around to provide me with company, even though they aren't aware of it, Kim won't be around much, and eventually I'll have to return to the place of anger and loneliness. The place that reminds me that I need to stay strong, for my sake and for the future that I envision for myself. And I will stay strong.

But while it lasts, I feel a bit of serenity amidst all my anger, temporarily engulfing it, hiding it from me so I can feel something else.

It's a nice feeling. Better hold on to it while it's still there.

"You think they care?" I ask Kim curiously.

"Who?" she asks me obliviously.

"The pigeons. People feed them all the time, but do you think that they're actually . . . grateful? Y'know, like they know that people are feeding them."

"Well it's . . . like you said," She starts to say hesitantly. "They only see food. I guess that's the only thing that matters to them."

"I like to think otherwise. Feeding makes me feel like I'm actually doing something good. Like I'm actually helping someone. Someone that can't help himself, so they need someone's help to eat."

"They have plenty of food. Trust me."

"Yeah, I know but . . . they like the food, and I like feeding them. I guess that makes it a win-win. Even if they don't actually appreciate it, I like to pretend that they do because it . . . it . . . uh . . . makes me feel like I'm useful to someone. Unlike what most people make me feel like."

I look at Kim, and I see her smirking. I didn't quite understand it at first, but I can't imagine it was a sign of mockery. Maybe she didn't quite know how to express it at first, but I'm pretty sure she had something sophisticated in mind.

"What?" I ask her, inquiring about her smirk.

"Hey . . . ," she starts to tell me calmly and compassionately. "You always have me."

"Yeah," I respond hesitantly.

I don't quite know how to feel about this. I'm not used to being with someone who actually gives a damn about my existence. Most of the time I'm just hating on everybody for whatever they did to me, which can't be described with a single sentence since it spreads across several years and different actions have been taken to ensure my misery. And then when someone is finally nice to me, I don't know how to approach it since this is uncharted ground for me. On one side, fear wants me to back away; on the other, a feeling which I cannot describe with one word tells me to delve into the unknown. I don't know which the right choice is, but I feel like either will eventually reveal itself to be a mistake.

Suddenly, just like that that without a warning, something black appears in my peripheral vision. It doesn't look like part of the environment I was currently in. It was black as tar and thin as a . . . that's when I realized it.

The threads! They are materializing. It's been a while since I've seen them, but they are here now and I realize that I'm about to lose it. I worry, as I try to remember that right now I only see one thread and so everything is still maintainable. But naturally, the threads won't settle for appearing by themselves.

With one thread after another, more and more join the scenery, swirling and twirling in different directions. It doesn't matter how narrow they are because they come in the lot, and a lot indeed. My sight is nearly obscured by their presence as more and more just keep materializing out of nowhere.

I feel like I'm about to lose it as my eyes open wide and I breathe slowly. My heart starts to pound as I try to hold the sweat within my body as to not leave a bad odor. It's bad enough that they've come at this time, but I wouldn't want to leave a bad impression on Kim.

"Neph?" I hear her worried voice.

I ignore her voice, as I'm currently trying to get myself together, as that would be the right thing to do. It would be good for both of us; I know she wouldn't want to see me the way I wouldn't want to see myself.

"Neph?" Her voice tries again to find me, drowning as my senses weaken.

The threads gather and gather, and become many with each second that passes. I see more of them now than the park that actually lies before me. Yet with their quantity, they still find room to move about.

I shut my eyes tight with every muscle I've got. I gently rub my forehead with two fingers, reminding myself what I must do right now as the gentle sensation eases my stress. It feels like a boulder sitting firmly on my shoulders, pressuring me to bend as I struggle to stand up straight. I can't shake off this boulder, as if it's tied to my body by the finest ropes.

I open my eyes for a moment and now the threads no longer gather crudely in front of me like chickens in a tight cage that are struggling to even turn their necks, but now they are everywhere. I look to my sides, up into the air and down on the ground. Not a single spot that they haven't contaminated with their presence. I grow even more nervous with this development. But what caught my attention this time was something even more peculiar: everyone was frozen still in time!

The families with their children on the swings; the man playing Frisbee with his dog; the pigeons mid-flight; Kim, standing beside me. Time stood still as everyone froze together with it and I'm the only one unaffected by it. I can't tell if this is actually happening or is just an illusion, as this is completely new to me. A new addition to the already terrible effects of the threads and it doesn't get easier.

The feeling that I'm about to lose it grows even stronger, as the boulder that I felt earlier gradually becomes a mountain that I must balance on my shoulders, and God forbid if it fell, if there were a God.

The stress on my body grows even tighter, and the threads don't stop multiplying. I feel like my brain is tearing itself apart as I try so hard to contain myself. I shut my eyes tighter than ever before. So hard that I feel like I'm about to rip apart my eyelids from pure exertion. But no matter how hard I try, I can feel that it's just getting worse as I can't hold it anymore!

It's getting the better of me! I can't do this! I CAN'T stand this! Fuck this! FUCK this world! I hate it! I hate everything! FUCK this shit! Everything everything everything there is to know about this world is shit and everything this and that they want me to lose it and fucking kill me over and over these people and filth and everything killing me hate it here fucking everything shit this and that nothing to do here want out fucking leave out just out need to escape fucking escape get out get out get out . . . . NEED TO LEAVE THIS SHIT!

"GET YOUR SHIT TOGETHER!!" a voice yells to me.

I open my eyes wide at the speed of light. Every person and animal in sight gets chopped up into cubic pieces. No blood and no gore, as if they were made from cardboard. The pieces that once made these creatures float about in the air, moving in random directions, each at its own pace. I am confused, but I feel suddenly so enlightened, as the fury that I felt a second ago is gone and the jumbled words that filled my brain have no meaning now.

Weirdly enough, the threads have also disappeared, and I am engulfed in complete and utter silence. I look to my sides, and the cubes continue to float and disperse further. I don't really know what to say about this. I'm nervous, not knowing what I'm dealing with right now, although I feel as though the rage has left me. I am left without any actions to take. I don't know what will fix this, and above all, I don't know what the hell is happening.

"Neph?" I hear a gentle voice calling me.

I barely pay attention to the voice as I'm trying to figure out if everything is OK.

"Neph?" the voice continues to call me, slightly raising its volume.

I continue to ignore the voice. I try to collect myself slowly as I gradually regain my calm, though I can't help but feel that something's amiss, which negatively helps to hold on to my feeling of discomfort. And yet with all this, everyone is still in pieces . . . floating pieces.

"NEPH!" the voice yells.

My vision distorts for a brief tenth of a second. I see clearly once more, and everyone and everything is back to normal, as if nothing has ever happened. I don't feel like I'm about to lose it again. Not now, at least.

I feel a gentle touch on my shoulder. I look to see where it's coming from, and I see Kim, worried as hell as told by the expression on her face.

"Is everything all right?" she asks me, compassionately worried.

I stare at her blankly, as the experience just now took the words out of my mouth while I still try to fathom what the hell happened.

"Of course," I finally tell her, although a bit hesitantly.

The look on her face clearly showed that she didn't buy it.

"Maybe we should call it a day?" she says regretfully with a sad expression.

I don't want to answer, but I know that she's right.

"Yeah . . . ," I say regretfully. "Maybe we should."

And with that, we each went our separate ways to finish whatever we had left with the day. Not that there was much to be done considering that it's already late.

She ended the date by saying that we could always meet another day, a day when I feel a lot better.

I used to think that all the people in the world are nothing but filth. But after meeting Kim . . . that still doesn't change a thing. She's an exception, and while there are many exceptions, they still can't compensate for all the garbage that fills this society. But meeting her . . . she's really nice. Not only is she really nice but she's also cool, accepting to go on a date with me, of all people, the notorious fire kid. The world could use more people like her, then maybe it wouldn't be such crap. I really enjoyed my time with her, although I can't promise that we will meet in the future, despite what she said and even though I want to.

But right now . . . it's time to end this day and prepare myself for the subsequent day. As I prepare, I still wonder what the hell happened today, as it never occurred to me. I mean, the threads always appear, since that's how I know when something bad's about to happen. But everyone being chopped into bits; now *that's* something new. I have this need to find out right now what it means, but something in me tells me to wait this out and let it figure itself out. Hopefully, the revelation will come one day so I can find out what this phenomenon was.

They always say: "tomorrow's a new day with its own problems." I just hope that tomorrow won't end up like the day before it, the same thing I wish for every morrow.

I don't think I'll summon the conjurer tonight.

CHAPTER III

A POWER I NEVER KNEW I HAD

Five a.m. in the morning. Monday. Time to take Grasshead out for a walk in Withers Woods, my favorite forest around this godforsaken town. Actually, it's the only forest around.

For reasons beyond my understanding, Grasshead only needs to go out once a week. He does look like a reptile so I suppose maybe there's some snake in those genes. I heard that snakes can go without food for nearly a year. This actually comes to my advantage because if I needed to take out Grasshead once a day it would be a bitch considering the amount of risk at hand. It would be harder trying to sneak him out of the house, even though it's quite easy early on in the morning seeing as how everyone's still in bed.

Come to think about it, I can't believe I've managed to pull this off for four years now. Four years without anyone, and I mean mostly everyone who lives in this town, finding out that there's a giant-ass monster-dog-thing hiding in this house. Can't tell if its luck or brains that's on my side; I'm just glad I don't have to deal with more bullshit because of this. The last thing I need is a shit-ton of commotion from this neighborhood. Heck . . . having the press here reporting about some kind of monster, it'll spread like wildfire and before I know it, DARPA or some random science department in the US government would confiscate him, and I really wouldn't want that. Then I'd truly be without friends, in addition to already having no friends.

Anyway, time to go the forest for some adventure. I get up from bed, dress, eat cereal, go back to bed to sleep an additional thirty minutes, get back up and put on my flip-flops, all just before leaving out of the front door. Then, I remembered I almost forgot Grasshead's blanket. I rush back to my room and grab the blanket and then back to the front door. It was already 6:12 by the time I left. I hope I can make it back before it's too late, otherwise I'll have to be creative about how I get Grasshead back in.

Just outside the front door of my house—or, more accurately, my father's house—I put the blanket on Grasshead to hide him from any suspecting eyes. In hindsight, I should've put it on him before I left the house. Good thing nothing bad happened, but I should learn from it.

But with everything at hand, we leave for the forest. Grasshead naturally just follows me, even though there's a blanket obscuring his sight, but I guess he compensates for it with his sense of smell. Must be a really good sense if he can smell from under a blanket; I guess that's where the dog part comes in.

I still can't believe that hiding Grasshead under a blanket actually worked for me all these years. It's a simple idea, but I guess my cautiousness is what assisted it in the first place. Of course, I wouldn't just conspicuously walk around in plain sight like this. I deliberately avoid everyone's eyes. It mostly works, although sometimes people manage to catch a glimpse from afar. Of course, nobody would dare ask "the fire kid" why is there an autonomous floating blanket following him around. I'm not even sure if they'd know what they saw. I'm not worried, though, since I know for a fact that they can barely see what's going on from where they stand. I never hear any word running around the neighborhood about my antics, which means that either people aren't talking to me about it, which is more likely, or nobody actually knows. Regardless, I don't give a shit.

Out of all the people that stared, there was one in particular that really caught my attention. It had to be about two months ago. I was going on my usual routine of taking out Grasshead to the woods under a blanket. In front of me I saw a bunch of people walking. As they came closer, it became apparent that it was a bunch of kids following an adult. It was as if the Pied Piper came to town, but of course that couldn't happen. As we crossed paths, the man that was leading the kids just stared deeply at the blanket as if he could see through and he knew what it was. Then he stared at me. Looking into his eyes with confusion, it looked as if he was filled with dread at the moment. Nonetheless, we soon disappeared from each other's sight, and I was left to wonder what the hell all of them were doing off the main road, which is where I was walking to avoid the eyes of suspicion. I have no idea what the hell that group was, but in the end I assumed it might just be a school field trip. Still, who the hell would want to take a trip to this shitty town?

Good memories, huh? No, not really. But as I continue to reminisce about redundant memories, I finally make it to the woods.

I pull the blanket off Grasshead and mount him as we venture deeper into the woods, for the fiftieth time already or something like that. If we ever get lost and we can't find our way out, I can always trust Grasshead to smell us out of here.

Like a dog excited to get off the leash, Grasshead just rushes forward. I've always believed that he could go faster, although he never gets the opportunity to do so because it would probably hurt to inadvertently ram his head into a tree. Hopefully one day I'll be able to truly witness how fast he is, but it can't be now.

"Whoa! Slow down, boy," I shout as I struggle to balance myself amidst all the jumps. "We're gonna stay here for a while so calm down."

Time passes by quickly as we enjoy each other's company, although I think Grasshead is more excited to just get out of the house after a long while, but whatever. The songs of the birds and seeing bunny rabbits hop here and there make it more than a joy to come out and be in this forest. Definitely better than seeing ugly-ass humans and hearing them talk on their cellphones all day. If they're not talking on the phone, then they have their ugly faces stuck to the screen. It only shows how humans aren't willing to compromise for nothing; it's one of the many banes of society.

I shouldn't fill my head with shitty thoughts while I'm out here, but I can't help but remember that when I'm done enjoying myself here in the woods, I'll have to return home to the usual shitty conditions in which I live. But for now, I should probably focus on what's important.

"Grasshead, y'know . . . I couldn't help but notice that you're not from around here," I jokingly tell him as we continue to walk in the forest. "I know this is a subject we've never brought up, but we've talked about so many things that I can't recall what we did talk about and what we didn't. And you always tell me that I'm right, which is good, but I can't help but feel that something's amiss, y'know?"

Grasshead simply responds with his unusual growl, which sounds like that of a chain-smoking wolf. Either they feed monster-dog-things with cigarettes where they come from or they have wooden voice boxes. Not that I can find out because, other than Grasshead, I haven't seen other monster-dog-things.

"Yeah . . . I guess you're right," I say, pretending that I know what he's saying. "You probably don't care where you came from. I don't really know what to say about that. It's weird because . . . I never tried to inquire where you came from either."

Grasshead growls in response.

"I guess I was just so preoccupied with whatever shit has been going on in my life that I didn't even care," I continue to say. "I mean, what the hell are you supposed to be anyways?"

Grasshead again just growls in response.

"Yeah . . . I guess it doesn't matter," I tell him. "But I definitely wanna know what's up with me. I mean, I live here, but I don't belong here in this town, in this world. Something about my life, no . . . my existence doesn't add up."

Grasshead once more growls in response.

"What I'm trying to say is . . . have you ever felt like the stork got the wrong address?" I say with emotions so deep they drown.

It's a question that comes to my mind every day since the moment it first came to me, and I just now get to share it with Grasshead. I don't know why I waited so long, but that hardly matters. I guess it just had to come by itself.

I don't think that Grasshead minds the question as much as I do. It bothers me every day, and I keep pondering about the meaning of my existence. And this will keep on as long as my life is shit, and I will be determined to believe that I never belonged here in the first place.

But as I continue to ponder about this question, with my head high up in the air while Grasshead just moves forward on his own accord, I suddenly hear footsteps coming from a small hill to my right. Three odd-looking creatures pop up from behind it, mounted by three people, all aligned horizontally. The physique of the creatures was something very similar to something I'd seen before. The body, the legs, the tail . . . and then it came to me that those creatures were . . . .

"Monster-dog-things?" I mutter to myself.

But each one of them looked completely different from Grasshead, with the most defining part being their heads.

The one on the left was white and had a head that looked like that of a koi, only with teeth. He had an unusual red crest on top of his head, kind of like those goldfishes that have a brain on their head.

The one in the middle was dark green and had a head that looked like a crow's beak. His lower jaw was split in two, with each half having a jutting spike curving upwards on the edge of it. His tongue was sticking to the ceiling of his mouth because he had nowhere else to put it.

The one on the right was light blue and had blue dreadlocks reaching down to the ground, covering most of his head, kind of like those dogs that look like mops. Only his mouth was exposed. Oddly enough, the dreads have at their ends what appear to be black barbs.

After inspecting all of the monster-dog-things, I turn my attention to the riders. All I see are a bunch of weirdoes dressed like . . . well . . . in all honesty, there's no metaphor that can sum up they're appearance. Only specifics can describe them.

They all wore these thin-looking jackets, colored differently based on their choice. Opposed to the choice of 'what color I should wear,' they all wore black baggy pants that seemed like they were made from leather. Two of them had these sturdy-looking boots, while the other one—the only woman in the group—had these sandals of sorts, which looked more like flip-flops but I couldn't really tell what they were because they were too far to see from here. Ironically, I could very well notice the paraphernalia on their backs, although it wasn't entirely obvious what they were carrying. The guy in the middle, presumably the leader, carried a sword, evident by the hilt that's poking out from his back. I could also see the cross-guard and, judging by its width, it's probably a claymore. The other guy had some kind of thingy which I couldn't tell what it was; all I saw was five prongs aligned like a pentagram, kind of like a star. The girl didn't seem to be carrying anything.

Putting aside their more obvious features, it's kind of hard to ignore how toned and muscular their bodies are. I mean, Christ! The girl is built like some supermodel-meets-ninja that came straight out of a comic book. I'm pretty sure she has like two percent body fat considering how lean her biceps look. And those collar bones are so prominent. The guys, on the other hand, put pro wrestlers to shame, or at least the leader does as the other guy is a tad slimmer, but he is muscular no less. And the beards. What manly beards! Their differences in styles clearly shows as the leader—which I still suppose he is—has a short beard, while the other guy sports a slim goatee.

The feature about them that catches my attention the most and the one that I find the most intriguing is that they all have tattoos on the right side of their necks. The tattoos are black and vary in shape, but they all seem to share an archetype of some sort of dragon or snake. I think this means that they might be from some kind of cult or a tribe or something. But if they come from the same cult, why would the tattoos look different?

The meaning of the tattoos isn't really an issue right now, as they are staring directly at me, clearly desiring something from me. I stand ready for whatever might come about.

"The creature in your possession does not belong to you," the leader suddenly exclaims in an unusual, somewhat Greek accent. "I suggest you relinquish him immediately"

"What?" I reply, confused.

"I will repeat myself: relinquish the creature immediately," he says with this cold, serious attitude.

I just stare at him with confusion as I try to figure out what the hell he wants with me.

"No," I reply, trying to maintain my cool.

"Do not force my hand," he persists with his behavior, pointing at me now. "Give us the creature. This is your final warning."

At that moment, I notice the long, armored bracelets on his arm. Four bracelets altogether; one on each bicep and one on each forearm. I realize that he came to fight, and he isn't going to let this down so easily. The fear alone of a blood-filled thought made me realize that his jacket is red. The atmosphere becomes tense as my desire is to just leave this place already and avoid a confrontation, although he doesn't seem to be fazed by the situation at all.

I don't respond, but instead quietly turn around and start to walk away. It might seem like a dick move to ignore him and just walk away like that, but I'd rather avoid a fight; I just don't have the patience to put up with this crap. Besides, I have no idea who these people are.

But just as I start to walk away, I hear him getting off his mount. I turn around and I see that they have all gotten off their respective mounts. At that moment, I realize that a storm is brewing.

"Keep that up and you'll end up like your jacket," I angrily threaten him.

He didn't seemed fazed by the threat at all; instead, he picked up the pace as if he was already looking for a fight. I really don't want to get into a fight. As I stand there, still thinking about what the right choice might be, I see the girl grab him by the shoulder as if she's trying to halt him.

"Asoron'in na. keika pawip'sok'em," he tells her as he gently removes her hand from his shoulder.

I have no idea what he said, but it was definitely in some weird language.

He then proceeds to walk towards me alone, with the other two watching him from behind.

"Seriously, what's your problem?" I say angrily. "Who the fuck are you guys, anyways?"

He continues to slowly walk towards Grasshead and me, completely ignoring my attempt to reason with him. He doesn't seem bothered by the fact that he's up against a monster-dog-thing and his badass owner, although without Grasshead I honestly don't know how well I would be able to keep up with this guy, despite my prowess and my history of fighting.

Grasshead and I just stand there, still thinking about the right choice as he slowly closes the gap between us. I feel Grasshead getting nervous, and as the tension in the atmosphere rises, we slowly start to walk backwards.

My heart starts to beat rapidly as I grow nervous. I deeply consider what my next actions will be. I hesitate as I consider my choices: if I run I'll get chased but if I stay . . . I might die. As he got closer, I realized that violence was inevitable, and then I knew what the right choice was.

"GET 'EM, GRASSHEAD!!" I shout

Grasshead then immediately charges at the guy and attempts

to crunch him down. The guy simply pushes Grasshead's head to the side and with a thrust of his palm, sends me flying off Grasshead like six feet away.

Grasshead then turns around and comes running to help me, worried for my well-being. But before he could get close enough, the girl appears out of nowhere and ties all of Grasshead's legs with a black rope at the speed of light; she moved so fast I couldn't see her. Grasshead falls to the ground, lying on his side. She goes on to place her hand on Grasshead's mouth while he struggles in an attempt to free himself; suddenly, a black muzzle made from leather and chains simply materializes around his mouth, locking it and preventing any necessary struggle.

"NO!" I yell.

From the ground, I grab a rock the size of my fist as I get up and throw it at them. It hit the leader in the back, but he barely budges. As he turns around to face me, I charge at him. I try to deliver a nasty haymaker, but before my fist could reach his face, he slaps it away like it's some kind of fly. He then punches me in the face and knees me in the stomach. I fall down on one knee, with him just staring at me, apparently waiting for me to get up. As I struggle to catch my breath after taking that blow to my diaphragm, I slowly start to get up. I finally stand straight on two feet, but before I can even stare at him, he push-kicks me away from him and I fall down on my back.

With that, he starts to walk away. He probably thinks that the fight is over, but I'm far from just yielding.

"Where the fuck are you going!? Get ba—"

Something suddenly hits me in the back of both my knees, forcing me to kneel. Then, in an instant, I feel something forcibly pushing my ankles into the ground. Then it constricts my arms together behind my back. The girl appears before me; the moment I see her, I know she is the one who did it. While she and the leader are part of the action, the other guy just stands there, spectating and seemingly enjoying the show.

All three of them start to gather in front of Grasshead, who is still lying on the ground.

"GET AWAY FROM HIM!!" I yell.

I can't get up; the chains on my feet bind me to the ground. I can't free my arms; the ropes lock them together.

"PLEASE!!" I continue to yell as they continue to ignore me.

The guy with the prongs coming out of his back walks towards Grasshead. Seeing him from a different angle, I can see what he has in his back, and it looks like some kind of star-shaped bag.

He gently puts his palm on Grasshead. Unexpectedly, a grey clay-like substance in the form of noodles starts to come out of the prongs of the bag. The clay gathers under Grasshead and acts like it's about to form into something.

"GODAMNIT! Leave him alone!" I continue to yell to no avail, nearly at the verge of begging.

The girl angrily grunts as she kicks the ground in front of me, throwing dust into my eyes.

With dust in my eyes, I am blinded and astonished by her reaction. That cold, heartless reaction. A reaction without sympathy or mercy. That really got to me. This is the straw that breaks the camel's back!

I frown with all the muscles in my face, eyes wide open with rage. I show my teeth for all to see as I hold myself not to grind them. Using sheer force alone, I start to get up, slowly ripping the chains that bind me from the ground. As I try to free my arms, I can slowly hear the ropes tearing apart. They look at me, shocked and without a clue to what's happening. They definitely didn't see this coming. How I was able to do this, I have no idea, but it didn't matter, because at that exact moment I had only one thought in mind.

"I said . . . LEAVE HIM ALONE!!!" I shout as I obliterate all the chains that bind my limbs, followed by a mighty airwave that creates a big dust cloud, the sound of my rage felt across the entire forest.

As the cloud disperses, I stand still in my spot, with little care to what I had accomplished at the moment, since all I care right now is to free Grasshead from his bonds. I can feel the rage boiling inside me as I breathe deeply. I grind my teeth and clench my fist as I look at them, and they look at me back with surprised expressions on their faces. As I trade stares with them and the tension rises between us, each of us stays still while thinking about what will be the smartest move to do next. They look at each other, probably frightened and not knowing what to do. And then . . .

The girl disappears in a flash with only a small cloud of dust left in her wake. Almost instantly, I feel chains wrapping around my arms, attempting to shackle them together behind my back. Before she is able to constrain my arms, I turn around, preventing her from finishing her move. I grab the chains with both my arms and start to spin them over my head while she stubbornly clings to them at the other end. I spin hard as I swing the chains with such force that her hands slip off and her body is slammed against a tree.

With my focus on the girl, I hear the sound of running to my right. I turn to see the supposed leader with his massive claymore over his head, barely a second away from embedding his sword into my skull. I catch the blade between my palms just before it manages to reach my head. I struggle to keep the blade away from me while he continues to press it down against my power. I can feel my hands shaking in the process. I can feel his hands shaking as he releases sounds of overexertion. Without too much thought, I shatter the blade with a slight twist of my hands. As shards of metal fly by my face, he stares at me with a terrified expression, as if he had just witnessed a cannibal feasting upon its meal.

"GET OUTTA MY FACE!!" I shout as I grab him by the face and deliver a nasty jab to his mug, sending him flying off to the tree behind.

Suddenly, something lunges at me with such force that it throws me to the ground. It painfully grabs me with what feels like teeth in the shoulder and I hold onto it with my arm. It feels like clay. We roll on the ground before I hurl it against a tree. The thing splits in two, with each part making a wide U-turn towards me, as it forms into what appear to be giant dragonflies with heads of dragons and a scorpion's stinger for a tail. They charge towards me, but I duck.

I turn around to see the dragonflies merge with a clay giant standing about twelve feet tall and as wide as an elephant. It looks like a reptilian killer whale with a mouth full of narrow, long razor teeth. It wears a loincloth around its waist and armor covers its head, shoulders, thighs, shins and chest, while the rest of his body is exposed, showing grey scales. It stands on its toes, each bearing a claw worthy of cutting through the toughest hide. The claws on its hands are no less vicious than the ones on its toes. In its hand, it holds a cleaver, with the hilt covering the entire back of the blade, while the blade itself has a sharp extension on the front half of its top, which curves backwards. But the worst sight of all was the other guy standing atop of it, manipulating it as if it were another appendage of his body.

The giant runs towards me and tries to swing down its cleaver upon me as I sidestep to dodge it. It then comes at me with a vertical slash, but I jump backwards out of its reach, followed by another overhead swing to ground, but I roll, dodging that one too. I grab the giant's leg and start to climb my way up to its head. Jumping from its leg to its waist, and then to its chest, all the while clinging by the edge of my nails to its clay hide while it attempts to shake me off. I can feel its torso turning clockwise and counterclockwise while my body flings against the air like a plastic bag. I launch myself into the air with a mighty pull up from its chest. I land gracefully on my feet on top of its shoulder, where I stand and confront the guy.

I try to deliver a punch, but he dodges. I try to punch with my other fist, but he falls back and sinks into the giant. I step forward onto the other shoulder to look over the edge, trying to figure out where he disappeared to. He pops up from behind me, right out from beneath the giant with a long morning star club. Before I have time to react, he swings it against the back of my head, shattering it immediately due to its brittle matter. I now have shallow punctures in my head due to the spikes, but that doesn't stop me. I come back with a backhand, but he crouches and subsequently pulls out a spikeless club out of the giant's shoulder. He swings it at my knee, making me fall down on it, still with my foot flat on the giant's shoulders. Clay noodles then come out of three of the most upper points of the star-like device on his back, squirming towards his hand and then forming into a survival knife. He tries to finish the job by stabbing me in the neck, but I slap the knife away with the back of my hand, shattering it against a tree. I then try to hit him in the face with a mighty hook, but he blocks it with his arm by grabbing me in the biceps. Clay noodles start coming out from the points of his device again; this time clay also comes out from the back of the giant and it's moving fast! The clay gathers around our arms and hardens, bonding them together. I try to deliver another punch, but he blocks that one as well. Clay forms around my other arm and it starts to harden.

Almost immediately, I can feel myself sinking into the giant while he pushes me further inside. As I sink, he stares at me with such determination that I can see the warrior inside him. Suddenly, his expression changes, showing softness and curiosity. He looked at me astonished, as if he knows me from somewhere. I return his gaze, but I have no idea what suddenly caught his attention. The only thing I want is to crush these people for humiliating me.

These thoughts distract me as my entire body sinks into the body of clay which is the giant. As total darkness envelops me and air escapes me, I know that can't stop me. I grab him by his foot, still inside the giant. I pull myself up, jumping into the air like a dolphin and freeing myself. I land steadily on both my feet on the shoulders of the giant, right in front of the guy, and deliver a powerful head butt. As I pull my head back, I can feel pain in my forehead as if something stabbed me. I then grab him by the head and fling him over my head, sending him flying hard against a tree as it topples over from the sheer force.

Finally dispatching all three, I jump down from the giant and run towards Grasshead, who is still tied up.

"C'mon, boy. Let's get the fuck outta here," I say as I start to rip apart the ropes holding his front legs.

I witness the raveled strings as the ropes tear apart, one after another. After four seconds, I finally break the ropes tying Grasshead's front legs. I go to his hind legs to do the same. After six seconds of breaking apart the strings that make the ropes, I can feel myself getting weaker. I exerted so much power over these guys that by the time I reached Grasshead I barely had anything left. I had to let my muscles relax. After three seconds, I break the ropes with one mighty pull of both my arms and finally free all of Grasshead's legs. I then proceed to disassemble the final piece that binds Grasshead, which is the muzzle.

"Don't worry, boy! Everything's gonna be all right!" I say as I grab the muzzle and prepare to rip it apart.

Just as I'm about to tear the muzzle apart, a force pushes me back several feet away and rolls me on the ground. I feel an object under my back as I forcibly stare at the sky and choke on something wrapped around my neck. The tips of my feet barely touch the ground as I struggle to keep the blood pumping to my brain.

I hear a soft voice exerting so much power in just taking me down. I realize it is the girl. I can feel how determined she is to choke me to death only by the noises she makes. I don't know what she has around my neck, but it feels like a rope as I desperately try to pull it away from me.

I feel my head falling lower and lower as the rope keeps pressing against my windpipe. I refuse to yield as I continue to pull it back to relieve the pressure, but I struggle to do so while the air escapes me.

Just as I feel that my life is about to slip away from my body and what a wonderful outcome that would be, something launches at the girl and I fall on the ground. I get up and look to see what was going on: it was Grasshead who charged at her.

I see the girl struggling in the clutches of Grasshead's maw and holding a rod between Grasshead's teeth while he attempts to crunch her down. The rod tries to extend but Grasshead's bite is too strong. As the rod gets weaker, pieces of it start falling off as Grasshead's teeth are touching the girl's stomach. Realizing her rod isn't enough, she desperately tries to push up Grasshead's upper jaw with her bare hands. As she keeps pushing without success, Grasshead's teeth start to pierce her belly and back. She screams in agony as tiny streams of blood flood out of her gut.

I stare a bit at the happening while panting, near-tired of this whole situation. Suddenly, I feel pressure in the air; I feel an object moving in the wind. My eyes open wide as I quickly turn around to see a tomahawk flying in my direction, with the leader far behind it. I catch the tomahawk with my hand as I turn around a whole circle, throwing it back at him. He does exactly the same, as he catches the tomahawk with his hand, turns around a whole circle, and throws it back at me.

I catch it again, but by the time I am about to throw it, he is close enough for me to engage him in close combat. As I feel the tomahawk firmly in my hand, I deliver a backhand swing to his skull, but he lowers his head to dodge it. He follows with a rising uppercut. I move my head back to dodge it. I grow impatient with this and I start to swing the tomahawk wildly in his face like a man holding a rolled-up newspaper desperately trying to kill a fly, with every swing of mine dodged by him with his quick reflexes. After several swings, he slaps away the tomahawk with a forehand slap. I grab him by the collar and throw him to the ground with a judo takedown. I try to choke him with both my hands, but he prevents them from reaching his throat with both of his hands. I can feel my pecs burning as I further close my hands on his throat. I frown and expose my teeth to show my power while his mouth is closed shut and eyes are wide open, constantly shifting their gaze from one of my hands to the other, always watching which is closer to crushing his trachea. As the two of us struggle against each other, I suddenly hear a masculine voice, but fail to make out the words as I ignore it and focus on what's more dire.

"DIM'IM!!" shouts the voice.

The eyes of the leader shift to the place where the voice is coming from, and then he looks back at me.

"Stop. Please," the voice says in an accent similar to that of the leader.

I can feel my hands getting closer to his neck faster than before. At that moment, I realize he's given up. As I loosen my muscles, he drops his entire body to the ground, closes his eyes and takes a series of deep breaths.

I look back to see what is going on, and there I see the other guy sitting down and leaning against a tree with his arm lifted up, gesturing to stop. He then swiftly drops it and takes a deep breath. He then starts to get up, rising with his leg, supported by a hand pushing his knee. When he finally gets up, he starts limping his way towards me.

"You" he calls me, gesturing with a point sign while panting. "Tell him to stop."

He then points at Grasshead, still trying to crunch down the girl while she's still pushing his upper jaw. The rod, surprisingly, is still there, despite crumbling to half its width.

"Grasshead. Drop her," I order Grasshead after a short delay.

Grasshead then drops the girl on her back. Covered in Grasshead's saliva, the girl writhes in her pain, clutching her stomach tight due to the bite wounds. The wounds aren't deep enough to kill her, but blood keeps spilling in small streams, one for each wound. This girl is a warrior tougher than any Navy SEAL or British SAS, combined or apart. I can see it.

The other guy then limps past me. He then stands still in front of the leader, who is still lying down, exhausted from the fight.

He looks down. They trade stares while the leader still pants. After taking a deep breath, he finally pushes himself upright to a sitting position. He looks down to the ground, sighs and then rubs his eyes. He then raises his head to look at his clay-loving ally. They look at each other while silence envelops the atmosphere.

"Heranga komo'in toma tang'ga na," the other guy says.

The leader looks down, holding his head with his hand, with his elbow sitting firmly on the knee of a flexed leg. He takes a deep breath.

"Kata oreka'in?" the leader asks his friend.

"Kata marang nayan'in iteke ke'sayan?" his friend suddenly says.

The leader then looks at my face. He then moves his head forward and slowly squints his eyes, closely inspecting my face. His face then shows an expression of disbelief.

"Kata heho'in?" he asks his friend.

"Akai'masak'nen," he says with a slight smirk on his face.

The leader suddenly bursts into laughter. As he quickly calms down from this moment of excitement, his friend, who is still standing beside him, frowns in disappointment.

The leader gestures his friend to pull him up from the ground. He gets up and proceeds to wipe the dirt off his clothes. He then turns his attention to me.

He starts walking towards me, with no limp whatsoever, as if the fight didn't even faze him. I am hesitant, as the tension of the battle disappeared, but I can't help but feel that something is brewing. I assume a defensive stance as I prepare for the worst.

"You can calm down," the leader suddenly says as he continues to walk. "You see, we don't plan on fighting anymore.

Clearly, this isn't an easy task as it should've been."

"Big words coming from someone who brought it on himself," I say with anger as I try to repress it.

He finally stands in front of me.

"Apologies," he continues to say. "But things didn't go according to plan."

"So are you gonna tell me why the fuck you tried to separate me from Grasshead?" I ask him as my anger slowly fades.

"We might . . . if you provide us with a place to rest. After all, our friend over there could use some patching up."

He then points at the girl, who is still lying on the ground with all those holes in her and blood coming out of her. I smirk as I look at her, proud of Grasshead and what he's capable of.

"Well she DOES have a lotta holes in her." I jokingly say.

I'm not one to end a fight with such pitiful results. But more importantly, I never attack someone who can't defend himself, which also applies if they surrender. That rule of mine is sacred.

Also, these people . . . there's something about them that I can't quite put my finger on. As much as I would love to continue and kick their asses, they're not trying to take away Grasshead anymore or kill me, so I guess it's sort of OK. Also, they apologized, and I don't remember when the last time was that someone apologized to me. This alone shows that there's something special to them. Something I must find out.

"You're not from around here, are ya?" I ask him.

"It speaks for itself. Don't you think?" he responds wittily.

"The fuck that supposed to mean?"

"I'd be happy to tell you if you would just take us to a hospital or something!" he raises his voice in impatience. "To'shin could die any second."

"Oh right! Of course, I almost forgot."

With that, we make peace with each other and it doesn't seem like there's going to be another fight, although I find it odd that they were able to forgive me so easily after I nearly killed them. Then again, the same can be said about me. I guess we have that much in common.

CHAPTER IV

DIVE . . . OR STAY AND LIVE IN MISERY

I open the door to my house, bringing in Grasshead and the three dumbasses that nearly killed me. I should remind myself not to be so forgiving next time this happens.

Everyone, and I mean that without exception, is exhausted and bruised from the fight, although others suffered a lot more while some are barely fazed from the injuries. The clothes are all torn apart and dirty like they were rags that had just cleaned a muddy floor. Everyone smells like shit, and now is definitely not the time to take a bath.

Good thing nobody's home yet. The dumb sisters are at school and the neglectful parents are at work. I got the entire house to myself right now, and I have nothing to worry about . . . for now.

Anyways, I open a bunch of random drawers until I find a first aid kit.

"No need for that," the leader tells me from behind.

I look back and stare at them with disbelief.

"Wait?" I ask, confused about the situation. "Didn't you sa—"

"I was bluffing," he interrupts me. "Besides, you'd need more than that toy kit. She has holes the size of my head."

I think he's exaggerating, but it's good to know that his sense of humor wasn't damaged.

"Well . . ." I start to say, "She's YOUR responsibility if she dies."

"She won't," he says with clear certainty.

So with that settled, I take them to my room. On my way, I notice that the girl with the holes in her belly can walk by herself, and she does it without even staggering. At this point, she seems completely unfazed by her wounds, despite how serious they look. I'm starting to think that fighting is second nature for these people.

Upon getting to my room, everyone takes a spot. The girl and the other guy sit on the floor, seeing as the only chair that I have is the one taken by the leader. It didn't seem to bother them much. Then again, it would've been childish to be bothered by it to begin with. Grasshead takes his spot at the corner of the room and immediately takes a nap, naturally. As for me, I sit on my bed.

"I never knew a paito'ga hiphomoy could be so powerful," the leader says while looking at the girl's wounds. "Usually it's the mosak'ga that cause so much damage, but a paito'ga wouldn't even measure up."

"And it's even worse for this one," the other guy adds to the conversation while looking at the girl. "I heard she neutralized a marbar. It's somewhat embarrassing."

"A marbar!" the leader remarks with surprise. "I've never actually seen one myself, but I heard they're really nasty. They have to be among the highest tiers."

"One tier before the highest, if I'm not mistaken."

"Shik'gao teng'karat," the girl suddenly exclaims in a pain-filled tone.

"Highest tier, it is then," the other guy says.

I just watch them talk to each other. Naturally, I have no idea what they're talking about. Should I care? Probably. But I have bigger things on my mind right now.

"What have you been feeding him?" the leader suddenly asks me.

"What? Oh. Dog food mostly," I say. "Sometimes I throw in a steak, too. Why? Am I supposed to feed him something else?"

"Nothing specific. Just a lot of meat."

"Hmm. You sure know your share of monster-dog-things."

"Monster dogs? They're called hiphomoys."

"Hmm . . . I never knew that."

"Well now you do. Although I don't think what you feed him makes him like this."

That vague sentence he made just now. In all honesty, I don't entirely understand what he's trying to get at, but apparently he seemed surprised by Grasshead's natural prowess. I assume by that that their monster-dog-things, or hiphomoys as I was told, aren't as powerful as Grasshead, making him special in some way. Speaking of which, I don't recall them bringing theirs with them on the trip here. Also, why the hell didn't they aid them in the fight? Whatever.

"So you guys wanted to talk to me about something?" I ask.

A silence envelops the atmosphere. They don't seem quite sure of what they want to say, as it just seems like they're thinking about it carefully. It makes sense since—considering that it's already established that they're not from around here—I might not entirely understand what message they might try to convey. I can't imagine how weird it can already get. One of the weirdest things in my life just happened to me a moment ago, or a few moments ago more accurately.

"Have you ever felt a calling?" the other guy vaguely asks me.

"A calling?" I ask, confused. "Like what?"

"Like . . . something was hidden from you? Something that never really . . . aligned with the place that you live in?"

I just stare with confusion. My expression alone says it as I blink several times to indicate how oblivious I am.

"I'm still not following ya," I reply with more confusion.

"I'm sorry," he tells me, somewhat embarrassed. "It's just that . . . I was always a great believer. But to think . . . he is actually real."

"WHAT IS?!" I start to get irritated over his vague wording.

"The composer!" he replies immediately with clear certainty.

"YOU'RE STILL NOT MAKING ANY SENSE!" The

annoyance gets the better of me.

Suddenly, the girl bursts into laughter. She continues to laugh, and it doesn't seem like she's going to stop any time soon, as she's really enjoying this laughter like she's just heard a really good joke. And then, she coughs violently, as blood comes spewing out of her mouth. She clutches her stomach as if she's trying to block the holes on her stomach from bleeding. She continues to cough, all the while staining my room with her blood, before calming down entirely. I guess she didn't want to turn it into a killing joke.

Weirdly enough, her friends didn't even seem worried for her wellbeing. They have to be either bad friends or they knew from the beginning that nothing bad was going to happen to her. Seeing how she's still alive with those holes, it's probably the latter. No human would've survived with those kinds of holes in them.

"Anyway . . ." he continues to tell his story. "What I am trying to say is . . . that there's this legend that we believe in. Well . . . at least some of us do."

"A legend?" I ask, not entirely understanding what he's getting at. "Like a prophecy?"

"No. not a prophecy. An actual legend. A story that spreads among our people like fire."

"And that is . . . ," I slowly lose my interest.

"Akai'masak'nen ka ojak'ga yopak'shik," he says with repressed excitement. "Or, in a tongue that you can understand, and in the tongue that we least use, *the composer of the calm horizon*."

I once more stare at him with a blank expression on my face, and this time it is blanker than a white paper.

"You expect me to understand what you're sayin'?" I tell him, growing tired of the vagueness of the subject.

"I'm sorry." he says, continuing to show his repressed excitement. "I haven't been specific enough."

"No shit."

"But it goes like this: we were sent here to retrieve back a lost hiphomoy. Conveniently, he's the one in your possession. Normally, such a task wouldn't be a burden: we remain hidden from the heranga and collect the hiphomoy without anyone noticing. Unfortunately, the mission took an unusual turn."

"I noticed."

"We encountered you. Normally, in such situations, we simply neutralize the target and proceed with our mission. But then, at that moment, when you broke through To'shin's bond . . . ."

Suddenly, he becomes silent.

"What about it?" I ask with mild interest.

"I didn't think about it first, because at that moment, I realized there was danger. But I couldn't help but think to myself: how can a mere heranga do such thing? They can't! And I kept telling this to myself over and over."

"Is there a punch line to this story?"

"It wasn't until the middle of the battle that I realized the answer."

"That I'm this 'hero of legend'?" I say mockingly.

"Yes!"

I just stare at him in disbelief, although I can see the seriousness that's just illuminating from his eyes. This whole assumption that I'm some legendary hero is just ludicrous. In all honesty, looking at my life, the ugly duckling would've been a better analogy.

"So, uh . . . ," I start to say indecisively, "what do you wanna do 'bout it?"

"Well . . . ," he starts to say hesitantly, "if it's not a problem with you, we think that—"

"What he's trying to say is that we want you to come with us," the leader suddenly interrupts impatiently as he stands up.

"Really?" I say skeptically. "And what makes you think I'll come so easily?"

"Well . . . you have no right to trust us, nor will it bear any positive results to take you by force. But . . . think about this," the leader says as suspense fills the room. "Have you ever thought that something was amiss of your life? That there are many answers beyond your reach? I'm certain that you've realized by now that there's a great power lingering within you. I'm also certain that we can provide those answers. Answers that will enlighten your life and above all, give it purpose."

"I see," I say, intrigued, but still somewhat skeptical. "Have you ever heard of the allegory of the cave?"

"I haven't," he tells me clearly. "But if you're saying that you won't come, then I suggest you weigh your options carefully."

I think for a moment about his words, thinking whether they were true and that they actually have an answer to my anguishes. I don't think even the greatest of shrinks could find a solution to whatever's going on in my head. That is, of course, if they actually tried to understand me instead of straight up throw me in a nuthouse. But I see these three and what they are capable of, I know they are beyond what this world has to offer. Maybe I will go with them. I mean, what the hell do I have to lose? Family? Friends? Please. Everyone wished they'd be rid of me. Makes room for a neighborhood with fewer worries of fire accidents. Despite this, I'm still afraid of the change. Will the change make things worse or better? Regardless, I have nothing to do here.

"Assuming I'll come with you," I say, slowly becoming sure of my decision. "How the fuck am I gonna explain this to my piece of shit family? Or maybe we're just gonna leave without an explanation?"

"Don't worry about that," the other guy says with clear certainty. "All we need to do is fake your death."

"Really? And how the fuck do you expect to do that? Make a guy get a few facelifts and then kill 'em?"

"Heh. Funny. But, jokes aside, all we need to make a fake body is my clay." His voice turns really serious at the end of that sentence.

He then gets up and goes for his star-thingy, which was

earlier placed at the side of the room. He throws it in between us all and next raises his hand, palm wide open, and then clay starts coming out of the holes, all gathering in a single spot. The gathering spot gradually starts to grow, constantly changing its shape while slowly taking on an apparent form.

I stare at the finalized form with astonishment, as all I see is me. Inch by inch, complete with the scars and everything else. Not a single flaw or blemish on my cursed vessel of a body was left out. It was even in full color, which surprised me the most considering that the clay was in fact grey, so where did the color come from?

"Hmm . . . ," I say upon seeing the fake corpse, almost impressed. "Y'know, it's nice that you invested so much into the details. Its true art but . . . this might fool some people at first but eventually, someone will find out that it's a fake before it reaches the grave. I mean whaddya think the autopsies will show?

"Again, you needn't worry," he replied without any concerns. "Normally during battles, we just create things out of clay because the result is hard enough to crush bones and we don't have too much time to make it harder, because then the enemy could use the window of opportunity to kill us fast. But with enough focus, we can apply more details into the clay, at the expense of more clay and the product losing its combat potential. This is also the reason I just ran out of clay. I assume you can see now how important this is to me."

He looks at me, and I look at him. I'm not one to tell people's desires by simply looking in the eyes. But logically, if he wasted all his clay just to fake my death and bring me with them, then I guess it has to be important to him. Well, at least to him, as I'm not sure what the girl thinks about this whole organization.

"Can you all use clay?" I ask him.

"No. Just me," he tells me.

"His clan uses clay," the leader spontaneously explains.

"Clans?" I say, confused.

"Yes!" he says like an excited child. "You see, we come from a land where every clan specializes in different techniques. My clan specializes in a variety of ancient weaponized fighting techniques."

He just GLOWS with pride as he continues to explain about his world. I think I can even see a smirk on his face.

"And To'shin over here specializes in non-lethal techniques for the purpose of incapacitating targets," he continues to explain . . . with pride!

"Non-lethal? She tried to choke me to death," I say, mildly annoyed.

"I would have if you would let me," the girl suddenly says aggressively.

I say nothing to her, as it will probably be wise to just leave her be for now. She doesn't seem too friendly. Although I can't help but say that I am somewhat attracted to her. I mean, she has a beautiful face, and that black hair tied into a ponytail, with spiky bangs partially obscuring her eye. And that body! But above all, she's a badass. I mean, I can see that she's amazing in every way. Well . . . other than the saltiness, that is.

"You're very pretty," I tell her with all honesty. "You know that?"

A smirk appears on her face. I think I just got her to lighten up a bit.

"Are all the clans just a buncha badasses?" I suddenly ask the leader.

"Most of the clans are," he starts to explain, showing pride once more. "You see, not everyone is mentally equipped for combat. And those that aren't fulfill non-combatant purposes."

"Interesting," I say in a not-so-interested way.

"Heh. This reminds me how I wanted to be an imarjen'ga when I was a child. I wanted to blast mountains with explosions that looked like jellyfish. Alas, it wasn't up to me what I would become."

"Whaddya mean?"

"We don't choose what to become; it is chosen for us."

"Hmm. that's kinda depressing."

"I eventually came to terms with it, so it wasn't much of a problem. The same goes for the rest of my people. Besides, I don't think a better purpose would befit me. If I like it and enjoy it, then that's the only thing one needs to contribute to themselves and their society. Nothing can be better than that."

Looking at his face as he says those words, I don't see just pride, but patriotism as well. It's clearly evident by how he talks about his people as if they're part of him and how one can contribute to their society. I wonder if all of them think that way, because if so, humans as a species could learn a lot from these people. Heck . . . these might be the people that I'm looking to be part of, although I can't be too sure.

Suddenly, I notice something peculiar on his face as he catches everyone's attention with his speech. I squint to look better at whatever I'm trying to look at, and what I see is something interesting: two small protrusions from under the skin, one between the eyebrows and one at the pinnacle of the forehead, shaped like small tiny horns. It looked more like an inverted beak of a falcon actually.

I look at the other two; I see that they too have those small beak-shaped horns, exactly at the same spot where the leader has his. I'm surprised I haven't noticed these before, but it was probably because I was too caught up in the fight to notice anything too small. I now know for a fact that these people aren't human, as if all the other things that happened until now didn't give that away. I also know what stabbed me in the forehead when I head butted the clay-using guy.

I decide not to ask them about it, since I don't think that there's much to ask. I mean, if a guy's head is bigger than the rest of his body, do you ask him about it?

Although I did notice that the leader had something that the other two did not: he has a pitch black spot the width of a coin just above the edge of his left eyebrow, close to the middle of his forehead. I have no idea if it means anything like the tattoos they have on their necks, since it almost seems like a tattoo itself. I decide not to ask about that either. I mean, if a guy has a giant mole on his face, do you ask him about it?

"Is everyone done resting?" the girl asks impatiently. "I want to leave now. I still have to get these holes closed."

"I'm waiting on all of you," I say.

"Well then, what are we waiting for?" the leader asks rhetorically. "Let's move."

He then turns his attention to me before any final preparations that might be.

"So . . . ," he starts to say. "Are you coming with us?"

"Pretty sure I said 'yes,'" I say with mild disbelief.

"Excellent! I'm sure you'll find yourself at home in the Novaverse. Wouldn't you agree, To'shin?"

He stares at her, but she doesn't say a word. She just seems disgruntled over the decision to bring me with them.

"You're both idiots!" she suddenly says in anger. "If it were up to me, this wouldn't happen."

"Then it's a good thing we live in a democracy." The leader wittily says. "Now if mind you all, I wouldn't like to waste any more time."

And with that, we leave the fake body lying on the bed and we move out to the forest, slowly walking, taking all the time we need. Naturally, Grasshead came with me, as he has nothing to do here.

As we walk, I think about my family. About the last time I saw them. About the last time they saw me. I wonder if I stayed longer, maybe one day we could've put our problems on the table and be a family like everyone else. Have my dad ignore that I killed my mother. And in turn, I would ignore that he ignores me. I could even be an actual role model for my sisters. Be the bigger brother that I'm supposed to be. But instead, I'm too bothered by my own puddle of mud. The kind found in the dirtiest, parasite-ridden swamps that you sink in until you reach chest height. And once you're there, you stop, and never sink again, making you stare at whatever's in front of you. You keep staring, hoping and waiting that something will pass by, but nothing ever does. But in all honesty, all these expectations for a better family life are nothing now, since my future suggests that the happiness I seek is without family. If such is the case . . . so be it.

As these thoughts continue to swirl in my head, we finally make our way to the forest. We pass by some squirrels and lichen, moving around trees and rocks, all while moving towards an undisclosed location. In four years, I don't think that Grasshead has missed marking a spot in this forest. He knows all the rabbit holes that came and went, all the trees that the woodpeckers use to annoy the other forest animals, and that one spot where the snails don't come to after the rain. What other secret does this forest hold that Grasshead and I don't know of yet?

"You guys never told me your names," I tell them as we continue to walk.

"I am Sowi'ga Krang'pegin," the leader tells me. "Or just So'krang for short."

"My name is Panar Prak'nen," the other guy tells me. "But everyone calls me Pa'prak."

So I know that the red jacket is called So'krang, and that the clay user is called Pa'prak. They both told me their names in sequential order, but the girl refuses to cooperate, as she just continues on riding without saying a word, pretending as if we're not even having this conversation. Unfortunate for her that I already know her name.

"And uh . . . To'shin. Right?" I ask politely, trying not to create tension.

"Totik'ga Shin," she says fast and aggressively.

I keep silent after hearing that as I notice that her animosity towards me hassn't gone away, although I think that she might've softened up since we first met, seeing as how she's even telling me her full name.

"How did you guys know that Grasshead was here?" I ask So'krang.

"Sometimes, our people come here for various reasons," he starts to tell me. "One of them informed us that there might be a hiphomoy here. Turns out he was right."

"That's impossible. I've kept Grasshead well hidden. There wasn't even a single indication that he even existed."

"Our world is made of the same elements as yours: air, land, water and all the other things. Except that due to its nature, our world is maintained with tiamtsat."

"Tiamtsat?"

"It is the fundamental power of all creatures, and the primal energy source that holds every material together. Without it, we would all fall dead to ground, assuming we could reach the ground before it would crumble to nothingness."

"Then shouldn't you be dead?"

So'krang reaches out to his lower back. I hear a chime, and then he presents something to me. The object was some kind of small glass container shaped like a lantern.

"This is called a hido'marash," he tells me while showing me the object. "We store tiamtsat in it so that it will sustain when we're in places that have no tiamtsat in them. Namely heratrang'ga pan, which is the name we give to this world."

"That's kinda small," I ask as he puts back the object behind his back. "Doesn't look like it can hold much of that tiamtsat."

"Well, for someone who is alone, it wouldn't be enough," So'krang goes on to explain. "But in companies, the tiamtsat cycles through anything with tiamtsat in it. This way, it preserves itself longer."

"I . . . didn't entirely understand that explanation."

"Well . . . tiamtsat always needs to move from one place to another, but it can only move to places that have tiamtsat in them. So for example, it wouldn't be able to cycle through these trees, but it will through us."

"That's nice and all, but that still doesn't explain how you knew about Grasshead."

"As beings that possess tiamtsat, we are able to feel it around us. Normally in the Novaverse, we aren't able to precisely detect where it's coming from, but with a huge absence of it and a more concentrated source, we can pinpoint the location of the object in question. Unless you are a barsher'ga, in which case you can do it even when there's tiamtsat everywhere."

"I see. Come to think of it, I do remember someone giving a suspicious look a while back."

"Maybe he was one of us."

"Well, he had a bunch of children following him."

"Children? Oh yeah! It was a jadak'ga who informed us of the lost hiphomoy."

"Hmm. I thought something was off about that guy. Still don't understand what he was doing there, anyways."

"Children of the Novaverse take field trips here once or twice during their tengora years to learn more about the nature of the heratrang'ga pan and its inhabitants, namely the heranga. These trips are meant to emphasize how the heranga lack organization and unity, and how they violently fight each other over nonsensical ideas, and the one thing that describes them all as one poor species: ignorance."

"And how exactly do you benefit from these field trips?"

"Well, then we teach the children that they are better than the heranga and some other things used to induce pride and a sense of tribal behavior, so that they may look out for each other as they grow up and become stronger, just like how I do with my friends as an adult. It's something that will cause the children to unite together to achieve a higher cause, although I don't know for how long those teachings persist after the trip. I mean, I barely remember what they told me when I visited New York. All I remember is a lot of car noises and two people fighting over mustard in a line to a hot dog stand."

"Yeah, well whatever they told you back then probably worked. Seeing how you fight, I can tell you're the product of hardcore brainwashing."

"It's not brainwash. It's just the mentality of the Natin. Instead of looking for ourselves, we look out for each other."

"If you say so," I reply sarcastically.

Eventually, we make our way to a pond located at the core of the forest, a pond I'm awfully familiar with, although I've never had the chance to swim in it. We stand at the edge of the pond.

So'krang turns his body around and then whistles. Suddenly, all three of their monster-dog-things, or hiphomoys, as I have learned to call them, come out from behind a bunch of trees, supposedly "parked" there while their owners do who-knows-what.

Seeing them again reminds me that they hadn't participated during the fight. I wonder what reason their owners would have had not to use their help in the battle. They easily could've turned the tide in their favor. Instead, they chose to have them on the sidelines. I suppose there's a reason for that, one that I may or may not find out in the future.

"This is it," So'krang says.

"You live in a pond?" I jokingly say.

"Actually, this is the portal to our world. I mean, at the bottom of it, that is."

A portal at the bottom of a pond? I was surprised to hear that the discovery of a new world could be so easily achieved. Not as stupid a location as if it were in a public place for everyone to see, like an airport or something, but I'm not the only one that comes here. Occasionally, people come here to swim. What if one of them drowned and someone dived to the bottom to save him? He could want to find out what that shiny thing over there was, for example, and end up in a completely different place. If that does happen, how do these Natin deal with accidental invaders? I wonder what would've happened if I did decide to swim here.

Would I have been invited to this world much earlier, or seal my fate outside of that world? Under those circumstances, I would've never been discovered.

"At the bottom, huh?" I say. "You know someone can just dive in and come into that world of yours."

"It has happened before," So'krang says.

"Really? And what do you do when that happens?"

"Well . . . the portal is opened and closed with password or a key. Sometimes, a Natin forgets to close the portal behind, allowing invaders to come in freely. When this happens, we knock the invader unconscious and send him back to where they came from. Sometimes they even try to tell their friends of their discovery. Of course, not that it helps them. After we close the gate, there's nothing to be found, leaving their friends to assume they were dreaming or something. Some persist on finding the portal again, but sooner or later they give up, much like the others."

"Of course, you want to keep your existence a secret. Fuck knows what will happen if the wrong people know where you live."

Just before the plunge, I wonder whether I should wait for them to jump in first or just do it already. Actually, when I think about it, it's kind of a trivial decision to make.

"Listen," So'krang starts to say, somewhat ominously, "you can still go back home. It's not too late, so I suggest you make one final decision before we jump."

I think about his words and I think about the dilemma one more time. But when I think about it, it's not too long before I am reminded that up until now that my life has been nothing but a disgrace. With that thought in mind, I want to find out the truth, and I believe these people might provide me with the answers. I wasn't brought to this world just to be the laughing stock of some nonexistent monotheistic deity. I came to this world for a cause, and I want to find out what this cause is. Then again, there really isn't much of a dilemma here, considering that the world is going to end in about eight months, so I might as well stay alive while I let everyone else get crushed by a meteor or something.

"No," I tell him clearly and directly, "I'm coming with you."

A silence envelops the atmosphere for mere seconds.

"Very well," So'krang says with a smirk on his face, seemingly satisfied.

With everything set, everyone mounts their respective hiphomoys and prepares to dive in. Standing behind them, I can see them each take a pair of goggles that just sticks to their bodies without any belt or strap to hold it in place. It just floats there, and at that moment I also notice that all their other paraphernalia is floating as well. So'krang's claymore, nicely sheathed inside the scabbard, was just sticking to his back. The same goes for Pa'prak's star-bag-thing. I suppose I should ask them how they do it, but I want to focus on the jump right now. For the time being, I'll just assume it's magic.

But as I continue to inspect their backs, So'krang and To'shin were already deep inside the pond. Pa'prak, who still hasn't jumped in, leaps onto his hiphomoy, puts on his goggles and moves away from the pond as far as he can.

"Kniya!!" he shouts.

His hiphomoy then dashes forward and jumps head first into the pond. I now stand alone as I mount Grasshead. Looking forward in the direction of the pond, gazing into the air, I think about how this moment will be the start of a new phase. A phase that will hopefully last an eternity.

I do not take a few steps back, as I am barely away from the pond. I take a deep breath before Grasshead jumps without moving back first to gain some momentum. We are now in the pond, and I can't see anything. Looking closer, I can see blurred images of what I suppose are Pa'prak and his hiphomoy. Suddenly, I see something azure shining in front of him. As I get closer, the shining grows, and he disappears into it. Now, I am as close as

I can get to the shiny thing and the immense brightness forces me to close my eyes. Only light to see in the front, and nothing to see in the back. I can't see anything, but I can feel Grasshead dog-paddling his way into the light as my body pushes through the water.

Seconds later, I can see the light weakening through my eyelids. We're past the light, yet I still feel water. I open my eyes to see that I am at the bottom of a water source, but it doesn't feel like I'm in the same pond, but rather a different one. Looking to my sides, I can't see the end, but that doesn't matter right now, because I'm in need to catch some air before I drown. Grasshead swims up as fast as he can, getting closer and closer to the surface, and back into sunlight's reach.

Finally making it to the surface, I take a deep breath to bring oxygen back to my lungs. Looking around me, I can see that, to my surprise, I am in a lake. In front of me, beyond the trees that block my view, awaits my greatest surprise yet. A world that has yet to recognize my identity. That world is . . . the Novaverse!

CHAPTER V

A NEW BEGINNING! WILL IT BE BETTER? OR WILL IT BE WORSE?

Grasshead dog-paddles his way to the land in front of him. By the time we touch the ground, the bunch are already waiting for us, dried out by the time we get to them. They all look at us, watching as Grasshead shakes off all the water from his grassy fur, and then they immediately dash into the forest. Realizing the situation, I tell Grasshead to get a move on. Grasshead bursts into speed and goes straight into the forest, jumping over every fallen tree and dodging those that are still standing upright. With a clear destination in mind, Grasshead runs faster than ever before.

We eventually exit the forest and enter an enormous meadow. I can see the trio on their hiphomoys far away from me; they were able to catch some distance while Grasshead and I were still swiftly moving around trees and rocks in the forest behind us. Suddenly, I feel Grasshead accelerate, moving faster than even before. With an opportunity finally presented to him, I can feel myself slipping off his back as he gains more and more speed. I was finally required to grasp Grasshead's fur with both my hands. It was always so convenient until now: gently hold onto Grasshead as he tries not to step on the other forest animals, but now there's nothing to step on, and he just reached full speed.

Moving at twice the speed of a falcon, we catch up to the others. I am now in the middle of the group, with Pa'prak to my left, and So'krang and To'shin to my right. Due to the intense speed, I had to wrap my arms around Grasshead's neck so I wouldn't fly away because of the intense wind that blows in my face. At one point, I couldn't look straight anymore because all the wind hurts my eyes. My head faces down so I can't see where we're going.

Suddenly, I get a pat on my shoulder. I look with squinty eyes and see So'krang offering me a pair of goggles. I gladly take them. I didn't even need to tie them behind my head. The wind pretty much glues them to my face, although I did have to hold them in case I looked to the sides, and by doing so, I was surprised to see the others positioned nicely on their hiphomoys, unbothered by the wind, and their palms simply put on their respective hiphomoy's head, without grasping any hairs. To them, it's just another horse gallop.

As we keep moving forward, I see in the distance a massive purple wall, probably 500 feet in height, spanning across several miles.

We finally reach the wall and in front of me stands a massive purple gate with a white symbol painted on it of that appeared to be a thick cobra with a whole set of dog teeth, rather than just fangs, and a dragon maw to boot.

Upon standing right in front of the gate, we get off our rides.

"Another pair of goggles, just for me," I say jokingly. "Well ain't that just fucking convenient."

"I always keep a spare," So'krang says. "Just in case."

"Heh. Look at you," I reply sarcastically.

Looking at the gate and seeing how tall it is, I nearly lose balance just from awe at the height.

"By the way, what is this place?" I ask.

"This is the clan of Awari." So'krang goes on to explain. "The Natin won't accept having a heranga live among them. You probably haven't noticed this yet, but here, everyone hates the heranga. Most of them would erase them entirely if they could.

"That's uplifting," I respond sarcastically.

"However, if we can convince the clanmistress of the Awari to allow you to stay here, then maybe we can relieve the animosity towards you to a certain degree."

"So basically they just go from wanting to kill me to tolerating me. Doesn't sound like it's gonna be any better."

"You needn't worry. If the clanmistress of Awari says something, people usually follow her. Na, people WILL follow her."

"I guess that makes her president of everything. Right?"

"Not really. It's just that the Awari have a perfect mind. In addition to being telepaths, they have complete self-control over their instincts and behavior. They are calm and level-headed. They base their decisions on logic rather than emotions. In fact, it would take something dire to break their minds."

"And how does that help us?"

"Well, as I said, everyone here hates the heranga. That's because they are selfish, self-destructive, impulsive, greedy, arrogant . . . and I could go on for an eternity to describe them even more. They just destroy everything they step on and are always at each other's throats, no matter how stupid the reason is. Gangra, just thinking about how they behave over and over, without learning ANYTHING from their mistakes sickens me!"

"You okay there?" I compassionately ask him, seeing as he just lost his temper.

So'krang takes a deep breath.

"Sorry," So'krang says after quickly calming down. "Despite the general consensus of my people, I, as an individual, keep an open mind to new possibilities. Especially if it could end this eternal war we're in."

"I see," I say gently, trying not to hit any weak spots. "But I still don't understand how this mistress gonna help us."

"Well, in short, when you're a telepath, it's easy for you to understand people's emotion and desires. And equally, it is easy to trust such people."

"Sounds like a good reason to make to her president."

"It wouldn't matter. The clanmasters have little to no authority and their roles are representative at best. They mostly assign clanmembers to missions and host public events. Take the queen of England as an analogy."

"No political authority? Then how do you pass laws?"

"Referendums, of course!"

"I see. By the way, are we waiting for something?"

"Well, the gates should have opened already."

So'krang then looks up to see what's going on. The rest of us then look up together after him. While the others knew what they were doing, I have no idea what I'm supposed to be looking at.

"WO!" So'krang suddenly shouts. "KATA NEN'KA ITEKA!?"

Suddenly, someone pops up from beyond the top of the gate. "Sirai," he yells in an apologetic, drowsy tone, as if he just woke up from sleep. "Marang kap'in."

The man goes back beyond the gate and a few seconds later a small door, merged with the giant gate itself, slowly starts to open. Inch by inch as the gap between the doors expands, I get glimpse of what appears to be a city inside. The gate finally opens.

"Great," So'krang says. "Now we just need to figure out how to get you through without causing a riot."

"Put this on," To'shin suddenly says. Without a warning, To'shin just throws some kind of blanket over my head.

"The fuck!?" I say out loud.

"Don't take it off," she says coldly.

Realizing that the blanket is just part of the plan, I reluctantly keep it on . . . for now.

I peek one time from the blanket to see where Grasshead is. I mount him and cover myself entirely with the blanket. I start to hear the hiphomoys moving. I can feel Grasshead moving as well.

I find this trip to be rather uncomfortable. The blanket smells like dead rabbits and feels like a cow's hide. It's thick and leathery and quite heavy. It's composition of hairy stuff causes my skin to itch, as strands of what appears to be animal hair keeps falling on me. It almost feels like walking back home from a haircut in the summer, with the stubbles of hair sticking like glue to my body from the sweat. The only thing I can see right now is total darkness, and the only things I hear are footsteps and the rabbling of voices. Despite all this, I suppose it's necessary for the time being. I just hope this trip won't last long.

But this trip feels like an eternity. I can't possibly tell how much time has passed since I put it on.

"Can I take the blanket off, already?" I ask impatiently.

"Na," So'krang replies in a straightforward manner.

Some more time has passed, and still no confirmation whether I can take off the damn blanket.

"How 'bout now? Can I take it off?" I ask once more.

"You can take it off when I tell you," So'krang says, somewhat annoyed.

A long time has passed now since I put on this carcass-smelling blanket. Finally, So'krang pulls it off me, and I am finally able to witness my surroundings.

In front of me is something that looks like a giant-ass mausoleum, painted in purple and preceded by a large surface paved with stone and some flowered bushes here and there. Two pillars stand taller than the mausoleum at the entrance to it. I assume this is the clanmistress's place, considering the size of it and that the blanket came off me when we arrived here.

I look back to see what I could've witnessed on my way here if it weren't for that blanket. Everything looks like a regular modern city, with buildings and whatnot, and although the buildings didn't have an intricate design to them, there was something unusual about them, and something that I wouldn't have seen back where I came from: they were frickin' wide! Wide enough to have a rhino move about in them without worrying that it would crush you against the wall. If I had a room that wide, I wouldn't have to worry about Grasshead breaking lamps all the time.

There is also something else that I noticed is unusual. There is a road high above the ground, possibly a highway of sorts. Just as I ponder what it could be, I see a creature from afar running on it, mounted by someone. It was hard to tell what the creature was, but it looked like a monster-dog . . . no . . . a hiphomoy.

After looking around, I turn back to face the mausoleum once more.

"So this is where the mistress lives?" I ask.

"Correct," So'krang says. "And it's *clan*mistress."

"Right. I'll be sure to remember that in the future . . . hopefully."

We start to make our way into the palace. I take Grasshead with me, while the others leave theirs behind. As I enter the building, I enter a large rectangular hall that serves as a junction area to who-knows-where on the right and the left. On top of the hall is a giant fancy chandelier covering half of the hall, sparkling of gold and shining of diamond, as if these people just throw their money at whatever they want, preferring it be invested in interior design instead of military and the like.

Random people move about in the hall, most likely employees of her royal majesty. I can't help but notice how different their choice of clothing is compared to the three accompanying me. A much less decent fashion than what I'm used to, men had wrapped bandages of various colors around their stomach, with everything above exposed. Woman, on the other hand, had a sleeveless fabric top that covered the breasts, showing shoulders and stomach, tied around the back and the nape while crossing itself at the sternum. Some even wear sleeveless jackets thin as rice paper, while everyone wears leather pants of various leg lengths, much like my friends here. I needn't even mention the horns that define these people and the tattoos that vary in shape.

What I find interesting is their footing. Flip-flop-like in appearance, it is only a flat sole connected by straps to a narrow cuff around the ankle. One strap came between the toes, while the other one was behind the foot. It seems as though these sole-exclusive flip-flops stick at the bottom of the wearer's feet.

Putting aside my grasp of how their fashion works, we move forward, entering a wide corridor. Eventually we make our way to another junction, confronted with a staircase and two other corridors leading left and right. We go left.

We keep moving. We finally make our way to the end of the corridor, and at the end stands a large door of refined wood. So'krang knocks on the door. A few seconds pass with no response. So'krang knocks again.

"Sotorek!" an almost-gentle, feminine voice yells.

So'krang opens the door and we all enter the office of the clanmistress of Awari. As we continue to walk inside, the room starts to get bigger, as if the room was narrower near the entrance, but getting larger as we progress. The room is fairly empty. I see two metal drawers embedded into the left wall, one next to the other. Each has a glowing green button on it on top of the handle. On the wall making up the end of room is a series of windows for all to see what's going on in the city from the top of the clanmistress's place. But the star of the room is the desk, located just near the windows, but not too close to block anyone's way of enjoying a nice view. And, of course, who is to be sitting in the desk but the clanmistress herself? Hard at work doing all kinds of paperwork, still with a big pile of papers to finish sitting on the desk to her right. Apparently she isn't doing all the paperwork alone, because to her left is a man sitting and helping her get it over with. Noticing that we're getting closer, she puts down her pen, moves her wrist up and down for some relief, and then sighs.

"Mark'nan Anji Akib'satra," So'krang begins to say. "I am Sowi'ga Krang'pegin of the Yasin, and these are Totik'ga Shin of the Shakten and Panar Prak'nen of the Heimareng. We recently came back from heratrang'ga pan with an important discovery."

With the clanmistress looking at us, she gets up from her office chair and makes her way to us, with her assistant following her. They finally come close to us. I am amazed by how elegant the clanmistress is.

She wears deep purple pants, the unusual flip-flops that everyone wears, and a very thin purple short-sleeved jacket over a black shirt. Her pants aren't long enough to hide her ankles, showing a bead anklet worn around her right one. She has black hair reaching down to her upper back and a bunch of tattoos, more than anyone I've seen so far. One is on the center of her forehead which looks like a diamond in between two crude-looking lightning bolts parallel to each other, with one mirroring the other. Another one is a slightly bent stripe on her left temple which starts at her eye and disappears into her hair. And of course, there's the tattoo that everyone shares: the neck tattoo. Being this close to her, I can see that it is the same as the symbol that is on the gate to the city. With the tattoos blocking her face, I can't help but notice that she is a bit angry to see me, but remains elegant throughout.

Her assistant is much taller than her, probably dwarfing her by a foot or so. He wears blue pants, the flip-flops and a thin black sleeveless jacket, like the one the clanmistress is wearing, over a scaly black sleeveless shirt. His neck tattoo is different than that of the clanmistress, a head of a creature. The other tattoo he has, which is unlike any I've seen so far, is a sleeve tattoo covering his right arm from the shoulder to his wrist. It has a tribal motif to it, with what appears to be a rope spiraling around his arm, and in between the large gaps were rain drops with curved tops. Each gap contained a top row and a bottom row, with the top row having the drops fall down, just the way they should be, while the drops at the bottom were inverted.

"Kata orim'in English?" the clanmistress asks in her calm demeanor.

"This is . . . uh . . . ," So'krang starts to say, somewhat confused.

"For fuckin' real!?" I reply, astonished. "You had all this time and didn't ask for my fuckin' name!?"

"I was too busy thinking about everything else."

"Well, maybe it's time you should ask."

"Of course. What's your name?"

"Neph Baker."

The clanmistress looks at me with eyes of disbelief. She knows she sees a human in front of her, but is desperate to deny that such a predicament might be. Maybe this one didn't want a tattoo? Maybe he broke his horn as a kid? All these self-imposed questions in an effort to avoid the truth had no meaning, because as much as she tries, I am but a piece of filth, standing on the surface where she doesn't want me, whether it be in her building or the world where she lives. But it doesn't matter where, as no one here will welcome me with open arms . . . or at least that's what I've been told.

"Kata heranga?" she asks, maintaining her calm demeanor as it slowly falls apart.

"This is Neph Baker," So'krang starts off. "We believe he may help us defeat the Airatsmeka once and for all. In fact, we believe he might be . . . ." So'krang suddenly pauses, as if a cat got his tongue. He takes a deep breath of anguish, holding his lips tight as he stares at the ground with uncertainty on his face.

"The . . . ," he goes on to say hesitantly, "composer of the . . . calm horizon."

The clanmistress turns around, looks up, then looks down on the floor, then back up, moving further away from us with each second she tries to understand the absurdity of the situation. After all, humans are never to come here. Otherwise, why would they, the Natin or whatever these people are called, feel the need to hide from those they consider filth? I guess it's because they wouldn't want to contaminate their precious land.

The clanmistress turns around hastily and rushes back to face us.

"DORA'KATA JANG'GA?!" she yells while flinging her hands in the air, breaking her calm.

"Please calm down, mark'nan," So'krang says while falling into a defensive position. "We have not forgotten the higher creed, but this is different."

The clanmistress stares at him curiously. She takes a deep breath, slowly calming down.

"Why do you respond to me in English?" she asks with a near-calm voice. "For the sake of this heranga? Their minds are fueled by a desire for murder and money. Have you forgotten that?"

"Not at all, mark'nan. But this one . . . he is . . . a fearsome warrior."

"Impossible. And above all: the composer!? You know fool well it's just a nursery rhyme. You are no longer a child, Yasin'ga. Start behaving like one!"

"Nursery rhyme?" I mutter to myself.

"It's true," Pa'prak suddenly interrupts. "We were sent to retrieve a rogue hiphomoy from the corrupted realm. And during our mission, this heranga defeated us in battle."

"How could a heranga defeat you in battle?" the clanmistress asked, confused and skeptical. "Those who were born and raised among warriors, lose to filth that walks on a path of chaos paved by his kind?"

"I love you too, ma'am," I say jokingly, although mildly angered.

"Mark'nan," Pa'prak replies. "Please read my mind."

The clanmistress sighs and then puts both her hands on each side of Pa'prak's head.

I stand there watching for a while. The clanmistress seems really focused with her eyes closed and all. After a while, she opens her eyes and blinks rapidly, showing enlightenment. She then rushes to So'krang and starts to read his mind, stretching her arms high to reach his head. Almost immediately after she finishes with So'krang, she rushes to To'shin, and then reads her mind as well.

After she's done reading the minds of all of them, she turns her head to me, and looks at me with astonishment. She no longer looks at me with the idea that I'm just another human, but as something else. Looking into her eyes, I can see that she believes a misplaced creature with a higher purpose, although I still somewhat question my identity.

She comes to me and attempts to read my mind with her usual "hands on head" thing. I notice her eyes twitching, and after a while she lets go. She then looks at me.

"So . . . ?" I ask. "What did you see?"

"I couldn't," she tells me, not surprised at all.

"Why not?"

"Because you don't want me to read your mind."

"What do you mean?"

"I cannot read your mind if you do not want me to."

"Heh. Didn't know telepaths work that way. I mean, I always knew they could disregard people's privacy, but this is some telepathic bureaucracy shit right here."

I smirk at her at her, as I find my own joke quite funny, but she isn't amused at all. My smirk slowly fades as I realize this.

"OK," I start to say, returning to seriousness. "You can read my mind now."

She attempts to read my mind again with the same hand motions, only to end up as confused as she previously was.

"You still don't want me to read your mind," she says.

"But I gave you permission," I reply, confused.

"You might have told me that you gave me permission, but subconsciously, you resist."

"How the fuck does that even work?"

"You have things that you wish to hide from others, and that is why your mind responds the way it does. However . . . seeing what your friends had to battle, I believe that you do not belong in heratrang'ga pan. Maybe you have a place here, and I am willing to give you a home if it means the benefit of your power.

After all, you wouldn't simply leave your family behind only to come here."

"Trust me . . . with my family, you'd wanna run away as far as you can and never look back . . . or kill yourself. Whatever comes first."

"You chose well. An untapped power lingers within you; something that could not be revealed by the resources of your inferior peers. A heranga that is able to defeat the Natin is not something to be ignored. But whether you are the composer of the calm horizon or not, only time will tell."

"Great. So how do we find out?"

"Your power will be put to test. But know this: should you fail to satisfy us, you will return to heratrang'ga pan, for both failures and outsiders do not belong among us."

"Little late for that; I already faked my death."

"That is not my concern."

That last sentence struck me hard, since despite her elegance, I couldn't help but feel the cold apathy emanating from her as those words came out of her mouth. I'm a bit startled.

"A little empathy wouldn't hurt you," I quietly mutter to myself.

A brief silence envelops the atmosphere.

"I had better prepare an announcement," the clanmistress remarks.

"An announcement for what?" I ask her, confused.

"For you. We can't simply have a heranga running freely without an explanation."

The clanmistress goes over to an intercom I happened to miss on the right portion of the office. She presses and holds a red button.

"Attention, everyone," she starts to announce. "I have a special announcement to make. Everyone is invited to be present in front of the mark'pani in two hours."

I can only imagine how confused they have to be when their leader isn't speaking to them in their native language.

"So we wait now, huh?" I ask. "What do I do in the meantime?"

"You wait." She adds, "I don't want you walking around until after I deliver the announcement. In the meantime, would you like something to eat? I suppose you're hungry?"

"As a matter of fact, I am."

"The kitchen and dining room are upstairs. All of you go have something to eat. Tell the Soparkat'ga I sent you and they will prepare for you something. Also, make sure they don't have any trouble with our friend here."

"Thank you for your generosity, mark'nan," So'krang says.

We turn around and leave the clanmistress's office. We're excited for a nice meal after the recent happening, as we wait for the clanmistress to prepare for the revolutionary announcement. Revolutionary by my standards, at least.

CHAPTER VI

LIKE IT OR NOT . . . HE STAYS

Two hours have already passed since the clanmistress told everyone on the intercom about her upcoming announcement. Immediately after that, we went to eat at the dining room, much like how the clanmistress suggested we do.

The food is very reminiscent of those five-star restaurants back on my world. In fact, it IS food from five-star restaurants, and despite how I enjoyed stuffing my stomach with those fancy meals, I couldn't help but notice the lack of exclusivity when it comes to Novaversian cuisine. Everything back on the table seemed to be borrowed from my world. I was expecting a filet mignon with dreadlocks, or maybe a giant koi stuffed with creamed potatoes. But no. You got the usual haute cuisine-looking steak together with the haute cuisine-looking soup, which is not bad in itself, but only reflects upon their culture when it comes to food.

After that, Pa'prak and To'shin left back to their rightful clans. As for So'krang, the clanmistress told him to wait by my side, even though he, too, didn't seem like he wanted to wait around much. She probably has big plans for him.

As for me, I'm napping on a sofa in the guest room, and the clanmistress suddenly approaches me just as I finally start to catch some Zs.

"Neph," she gently addresses me.

I open my eyes. I'm still drowsy and my eyes are only half open. I find the desire to go back to sleep, but I understand that there are more important matters to tend to. Reluctantly, I get up to sit on the sofa as I slowly collect myself for the upcoming task at hand.

"It's time," she gently says.

Still drowsy, I rub my eyes and face to stimulate the nerves as the feeling of numbness gradually goes away. I slowly get up from the sofa by pushing against my knees as my legs are on the ground. I stagger, but quickly regain balance. I find the desire to get back on the sofa, but I hold myself together as I prepare for the more important things at hand.

I witness the clanmistress leaving the guest room as she elegantly makes her leave. So'krang suddenly appears to me by my side, already on his feet. I have no idea where he popped out from, seeing as I was asleep most of the time.

"Let's go," he tells me.

As I stand on my feet, we both follow the clanmistress to wherever, with Grasshead and the assistant following behind us. We go down the stairs, through the hall near the entrance, and then outside to the paved area just outside the entrance. This time, I see stairs in front of me leading somewhere upwards. We go up the stairs, which brings us to a large square platform cut out from the paved area beneath it. We make it to the edge, and to my astonishment, an enormous crowd stands in front of us, like these people wouldn't settle for hearing this thing on the television, assuming they have one, of course.

I look over the balustrade to find out that the surface I'm standing on is floating, and that there is a missing piece in the pavement below, further justifying my speculation that this floating surface is, in fact, cut out from the floor. Grasshead rushes to see what's beyond the balustrade like any normal dog would do, even though he's actually a hiphomoy. But even with all this excitement, I still can't figure out where the balustrade came from.

The clanmistress stands in front of this weird-looking microphone that looks more like a swarm of greenish-yellow fireflies. As she tests to see if it's working by flinging her hand across the glowing area which is the microphone, bubbling vibrations can be heard across the entire area. My ears hurt a bit as I stand to her right. On her other side, I can see her assistant standing to her left.

As she faces the enormous crowd, she seems well-prepared to give her speech. Back where I come from, I don't recall ever seeing a crowd like this being so still and silent during a speech. Most of the time the crowds that I witnessed just made a lot of noise and trouble. Heck . . . sometimes someone would try to jump on stage and beat the shit out of whoever was giving the speech. But these people right here . . . I can see that they're a proud collective with such discipline that they respect not only their higher-ups, but each other as well.

And it shows quite strongly, as the silence lasts for several seconds, and no one can tell when the clanmistress will start to talk.

"Good afternoon, Natin . . . ," she suddenly says.

The crowd rabbles in confusion, most likely because their beloved clanmistress is speaking in English.

"Today . . . is a day of change. Not necessarily revolution, but change indeed. This change will relinquish our need to wait. To wait . . . because the great Awari told us so. She only told us to wait. She didn't say why. She didn't say when. She didn't say what. She knows all, yet all we know is to wait. Are we waiting for the Messiah? Are we waiting for Jesus? We abhor such ideas. We CONDEMN such ideas. The higher creed says only that which has proven itself can be acknowledged, and I have received today a most informative message that might finally bring us the answer we've been waiting for. This . . . is Neph Baker. Back in heratrang'ga pan, this heranga defea—"

The crowd starts rabbling in anger before she could continue her speech, with shaken fists and fingers pointing at her.

"SILENCE!!" she shouts. "I will finish my speech!"

A moment of silence occurs. The crowd is reminded of their position as they become quiet once more.

"This heranga defeated a Shakten'ga, a Yasin'ga and Heimareng'ga, all on a mission to heratrang'ga pan. His powers were unexpected. A heranga displaying the capabilities to fight against us, the Natin. Never before has it been heard that a heranga can spar with a Natin . . . until this day. This heranga holds inside him a power yet to be understood. A power that is even beyond ours. A power that far exceeds what we have created and developed in more than six centuries. Through him, we will no longer have to wait, for he is akai'mask'nen ka ojak'ga yopak'shik, the composer of the calm horizon."

The crowd slowly starts to fill with laughter

"TOMADIM!!" she yells.

Everyone becomes quiet at an instant, without even a tenth of a second passing since the clanmistress shouted.

"You might think this is a joke . . . but this heranga that you so much despise at the moment answers to all the criteria. Right now you mock him . . . but he will prove himself. And if he proves himself, then he has answered to the higher creed. Their god has disappointed them, yet they still believe in him. This is the reason why we have become what we are today. And it is the reason why the higher creed exists. Because everything that we found ourselves on has proven itself. And this heranga will prove himself as well."

She pauses for a couple of seconds.

"Why do you fear? Why do you doubt?"

Again, a pause, only this time for three seconds.

"Do you have something to lose? Does this heranga threaten you? There can only be two results: if he lives, then he shows that he might have a place in here. If he dies, then he has proven himself as filth that is unworthy of our respect. None of you should care for either, because it is time's responsibility to handle his fate. All of you will continue your lives while they go, uninterrupted by this heranga. In the future, you might recognize him as one of us. Regardless, and at this moment, we shall accept him as one of us, because he is not like his kind. If he was, then he wouldn't be standing here today. You do not have to be his friend, but you may not persecute him. Persecution is for the ignorant, and we pride ourselves on being a collective free of bigotry, for all those that possess bigotry belong elsewhere, in a place where it synergizes well with corruption and evil. I suggest that all of you greet this heranga well, and see him not as another heranga, or makis'bak as some of you prefer to call them, but as part of the united clans."

She pauses for the last time.

"Thank you for your respect, everyone. You may all retire to your previous assignments."

And with that, the crowd disperses. Everyone turns back and leaves to what they were doing before.

"Come with me, Neph." the clanmistress says while gently putting her hand on my shoulder.

We both turn around and head back into the building, followed by Grasshead, So'krang and the assistant. On my way in, I hear the sound of a stone door closing as if it is dragged by a mystical force on a hard ground. I look back to see the floating stairs and surface slowly descending into the ground, filling the gap they created in order to prepare the stage. Quickly, the stage disappears and reverts to what it was when I first came here, although the balustrade stays. I suppose it will be removed later by other means.

After witnessing the magical sight, I proceed to follow the clanmistress.

At her office, she sits behind her desk, her assistant leaning on the wall, and I'm standing in front of her with Grasshead and So'krang to my side.

"They didn't seem very satisfied," I say.

"They are not used to accepting outsiders," the clanmistress calmly says. "But over time, they will recognize you as one of us."

"Don't be so sure. Besides, 'they'? You say it like you don't share their opinion."

"I've already seen your capabilities from the eyes of your friends."

"Friends?" I say with disbelief.

"Listen . . . not everyone is able to understand this, and it would be even harder to accept it. What I have seen is what most people won't see, and I believe, as the mark'nan of the clan of Awari, that you might have a place here, and I want to give you the opportunity to prove yourself."

"And what about everyone else?"

"Give them time, and they will learn to accept you. Or at the very least tolerate you."

"Gee, that's encouraging," I say sarcastically.

"Neph . . . don't worry. In the end, I'm sure everything will fall into place."

"Easy for you to say," I start to say, mildly annoyed. "You already have a place, and a fancy chair to sit on. I have NO PLACE. Why do you think I came here to begin with? Just so I could be demonized by more people? No! It's cuz I thought I could get away from the puddle of shit I was sinking in. But now . . . I don't know if this is what I want."

"Then let me ask you this." The clanmistress's tone changes to seem more sentimental and compassionate. "What do you want?"

Feeling the empathy I so desired from her, I put aside my mild rage and think seriously about her words, for a seriously emotional question deserves an equally emotional answer.

"What do I want?" I ask myself. I think about it a little more, until it finally comes to me.

"To find a place where I belong." I start to say, full of emotional thoughts. "To find a purpose in life. To be useful . . . unlike how everyone makes me feel. Basically feel like I didn't waste my mother's eggs just so she could die when I came outta her v—"

"All right, enough," the clanmistress rushes to cut me short. "I understand your desires."

As she says those words, she gets up from her chair and slowly walks up to me, moving parallel to her desk as she smoothly passes her gentle feminine fingers on its flat surface.

"However, in time you will discover . . . ," she goes on to say.

She finally stands in front of me. And as she stands a head shorter than me, she presses gently at my sternum with her index finger, supposedly trying to reach my heart.

"That 'useful' is what you make of yourself, and not what others make of you," she finishes. "Which is why I am confident you will do everything in your power not to fail."

"Because if do I'll go back to shit," I say, a tad afraid.

"Yes," she says, sounding rather confused as she rolls her eyes to the sides. "That is . . . one way to put it."

Even when the mood of the conversation changes, I now know that I must do whatever it takes to stay here. Or, more accurately, make sure I don't return to the shit. I have no idea what awaits me here . . . but I'll get through any trial they'll put me through.

"So'krang, I have arrangements for you," she suddenly addresses So'krang.

"Yes, Mark'nan. How may I be of help?" So'krang says, displaying the uttermost loyalty.

"You two seem attached."

"Not really," I quickly say, passive-aggressively.

"I would like you to be his mentor," she continues.

"I dunno about that. I don't quite attach myself to people who try to kill me."

"Don't worry," she replies. "You'll learn in time how death is a part of the life of any tak'nen. Besides, someone has to teach you the basics of our world."

"What's wrong with the other two?"

"Nothing. To'shin has captured a highly wanted marbar and Pa'prak taught several Natin the techniques of Heimareng. Basically, they are exceptional at what they do and the same goes for all Natin, something that you will learn over time. But out of the three, So'krang is the most suitable, seeing as how he was an acclaimed student in his tengora years and afterwards went on to kill more than 200 Airatsmeka as a Yasin'ga and has led several expeditions. Also, he is surprisingly knowledgeable of our world, which I believe will be of use for you so that you may know how the Natin function."

"Murder on the resume, huh? That's definitely not a good impression."

"Besides, neither you nor I have the time to wait for a mentor to be properly selected and assigned to you."

"Hmm . . . then I guess we don't have much to go on."

I don't necessarily refuse to have So'krang teach me about this world and show me around, but I don't really understand how anyone else couldn't do the same job, if not better.

Suddenly, I feel a strong force falling on my shoulder, pushing me down as I resist. I look to my side and I see So'krang, putting his heavy hand on my shoulder, joyful as ever with a stupid smirk on his face.

"So where do we start?" So'krang asks, mildly excited as he tries to hide it.

"For now, you can retire to your home," the clanmistress says. "Afterwards, do what you feel is right. Teach him or send him into battle. You have full liberty on how to handle the teaching of this young man."

"I undertstand. Thank you, Mark'nan."

"Now please, leave me be. I have matters to attend to."

"Of course, Mark'nan."

And with that, we bid the clanmistress farewell and start to make our way out.

"Come," So'krang tells me.

As I see it now, I have a ton of adventures ahead of me. What these adventures hold, I have no idea. Regardless, I know that these adventures are going to be tough and ruthless, and that I must withstand whatever they might throw at me. I will be put through trials to test if I am indeed the composer, and I intend to prove such, for any and all failures will throw me back to a life of condemnation, back into the puddle of shit that I was endlessly sinking in, and the one place I do not want to go back to. It is so important for me to stay away from that place where people kept staring at me with demonizing eyes that the title of the composer doesn't really mean much to me, but the fact that I am given a new home with the opportunity to start my life anew does. Such an opportunity I do not intend to just throw out the window. I will hold onto this opportunity with my teeth, and I will not let go until I am dead. That is how important this is for me. But I have no idea what these people are capable of, and how hard their trials will be. I may withstand, and I may not. I just hope that if I fail, then I will die too, since death is more pleasing than going back to being a bird in a cage. And in the end, whether these people will accept me or not, I cannot tell. But one thing is for certain: I'll be the only person here with an American accent.

CHAPTER VII

WALKING AND TALKING IN THE WESTERN SULFUR VALLEY

Now the hiphomoys are walking up some rocky hill, as opposed to the last 1000 miles where they just ran like crazy. It was quite neat, considering that I've never seen Grasshead run that fast for so long, except for that other time when we first arrived. There isn't even a single indication that they're exhausted; it's like they have some kind of magical mechanism of infinite energy hidden inside them.

We reach the top of the hill, and beyond that we see a valley of rock, accompanied by the smell of sulfur. We go downhill into the valley.

The valley is mostly brown with some yellowish stains here and there. It is completely devoid of plant life, and I can't see any animals either. It is very hot here as much as it is dry. But above all, it is so huge that I can't see the end of it unless I count the deep-blue, completely opaque ocean to the right as the end, because as it would suggest, we're at the border of this land. I can already understand that it's going to be one literal hell of a journey.

"Being the mentor of the composer," So'krang suddenly tells himself, sounding somewhat despondent. "If it were only rewarding in some way."

"You don't seem too excited about this job," I reply curiously while trying to sound indifferent.

"Well frankly, it is unprecedented. I don't think anyone would've known how to react to such a situation. More so, I don't know how to approach this myself."

"Be creative. What can I say?"

"I'll tell you this too: I don't actually believe in the composer. To me it's just a legend that exploded out of proportion and made way for bedtime stories and a fanhood of ridiculous believers."

"Really. You didn't seem to have a problem with it when we nearly killed each other. Well . . . after that, actually."

"Well, I didn't really have an opinion on the matter. I almost never take missions in heratrang'ga pan, and I wanted to get it over with. Besides, I knew that Pa'prak wouldn't let it go, and seeing how strong you are, it was the only way to bring back your hiphomoy, and therefore finish the mission."

"Hmm . . . so I understand it was more of a technicality that I came here, rather than a true passion for . . . whatever the fuck this composer is. Y'know, come to think about it, you might've actually been the best pick for a mentor after all."

"That's . . . complimenting. I suppose."

We continue to ride further into the valley. Silence continues to envelop us as we move on. I don't really know what to talk about, and he doesn't really seem in a mood to talk.

"So, uh . . . ," I start. "Doesn't it bother you we tried to kill each other a while ago?"

"Na. Don't worry about it," he says, taking it easy. "I've been on the verge of death several times. It's basically part of my job, and the same could be said for every tak'nen. I mean, if I held a vendetta against every Airatsmeka that tried to kill me, I'd have a list that I would never be able to finish. Besides, most of them meet their end sooner or later."

"What's a tak'nen?"

"Members of the warrior clans. The clans are categorized into two types: tak'nen, the ones who fight and prevent the Airatsmeka—or haa'bak if you really hate them—from gathering outside of Horei, and the tak'na, the ones that don't fight and . . . do what non-fighters do."

"And how many clans are there?"

"Two hundred and twenty four. They are Kriya, Sihok, Magaiba, Wab—"

"Whoa, whoa, stop! I didn't ask for their names. I just wanted to know how many. But man . . . two hundred and twenty four. That's a fuckin' lot. And you can name all of them?"

"It's mandatory for all tengora'nen to memorize the name of all the clans before komo'kea'ka."

"Fuck! I can't remember the fifty states, yet you can name me over 200 clans."

"States of what?"

"States of America."

"Oh right. I didn't pay much attention at heranga civics back then."

"Back then where exactly? And what's tengora?"

"A tengora'nen is a young Natin before komo'kea'ka. You can say it is the equivalent of a school student in heratrang'ga pan. The tengora years are the most academic I had. Now it is just fighting. Always fighting."

"Hmm. Don'tcha ever get tired of fighting?"

"I was pre-destined to fight. That's reason alone why I am a tak'nen."

"So, ever feel like doing something else? Like . . . even once?"

"It wouldn't matter. Nobody here chooses what they desire to do. Their purpose is bestowed upon them by a higher force."

"So you mean nobody gets to choose anything here? Not just their jobs, but literally everything?"

"Na. Sorry but I wasn't being precise. You can choose. You can choose things like hobbies, what you want to eat for dinner, what you want to do the afternoon, what bar should you go out to have a glass of safik with friends, and so forth. What you can't choose is your purpose. But that shouldn't prevent you from building your future."

"What if you're not satisfied with your purpose? What if you want a career change?"

"There's no such thing. Every Natin at the age of fifteen, after completing nine years of tengora'pani, undergoes the ritual of komo'kea'ka, where they are integrated into one of the many clans. The idea is that everyone has a calling, and the ritual of komo'kea'ka is meant to find that calling for you, because it's what you'll do best, and therefore allow you to benefit your society to the fullest."

"Age of fifteen, huh? So it's a quinceañera."

"I don't know what that is, but I promise you, it's nothing like any rite of passage you may know. You see, unlike the things you're used to, komo'kea'ka is not only symbolic, but bestows one with a clear purpose."

"What if you ended up doing something that isn't your calling?"

"That never happens."

"And what about you? How did you take it when you found out you were gonna be a uh . . . Spartan warrior . . . of sorts?"

"Like I said, I was pre-destined to become a Yasin'ga. Besides, they prepare us in tengora'pani that we don't choose what to be, but whatever we may become, we will be ideal at it."

"Why not just let you choose what you want to be?"

"Well . . . nobody actually knows what's good for them, because at that age you're not entirely sure what you want to do. You see, there are so many directions you can take, but you don't know which one is the best. You start to take one direction, and then you don't like it, then you go back and take another one, and then you don't like that one too and slowly you just get angrier. That is why the ritual of komo'kea'ka always attunes us with our calling. So that we'll always end up doing what we do best."

"Wow. That's . . . actually kinda awesome. A society that gives you the best possible job for you. Humans can learn a thing or two from your people."

"They would probably just stay with their ideals, anyway."

We continue to walk in the valley. We climb up yet another hill, only this time, once we get to the top, beyond that was a sight to see: a giant lizard that bears the appearance of a dragon, only without wings. Bigger than a rhino; smaller than an elephant. Teeth as sharp as katanas with a thick grayish-black hide to boot. Standing on the toes of each of his four legs, with each toe bearing a razor nail the size of my palm. I knew it couldn't be a dragon judging by how he kept his head low at shoulder height, as opposed to how dragons present themselves, with their heads high above their bodies. Besides . . . dragons? Dragons are awesome but they don't exist, not even in parallel universes.

"That's a noomthey," So'krang says.

"It isn't . . . some kind of dragon, right?" I ask.

"Please. Dragons . . . ," he says jokingly and somewhat in disbelief.

"He isn't gonna come here, is he?"

"They usually keep to themselves, unless they're hungry. Good thing this one didn't notice us yet."

"But he won't come after us, right?"

"Na. Well . . . usually they don't."

The noomthey turns his attention to us. He seems alarmed but stays in his place.

"Like I said, don't worry," So'krang says, almost nervous. "Hopefully another one will come and they will try to eat each other."

"What are they, cannibals?"

"The western noomthey is. Because the western sulfur valley is mostly lifeless and the only ones that survive here are the noomtheys. That's why they had to resort to eating each other. The eastern sulfur valley, on the other hand, has more life, so the eastern noomthey has more things to eat, like the golden-feathered xiphorynch, or the draggas, or the golden-bearded hookhorn, among other things. Because of this, the western subspecies is much stronger because it had to develop strong teeth and a thick hide to survive against other noomtheys."

"So if you were to put a western noomthey against an eastern one, then the eastern one wouldn't stand a chance, right?"

"True."

"So . . . if this is the western sulfur valley, then where is the eastern? I mean, I can see the ocean from here. So shouldn't this be the eastern?"

"The eastern sulfur valley is located exactly east from here on Hingshasra between the clans of Sihita and the clan of Tarten."

"Hmm . . . you sure know a lot . . . for a warrior who's supposed to fight all the time, that is."

"Why, thank you," he says cheerfully with a smirk on his face.

The conversation becomes interesting and friendly. In fact, we're probably starting to bond, although I'm still somewhat reluctant to be with friends with someone who nearly killed me. Normally, I would hold a vendetta against people who do me wrong, but since he apologized, it gives our relationship a whole different meaning. I don't remember when the last time someone apologized to me was, let alone for trying to kill me. I'll just let time do its part in this relationship.

Right now though, we have a bigger problem. The noomthey is still staring at us, I have no idea what he's going to do, and I'm in no place to call any actions regarding the matter.

"So what should we do with him?" I ask.

"Taking him head on is a bad idea," So'krang says.

"Do you usually fight these things?"

"Never. They aren't the enemy. Unless they attack for some reason, then we just neutralize them."

"Maybe we should move around him."

"That would be a grand idea."

We back away from the top of the hill from which we can watch the noomthey and we start walking left to move around him. Although this extra trip would be more bothersome, it's probably worth our safety. I didn't come all this way to become noomthey chow.

We continue to move on, with that noomthey way behind. I feel we're slowly exiting the sulfur valley, judging by the weakening smell of sulfur. Although I still can't ignore the lifeless biome which surrounds me, I do feel like we're making progress. Hopefully, I will discover my purpose here sooner than I can expect.

"I wanted to ask you: what do you exactly do in tengora?"

"Well . . . it's not much different from what you may expect. We enroll at the age of six until the age of fifteen. There are mandatory classes; most of them are academic, such as civics, math, English. Mandatory classes are not limited to just academics. Among the other non-academic are equestrianism and . . . other stuff I can't really remember."

"You guys are taught to ride horses as a mandatory class?"

"Hiphomoys. I don't know if you noticed, but we don't drive cars here."

"Actually, I didn't."

"Anyway, the other types of classes are the selective classes."

"What are those?"

"Well um . . . how should I explain this?"

"In the most natural way possible, of course."

"From the moment we enroll in tengora'pani, everyone starts with the same classes."

"Yeah, I already got that."

"Based upon our performance throughout the years, we are assigned to the class we will be most efficient at. Basically, the tengora'nen are divided into different classes based on what they are best at. The purpose of this is to stimulate the callings of the tengora'nen in order to estimate which clan they will be integrated to upon reaching the age of fifteen."

"Isn't a calling something you're born with? I mean, it will pop up by itself eventually."

"Yes, but the calling remains dormant in our early ages. You see, the tiamtsat is product of the Gangra, the progenitors of our world and the suppliers of tiamtsat. There are two hundred and twenty-four Gangra, therefore two hundred and twenty-four clans, therefore two hundred and twenty-four types of tiamtsat."

"Wait . . . there are types of tiamtsat? And I assume each one is representative of its respective . . . uh . . . gangrene, was it?"

"Gan*gra*. But yes. You see . . . each type of tiamtsat is concentrated the most in a large patch somewhere in the Novaverse. This happens because Natin of the same tiamtsat type gather in that patch for whatever reason. And because tiamtsat is an itinerant energy . . . ."

"We talked about it; how it moves from one to the other."

"It moves to all the things surrounding it. That is how a single type of tiamtsat concentrates in a single area. If the Natin who currently live in that area were to disperse, then the patch would slowly revert to its original formation."

"Original formation?"

"A patch containing many types of tiamtsat. That is exactly with Hanghidobanei, which is the archipelago where all the families live."

"Families?"

"Yes, families. I don't need to explain to you what a family is, right?"

"Oh. No, I just thought . . . you meant something else. Never mind. So you were saying that these families are relocated there?"

"You're starting to grasp it. You see, when a child is born in the Novaverse, they absorb tiamtsat from their surroundings. Because they absorb several types of tiamtsat into their system, stimulating a single type of tiamtsat helps develop that type. With that, that type of tiamtsat grows and pushes the other types out of the body in the progress. From there, the calling slowly starts to manifest.

"That's great and all, but I still don't get why they have to move to Hanghoo . . . whatever it's called?"

"The people have decided that all births will happen in Hanghidobanei to prevent any form of selective birth location so that the population of every clan will have a fair amount of disciples. And because Hanghidobanei includes all types of tiamtsat in a dense and relatively small area, it would only be fair to place families there."

"I don't think I'm entirely getting you."

"Well . . . let's take the clan of Mahasa for example. The Mahasa'ga has the potential to become theoretically any clan they want and in the early days, they were among the most-demanded clans. Women intentionally moved to the clan of Mahasa to give birth there, and the resulting child would be a future Mahasa'ga. The people noticed this pattern of behavior, so before the Mahasa'ga could overpopulate the Novaverse, the people have made a law that requires all pregnant women to give birth at a location that has at least fifty-seven different types of tiamtsat. And to make things easy, they just go to Hanghidobanei. Of course, they could always give birth in the wild, but the trelyks might come and eat them, or if I dare say, a homong. Actually, come to think of it, nobody would let a pregnant woman in an area with a homong in it."

"The Mahasa'ga sound awesome. Are they kings?"

"Bak'tes. There are no kings. Was I not clear enough the first time?"

"First time? There was only ONE time."

"Everyone here is equal, but each have different purposes. That is all."

"Except for the clanmasters, who rule all."

"Again, they don't rule; the people rule. They merely organize everything."

Slowly, as we still talk, I start to notice more grass coming our way, even some flowers. The smell of sulfur is near-dead now. Looking forward, I see more green than the last two hours I spent in that valley filled with cannibalistic rhino-dragons. Never was I so glad to have the scent of flowers fill my nasal cavity with aromatic stimulants. As I breathe the scent of the oncoming green surroundings, with a touch of sulfur, I feel my shoulders relaxing, knowing that we are a few steps away from leaving this wretched rock, and a few more steps toward reaching our destination.

"The road ahead of us is flat again!" So'krang exclaims.

He and his split-jawed hiphomoy immediately gallop forward into the green, and out of the sulfur valley. They didn't even warn me.

Realizing what just happened, me and Grasshead dash forward to gain on them. Within seconds, we catch up with them. I look at him, and he looks at me. I give him an expression which is supposed to deliver the message, "What the hell, man!?" and in response, he smiles at me, which might be translated as, "Lighten up, will ya?" even though So'krang would never say it that way.

As we dash, I just hope we're not too far from wherever we're supposed to be going, because I could really use a nap right now.

CHAPTER VIII

A PEEK INTO THE LIFE OF A NATIN BEFORE BATTLE

We finally reach So'krang's home after several miles. It is called the clan of Yasin, because apparently every "city-clan" needs to be named after their respective gangra, that or the lack of creativity.

We stand in front of the giant gate leading into the clan, similar to the gate at the entrance to the clan of Awari. This gate, too, has a white symbol of a dragonesque creature, although this one seems to have a helmet on. Also, the gate to Yasin is beige-colored, as opposed to purple. I still don't know what these creatures are and what significance they might have to use them as symbols.

"WO!!" So'krang shouts. "AAM'IN GARI'AAM!!"

A man peeks from behind the giant walls to see who is coming. He looks like an ant from down here.

The man retreats behind the walls and the gate opens a few seconds later. As the gate opens, we start to make our way in.

The city didn't look too different from that of the clan of Awari, with wide buildings and whatnot. Although the collective design of the architecture here was more rural with a bit of old-school, probably to coincide with the whole "ancient" thing.

On our way to So'krang's house, I witness some really indecent behavior. Men and women alike were scratching their crotches like a bunch of cavemen that failed to integrate into society as part of some messed-up social experiment. I suppose the reason why they never cut their nails is so that they can relieve themselves of the itch through those thick leather pants.

"Y'know . . . ," I start to tell So'krang as we continue to ride. "I couldn't help but notice that nobody here gives a fuck."

"About what?" So'krang asks.

"About decent behavior. That's what."

"Heh . . . you know . . . our culture is a lot different from anything you might know. I think that's something you'd have realized . . . I assume by now."

So'krang just smirks after that. Of course, I never expected him to apologize for his people. I don't respond to what he just said, but instead just look forward as I continue to ride, thinking about those words. In all honesty, he's right. What I'm used to is something that's a lot different than what goes on in this world. And whatever goes on in this world, I'd better get used to it, because I'm going to stay here for a while.

Finally, we leave the urban area and enter the living quarters. Hard to call it urban considering the city's design, but despite the archaic features, it had pretty much what I'd expect from a modern city: shops offering various items, restaurants and everything else.

Riding through the living quarters, I bear witness to rows of houses of similar design, wide like all the other buildings, with just one or two features differentiating one from the other. They were quite big in general, with fancy metal fences separating them from one another. Must be nice where all the people get to enjoy a comfortable house with enough space for everyone.

We finally reach So'krang's house. Big, wide and rural like all the other houses. Nothing extraordinary about it but for one or two design bits I can't quite put my finger on, but I know it's there.

We get off our respective hiphomoys and start walking down the small stone path leading straight to the entrance of So'krang's house.

"Tem'wok'in bawit'in jei na," So'krang says to himself.

"What?" I ask, confused.

"I can't wait to change my cloth."

So'krang opens the door to his house, with no key or even knocking on the door. He just opened it as if it were a public venue for whatever.

"Don't you lock the house?" I ask him.

"No need," he says simply.

"Heh. Well . . . good luck with burglars. I just hope for you that you won't have any."

"What are burglars?"

I'm mildly shocked. I look at his face, and I can't find any signs of sarcasm. Through that statement alone, I can already see how awesome it is to live in this glorious world.

"Never mind."

We enter So'krang's house. Nothing out of the ordinary. Straight to the right of the entrance, there is a staircase. I don't know where the stairs lead, nor is it my business. Otherwise, the entrance leads straight to the living room. There is pretty much everything one would expect from a living room. You got a sofa, a bunch of other furniture and of course, a television. The TV, unusually though, looks like a metallic cube. It has a bunch of outlets on its left side, circular in shape and varying in color, mostly green and red. Seeing the house on the inside, I don't think the Natin are trying to differentiate themselves from humans, at least not when it comes to interior design.

"MARMELLA!?" So'krang shouts.

Suddenly, I start to hear footsteps, and from the staircase, a woman comes down dressed in conventional Natin fashion and a neck tattoo shaped like some kind of beast like all the others I've seen so far. She has the eye tattoo similar to the one the clanmistress of Awari has. I'm slowly starting to understand that each tattoo signifies something, but her feature that caught my attention the most was the absence of her left ring finger, cut off at its knuckle.

The closer she gets to us, the faster she comes down the stairs, and the big smile on her face became clearer and wider.

She approaches So'krang with a hug, followed by a French kiss. Through this trade of actions, I understand that this is So'krang's wife.

They then look at each other with a smile.

"Wo, marmel," she says. "Kata tidrai?"

"Ai'ga," he responds.

I couldn't quite understand what they were saying, but judging by the context and how conversations start when the man comes back home, she probably asked him how his day was, or how the mission went, to which he replied that it was good, clearly telling her what she wants to hear.

"Kata nen?" she asks while looking at me.

"This is Neph Baker," he responds. "I think he would like it if we spoke in English."

"Ah, yes. The one they say is the composer."

"You already know that?" I ask.

I was surprised by the fact that someone who wasn't present at the clanmistress's speech had already heard of my coming.

"It was everywhere," she starts to say. "Moments after An'a gave her speech, it was all over the Techno and the Psychopool. I would never think An'a would be generous enough to speak English for your sake."

"Yeah," I reply. "She's quite amazing, if I do say so myself."

"She really believes in him," So'krang says. "Unlike the masses."

"Well the Awari see things that we can't. I just hope that she did the right thing."

"I guess we'll just have to wait and see what happens," I say jokingly.

She looks at me silently, and then looks at So'krang.

"I made chow mein," she says. "It's better than last time."

"Well then I can't wait," So'krang says cheerfully.

He then lifts her in the air as if she were some kind of doll as he spins around. Her hair whips in the air as she just laughs with joy. The love between the two just radiates all over the house.

"Put me down," she says while laughing. "You won't like what I can do when I get spinned."

"Trust me, marmella," he says cheerfully, "I'm used to it by now. It won't work anymore."

"Kata ee?" she says joyfully.

She then throws So'krang's arms apart as she flies away from him from the momentum, hitting the wall right beside her. She clings to a cuckoo clock right above her as she grabs So'krang's head with her legs. He then pushes her against the wall as they still laugh. Caught between the wall and the big piece of meat that is her husband, they kiss wildly, infatuated like animals in mating season, with pheromones in the air and hormones in the blood.

I just stare at them without knowing what to do. Clearly, they have no regard for decency when it comes to guests. Then again, I shouldn't be surprised.

In the end, I decide to pat So'krang on the shoulder.

He quickly returns his wife back on her feet, as they straighten up their clothes and return to the conversation before they started all this.

"Sorry," So'krang says. "I don't usually have guests."

"I don't think it woulda made a difference," I jokingly say.

"Let's go to the kitchen," So'krang's wife says.

She starts to head out by herself. So'krang and I stand by one another before following her into the kitchen.

"You like chow mein, huh?" I ask So'krang in a relatable way.

"Well it really depends on my mood," So'krang partially agrees.

"Hmm . . . maybe we're not so different after all."

Sitting in the kitchen, we feast on chow mein, and it is surprisingly good. I know I'm satisfied, although the meal keeps reminding me of the lack of cuisine in this universe.

While eating, I bear witness to some unusual table manners. So'krang and his wife ate with their mouths open. Chewing noises in the background caught the ear while the stains of sauce around their mouths caught the eye. I wouldn't expect otherwise from these people who scratch their crotches in public. Clearly the Natin have no regard for modesty. It's probably an attempt to differentiate themselves from those that they do not want to be associated with, the heranga, or humans as I am used to calling them. I really don't know what to think of this, but I'm going to spend the rest of my life with these people, so I might as well get used to it. If it's any consolation, they're using a fork and not their hands.

"What's your name?" I ask So'krang's wife.

"Ka'ka'pan," she answers with her mouth full.

"And your full name?"

"Kari'maik ka pan'totik."

"I must say," So'krang starts to say, also with his mouth full. "These noodles are definitely better than last time. But I can't help but feel that it's still lacking something."

"Really?" I disagree. "Cuz I think it's OK."

"Don't get me wrong. It's still good, but I feel like it needs a tad bit of . . . something."

"Try salt. Maybe that'll work."

"I'll be sure to make it even better next time," Ka'ka'pan says lightheartedly.

"Oh no. Don't bother," I start to say. "Don't listen to what this guy has to say. It's fine."

She chuckles a bit. "You're funny," she says gently.

"I try to be," I say jokingly with a smirk.

Overall, the chow mein made a nice meal. I know I'm satisfied.

"Well . . . ." So'krang goes on to say while wiping his mouth, "I think I'll take a nap."

"Shouldn't you take a shower first?" I ask him, confused about his priorities.

"I haven't forgotten, but thanks for reminding me. What do you want to do in the meantime?"

"Dunno. What's there to do?"

"Well . . . I suppose you could watch technovision."

"What's technovision?"

"It's basically our equivalent of the TV. I would also suggest if you want to use the Psychopool, but you wouldn't probably know how to use it."

"Well, I guess I could watch TV."

So'krang and I head to the living room, where the technovision is. Turns out the technovision is the metal cube sitting on a table strong enough to hold his massive shape.

I sit on the couch, while So'krang grabs what I think is the remote control. It was purple in color and looked like an octagonal cylinder with a bunch of buttons all over it.

"Is there something you want to watch?" he asks me.

"Ugh . . . ," I wonder out loud, "is there . . . a nature channel, maybe?"

"Nature channel? You mean with animals?"

"Or geography. But yeah . . . something with animals would be preferable."

"So you want something with animals? I think I might have something here."

So'krang opens a drawer under the TV. Out of curiosity, I go over there to see what he's doing, because I'm pretty sure that channels are in the TV, rather than being in a drawer. In there, I see a bunch of finger-sized cylindrical thingies that look exactly like those already connected to the side of the TV.

He inspects their writings, and after a few inspections, takes one out and connects it to a vacant outlet in the "outlet interface."

He goes back to take the remote. I go back to sit on the sofa.

He isn't even aiming at the TV, and he already starts pressing buttons. Zapping between channels, he finally stops at the one with a weird-looking animal in it. He puts the remote down on the sofa near me.

"Enjoy," he says while making his way out of the living room.

"How am I going to understand what they're saying?" I ask him, mildly irritated.

"I don't know. You said you wanted animals, so this is what I had. If you want channels from heratrang'ga pan, maybe we can buy them later."

So'krang then leaves the room.

Hearing him, I understand that this is the best option I have right now. Worst case scenario, I'll just try to understand what the animals here are doing with my imagination. If not that, then I'll just have fun looking at them.

The first documentary is about a symbiotic relationship between two creatures called dob and zeeb. I know they're called that because those are the two words that are repeated the most, as opposed to all the other mumbo jumbo, though I can't tell which one is the dob and which is the zeeb.

The second documentary is about a swamp creature called the bunye. The name and nature of the creature bears similarity to the Australian myth of the bunyip. I suppose that's where the creature gets his name.

The third documentary, and the most interesting so far, is about some kind of pink wolf called the gonglik that behaves pretty much like all wolves for most of the time, except for just before the winter. At that time that he doesn't behave like a carnivore at all, but eats sugar cane and cocoa. In the winter, he grows a pink coat of wool all over his body, making him look like a sheep with teeth. The second part of the documentary focuses on farmers trimming the wool from them and then some factory contraptions, and then a bunch of people were shown eating colored dough. I suppose the dough is a product of that wool, kind of like how ice cream is made from milk, which in turn comes from cows.

The shows were rather lengthy, with each lasting an hour or so. By the end of the third documentary, So'krang approaches me, awakened from his nap and dressed appropriately for a Natin.

"Hey. Get prepared. We're going," he tells me, mildly drowsy.

"Where?" I ask him.

"We're going outside to eat."

"But we just ate."

"That was three hours ago. Besides, it's almost dinner."

I am surprised that he said that. I look outside to the garden and I'm surprised to find out that dusk is near approaching. I didn't really feel time passing by because I was mostly caught up in the documentaries and all the lights are on. Apparently, they have complete disregard for electrical bills, assuming they even have to pay them.

But with everything prepared, we make our way out to the city. So'krang leaves his hiphomoy behind, while I, naturally, take Grasshead with me. I suppose people here usually walk when it comes to in-city traveling.

Outside the living quarters in the main area of the city, I can see some people walking. Some are walking with their hiphomoys following them, and some are riding their hiphomoys. Indecent fashion and indecent manners don't bother anyone but me. I'm still trying to adjust to this new status quo, although the signs here, written in a language that I cannot understand, almost make it hard. I'm sure I'll make it through though.

We keep walking until So'krang turns his attention to a certain restaurant.

"Let's go in here," he says.

Inside, I find what anyone would expect from a restaurant: tables, a counter, and a lot of people. Of course, the interior of the restaurant is wide like all the other buildings here. We make our way to the first vacant table we spot, and we sit down immediately.

I look around the restaurant and notice how people eat. The table manners here haven't changed from those at So'krang's house. I assume that these are the universally accepted table manners. Thinking further into the purpose of these manners, I realize that they enjoy food more than what humans do, mainly because they aren't concerned with what others think about them and more about just eating.

I notice some additional behaviors at the restaurant. Some spit out their food to the corner of the plate as if they have a funny taste in their mouth, or maybe it is a bone that poked them in the cheek. Many drink what appears to be a thick yellow juice, and some, like a girl sitting with her friends across the corner, after spilling some of the juice out of her mouth, merely pick it up with her finger from the table and put it back in her mouth, all while she is laughing and smiling with her friends. Chewing noises, complete disregard of table manners and a mouthful of stolen recipes all contribute to a joyful meal.

"Why aren't we eating at your house?" I ask So'krang.

"Nobody made food for dinner," he answers. "Ka'ka'pan just left for an expedition, and I prefer to buy my food rather than cook it."

"What expedition?"

"It basically refers to missions where tak'nen form groups and then they make their way to a location to destroy a group of Airatsmeka. Expeditions usually take between four to five days."

"Hmm . . . bogus."

"Which brings me to my next topic."

Suddenly, a man wearing a dirty white apron with a sleeveless shirt approaches us.

"Wo," he says. "Kata em'in?"

"Domae itiki . . . ," So'krang replies.

So'krang then turns his attention away from the man to me, and stares at me for a couple of seconds.

"I would like a tirasartan," he says after turning his attention back to the man. "Give one for my friend too."

The man then looks at me, and continues to give me the stare So'krang gave me a second ago, only this look tells me "it's that damn heranga from TV," rather than "I'm supposed to speak English for his convenience."

"Of course," the man says.

He then returns to behind the counter and into the kitchen.

"I suppose that was the waiter?" I ask.

"You suppose correctly," So'krang says in response.

"He didn't look like one."

"That's because he's also the cook."

"Why? Are they on a budget or something?"

"No. You see, those that make the food also serve it. There's no need for waiters."

"Is that so?"

"Trivial matters aside, I would like to talk to you about what will happen in the coming days."

"And that is?"

"I am supposed to leave on an expedition tomorrow."

"So where's the problem?"

"I do not know whether I should take you with me or leave you to yourself. Frankly, receiving the task of the mentor came to me as a surprise, and I'm quite oblivious as to how to approach this."

"I don't see the dilemma."

"Well, you see . . . you're not trained in our arts. If I take you with me, there's a chance you might die. You have never seen an Airatsmeka, and you have no idea what they're like. The strategy of the Airatsmeka may be predictable, but they are powerful, and I am not confident that you are capable of handling them. But then there is leaving you here, and though you might use that time to train in our techniques, but I don't want to leave you in the care of someone else."

"Why not? There shouldn't be a problem with that. Should there? I mean after all . . . hehe . . . I did kick your ass."

"Don't let your ego bloat. The clanmistress of Awari tasked me with your progress, so it's only fair that I live up to her expectations. Also, not many may show tolerance when dealing with a heranga, so leaving you in the care of someone else could be bad."

"You seem to handle it pretty well."

"That's because I'm special. Heh. Na, I'm just kidding. But jokes aside, we really need to figure out this problem."

Suddenly, the waiter-cook comes back with our orders, one dish in each of his hands.

"Here are your orders," he says while putting down the plates of food. "Enjoy."

He then presumes to return to the kitchen.

"Can everyone here speak English well?" I ask.

"English is the second-most spoken language in the Novaverse," So'krang goes on to explain. "Right after our official language, hang'pan'rika. You see, it is mandatory to learn English for . . . political reasons, I guess. As for the actual reason: I have no idea.

"Fuck politics, right?" I say jokingly with a smirk.

"English is also researched by some clans, among other languages, because it is the most spoken language in heratrang'ga pan."

"The most spoken language is Chinese, actually."

"Oh. Well . . . only the jadak'ga would know that. If anyone knows why we have to learn English it's probably them. But enough talk. Have you seen what's on the table?"

"Yes, I noticed. Don't really know what to say."

What I see before us is something cylindrical inside a white paper bag. Beside that is a glass filled with the same yellow stuff that girl had been drinking. I lift the bag and partially take out what's inside just enough so that I can still hold the bag with the thing inside without getting my hands dirty. What I see is a big cylindrical chunk of yellow meat. It is soft to the touch.

"The fuck is this?" I ask.

"It's called tirasartan," So'krang says. "Try it."

I take a small bite from the top of the chunk.

"Oh wow!" I announce as my taste buds explode with joy and flavor. It tastes like shrimp flavored with butter and corn. I fall in love with the thing at first bite, for never have I tasted something like this. I am quite surprised that despite the small variety of Novaversian cuisine, they have really delicious meals, assuming they have more than just the tirasartan, of course.

I pay attention to the yellow stuff in the glass, hoping that it will exceed my expectations like how the tirasartan did. I take the glass and start to drink. Of course, being a thick and sticky substance, it took a while for it to reach my mouth.

"What the fuck?" I respond to my disappointing discovery. "It's just cheese!"

"Melted cheese," So'krang corrects me. "It is called gnabits."

"So it's basically fondue in a glass."

"Just drink it," So'krang says, mildly annoyed.

After ten minutes, I have utterly devoured the tirasartan and sapped the glass of fondue empty. I can't help it, for never have I tasted something like this; with every bite, I just feel like I want more and more. Alas, the meal is gone and currently moving in my stomach. The same way I should be moving to talk about more important matters.

"About your dilemma . . . ," I start. "I've made up my mind."

"Yghou dghid?" So'krang says with his mouth full of tirasartan he still hasn't finished eating.

"I'm coming with you."

So'krang swallows his food just before going on to say, "Are you sure about this? You might die."

"I've never been more fuckin' positive in my life. I don't think I have anything better to do, anyways."

"You can still stay here, and I think it would probably be for the best, considering that I don't have a plan."

"Think about it like this: if I stay here while you're out fighting, then I can either train or slack off at your home. Training means being under the responsibility of someone who might be intolerant to me, which doesn't help our cause, and staying in your house is just procrastinating. Either way, I wouldn't be getting anywhere. And I really don't wanna give the clanmistress a reason to hate me, considering that my residence here is at stake, which basically means that I'll have to go back to the shithole I came from."

"Those are interesting perceptions . . . but these are the Airatsmeka we're talking about. They are not to be underestimated, and if they were to put more thought into their strategy, maybe there would be fewer casualties for them and more for us."

"Death means nothing to me at this point. Heck . . . I could actually benefit from it if it happens. I wouldn't have to worry about going back to shit and everyone here wouldn't have to put up with me. It's actually a win-win when you think 'bout it."

I sigh as I think about the seriousness of the issue, despite how humorously I've presented it. My state of mind suddenly shifts from being semi-cheerful to being consumed by deep thoughts.

"But in all honesty, it's what happens if I live that concerns me the most," I say in a more melancholic tone. "I don't wanna fuck this up, and I don't wanna waste time. I'll do everything in my power to stay away from . . . ." I sigh once more. "From the cage that I wasted my life in for so long." I say as my tone becomes more dramatic. "I WILL prove myself!"

"I see . . . ," So'krang says, seemingly intrigued and somewhat moved.

Silence. So'krang looks down at the table, thinking about something.

"Tell me, Neph," he says after raising his head and looking back at me. "Do you believe in fate?"

"In all honesty, at this point I don't know what to believe in anymore," I tell him, slowly regaining my good mood. "Besides, there's no going back now."

So'krang again looks at the table, thinking, then back at me.

"I agree with your statement," he decides. "We will go together tomorrow."

"Great," I reply calmly.

I look around me, thinking about the future and what it may hold. Thinking about tomorrow and what will happen. Will I die? Will I live? Either way, I'll make this work.

"Where's the bathroom?" I ask.

"Over there," So'krang tells me while pointing in the general direction.

I stand in front of the bathroom door, and to my surprise, there is only one, and not two like one would expect. Then again, gender-neutral bathrooms are only a sign of how perfect this world is. Being able to put gender differences aside is quite fitting for the people who constantly display no modesty whatsoever.

Opening the door to the restroom and staring at it, I can see that it's much larger than a restroom I would expect. At this point, I'm not even surprised. There is a large row of closed stalls, and right in front of that, there is a large row of sinks and soap dispensers. It's basically just a casual restroom, but longer.

I go in a vacant stall. Luckily, the first one in the row was just that, so I don't have to waste my time going further into the restroom and searching for an empty stall. I go in the stall, lock it, and take a piss, flushing the toilet afterwards.

Leaving the stall, I head over to a sink to wash my hands. Beside me, a Natin guy is also washing his hands; he belongs to a clan I have yet to know of. We trade stares while washing hands, and then we look away, although I could still feel that he was looking at me. I continue to wash my hands, and he is about to leave, yet he turns to look at me one more time, and then he just stands there.

"You're the so-called composer . . . am I right?" he suddenly asks me.

"That would be me, yes," I reply to him just as I finish washing my hands.

He then smirks. A smile of disbelief and annoyance. He clearly isn't satisfied with something.

"You may have been accepted by the mark'nan of Awari, but don't rush to consider yourself one of us," he says passive-aggressively, dropping the smirk off his face.

"Who says I'm one of you?" I reply, returning the same amount of passive-aggressiveness. "I'm me. That's all there is to it."

He starts to walk towards me slowly.

"You are lucky for the generosity of the mark'nan," he continues while walking slowly toward me. "I want you to know that if it were up to me, I'd let a herd of konlaby come in to my home before I would let the likes of you come in."

He finally stops walking. We are now facing each other point-blank, staring deep into each other's eyes. The guy dwarfs me by a head.

"Well then, I guess it's good that I didn't meet you when I came here. But listen . . . I'm not looking for trouble."

"And that's coming from a makis'bak," he says, moving from passive-aggressive to borderline aggressive. "But if you really want to stay here, just don't infect us with your ignorance. But know this: I will never accept you as one of my people, and you will never belong in this worl—"

Suddenly, a hand grabs him by his shoulder. Behind him stands a girl, who was probably using the facilities while we were talking. I was so busy arguing with this guy that I completely forgot that this is a gender-neutral bathroom.

He turns his head to look at her, his clothes soaked in water from the hands she just washed. Clearly, she is nervous to end this fight as soon as possible.

"Ting'ga na," she tells him.

He slowly starts to turn his head to me. We're back to trading stares with each other.

"You're right," he agrees, slowly calming down. "He's not worth it."

Both of them leave the bathroom. I am now alone.

This interaction made me wonder: were it not for the mark'nan, would this guy kill me? What am I to these people? Am I a burden, or am I someone to look up to? But more importantly, what is my purpose in life? I will move one step closer to finding the answer to all these questions tomorrow, when I get to kick some ass and show my fighting prowess. But for now, I just want to leave this joint and take a nap.

CHAPTER IX
INTRODUCTIONS ARE MANDATORY!

Its eight a.m. in the morning, and I find myself drowsy, barely waking up from sleep, and clad in the same clothes I came here with. I'm not willing to wear Natin fashion yet; I prefer to recycle for now. So'krang, looking like he woke up with coffee injected into him, clad in his leather gear, with the bracelets and whatnot, together with a crossbow on his back and a newly forged claymore beside it. Basically, he doesn't look any different now from the moment I met him, except that today he's wearing a thick armored short-sleeved jacket. When I asked him why he didn't wear it when we met, he said that it's because that mission wasn't supposed to be a hard task. Emphasis on "supposed," because as it proved, it was very hard, and I have myself to thank for it.

That was just before we left his house. Right now, we're riding on our hiphomoys to the airport.

Once reaching it, the airport reminds me more of a military base than an actual airport. No buildings; just one huge open area. People are moving everywhere, whether it is by running or riding hiphomoys, trying to reach their designated flight. Adults and children alike are directed by operators on the field who tell them in which direction their flight is located. The place feels more like a bazaar than an airport.

The planes aren't even planes. They are giant metallic silver wagons on four wheels connected to an even bigger feathered lizard. These giant lizards bore the appearance of a feathered dragon, with bird wings made of feathers, rather than dragon wings made of membrane like one would expect. Quantities of feathers are more dominant in the head and upper back areas, whereas the rest of their bodies are quite lacking, as if the feathers withered away. How these "wagon-dragons" connect to the wagon is the most interesting: the tail is inserted into a ring, which is a component of the wagon, and then the tip of the tail is tied to the base of it. This way, the people here don't have to wrap chains around the creatures to carry the wagons.

"Where the fuck are we supposed to go?" I ask impatiently, bothered by the massive crowd.

"Uh . . . all right," So'krang says, struggling to find the right words. "It's this way . . . I think."

"You think!?" I say in disbelief.

"What do you want? It's hard trying to find a flight that still has room for passengers."

"Wait . . . so you're telling me we're not actually looking for a specific plane? Then why is it 'this way'?"

"I don't know. You asked where we are going, so I thought there would be a flight with room over there."

"Then we'd best get a move on."

Riding on Grasshead, I move ahead to wherever So'krang is pointing. He follows me on his hiphomoy, whose name I still don't know.

We continue to zigzag through people while we watch wagon-dragons rise into the sky, as they soar to their destination. Hopefully, we might catch a flight in time before someone else takes our seats.

"Neph!" So'krang shouts to me from far behind me.

Grasshead U-turns so that I can see what's going on. I see So'krang waving to me from afar, next to a wagon-dragon. I suppose he found one with empty seats.

Grasshead and I dash to him.

"Wait," he tells me.

So'krang dismounts his hiphomoy and starts walking to this guy, clad in nothing extraordinary of Natin fashion but sporting a big green badge on his jacket. With his hiphomoy following him, So'krang takes out a piece of paper and hands it to the guy. The guy looks at it, and then goes on to mount So'krang's hiphomoy.

"KNIYA!" the guy shouts.

So'krang's hiphomoy then gallops away into the distance, moving between people and eventually out of the field, although by the time he did that I couldn't see him anymore.

"Who was that?" I ask.

"That was the rang'rarik'nen," So'krang says.

"The who?"

"Soparkat'ga at the airport responsible for returning hiphomoys to their rightful homes. I suppose the most accurate analogy would be a valet."

"Hmm . . . So I suppose you differentiate between the clanmembers by putting 'ga' at the end?"

"'ga' simply means that the word is an adjective. It's like how one would say American or European."

"I see. By the way, valets bring your rides to you, not take them away from you."

"Semantics," So'krang says, although I can't tell if he is joking or not.

Done talking about grammar and valets, we climb up to the giant wagon via a ladder. Grasshead just jumps inside it from where he was standing. I didn't even know he could jump that high. But then again, he can run really fast, so that just goes to show how strong his legs are. I wonder if he can also scale walls with those claws of his.

There, we see several Natin sitting on a flat surface, some with children and some without. There are no seats; kind of like how fugitives sit in the back of a truck when trying to escape authorities, or maybe public transportation in third world countries. Either way, this is unfitting for a modern and somewhat technologically advanced society such as the united clans, but what do I know?

All three of us sit down. So'krang puts down his claymore and crossbow by his side as we lean on the walls just like everyone else. Nobody sits in the middle. Everyone stares at the newcomers, but at me especially. They look at me with eyes that say "oh, it's him," and in response, I look at them defensively. I didn't come to impress any of them, just to run away from home.

"Are we leaving soon?" I ask So'krang, uncomfortable with all the stares.

"The pilot has yet to arrive," he says.

"When is he coming?"

"Eventually."

I look away from So'krang into the air.

"Some answer," I mumble to myself.

After a while, the pilot finally arrives, climbing onto the wagon-dragon, and then approaches everyone in the wagon, but without entering it. The wagon is already full, if you only include the sides without the middle.

Everyone approaches him one by one as he puts one leg on the edge of the wagon, while the other one remains on the dragon. Everyone gives him some kind of ticket thingy, rectangular in shape and solid in touch. After collecting all of the ticket thingies, he proceeds to turn around and prepare for lift-off as everyone else returns to their seats.

"What did you give him?" I ask So'krang

"I gave him the name of our designated waypoint," So'krang answers simply.

"Waypoint?"

"Groups of tak'nen meet in various waypoints outside of clans. Our waypoint is nen'ma prak'satra. And it's not a mountain full of monkeys like it would suggest."

"I don't even know what that means."

As everyone takes their flat seats on the edges of the wagon, the pilot sits forward on the wagon-dragon.

"KNIYA!" he shouts.

The wagon-dragon starts to move slowly, accelerating with each second and dragging the wagon with him. Finally, when it reaches enough speed, the wagon-dragon soars upwards. The angle at which the wagon-dragon rose to the sky causes an inertia which would normally push all the passengers to the back of the wagon, if they aren't prepared, of course. Contrary to everyone else, I am not prepared. I slide straight towards two passengers sitting at the back of the wagon. Seeing me coming, they both move sideways as I slam against the wall, landing me right in between them. I look at them with mild embarrassment, while they look at me with indifference. I struggle to make my way back to So'krang's side over the slippery surface, but eventually I make it.

Now in the air, I can feel the wind blowing on my face. This is probably the closest I'll get to ride a "convertible plane."

All is quiet in the wagon. I wonder if it's always this quiet. I suppose it has something to do with the amount of discomforting stares I'm receiving. Of course, I don't blame them for not wanting to share a ride with me, or maybe not wanting to share the pride of killing all those Airatsmeka with me. Regardless, they will get used to me in the end.

"Wo," someone sitting in one of the corners calls to me.

I turn my attention to him.

"Aren't you the one they say is the composer?" he asks.

The guy next to him, supposedly his friend, pays attention to our conversation.

"That would be me," I respond with certainty.

The two start to laugh subtly.

"Imas ai'gao heho naidi'in hang'ron'ga." his friend tells him in a gleeful manner.

The two then start to laugh their asses off, before almost immediately settling down. Some of the other passengers smile to themselves over the statement, while others are annoyed, remaining to themselves.

"Don't worry," So'krang says. "I believe that one day, the Natin will accept you as one of their own. Like I have."

"Like you have?" I say, confused.

"I've seen what you're capable of. You're more than welcomed in the Novaverse. You have a calling here. But we have to discover what this calling is before we know it."

"Doesn't stop them from laughing at me, though."

"I don't know what the future may hold, but being laughed at is better than being hated."

We've been in the air for quite a while now. The passengers have been jumping freely whenever they get to their destination, and only a few are left. I'm just glad those two jackasses left. Even with them being silent, their presence annoyed me.

Suddenly, the wagon starts to descend fast at an angle. This has always been happening just before someone jumps. I suppose this is a notification when the flight reaches a certain destination of one of the passengers.

With this, So'krang looks over the wagon to check if it's our destination. I don't do it because I know he'll do it.

"This is our waypoint." So'krang tells me while patting me on the shoulder and grabbing his stuff.

I get up from the flat surface of the wagon. Before I turn around to prepare for the jump, So'krang approaches Grasshead, who is already on his feet, and reaches down to his chest and thrusts his palm forward. It was hard to tell what he did exactly, but I trust him enough to know that it's not harmful. He then hands me a silver square-shaped thingy with a blue orb embedded in the middle of it.

"Stick this to your chest," he tells me.

Just like he said, I place the thingy firmly on my chest. I feel a slight sting, and then it just sticks there like glue.

I turn around, facing the outside of the wagon. So'krang is already sitting on the edge, combat-ready with his signature claymore on his back and prepared to jump. I wonder how the wind isn't blowing him off. Is it that he's too strong or the wind is too weak?

"JUMP!" he shouts just before jumping.

"LIKE I HAVEN'T FIGURED THAT OUT YET!" I shout back at him.

Without thinking twice, I just leap over the walls of the wagon like a regular base jumper. I am now sinking into the sky, as I feel the wind splashing against my face.

I can't feel the time passing by, as I get closer and closer to the ground. Seeing myself about to get turned into mashed potato, I start to panic over my lack of parachute. But before I can even get close to dying, a blue substance starts to form out of the thingy wrapped around my chest. The blue substance looks like gel, and quickly develops to encase my entire body. Before I realize it, I was inside a giant blue gel cube, which, for some reason, I could breathe through.

The gel collides with the ground, completely softening my fall to the point of no harm. The gel then proceeds to slowly dissolve.

It takes me a while to get out and stand up from the still-dissolving gel. Upon standing up, I notice So'krang approaching me, who, by now, has already managed to get out of his gel.

"Gelatinized fluorocarbon," he says.

I immediately understand that he is telling me the name of the substance, but in the moment of panic that occurred, I forgot that the Natin don't "do" earth stuff, or hertatrang'ga pan stuff more appropriately.

Upon turning around, I see in front of me five combat-ready individuals. All Natin, of course, two guys and three girls, clad in Natin fashion with different styles. One of the guys wears a thin silver jacket, the unusual flip-flops that everyone loves to wear and baggy pants made of soft material which I could not identify. He has a device near his hip containing rolled-up wire and a sheathed katana glued to his back by nothing, kind of like how So'krang does with his claymore.

Wearing a sleeveless leather jacket which he keeps unzipped and the usual leather pants I always see everyone wearing, the other guy dwarfs everyone else, standing seven feet tall at least. No weapons of any kind on this massive specimen of a dude, although I suppose those sturdy-looking boots he's wearing could be used as a blunt weapon.

And then there are the girls. The first one is clad in an all-white shirt under an all-white heavy leather jacket combined with black leather pants down to the knees, showing her calves to everyone as well as the flip-flops she's wearing. She wears a belt with a bunch of vials hanging from it, together with a small sheathed knife behind it. The vials contain some kind of green powder. She carries a sack on her back tied by a belt around her shoulder. The colors on her clothing really catch my eye, because together with the vials, the first analogy that comes to my mind is that she is the paramedic, or at least that's what I assume.

The second girl seems gloomy in appearance. She keeps her head down and her hands in her pockets. She wears a light blue body-length lightweight jacket and leather leggings, which seem weird yet unusually attractive together with her flip-flops. At one point, she adjusts her straight bangs from her dark brown hair, probably in a poor attempt to hide that white eye patch she is wearing. Sadly for her, the eye patch is too prominent, so it doesn't really do her good to try and hide it. Other than that, she isn't carrying any weapons.

And of course, there's the last girl on the team. She's wearing a purple leather jacket, full-length leather pants, covering almost the entirety of her boots, and has back-length black hair. But the feature that catches my eye the most is her neck tattoo. Looking at it from where I'm standing, it looks similar to something I've already seen, or more accurately, something that I'm always seeing, but right now, I can't quite put my finger on it.

I approach her slowly, but with eagerness at the same time. I look at her, and she looks at me.

"Can you . . . maybe . . . tilt your head a bit," I ask her while gesturing her to tilt her head.

She looks around at everybody, probably embarrassed. But in the end, she tilts her head and pulls her collar just enough for me to accurately look at the details of the tattoo. The tattoo bears the appearance of a creature with pointy fur, assuming it is fur. And then it came to me: it's Grasshead! At that moment, I realize that all the neck tattoos are actually the heads of all the breeds of hiphomoys, each representing their respective clan. I guess this is how much the Natin love their dogs.

That moment of realization makes me forget about everything. It didn't seem like just a tattoo to me anymore; it looked to me like Grasshead. I grab her by the shoulder and move her a bit to get a better look at the tattoo; I'm so amazed at that moment of realization that I forget that I'm forcing someone to do something she doesn't want to. Immediately, she slaps my hand away from her and returns to her original position of looking straight ahead while straightening her collar. I could then see her discomfort.

"I'm sorry. I'm sorry," I say quickly and apologetically.

She looks from side to side rapidly, and then slowly relaxes.

"It's OK," she tells me calmly.

I take a few steps back to So'krang's side, and the team went back to normal.

Among the conclusions I've reached upon inspecting this team is that the Natin really love jackets and leather. The leather is understandable, considering that it's thick and protects well. As for the jackets, I can't quite understand their purpose. I hypothesize that it's easy to remove when dropping weight to gain speed when fleeing the enemy. If not that, then they're probably for some other situation. Between the boots and the flip-flops, I think the footing of choice comes down to whether you're fast and agile or slow but hit hard. Boots are heavy, so it only suits the ones that can deal with slow speed, such as the big guy, while the flip-flops are lighter so they allow their wearer to move fast.

"All right!" So'krang says while taking some steps forward. "We're going to be a team for the next few days, so I suggest each of us introduce themselves."

"Kata orim'in English?" the guy with the sword asks.

"Well, yes, since our friend here does not speak our language, I thought it would be best if we speak English. As much as I understand that some of you see this as unfortunate, it is imperative that we take all the necessary steps to create sufficient teamwork in the upcoming mission."

"He is the makis'bak that is believed to be the composer. Is he not?" the big guy asks.

"Yes. This is Neph Baker," So'krang adds, "as you already know."

"I remembered the composer, but not his actual name."

"Well, you can start by remembering it now," I interrupt their conversation.

"I wasn't talking to you," the big guy tells me passive-aggressively.

I become cautious, as I can feel the tension growing in this team.

"Calm down. Now!" So'krang exclaims in a mighty voice. "I will not tolerate disorder! I do not care who is on the team and what you think about them, we WILL complete this mission! Any further misconduct will result in reduced points upon mission completion."

Everyone pulls themselves together immediately. So'krang easily reminds them where they stand and who is the commander here. They seemed frightened, but respectful at the same time.

Until this point, I was skeptical about So'krang's potential regarding mentoring . . . not anymore!

"Let us introduce ourselves. I will start: I am Sowi'ga Krang'pegin of the clan of Yasin. Twenty-three years of age. I have been on 165 expeditions; on thirty-seven of them I have been the leader. My kill count stands at 167. Who wants to go next?"

Everyone contemplates whether they should be next or wait for later. Then sword guy steps forward.

"I'm Sadidi'ga Anim of the clan of Sokokit. Nineteen years of age. This is my seventeenth expedition. Up until today, I have killed fifty-six Airatsmeka."

Sadidi'ga Anim steps back, and forward comes the big guy.

"Riwaja Tang. Twenty. I come from the clan of Kirtiami, the manliest clan. I've been on twenty-five expeditions and killed forty-eight haa'bak."

Riwaja Tang steps back, and forward comes the paramedic, assuming she's actually a paramedic, of course.

"I am Hiyan'kea Ka Ojak of the clan of Okati. I am nineteen years old. I have been on twenty-seven expeditions and killed only seventeen Airatsmeka. I look forward to a successful mission."

I couldn't help but notice how soft her voice is. Almost soothing in its pitch.

Hiyan'kea Ka Ojak steps back, and forward comes the girl with Grasshead on her neck.

"I'm Pang'ga Bara, and I am a Paito'ga. Twenty years of age, been on twenty-four expeditions and killed exactly fifty Airatsmeka."

Pang'ga Bara steps back, and forward comes . . . nobody. Everyone looks at the gloomy girl, and she looks back at everybody. With the need to fulfill everyone's expectations, she steps forward reluctantly.

"I'm Kari Wen Yai of the clan of . . . um . . . uh . . . Amroro. I'm nineteen. I've been on nineteen expeditions and killed . . . um . . . I killed ninety-one Airatsmeka."

Kari Wen Yai steps back, and I'm the only one left to introduce. As if there is actually any need to, but I'll do it regardless.

"I am Neph Baker. I'm fifteen. This is my first expedition and so far, I've killed nobody. I would go on and say where I come from, but you already know that."

And with that, everyone is done introducing themselves. Hopefully now we can get along.

"All right," So'krang continues. "Let us talk about the mission details: there are five Airatsmeka approximately 200 shiandon from here. The journey will take us approximately four to five days from now. Our mission, as you know, is to kill them. Nothing special from what we usually do. Any questions?"

Riwaja Tang raises his hand.

"How come he gets to go on an expedition on the age of komo'kea'ka?" he asks. "It took me four years before I could go on my first expedition, and I trained hard for it, yet he is barely prepared, if at all."

"I understand your frustration," So'krang starts to answer his question. "But may I remind you, Neph is not a Natin, and he will be treated as such. Any more questions?"

Pang'ga Bara raises her hand.

"Why is a Paito'ga hiphomoy among us?" she starts to ask. "They aren't fit for battle. Maybe if it were a Mosak'ga then it would be OK, but anything else is a liability. Unless you want to tell me this is a Hikama'ga. If so, where's his armor?"

I think about her words. That is the second time I hear the word "Mosak'ga," and the first time I hear the word "Hikama'ga." I don't know exactly what that means, but from what little I know of the Natin until now, I think that it's a clan that specializes in training hiphomoys for combat. Alas, Grasshead was never trained for combat, but his enemies are dead before they even know it if they underestimate him.

"This is no regular hiphomoy," So'krang answers. "He possesses power beyond our understanding. In fact, he nearly killed one of my teammates during my mission to heratrang'ga pan."

Looking at her, she seemed mildly shocked over that statement, but skeptical at the same time.

"Any more questions?" So'krang asks.

Everyone is silent.

"Good," So'krang says. "Then I suppose we can move forward."

So'krang starts to walk, and everyone starts to follow him. I couldn't quite tell whether we're going west, south, north or wherever, considering it was a giant open field. Truth is, I don't need to know the direction of the wind. Just tell me if it's left or right and I'm fine with that.

While walking, what I see is this: So'krang in the front of the formation, being the leader, of course. The five Natin that joined our team follow behind him. And then there's me and Grasshead, behind everyone else. Normally I would take So'krang's side, being the only person I actually know here, but seeing the lack of trust in the eyes of everyone else, I prefer to be by myself and keep a low profile. At least I get to enjoy the wind quietly.

We walk until the night comes, and then we stop at some random grove to settle down. Everyone takes their place; some decide to sit down, leaning on a tree or otherwise; some decide to remaining standing; some decide to lie down. Most of us sit near each other in a single location.

"All right," So'krang says. "We will rest here for the night. I am going to contact the clan of Doamar for food delivery. What would you like to eat?"

"Pork!" Riwaja Tang exclaims.

"Tirasartan," Pang'ga Bara says calmly.

"Sushi, please," Hiyan'kea Ka Ojak requests nicely.

"Just yogurt," Kari Wen Yai decides in a gloomy manner.

"I'm not hungry," Sadidi'ga Anim says quietly but surely.

"All right," So'krans starts, as usual. "And I will have chow mein for myself. Neph, would you like anything to eat?"

I was confused at first, trying to understand where the food comes from. "Uh . . . ," I hesitate. I realize eventually that it doesn't matter where the food comes from, since the Natin can get the job done. "I'll also go with chow mein."

So'krang writes down all the food requests on a notepad, and then proceeds to take out a device resembling a TV remote control. The kind from where I come from, not the dumbbell-looking giant one that's more of blunt weapon than a remote. He then takes out another smaller device which resembles the finger-thingies he inserted into the TV at his home, although this one is longer. He then proceeds to put the notepad on top of the bigger device with the writings facing the device, and then inserts the smaller device into an outlet on the side of the bigger device.

A bunch of blue lights flash from the bigger device. So'krang then stands up and starts walking away, deeper into the grove, probably just to take a piss. He just leaves the device by itself. I suppose now we are waiting for something.

I go to sit down and lean on a random tree. Coincidentally, Sadidi'ga Anim is leaning on the same one, right beside me. From the back of his belt, from which he hangs all his tools and weapons, he takes out a long, purple cigar-like thingy, the end of which looks like a small purple cloud relative to the size of the cigar thingy. I didn't see that he had that with him, probably because it had been hidden behind him.

He then proceeds to take out this small salt shaker-like container with a very small hole on top of it. He holds it over the small cloud-ended cigar thingy and shakes it twice. The small cloud starts to ignite like a cigarette would. Sadidi'ga Anim then inhales from the cigar thingy, and the small cloud ignites even more because of the air, further clarifying that it is some kind of cigarette. After finishing inhaling and taking everything into his lungs, he then exhales purple smoke from his mouth.

"Want some?" he asks me while trying to hand me the thingy.

"I don't smoke," I tell him while gesturing to decline his offer.

He then looks away, back to minding his business, while I look at the thingy, trying to understand what it exactly is.

"What is that? A cigarette?" I ask Sadidi'ga Anim.

"It's called saglashin. And yes, I suppose this would be our equivalent of what you call a cigarette, only that it doesn't kill us so fast. We can always clean our lungs so it's toxicity doesn't really matter."

I'm trying to understand the phrase "clean our lungs." There are meanings I don't understand about their terminology. Marbar? Safik? Psychopool? I never bothered asking about those because I knew from the beginning that there would be many things I wouldn't understand, but I will learn their meaning eventually. Why didn't I bother to ask about them when I first heard them? I never really cared.

Suddenly, a dark purple rift in space forms near us for a split second, and from it appears a Natin, carrying a giant sack.

"Em itika!" he says, whatever that means.

Everyone, from wherever they are resting, rushes to the man, who by now I understand is the guy who brings the food. The only one who remains in his place is Sadidi'ga Anim, who clearly stated before that he was not hungry.

One by one, the man gives out the food to the person who desired it. After everyone but So'krang and I have taken food, I approach him next. He is just about to give me my chow mein, but before the delivery can reach my hand, the guy stops and stares at me point-blank, bewildered. It takes him two seconds to fathom that he is looking at the so-called composer before he gives me my dinner. He then turns around, preparing to give So'krang his food, who is the last to collect his delivery.

"Kata akai'masak'nen?" the delivery guy asks.

"Ee," So'krang responds with confidence.

"Kata tidrai?"

"Ai'ga."

The guy then nods his head once, and leaves in the same purple void that he entered from.

I approach So'krang before I open my box of chow mein. "So what, you have an entire clan of pizza delivery guys?" I ask sarcastically.

"They do more than just bring food," So'krang explains. "They save lives too."

"Really?"

"Yes. We might need to call one in our upcoming battle."

"I just hope it won't be me that needs his life saved."

"Don't fill your mouth with carambola. It might just happen."

"What?"

"It's an idiom. Marash'in itoke orim ba bar'pa na. Carambola is otherwise known as the starfruit."

"I know what carambola is; I just didn't understand that thing you said."

"It basically means that when you are saying something that didn't happen yet, it might just happen because you said it."

"So it's kinda like jinxing?"

"Well . . . I don't know what jinxing is, but I suppose it is of similar meaning."

"It's cool. You don't have to know what it means. I understand now."

Afterwards, I make my way to sit and enjoy my food.

"All right, may I have your attention before we start eating?" So'krang asks just before I find a spot to settle down. "It's night, so we are going to take shifts guarding. Every hour, someone will replace the one currently guarding. Who would like to volunteer to be the first?"

"I could do it," Sadidi'ga Anim immediately responds from the tree he is leaning on, still smoking his saglashin.

"Very well," So'krang says. "Neph, I just want you to know that . . . you don't have to participate if you don't' want to."

"I have to. I'm part of the team," I respond objectively but mildly insulted.

"Very well. All right, everyone. Ma mark'asmi!" So'krang exclaims.

And with that, everyone starts eating their meals, like lions feasting on a wildebeest.

I'm still trying to fathom So'krang's remark about whether I want to participate or not. I AM part of the team, so why is it a privilege for me and an obligation for others? Maybe it's because he's worried for my wellbeing because I'm not prepared for what's ahead. Or maybe it's because they still haven't accepted me as one of their own, so he wants to keep everything easy for now. It's not my fault that everyone hates me here. Regardless, I am going to prove myself. And after I prove myself, no one will doubt me anymore. But until then, I will bide my time.

CHAPTER X

MY FIRST BATTLE

For three days, the team walks in order to kill the Airatsmeka that await them in some random location on the continent of Wotaiga, the largest continent among the six. Some show more patience, others less. It is important to organize several miles away from the targets and walk there, because if one would approach them from the sky, they would simply blast them into oblivion. Hiphomoys are generally considered a liability in battle; even though there are exceptions, such is the case with this mission. There are no ran'rarik'nen where the battle happens, so sending them off home by themselves will just get them lost. Basically, this is the best way.

But finally, after three days, which is less than what So'krang estimated, the team reaches their destination, and the Airatsmeka are right where they want them.

Approaching them silently as not to alert them, the team hides behind a giant rock. Preparing for the fight to come, Neph gazes upon an Airatsmeka for the first time. "Holy shit," he mutters to himself.

Despite his surprise, the Airatsmeka don't look much different from the Natin, except for the random black marks of various size and number all over their bodies and the slightly bigger horns on their faces. Everything about them is black, from deep black hair to deep black eyes and black fabric attire. Their choice of wear isn't just black, but is also dirty and its age is very apparent, as it is the hides of the animal corpses they desecrated, whether they murdered them or scavenged their dead bodies. If it isn't enough that their clothes are an insult to nature, being the bloody dirt-ridden skins of the animals, but the Airatsmeka wear it in a far more indecent and revealing way than the Natin, both due to the scarcity of resources that the Airatsmeka suffer from and as an expression of their brutal, ruthless nature. Need it be mentioned that the black marks on their bodies give them the appearance as if they are rusting, hence the pejorative "haa'bak," where "haa" means rust and "bak" is a word that should not be spoken?

These Airatsmeka are a group of five: four men and one woman. The men don't bear much difference in appearance. They are muscular and manly, and above all ugly, but their appearance suggests nothing of their combat skills.

For this reason, they are referred to as numbers 1 through 4, since the lives of the Airatsmeka bear no importance to the cause of the Natin, that and they are definitely not interested in wasting time collecting dossiers about their enemy, who constantly and endlessly pop up at random locations in the Novaverse. The Natin wouldn't be able to collect that much information even if they wanted to. Basically, to the Natin, the Airatsmeka are not even a thing to consider.

But an even more objective reason as to why they are called such is because they are pawns. If they were any other classification, they would have enough importance for the Natin to differentiate between them, but they are all pawns, so they won't receive that privilege.

Pawns are the weakest form of Airatsmeka, who are mostly first-timers that have been recently released from Horei, their home continent, to collect food and kill Natin. They are perfect for relatively new tak'nen to take on.

In contrast to all the pawns on their team, the woman is not a pawn. The woman is a classification known as the natra, because even the most non-strategic of races need to have some variety in their team.

The natra specialize in poisonous attacks they deliver via their sharp synthetic nails and stealthy combat techniques where they approach their opposition without being noticed, or at least they try not to, sometimes succeeding and sometimes failing. The natra isn't a role exclusive to females, although men won't rush to take that role, given concerns for their manliness and self-proclaimed awesome demeanor.

Fortunately for this natra, she isn't simply a number in the eyes of her opposition. She is different and makes this whole mission a bit more challenging. But were there to be more than one natra, then there would be natra 1 and natra 2.

Other than how they fight, based on what they look like, not much is left to say about their current actions. Do they anticipate the arrival of the Natin, or do they just not care about what's to come? Seeing how it looks like right now, it's probably the latter.

Sitting there on a bunch of trees they ripped from the ground and put sideways, they seem calm but bored. They seem to have walked for days, collecting food and killing Natin if they could. They now rest before continuing their journey, assuming they would live long enough to do so.

With the team still behind a rock, watching them closely, they plan their attack.

"All right," So'krang begins. "Hi'ka'o, I want you to stay in the backline in case someone needs care. Your offensive capabilities aren't sure enough to fight together with us, so it is important."

"Understood," Hi'ka'o responds with doubtless loyalty.

"Neph, I want you to stay with Hi'ka'o and watch. I want you learn what we are doing."

"I won't learn anything from watching you guys fight," Neph responds skeptically. "I'd rather just fight with you."

"These are the Airatsmeka," So'krang explains. "This isn't like when we fought. They would decimate you in seconds."

"Fine. But don't come whining to me when you need my help. Don't forget how I beat the shit outta ya and the othe—"

"This isn't the time for reminiscing," So'krang says, somewhat embarrassed. "Just . . . do what I tell you. For the sake of the mission."

"For the sake of your fuckin' ass, maybe."

"THIS IS DIFFERENT!" So'krang begins to lose his temper.

"He beat you in combat?" Sa'a suddenly interrupts their conversation, confused and in disbelief.

So'krang lets out a grunt of despondence while rubbing his eyes. He then sighs as he fears for the sake of the mission.

"Any questions before we start?" he says despondently.

Everyone remains quiet and trades stares with each other, seeing if the person has a question, because everyone knows for themselves that they don't have one.

"All right," So'krang remarks over the quiet. "Who wants to initiate?"

Everyone again trades stares with one another, seeing who will volunteer to initiate. Everyone hesitates, not out of fear, but out of the question: who is the best to initiate?

"I'll start," Sa'a says, seeing that no one else will take the initiative.

Sa'a unsheathes his katana and holds it in his left hand. He positions himself as if he's about to jump forward with mighty force. Right hand on the ground, he looks left and right one more time, looking at everyone in the eyes and gesturing them to prepare for what's coming ahead. He then looks forward at the Airatsmeka, and then . . .

Sa'a disappears in the blink of an eye! A gust of wind can be felt in his wake. The power that he gathers to thrust himself forward with incredible speed brings him close enough to No. 1, but not to the rest.

With every second that counts, Sa'a swings his katana at No. 1, cutting him in the chest. No. 1 rolls backward while the rest of his team jumps high in different directions, escaping the fight between them.

No. 1 gets up quickly from the ground, unwavered by the deep cut to his chest. He forms black smoke into the palm of his hands, which grows and grows until it becomes as big as him. Covered in this black smoke, he hurls it towards Sa'a.

With it being too late to escape, it all seems doomed for Sa'a. But suddenly, several tree roots launch themselves in Sa'a's direction, encasing him and protecting him just in time to save him from the black blast. Sa'a breathes fast, realizing he was just seconds from being blasted into oblivion.

Suddenly, another black blast decimates the roots that had protected Sa'a, flying over him just enough to burn his cheek.

From a mighty jump, No. 1 lands straight onto Sa'a and in between the parts of the roots that weren't decimated. Still lying on the ground with the roots that protected him, Sa'a watches as No. 1 forms yet another patch of black smoke in the palm of his hands. Before No.1 can do anything, Sa'a stabs him in the chest with his katana. No.1 flinches a bit, but almost immediately breaks the sword with his bare hand, as if it were a twig. Now, in no position to protect himself and with No.1 preparing to blast him point-blank, Sa'a feels his death coming.

Suddenly from the sky, Ri'tang lands on three points, with his giant fist hitting hard in No. 1's back. Ri'tang then grabs him with his other hand and throws him to kingdom come. Ri'tang then climbs on the remaining patch of roots and begins to rip the biggest root in the patch. With the root in his hands, three times as big as his body, he prepares to throw it in No. 1's direction.

No. 2 comes flying at Ri'tang, pushing Ri'tang and himself all the way to the nearest grove and removing the giant root from his hands. Ri'tang and No. 2 both fall to the ground, but immediately get up. They face each other, and continue to run at each other for a fight at close combat. Trading punches like two boxers with rockets up their asses, each one tries to pummel the other's face into a bloody stain.

No.2 manages to hit Ri'tang in the stomach. Ri'tang clenches at the pain, but immediately regains control. Before he can do anything, No. 2 kicks him in the chest, shatters his sternum and sends him flying, hitting hard against a tree. Ri'tang wastes no time and gets up. No. 2 rushes at him, but Ri'tang grabs him by the shoulder as soon as he gets close enough and throws him through several trees. Numerous broken trees are created in the wake of No. 2, who flew through them like a race car driver flying through a windshield. Ri'tang then pursues him, searching for him in the mess left in his wake.

While Ri'tang is off searching for No. 2 to continue his fight, his teammates fend for themselves against the other Airatsmeka, like So'krang, for instance, who is fighting against No. 3.

So'krang swings his sword a number of times at No. 3 as No. 3 dodges every hit, until he just grabs the claymore by the blade with his hand, cutting it. Blood dripping from his palm, No. 3 struggles to keep the blade away from his face with one hand, as So'krang forcibly pushes it against his might. Realizing this contest of strength is a waste of time, So'krang drives his elbow into No. 3's face and then, with a window of opportunity, swings his claymore at No. 3. That window is for naught as No. 3 just slaps the claymore away out of sight.

No. 3 starts to form black smoke into his hand to enhance his punch, but So'krang distracts him, shoving his index and middle fingers into his eye, with the uncut nails making the damage even worse, as he runs away from No. 3 in an effort to find his lost sword. Wincing in pain over the eye that he just lost, No. 3 bides his time while So'krang runs between trees and looks under the dirt to retrieve his weapon of choice, and his most efficient tool for fighting.

Finally finding his claymore embedded in a tree from the power of the slap, he proceeds to pull it out of the tree with haste to return. With the claymore now back in his hands, he prepares to return to the fight that he left. Unfortunately for him, No. 3 wastes no time and lands with a black spear created in his hands and stylized to his liking. So'krang rolls away from the landing attack, and No. 3 embeds the spear in the ground against his intentions.

So'krang swings his claymore through the spear, shattering it and cutting No. 3 in the chest. The spear blocks the brunt force of the attack; had it not been there, No. 3 would've been cut in half.

So'krang prepares for another swing, but just as he's about to deliver, No. 3 collects all the power that he can in less than a second to blast So'krang away, leaving behind a trail of black smoke.

Flying several feet away and landing on his back, So'krang now lies on the ground with his eyes to the sky. Exhausted from the fight, So'krang cuts himself some slack to stare at the sky. It is only when he sees No. 3 falling at him from the sky that he pulls himself together and grabs No. 3 by the neck as soon as No. 3 lands on him. So'krang rolls backwards, still holding No. 3 by the neck, and positions himself on top.

Now mounting the disadvantaged No. 3, he holds his claymore tightly with both his hands and prepares to drive it through his heart. But as So'krang holds the claymore high in the air to gain momentum on the finishing blow, No. 3 blows him away into the sky with a black blast. As the black fog from the blast fades, So'krang is nowhere to be seen. Breathing in relief over his supposed victory, No. 3 lies on the ground, taking a moment to relax.

Suddenly, arrows come falling from the sky. No. 3 rushes to get his wits together as he dodges every arrow that comes, all while still lying on the ground. Four arrows miss, while one pierces No. 3 in the chest. Before he can even think of taking it out, So'krang lands, claymore first, ready to stick its gigantic blade into No. 3, but No. 3 rolls sideways and immediately gets back up.

Again, So'krang finds himself trying to pull out his sword from something other than his target. No. 3 tries to seize the opportunity by engulfing his fist in black smoke to enhance his punch. No. 3 gets close enough to deliver the awesome punch, and So'krang has no time to pull out the claymore. Knowing this, he breaks the sword in half, and cuts No. 3 in the chest before No. 3 can hit him. Losing focus, the black smoke fades from No. 3's arm, as So'krang stares at his now broken sword.

"Dora bak'tes!!" So'krang remarks loudly, annoyed over the fact that he broke his favorite sword for the second time.

No. 3 shouts. So'krang runs away from No. 3 to reorganize himself and come up with a plan, seeing as his main weapon is now broken. No. 3, without a question, runs after him.

Up until now, So'krang seems to be handling himself pretty well. But can the same be said for the others?

Pang'ba is fighting No. 4 somewhere surrounded by a bunch of trees, out of sight and away from the company of her friends. If she calls for help, they may not hear her. But Pang'ba needs no help, for not only does the tak'nen show no sign of weakness during battle, but her control over flora gives her an advantage over the fight. Of course, No. 4 has just enough explosive power to destroy every flower that Pang'ba throws in his direction, but for how long can he keep that up?

No. 4 runs at Pang'ba at full speed, but Pang'ba summons thorny vines from the ground to wrap around No. 4's leg. Held in place by vines holding him tightly, each movement of his leg tears his flesh even more. Pang'ba creates thorny vines around her arm, with the thorns facing outwards, making it look like a gauntlet of thorns. She rushes at an ensnared No. 4, and then tries to punch him in the face, only for him to dodge. She follows up with a backhand swing, but he grabs her by the forearm, holding her in place.

Now both locked in place by each other, No. 4 conjures big nails of black glittering stone on his free hand to pierce the face of Pang'ba, but she extends the vines onto his arm, wrapping them around it. Now with the vines around his arm, Pang'ba contorts them against his elbow, breaking his arm and tearing his flesh in the process. With No. 4 screaming in pain, Pang'ba seizes the opportunity to punch No. 4 in the neck with another gauntlet of vine and thorns she creates, piercing No. 4's neck.

Out of anger and pain, No. 4 wastes no thought as to blast Pang'ba away, leaving behind a trail of black smoke. Pang'ba hits hard against a tree, breaking a few ribs in the process.

While she writhes in pain over her new wound, she breathes hard to collect herself for the next attack. Before she could finish her preparation, she sees something black in the distance making its way toward her. As it gets closer, it's apparent that it is bigger than it seems, and as it destroys every tree that stands in its way, it is very apparent that it is a giant black spear.

Now almost close enough to skewer Pang'ba like a shish kebab, Pang'ba uses her powers to mutate the tree that she is on to extend its wooden hard material to protect her. Thick, wooden tendrils form from the body of the tree, making their way to the spear as it approaches Pang'ba, moving fast enough to wrap themselves around both Pang'ba and the spear, protecting the former and halting the latter. Now completely encased in wood, the spear is held in the air by the wooden tendrils, with the tip of it barely touching Pang'ba's throat. A drip of blood can be seen falling from the cut, for only her head is exposed among the tendrils she is covered in.

Suddenly, No. 4 appears before Pang'ba, who lunges at her at the speed of sound. Standing on the tendrils while he sticks his nails in the tree to balance himself, he looks at Pang'ba, smiling, for he knows that she is immobilized, and a window of opportunity is right there before him.

While No. 4 is taking his time, excited over this glorious opportunity, Pang'ba further mutates the tree to form a sharp wooden stake, coming out from the side of her head, moving fast with the aim of piercing No. 4's face. Alas, No. 4 tilts his head sideways, completely cutting his cheek. Pang'ba only missed because No. 4 saw the stake coming at him in the last tenth of a second; had he been a tad slower, he would have his brain on a stick right now.

Angered over his lost cheek, he didn't even think twice about blasting Pang'ba through the tree and away.

Pang'ba recovers from the blast and gets back up on her feet, which remain almost completely unharmed thanks to the tree that protected her, except for a broken collarbone and a cut on her forehead.

No. 4 runs fast at Pang'ba, leaving her no time to prepare for her next attack as she recovers from the blow. He prepares to leap into the air and dive at her with a haymaker straight to her face to end her once and for all.

But before he can do so, razor sharp leaves come falling down suddenly from the tree above him. Some hit the ground, while others successfully hit No. 4, cutting him and embedding themselves in his body.

No. 4 halts over the realization of danger and the idea that something is lurking and trying to kill him. He looks at the razor sharp leaves stuck in the ground, and then he looks at the trees shading him from the sunlight. He tries to understand where the leaves came from, but he can't seem to figure it out.

Suddenly, Sa'a comes falling down from the trees, leaving no clue to what he's done with his previous opponent. He can be seen holding a bunch of leaves in his hands, as he stands up straight upon landing. He throws all the leaves on the ground, leaving only six in his hands. He slowly swipes each one of them between his thumb and index finger, making them razor sharp. He then puts them between each of his fingers on both hands except for the thumbs. Now, Sa'a is ready for combat, equipped with makeshift claws that are ready to punch and stab at the same time.

Sa'a rushes at No. 4 and delivers a flurry of punches. A quick jab and another jab, each intent on piercing flesh and moving fast like the swing of a flyswatter. Alas, as quick as Sa'a may be, for he has trained to be fast and swift, he can not land a single hit on No. 4, who dodges each punch that came from the flurry.

How did Sa'a miss all of his punches? Perhaps he is already exhausted from his previous fight. Or maybe No. 4 is just too fast for him. The former sounds more reasonable, but regardless of what the reason may be, Sa'a isn't getting anywhere with these punches.

Already tired of evading the punches, No. 4 counters Sa'a and punches him in the lower ribs with a fist-sized point blank blast of black smoke, completely removing a small patch of flesh, just big enough to show some shattered ribs.

Bleeding heavily from the wound, Sa'a starts to waver. No. 4 sees an opportunity. He walks slowly towards Sa'a, but as he gets closer to him he picks up the speed. As he reaches Sa'a, who just wavers there, he stands above him and smiles, for this will be a glorious kill, or at least that's what he thinks.

No. 4 is about to deliver the final blow as he raises his hand high into the air. But before he could do anything else, Sa'a, still wavering, delivers a punch flurry straight to his stomach. A quick jab and then another jab No. 4 doesn't see coming. A punch to the stomach and a punch to the chest, Sa'a doesn't even think; he just punches as he pierces the skin of No. 4, filling him with holes. Completely filled with holes and dripping with blood, No. 4 looks more like Swiss cheese than anything else.

No. 4 falls to his knees. Sa'a stands up straight and breathes hard, trying to collect himself from all the blows he. Pang'ba approaches him and stands by his side. They both look at No. 4, near dead from exsanguination as he remains on his knees, staring into nothingness in front of him because of his blurred vision.

Sa'a and Pang'ba look at each other, and then Pang'ba looks at Sa'a's exposed ribs; in response, he looks at them too. They could just let No. 4 die from the bleeding, but then that would mean that the kill belongs to Sa'a. Knowing that the kill rightfully belongs to Pang'ba and treating his wound is more important, he smiles at Pang'ba and runs off to wherever Hi'ka'o is for treatment.

Now alone again with No. 4, Pang'ba stands in front of him while he is still on his knees. There's no indication that he is planning anything, as right now all he does is stare at nothing with an open jaw that gushes out a waterfall of blood.

Pang'ba slowly crouches and commands the soil on which she stands to sprout a plant with a razor-sharp blade as a flower. She plucks the plant out of the ground, and slowly rises back up.

Holding the blade-plant by its stem, she stabs No. 4 in the ear and through the brain, finally finishing him off after a tiresome fight.

But while Pang'ba has finished her fight, others are still having theirs.

Like Ri'tang, who grabs No. 2 by the leg and slams him against the ground with all his might. The earth shakes as No. 2 sinks into the ground. The shake is so strong it's felt across the entire battlefield.

Ri'tang mounts No. 2 while he is still on the ground. Ri'tang starts to pummel his face. A left punch and a right punch, repeated over and over. The punches are so strong the sound waves they produce can be heard up to two miles away, far enough to be heard by everyone currently fighting, much like how earth shook moments ago.

But, no matter how many times he punches him in the face, No. 2 won't die. Ri'tang doesn't give up just yet, as he keeps punching and punching until he feels No. 2's brain matter on his knuckles.

Ri'tang suddenly stops punching over the sound of a chuckle. He looked at No. 2. A nose broken sideways, a jutting bone coming out of the jaw, and half of his teeth missing, No. 2 looks at Ri'tang while he lies on the ground and starts to laugh.

He laughs for a while, as Ri'tang stares at him in confusion, and then starts to choke on his own blood, for it has been draining into his throat while he laughed.

Ri'tang, frowning with anger, prepares to deliver another punch, this time more massive than all the ones before. But before he could land the blow, No. 2 blasts his fist point blank, just as Ri'tang is about to hit him.

From the force of the blast, Ri'tang immediately gets back up and staggers backwards, regaining his balance in the process. He looks at his fist and sees the bone of his knuckles exposed without any skin or muscle and covered in blood.

Ri'tang pulls himself together and gets back to the fight, but the fight is coming to him, for No. 2 is already on his feet and charging full speed at Ri'tang.

Ri'tang tries to halt the charge with all his might, scraping the soil under his feet in the process. The charge hits Ri'tang like a truck at full speed, but even a truck can only keep up with Ri'tang for so long, as he gets pushed back several feet before completely halting No. 2.

No. 2 is still pushing forward at full speed, but is unable to even budge Ri'tang at this point. Ri'tang then swings No. 2 over his head and throws him behind him, using No. 2's momentum against him as he crashes into several trees in a row.

Ri'tang runs half a mile to where No. 2 stopped his charge and sees him lying on the ground, motionless. Ri'tang wastes no time at thinking twice whether he's alive or dead, as he rips the massive tree beside him from the ground and slams it onto No. 2, crushing him.

With only his arms and legs visible, No. 2 leaves no sign as to whether he's alive or dead. Ri'tang stares at him under the tree and tries to figure if it is done or not. He wants to know for himself whether he can leave, but he can't decide what to do. But Ri'tang, impatient as he is, eventually decides that he should leave, and so he does. He turns around and starts to walk away, declaring to himself that No. 2 is dead.

Suddenly, Ri'tang hears an explosion behind him, but before he turns around, he gets thrown away as he gets hit hard in the back. Ri'tang rolls and gets back up on his feet, as well as the thing that hit him.

With no surprise at all, it was No. 2, now completely looking like a Picasso painting. Even as the bloody smear that he is now, a smile can still be seen from what skin flap he has on his face that isn't dangling.

Finishing his laughter, he yet again charges at Ri'tang at full speed. Ri'tang, already familiar with the move, dodges the meat bullet and grabs him by his leg.

Ri'tang then goes on to spin around, gaining speed with each spin. No. 2 is left helpless, for he cannot move even slightest given the massive speed. After spinning for ten seconds, Ri'tang finally lets go, sending No. 2 flying off miles away.

As No. 2 starts to descend, he gets stabbed through his heart, impaled on what appears to be one half of a pair of scissors. He grips the sharp edge of the blade and tries painfully to pull himself out of it. But before he can free himself, a pair of giant scissors, colored deep blue, forms around him and closes on him, cutting him in half as his lower body falls to the ground while his upper body remains skewered on a blade and hanging in the air.

But where did the scissors come from? They came from Ka'wen'yai, for she has the power to conjure razor sharp scissors of varying sizes, entirely or partially.

Ka'wen'yai, who just finished off No. 2 and therefore stole Ri'tang's kill, is leaning on a tree as she is bleeding from the shoulder. She seems like she wants to rest rather than fight, and why she is not fighting right now like she should is a question that should concern everyone.

But, alas, her rest will not last forever, for a giant horizontal vortex of black smoke comes flying her way, destroying everything in its wake. Ka'wen'yai, realizing the situation, ends her rest and gets back up on her feet. She forms a pair of blue giant scissors and then breaks them in half, holding each half in her hands. As the tip of vortex is just about to touch Ka'wen'yai and rend her to shreds, she stabs it, and is sent flying backwards.

Getting up from the ground, now with an exposed and broken sternum to boot, she breathes deeply but slowly as she looks at No. 1 lying there on the ground with one half of the scissors lodged deep in his shoulder. He slowly starts to get up from the ground. Ka'wen'yai slowly makes her way to No. 1 with the one half of the scissors still in her hand. Now back on his feet, although still with a giant blade in his shoulder, No. 1 is now ready to fight again. Before he can even think about it, Ka'wen'yai impales him in the stomach with her remaining half of the scissors. A grunt of pain can be heard from him as she proceeds to tightly grip the other half stuck in his shoulder with both her hands, and push it down deeper, cutting his flesh even more from the inside. He falls to his knees and shuts his eyes tight over the excruciating pain, as Ka'wen'yai conjures a pair of scissors around his neck, closing and cutting his head off, ultimately killing him.

With two Airatsmeka dead by her hands, she desires to fight no more; she makes her way to the nearest tree to once again rest, for the tree that she rested on before was no more. But no worries, for Ka'wen'yai hasn't forgotten her duties. She just needs a little breather, and then she'll come back for her friends.

But while Ka'wen'yai is resting on some random tree, Sa'a is just arriving at Hi'ka'o's location to seek help over his wound. He looks at her, and she looks at him, and then his wound.

"An'tar'in," Hi'ka'o says, seeing the severity of Sa'a's wound.

Sa'a then proceeds to lie down in front of her, hurting in the process due to his broken ribs. She aids him in lying down.

Now completely on the ground, Sa'a is ready for treatment. Hi'ka'o repositions herself to treat Sa'a's wound from the right angle. She starts by holding her hands above his wound, and slowly, a green light emits from her hands, following by glowing green particles floating in it, making them look like fireflies.

But as Sa'a is being healed, So'krang is still fighting the good fight.

He runs away from No. 3 as he shoots at him with his crossbow. Standing a fine distance away, So'krang either misses entirely or hits No. 3 somewhere on his body, the latter of which barely does anything to him.

Closing the gap with a swift of movement, leaving behind a trail of black smoke, No. 3 stands in front of So'krang. So'krang fires his last three arrows at No. 3 from point blank, and No. 3 stands still, taking them all to his chest, and then smiles a little. Out of practical options, So'krang swings his crossbow at No. 3's face, but No. 3 grabs it in his hand without too much effort and crushes it with a clench of his palm.

Now with no options at all, So'krang is doomed for sure, as No. 3 instantly conjures a knife in his hand, grabs So'krang's neck with other, and prepares to stab him in the face. But just before he can thrust, the hand which is holding the knife is grabbed by a thorny vine as it continues to wrap itself around the arm.

Struggling to free himself, No. 3 pulls against the force of the vine, as the vine pulls itself back in response. The vine shortly after manages to pull No. 3 to the ground onto a small patch of spiky grass, puncturing his back as if it were a pin cushion.

Pang'ba appears from behind one of the trees and runs to stand by So'krang.

"Good," So'krang smiles. "You came. I could use a little help."

"Neph itika na, jek'in," she replies.

"Oh right. I got used to him being around me all the time. Anyway, I am out of weapons."

Pang'ba crouches and puts her hand on the grass. Slowly, she pulls out of the ground a ten-foot long vine with long blade-like thorns protruding from the sides of it, stylized like a bladed whip. She hands it over to So'krang.

"I was never the best with the scourge," So'krang remarks to himself. "But I suppose this will suffice."

"Orim'in hang'pan'rika, emai," she tells him, mildly annoyed.

"I'll try," he tells her, smiling at her and trying to keep the mood up.

So'krang gestures for her to leave and help the others with a gentle tilt of his head sideways. She nods her head in response and leaves the battle between him and No. 3.

With a new weapon in his hands, he turns his attention back to No. 3, who is now collecting himself to get back to the fight. Without the use of his arms, No. 3 pulls himself back up with his legs alone, and with his back full of holes, he is now ready to get back to the fight. So'krang demonstrates his whip skills by flinging it in different directions, and finishing the performance by whipping the ground, sounding a whip cracking. No. 3 is wary, but remains brave to fight So'krang.

The two run at each other, and halfway, So'krang flings the whip at No. 3, wrapping it around his arm. They switch sides during the clash, and So'krang pulls his whip in the process, using the momentum to his advantage and tearing the flesh of No. 3 right off his arm.

No. 3 looks at his arm in astonishment, and then looks at So'krang, once again demonstrating his skills with the whip, smiling and proud.

But like he said, and unbeknownst to No. 3, So'krang was never really good with the whip, or scourge as he likes to call it. However, seeing as it is his only weapon now, he doesn't have a choice, and will have to make the best of it.

But as So'krang tries to figure out how to properly whip the blood out of No. 3, Sa'a is still being treated by Hi'ka'o, who finishes healing Sa'a's wound with her hands. But while the bleeding stops, the wound is still open and shows a fine display of broken ribs.

Hi'ka'o takes her bag off her back and puts it to her side. She opens it and takes out a small bottle of sihoronpa, a thick, green fluid created from the tiamtsat of the sihoni'ga, whose regenerative capabilities are the second best in the Novaverse, right after the samish'ga. The sihoronpa is used to create a temporary patch to cover wounds and stop bleeding until the wound receives permanent treatment.

Hi'ka'o pours the sihoronpa onto Sa'a's wound as it drips further down, slowly covering its entirety. But seeing as gravity can't do everything by itself, she slides her hand between his back and the ground and pushes upward, signaling him to turn on his side. He grunts over the pain.

"Dora sirai," she apologizes in her sweet, gentle voice.

She pours the liquid on the remaining areas where she couldn't reach before. Now the wound is completely covered in sihoronpa, and Hi'ka'o starts to blow gently on the patch of thick liquid. It slowly starts to dry.

"Hey, uh . . . guys?" Neph says in confusion while staring at the site where the Airatsmeka settled down originally. "I just remembered something, and it kinda bugs me: when the fight started, everyone grabbed someone to fight against. But no one grabbed the girl. Also, she didn't jump into the air like the rest. Does that mean something?

Hi'ka'o raises her head up, putting aside Sa'a's treatment for a moment and trying to realize the events currently unfolding while looking into the air. Thinking, she soon puts on a worried expression.

"Is everything OK?" Neph asks her.

A slight pause, and still no answer from her.

"WE NEED TO RUN!" she exclaims in a loud voice, with no indication to where her soft voice disappeared to.

Sa'a gets up from the ground, and together with Hi'ka'o, Neph and Grasshead, they all run off to somewhere deep into the closest woods. They keep running, until they settle in an area where the trees completely block the sun from shooting her rays of light.

"What's happening?" Neph asks, confused.

"Keep your back to a tree," Hi'ka'o vaguely answers his question.

Seeing how serious the situation is, he takes the question as is with no need for bickering, and takes the closest tree to keep his back against. But that doesn't stop the danger from coming, for they hear a womanly laugh in the air.

A suspended silence engulfs them as they look around. At the trees. At the ground. At the air. Trying to figure out where the source of the laugh might approach from. It can't approach them from their backs, because there's a tree in the way, but it can come from the front, but that will just be an invitation for a fight. Does the source of the laugh want to end things discreetly, or does it want a challenge?

The silence still persists, and nobody knows what will happen next.

Suddenly, Grasshead can be heard sniffing. He then growls, and immediately leaps forward in front of Hi'ka'o and bites the air. The natra appears in his mouth from nowhere. Caught between his teeth, she scratches his face while trying to free herself before she gets crushed. She tries to scratch his eyes, but Grasshead's constant movements over her self-defense proves impossible for her to do so, but it does break his focus long enough for her to stay in his mouth without him just finishing the job.

As the two continue to struggle over who'll kill who first, Neph yanks Hi'ka'o's knife from the back of her belt and charges at the natra. Trying to cut her with a swift swing, she frees herself in time to escape his attack.

She now stands in front of Neph, and the two stare at each other. Without further thinking, she turns back and runs deeper into the woods, turning invisible in the process.

Neph runs after her, and Grasshead follows.

"No, Grasshead," Neph orders. "Stay. Protect them in case something happens."

Grasshead complies with Neph's request with a quiet growl indicating so. With that, Neph ventures on into the woods to find the natra and finish her off, assuming he can actually do so.

Running without knowing where he's going, he suddenly stops over the sound of the same laugh once more. He turns around as he looks around to find out where she is.

Even though he is not entirely capable of fighting Airatsmeka, he'll do so anyway, as he seeks to prove to himself that there is a reason that he left his old life to start anew. There might be a chance that he doesn't succeed, but he has to prove himself no matter what!

As he turned around some more, there in front, point blank, stood the natra. Not a split second had passed since she appeared, and she had already stabbed him in the stomach.

Tipped with poison, she knows he's done for. She relinquishes her worries as she gently swipes her nails on his face while he stands there motionless.

"Kata heranga?" she remarks to herself.

This is the first time Neph heard an Airatsmeka speak. Although both the Natin and Airatsmeka spoke hang'pan'rika, their accent is different than that of the Natin. They speak with longer syllables and their Rs sound as if they are gargling water.

"Keika itiki na'hin akai'in seda'bak kata'in to dobi tom heranga," she continues to talk as Neph is forced to listen. "Prak'jadak'in toma eteki bak."

As she finishes swiping his face, she leaves him with tiny scratches that seem almost innocuous. She then goes to lick his blood off her nails and subsequently puts her nails in her mouth as she sucks on them in a provocative manner. Seeing no danger in front of her, she smiles while doing so.

Neph swiftly grabs her by the wrist and shoves her fingers deep into the back of her mouth!

Staggering backwards a bit before falling face on the ground, she is now painfully spitting blood. She did not see this coming; she underestimated him.

Neph does not give her any chance to retaliate as he jumps on her back and holds her in a headlock. Holding her tightly between his arms, he twists his hands in opposite directions and snaps her neck, killing her.

Neph rises up on his feet, breathing hard due to the poison in his system. He looks at her miserable dead body.

"Bitch," he mutters to himself silently as he spits out some blood.

He then turns around and starts to walk. He takes one step, and then another step, and then another step. Four steps altogether, he suddenly stops in his place. He slowly falls to his knees, and then he falls completely to the ground. With his face on the grass, he turns around to lie on his back, as he stares at what can be seen of the sun through the trees that block her. Lying on the comfortable grass, Neph is left to wonder: will he succumb to the poison and die, or will he live and prove himself?

But Neph's fate right now all depends on his teammates; whether they can finish their enemies in time to save him, or will they die too? Seeing as the numbers of the enemy have dwindled to one, they are very likely to succeed.

So'krang, who is still fighting the troublesome No. 3, runs around in the woods to find out where his opposition has disappeared to, because somewhere during the battle, No. 3 decided that it was the right thing to run away.

Stopping at some random area in the woods, So'krang tries to decide in what direction he should go next, for he cannot find No. 3. But suddenly, No. 3 appears from above the trees, descending towards So'krang with a spear in his hands. No. 3 lands and So'krang dodges the attack, making No. 3 embed the spear in the ground.

So'krang tries to whip No. 3 from close range, but No. 3 grabs his arm and kicks him in the knee, breaking his leg.

So'krang hops backwards and tries to balance himself. Balancing himself on one leg, So'krang tries again to whip No. 3, this time at a fair distance. But No. 3, already used to the whip by now, grabs it as it swings and pulls So'krang to him. So'krang, flying in the air towards No. 3, gets kicked hard in the jaw as he is sent flying away even further in the opposite direction.

Landing after a long trip, he gets up and sits on the ground. Now with a leg that looks like a noodle and a broken jaw hanging loosely by his mouth, it is doubtful whether he can win now, for No. 3 is the toughest one in the group, or at least so he's proven by being the last man standing on his team. Regardless, the Natin will fight until death and with complete disregard to who has the better chance of winning. With this idea in mind, So'krang stands up on one leg and the vine-whip tight his hand. He prepares for another round as No. 3 charges fast in his direction.

Shouting loudly over his obvious to-be victory, No. 3 prepares a punch so hard it will go through So'krang's face.

Suddenly, an object moves so fast in front of No. 3 it is hard to tell what it is. As he continues to move forward at full speed, No. 3 fails to see the floss-wide wire as his head is cut clean off his body. His body falls straight to the ground and his head rolls off to wherever.

So'krang looks to the direction the fast object went, and sees Sa'a standing there. Of course, So'krang knew it was Sa'a, as it was no surprise to him.

Sa'a approaches So'krang, as Ri'tang, Hi'ka'o, Pang'ba, Ka'wen'yai and Grasshead all gather up in the same place.

"Marang smek'sowi'in nihire," Ri'tang tells Ka'wen'yai, a bit irritated.

Ka'wen'yai just looks at him in a gloomy fashion with nothing to say.

"Kihllz beluhng thu evurywahn!" So'krang tells Ri'tang through a broken jaw and excruciating pain. "Yhou dohn't steahl dehm."

Grasshead growls, attracting the attention of So'krang. Upon looking at Grasshead by himself, So'krang realizes something.

"Whehr'z Nefff?" he asks everyone.

Everyone remains quiet, looking at each other, hoping that the person next to them might have the answer. They all rush off together to find Neph.

It doesn't take them long to find him there lying on the ground, breathing hard, trying to fight the poison that is destroying the cells in his body.

Hi'ka'o wastes no time as to take her hands and put them atop of Neph's wound. Her hands can be seen shaking from all the power she exerts to save his life in time, as a green liquid can be seen being extracted from his wound. Slowly, the drops of the liquid that come out of the wound gather into a liquid ball above Neph. Hi'ka'o throws the ball away. She repeats her actions as another ball of green liquid is formed, and throws that away, too.

After there is no more liquid to extract, Hi'ka'o then proceeds to close the wounds with her hands, as a green light emits from them and green glowing particles appear too, similar to what she did with Sa'a earlier.

With everyone gathered in the same place, it is safe to say that all the Airatsmeka are dead. Gruesomely, brutally dead.

This team of Natin will come home with shattered ribs, torn tendons, ripped ligaments, broken jaws, bent limbs, cracked sternums, ruptured cartilage and a river-worth of blood lost. After all this, they are still alive and kicking. The Natin have proven themselves to be the epitome of badassery.

CHAPTER XI

ONCE, AN INCIDENCE

I lie down in a pool of small balls of the softest material, reminiscent of the finest mattresses of the utmost quality and ergonomic design, because apparently this is what they have instead of beds. It's quite comfortable actually, and it's definitely more comfortable than a regular hospital bed.

Speaking of which, this hospital looks like just any other hospital. You got the beds, the machines used to check if you aren't dead yet, and everything between those. Basically, nothing special to look at. This prompts me to look at the ventilator on the ceiling in the room that I am in. Good thing it isn't a light-bulb. Otherwise I would be led to believe that I'm dreaming and I'm seconds away from waking up in a bathroom. But I know for a fact that there's no way that's going to happen, and even though I was close to death, I believe this is a path to a better life.

Speaking of death, I just woke up. I find myself connected to a tube through my nose and some painkiller infused into me through another tube in my arm. It's quiet in the hospital, but I'm raging inside. Just thinking that I almost died makes me angry, although I can't help but feel that I should be happy for this, but it's not happening.

The last thing I remember is the word "bitch" coming out of my mouth, and that's it. The next thing I remember is what's happening now.

Of course, nobody came to visit. I am mostly by myself except for the company of two: Grasshead, my ever-loyal companion, napping on the floor beside my bed, and So'krang, my committed mentor sitting on a chair on the other side of the bed, with no battle scars or any indication that he was in battle except for the torn clothing.

We both remain quiet. I do it because I'm angry and want to calm down, and he does it because . . . I'm not really sure why. Probably because he sees how I'm working all my face muscles to frown, realizing how angry I am, and judging by the silence, he probably thinks its best that he doesn't talk.

I think it's the best for now. I enjoy the silence. The only thing I can hear is the sound of the ceiling ventilator spinning and Grasshead snoring. Any attempt to address me right now would be a mistake, for it will trigger an undesired reaction.

"You know . . . ," So'krang starts to say, breaking the silence.

"SHUT UP!" I yell at him as I straighten up to sit down on the bed. "JUST SHUT THE FUCK UP! OK!?"

I immediately slam my body back onto the soft pillow of the bed, going back to lying down. I take a deep breath, trying to regain my calm I lost almost immediately.

"That was quite impressive, you know," he exclaims quietly.

"What wass?" I respond curiously.

"How you killed her."

"Yeah, well . . . she fuckin' underestimated me."

"They underestimate all of us. That's why their death toll is higher than ours. But I must say, using her own nails against her . . . I haven't seen that one yet."

"She had them in her mouth. That was stupidest thing I've ever seen."

"Although she did nearly kill you. The venom was almost at your head. Had we gotten to you a tad later you would probably already be dead."

"I guess that makes me lucky. Heh . . . although I'm not sure "lucky" would be the right description."

We stop talking at this moment for a while. I wanted to go back to resting, until something came to me.

"Wait a minute, how do you know all this?" I ask him. "You weren't there."

"Retrocognition," he tells me in the simplest manner.

"The fuck is that?"

"It's the technique used by the Awari'ga to see events that happened in the past. Basically, it's the opposite of seeing the future."

"Oh really. Why do you need to do that?"

"To collect information so that I can submit my report about the mission. You see, as team leader, I am commissioned with informing the clan of Karis with everything that happened during the expedition. Unfortunately, I can't be everywhere, and so the Awari'ga are required to see the events happening where I wasn't present."

"What are you supposed to report about?"

"Basically things that concern the individuals in the group. Things like individual's behavior, skills, cooperation with teammates and so forth. This information is collected and based on that, points are distributed to the individuals' profile."

"Are points important?"

"They are, if you want to get rewarded nicely. That and it allows you to participate in more difficult missions the more you accumulate."

"And these Karis . . . I suppose they are supposed to be bureaucrats?"

"I guess . . . that would be the closest equivalent to them . . . so, yes. We don't like to complicate things, but I suppose you can call them that. Although they mostly organize the Natin's profiles and uh . . . everything in between, I suppose."

"You don't know exactly what they do?"

"It's not for me to know."

"And how's your report going?"

"Already finished it."

"Hmm. You must be a fast writer then."

"Not really. It took me an entire day to write. Last time I checked, the average time it takes to register a report is far less than that."

I straighten up on my bed as my face shows an expression of surprise.

"Wait. An entire day? How long was I out?"

"Two days."

"Two days!?" I find this fact hard to fathom. "Shit . . . I thought I was a sleep for a few hours."

Just as I go back to lying down, a Natin woman comes to our room. Dressed like any ordinary Natin, there is no indication whether she is a staff member or just someone who wants to say hello.

"Hello, Neph," she says as she holds her hands together. "Is everything OK?"

"Everything's fine, thank you," I reply impatiently, although it's not her fault.

"Do you need more painkillers?"

"Nah . . . I'm fine."

She then turns her attention to So'krang.

"Kata Tashin'karat?" she asks him something that, of course, I cannot understand.

"My jaw is fine, thank you," he answers.

She nods her head and then proceeds to leave the room quietly.

"What's wrong with your jaw?" I ask him.

"I broke it," he tells me simply.

"Really? Doesn't seem like it."

"It didn't take too long to fix it."

"Really? Usually it takes a while. It takes some rubber and a bunch of hooks in your mouth. Kinda unpleasant."

"Not in the Novaverse. Hospitalization doesn't take too long, unless it's something serious."

"I was wondering how you aren't without a single scratch. By the way, who was she?"

"I thought you knew by now. She's the doctor."

"Yeah well . . . it didn't seem like it."

"The clan of Kahatasmar is in charge of all the medicine in the Novaverse. You see, in the Novaverse, there is no differentiation between staff members. An orderly can be a surgeon and vice versa, although it is expected that rookies take care of the easier tasks."

"So that just gives them the privilege of not wearing uniform?"

"No need for uniform. The sash on the arm is indication enough."

"A sash around the arm? I didn't see that."

"That's because you're an idiot."

"And you're an asshole."

We both laugh a short, quiet laugh, realizing the harmlessness in each other's words as the relationship goes from mentor and subordinate to that of two friends.

"But seriously, can we make sure this doesn't happen again?" I remark suddenly in a playful tone.

"You're the one who insisted on coming with me," So'krang responds in an equally playful manner.

"Well it seemed like the most optimal choice. But the real problem at hand is that I'm still alive . . . and I haven't done anything to advance in my goals."

"What are you trying to say?"

"I need to prove that I'm the composer, and it doesn't feel like I'm getting there. So is there any way to do this faster?"

"Frankly, I'm not sure. Although . . . ," So'krang suddenly stops short, seemingly intrigued by whatever crossed his mind at that moment.

"What?" I ask him nervously, eager to know what he's thinking about.

"Maybe killing Sima Brak would be the fastest way to gain the respect of the Natin," he says indecisively.

"What's that?"

"But then you would definitely fail, and you will be kicked out of the Novaverse faster than you can realize it."

"You make it sound like it's a longshot."

"Well . . . ehm . . . right now, it is nigh-impossible."

"Hmm . . . well . . . maybe it's not the best idea then."

After that, we stop talking for a while and the silence takes over. I use this silence to think about the future. What's going to come next? When will I leave the hospital? Not that it matters because the future will come by itself, because if there's one thing I've learned is that you can fantasize as much as you want about the future and what you're going to be like, but the reality is always worlds apart from the fantasy. Then again, it doesn't mean that what reality has to offer in the future is always unsatisfying. I always held myself together for the day that things will change for the better, but no one told me that I would make my place in a parallel universe.

Putting aside the silence, as much as it puts me at ease, I wish to speak again with So'krang, for there is something I am curious about. It's funny how most of our conversations involve mostly me asking questions and him answering accordingly. Although once I know everything I need to know about the Novaverse, we can start having real conversations . . . hopefully.

"So where are all the others?" I ask him.

"They all went their own direction," he explains. "The mission is over, so they have nothing to do here anymore."

"Gee. How caring of them," I reply sarcastically.

"Actually, some did stay. The Okati'ga and the Amroro'ga. What were their names again?" he asks himself, trying to recall.

"What did they look like?" I ask him in an attempt to help him recall.

"The one that you stood by and the one that conjures scissors."

"Scissors?"

"Yeah, that's what she does."

"Well, I hadn't seen any scissors during the battle but I believe the other one was . . . yeah, I can't remember her name either. Maybe if it was shorter it would be easier to remember. Although I do remember that she had a beautiful voice."

"Is that how you remember people?" he asks me, confused a bit. "By their voice?"

"Actually, I remember people by how shit they were to me. Heh."

I put on a smirk as I think about what I just said. But funny as it may sound, it's actually quite sad to think that someone has to remember others by how cruel they were to him. Then again, that probably applies to everyone. In all honesty, I think people put more emphasis on the shit over the good. But then again, that's just human nature. How the hell human nature even works or how you can fix it is beyond my understanding, let alone my interest.

As I have those thoughts run around in circles in my head, I wipe off the smirk from my face almost immediately and I return to put on a neutral expression.

"So you're saying only two came to visit me?" I say as I sigh.

"Yes."

"Hmm . . . y'know . . . that's actually quite comforting. T'know someone actually invested some of their time in finding out about your wellbeing. The others could learn something from them, although I didn't expect much from them to begin with."

"Don't blame the others for their behavior. Generally, the Natin have been educated to hate the heranga, and many have a hard time making an exception for you."

"The clanmistress of A-whatever didn't."

"Don't expect everyone to share the same opinions, either. Some are more tolerant than others." So'krang takes a deep breath, exhales, and starts to get up from his comfy chair. "Anyways, it shouldn't be long before you're released." he adds. "So we'd best get prepared."

He then takes a bunch of clothing, nicely folded and probably ironed as well, with a pair of Novaversian flip-flops right on top of them. He stands high above me, as I'm still lying down in this tub of balls.

"Here's a we'jei, a pair of rekarakib, and a pair of na'sho," he says as he throws at me the rice paper-thin Novaversian jacket, the Novaversian leather pants, and the Novaversian flip-flops . . . in that order. "Put these on."

"Put these on?" I remark in confusion. "Wait . . . where the fuck did MY clothes go to?!"

"You came to a hospital in an emergency. Where do you think they went?"

As he implies what happened to my clothes, a stupid smirk appears on his face, further indicating what happened to them. seeing as I'm in a hospital, and seeing as I'm wearing nothing but my briefs, I realize now that I won't be getting them back, as I'm forced from now on to wear whatever every other Natin wear.

"Fuck!" I remark to myself.

"Don't feel bad," So'krang continues, mildly cheerful in a provocative manner. "At least you get to keep your underwear."

After that stupid remark, he proceeds to leave the room.

"Wait," I call to him just before he exits. "Where are you going?"

"I'm going to get some food. You want something?"

"Yeah. Get me that tura . . . tira . . . uh?"

"Tirasartan."

"Yeah, that. I loved that."

"Very well."

So'krang proceeds to leave the room. I am now by myself with Grasshead, who is still napping by the way. His breath can be heard as he calmly sleeps, lying there on the floor.

The silence has once again enveloped the room, and I am now free to enjoy it. I put my hands behind my head as I lie down and stare at the ceiling, since I have nothing better to do. I wonder what awaits me next.

CHAPTER XII

TRAINING IN THE NOVAVERSE IS NO VIDEO GAME

I have been released from the hospital where I was treated one day after I awoke, but after three days in total. It was nice of So'krang to provide me with the casual wear of his people, but it was probably mostly due to the fact that my original clothes were no more. At least now I know what they're called, and I no longer need to refer to them as leather pants or flip-flops or whatever. The we'jei is silky in its touch and feels almost like I am wearing nothing at all, which sounds reasonable considering how thin it is. The rekararib are surprisingly comfortable despite being made of leather, although I wish I had them shorter since it doesn't synch well with the heat. And the na'sho don't even feel like flip-flops; I don't even feel like I'm wearing any kind of footwear, although the straps press a little too hard between my toes. So'krang said the feeling should subside in about a week. If he says so then it's probably the best advice I'll get regarding the issue, although I still yearn for my old clothes.

But much like how I did with my old home, I have to move on, and with So'krang and Grasshead by my side, we make our way to one of many training grounds of the clan of Maga, which is where I was hospitalized.

Apparently the clan of Maga specialize in martial arts and close combat. I don't know what kind of martial arts they teach, but it has to be pretty badass if they have warriors running straight into the face of the enemy just to karate-chop them in the face.

"Why are we doing this again?" I ask So'krang.

"We were already here, so I thought it would only be right to take you here to see how the Maga'ga trains," he tells me, with little regard to what relevance this has to my "journey" of becoming the composer.

"And what purpose does this serve us?"

"We didn't get much opportunity to train . . . ."

"We didn't get ANY opportunities to train."

He stares at me with a "what the hell" expression, and then stares forward as we continue to walk towards the training grounds.

"I wanted you to witness how we train," he continues. "You will find that the way we do things here are quite . . . uh . . . hardcore."

"Hmm," I respond to him, intrigued but skeptical at the same time.

We finally reach the training grounds. What I see before us is a humongous grey dome held up high by four metallic pillars, standing tall at each of the dome's corners. The interior is covered by large black curtains, with a separate black tunnel and doors big enough to have an elephant come through leading into it. The architecture suggested that it was an open area, although the black curtains are supposed to make it look otherwise, but I'm not convinced.

Upon going through the tunnel, which felt like crawling through one of those plastic tubes they bring to some six-year-old's birthday party, but without the crawling, I bear witness to what's inside.

The entire training area looks like they are invested in producing the most blood and sweat, but never any tears. There are punching bags on the left, adjacent to those are a bunch of trees, some arenas in middle, and on the far right is a gym or something. I found it hard to tell due to the distance.

Several Natin are training relentlessly at everything in the arena. Punching the trees, each other, and everything that can get their knuckles to be tougher than iron. Of course, they didn't limit themselves to just punching, because they are also kicking a lot, and there are a lot of knees and elbows too, along with bone-breaking grapples and whatnot. But being a punch-oriented kind of person, I couldn't help but notice all the fists flying in the air.

But the most interesting aspect of the arena was the fact the floor was, in fact, the earth itself.

"I assume the budget didn't cover the floor," I jokingly tell So'krang.

"What?" he responds obliviously.

"The floor. Why is there no floor?"

"Oh. That. Well . . . it would get crushed under the immense weight. So there's no need for it."

"Weight of what?"

"Training equipment, of course."

I look at him with doubt. He says it like it's obvious.

The only assumption I could make is that the dumbbells exceeded 100 pounds each. In which case, what would that be like? 40 tons? Whoever could lift so much would create a whole new league of lifting, and with all due respect, I don't think anyone here can do that. Not this clan, at least.

So'krang suddenly turns his attention to one of the arenas, where two people are fighting. He starts to walk by himself and then gestures me to come along. I do as requested, seeing as I have nothing better to do.

Looking from afar, I can see that the arena has no proper borders, but a white circle around a large patch of dirt indicating its limits. A number of people are standing around it, witnessing the fight. While I walk towards the arena, one of the fighters is thrown out of the border, to which one of the audience responds by lifting them back up on their feet and pushing them back into the arena, like it's a bunch of bullies lynching a weaker kid.

Upon getting close to the arena, I look at a girl and guy fighting each other. Both the girl and the guy had well-toned, combat-ready physiques, much like you would expect from the warriors around here, regardless of gender. Both wore blue bell bottoms, thin as the jackets that everyone loves around here. But while the guy was shirtless, the girl wore that breast-covering piece of clothing that I see the women here walking around with. And then there are the neck tattoos. Always the tattoos.

But despite all this, the guy still looked like he could destroy the girl. But that's coming from a person who comes from a world where the women are, in fact, weaker on average. Clearly, the Natin experience things differently, so I have to approach this view from a different perspective now.

With my opinions on my side, I watch what appears to be some pretty ruthless fighting. The fighters' faces are bleeding from a broken nose and a busted brow, their bodies filled with bruises, deep purple like a puddle of grape juice. As if their fight hadn't been brutal enough before I got there, it just gets worse.

The girl delivers a series of punches, left and right over and over, with the guy blocking each hit with the palms of his hands. Finally, he counters by grabbing one of her punches, pulling her and then delivering a rising knee straight to her stomach. She holds her stomach tight, sitting down from the impact, as he approaches her fast to land an overhead punch. Suddenly, she gets up and kicks him in the face so hard that he staggers backwards. She rolls forward, jumps in the air and hits him hard in the side of the head with a nasty spinning kick. She wastes no time to grab him by the hair and punch him repeatedly in the stomach. A punch and another and then another punch, before he grows tired and grabs her by the wrist, throws it away and then immediately proceeds to grab the entire half of her face in what appears to be an attempt to gouge her eye with his thumb. She then throws back her head to avoid his thumb.

Using his unfortunate position against him, she maneuvers herself across his body to put him in an arm-lock, all while he's still standing. She gives her all to break his arm as he grinds his teeth just to keep his arm intact. Suddenly, in a bold move, he stops resisting. She swings back fast as he uses his other arm to grab her by the throat behind his back. He spins radically to relinquish any remaining grip she has on him, using the momentum to lift her high by the throat and then forcefully throw her down on his kneeling knee as she bounces off slightly from the impact. A crunching sound could be heard from the hit, and the girl now lay on the floor with the entire side of her ribcage broken. Now the fight is over . . . or so it seems.

As he walks slowly due to the hard hits he suffered in the intense fight, he prepares to end it. The girl is still lying on the arena floor in pain, and there is no sign that she'll take the victory.

The guy starts to gain speed approaching her. He now runs, preparing to deliver a kick to the head, shouting to exert any remaining power he has to obtain this victory. But before he can land the finishing blow, the girl rises up fast and pokes him hard in the chest with three fingers. The guy flies backwards, landing hard on the floor, and staying there. Now, the victory belongs to the girl.

After a while, people rush into the arena to pick up the now-unconscious guy and take him to wherever, presumably to the hospital. The girl is left by herself, perceived as "all right" by her peers, but I see differently. She was breathing really hard, clutching tight the side of her ribs, yet for some reason she can stand.

She then stares at me. I found it hard to decipher what she is thinking of me. Does she see me like that guy in the toilet I met back then or does she have a different opinion about me? Suddenly, a slight smile can be seen on her face. I guess not everyone here thinks the same.

She is then approached by her peers. The crowd of people blocks my view, but I guessed wrong about them neglecting her.

I look at So'krang, who is still standing there like a chicken staring into the blank air.

"So what'll happen to him?" I ask him, interrupting his "chicken trance."

"She severed his spinal cord," he says calmly.

"Oh shit!" I respond, shocked. "I assume he won't be able to fight again?"

"Na. Six weeks from now and he'll be fully functional."

"I see." I look back at the arena. "They looked young." I remark.

"They're ani'man," he tells me.

"What?"

"They're first-years. They're fifteen."

"Really? They looked young, even with that small bit of facial hair that guy had."

"We shave early."

"Aha. They fought kinda rough for their age, don't y'think?"

"Actually, I don't think that at all. This is how we do it. If you can't do it like this then don't do it at all. Eventually they will have to face the enemy anyway and they will have to know what it feels like. So it starts now."

"Hmm. You weren't kidding when you said you do it hardcore."

We remain quiet for a while.

"Anyways, what do we do now?" I ask him.

"Go fight her," he tells me simply.

I quickly turn my head to look at him, as anyone who just saw my face will interpret it as the facial equivalent of "what the fuck?!"

"Fight her?!" I ask, refusing to believe it. "You're shitting me!?"

"Far from that," he tells me with confidence. "Now go fight her."

"I dunno, man. I dunno if I'm up for the task. I mean, you saw what she did to that guy. Besides, I don't think she's up for it herself. I mean, look at her. In her condition, I might kick her ass."

So'krang snickers quietly. I stare at him with confusion as an ominous feeling flows through my shoulders.

"Worry about yourself," he says, suddenly putting on a serious expression. "She'll be fine."

"Yeah . . . ," I say, hesitantly and doubtfully. "I'm not sure you know what you're doing."

"I'm you're mentor. I think I know PERFECTLY what I'm doing. Besides, I'm the best you have right now around here."

"Great, now you're just being abusive with your position."

A quiet comes between us amidst all the noise that surrounds us, a slight feeling of tension between us as we seem to have hit a bumpy spot in our relationship. We look at each other seriously as we hope to quickly solve the problem.

"Have a little faith in me, Neph," he tells me empathetically with a serious face.

I try. I really do. But being who I am, it's hard for me to find trust for others.

"Shouldn't we . . . at least get permission," I ask him compassionately. "It's not like I can just waltz in there and start fighting. Can I?"

"If permission is the problem then don't worry. I got it covered," he tells me seriously.

He turns around and makes his way to a man with muscular features, wearing the stomach bandages I see on men everywhere and black leather pants, but barefoot. I assume this is the guy in charge around here.

The man is just tending to a Natin, possibly still a first-year who had been punching one of the many trees in the arena. The Natin, who is possibly a disciple still in training, is already exhausted from punching and kicking the tree, as he lies on the dirty, sweat-soaked soil that is this arena's floor as if he were some kind of rag. The sweat just drips slowly from his arms as it sticks to his clothing and soaks the dirt beneath him. The man in charge of him yells at him as spit launches from his mouth and pumped veins fill his forehead. The yelling continues for a while, and I couldn't possibly understand what he was saying because of the distance and all the noises around here that muffle out whatever he might say, even if I did understand the language. And then, all of a sudden, the man kicks the disciple in his stomach as he flips over on the ground and immediately pulls him back up to stand on his feet. The disciple staggers a bit before returning to punching and kicking the tree, as if he had never been exhausted to begin with.

From that interaction alone, I can understand how brutal the training sessions here can be, although I wonder if it's the same for the rest of the clan. I wonder if anyone has a problem with that. Then again, if someone did have a problem with the training, then they probably wouldn't have ended up here in the first place.

Just as the man, who I would like to think is hiding a compassionate soul behind a ruthless demeanor, finishes his interaction with the disciple, he is approached by So'krang. So'krang puts his hand on his shoulder and tells him something which, again, I couldn't possibly understand because of the reasons I mentioned earlier.

They then both look at me, and then the guy in charge looks back at So'krang, nods his head and moves away from him. So'krang then comes back to me.

"Get in the arena," he tells me while pointing with his head toward the arena.

I approach the arena. Grasshead attempts to follow me.

"Grasshead, stay," I tell him calmly.

Grasshead stays by So'krang's side as I enter the arena. Once inside the arena, I wait for orders.

"Shoes!" So'krang yells from behind me.

I look back to see him, not entirely satisfied with the way he conveyed that message. Regardless, I take off my shoes, just as he wanted. I then proceed to get in the arena . . . again.

"And shirt!" he yells again from behind me.

I do as he says and take off my jacket and shirt, and throw them at him. He catches them.

"Any more and it'll cost ya," I jokingly tell him with a smirk.

He looks at me dead serious in response, probably unsatisfied with the joke.

"Never mind," I say, a tad afraid and wiping off my smirk. I now stand in the arena, bare feet and shirtless and waiting for someone to approach me.

Suddenly, a girl walks up to the arena, sporting the same attire as the last girl who beat the hell out of that one guy. She has black hair, tied into a ponytail reaching down to between her shoulder blades, and three bulges on the skin of her right shoulder, shaped like spikes and positioned in an inverted triangle. Underneath the spike are three white stripes, placed one after the other all the way to her elbow.

A different form of body modification, I presume. One that I haven't seen yet, which is logical considering only the Natin have such a fad.

Regardless, I look at her, and she looks at me. I then look at So'krang, and then I look at the guy in charge, while she continues to look at me without moving her eyes. I'm waiting for the cue to start, if there is one.

I look at So'krang again, waiting for my cue, and in response, he gestures me to pay attention to her. I do so, and get closer to her.

We are now something like two feet away from each other, me and the girl. I understand that there is no cue, and the fight just starts by itself.

I assume a boxer's stance, putting my fists in front of my face. On the other hand, she doesn't seem to have any stance at all. She just stands upright with both her arms at the sides of her body slightly bent, and her palms partially open.

She strafes right, and in response, I strafe left. She does nothing, and I'm too hesitant to take action, knowing that she'll just counter me, being skilled in martial arts. This goes on for a few seconds.

Suddenly, she starts waving her hands in my face. I stay cautious by not doing anything, and then she slaps me. Startled, I try to punch her, but she just throws it to the side, followed by a jumping roundhouse straight to my cheek. I fall down to the ground, but get up immediately.

I return to stare back at her face, assuming my boxer's stance again while she remains in her unusual stance. I prepare for the next time she will attack me, and try to remain defensive, waiting for the right moment to strike.

Again, she waves her hands in my face, but she won't get any response from me this time. Regardless, I can never find the right moment to strike.

Suddenly, she comes at me with a fast flurry of fists right to the chest, Strong enough to hurt but weak enough as to not break my ribs.

I push her back and proceed to try to punch her again. She counters me by throwing my fist away, holding it, and tripping me with a sweep of her leg. Now directly facing the ground, she axe-kicks me on the back of the head, followed by a somersault kick straight to the face. I fly backwards, landing on my back. I waste no time to roll back and get back up on my feet.

I can hear laughter in the audience, but that won't stop me.

We face each other again. What this fight has in store now, I cannot expect. This time, however, she didn't wave her hands in my face. I don't know what she will do next. But we just stand there facing each other, with her clearly knowing what she's doing, while I don't.

She then punches me left and right in the face. I retaliate with a straight punch, but she just grabs it, headbutts me in the nose, pulls me to her by my arm, and then delivers a straight kick to my face, with the momentum making the impact even worse.

I roll back, and like always, immediately get back up. Without a second to think about it, I see her running at me at full speed. She then attacks with me a flurry of punches. Punches to the chest; punches to my face. And then, a hand-chop to the jaw. I almost fall to the ground again, but I stop it with my arm. Holding myself in place, I take one fast breath before rising fast back up on my feet, with a punch ready to sink into her face. I can feel her hands on my arm, ready to counter me in some way I can't predict.

But she can't stop me, and her hands are holding my arm tight as the punch goes straight to her face. She staggers backwards from the force, turns around and falls forward. She gets back up, holds her mouth and looks at me, surprised and, if I can say so, mildly afraid. I can hear mumbles in the audience, probably trying to understand what just happened. I smile at her, knowing that now it just got real!

I run at her at full speed. Just as I get close enough to her, I jump in the air and thrust both of my feet forward, aiming straight. I can't see what's going on because my face is looking at the ceiling from the position I'm in, but I can feel her gripping my ankles and pulling herself closer to me. I can now feel her feet on my back, pushing hard as she propels herself closer to my head. Using the momentum to my favor, I flip backwards in the air, grab her by the ankles, pull her, and hold her hard by the thighs as her body is parallel to mine and her back is facing the floor, positioned in a nasty power-bomb. We both fall down and she gets slammed hard against the arena floor.

Now lying flat on the ground, I mount her like they do in those MMA fights. With her legs wrapped around my waist, she is in no position to retaliate as I punch with my left fist and hold myself in place with my right arm pressing against the ground.

After the second punch, she grabs me by the hair and starts punching me in the face. I move my head backwards to avoid her fist and make things harder for her, as if attacking in that position of hers isn't bad enough.

I grab her punching arm and throw it away. I get closer to her from my mounted position and continue to punch her. Three punches, and then she holds my face with her thumbs on my eyes. I pull my head back to keep her from gouging my eyes out. I struggle to keep her on the ground and keep my eyes intact at the same time.

Having enough of this, I throw her hands sideways, wrap my arms around her legs as I get back up to a standing position, and deliver a wheelbarrow suplex by throwing myself backwards as she flies over me and finally lands hard on her face.

I get back up immediately and turn around. I see her rolling forward and then moving fast on all four limbs on the edges of the arena. She gets back up on her feet, and I can clearly see her nose bleeding profusely.

She stands in place and seems hesitant. She breathes deeply, trying to figure out how to approach me next; the unpredictable adversary who knows nothing of martial arts, but compensates with relentless determination. I smile at her. I 'm excited about how things are unfolding.

And then, she runs at me at full speed. She then jumps, spins in the air, and tries to deliver a spinning kick. Unfortunately for her, she is too slow for me, as I grab her by the ankle and proceed to spin her around me.

"AAAAAGGGGHHHH!!" I shout with every remaining breath in my lungs, anxious to win this fight already and prove my worth.

Suddenly, I see her bending toward me while I spin her. Softly, I can feel a pair of hands grabbing me, one on the back of my head and the other on my chin. I can feel my head turning. I hear a crack, and then I fall hard to the ground. I can't move anything, nor can I feel anything. My vision is getting blurry, and my hearing is getting muffled. And then . . . everything just fades to black.

CHAPTER XIII

TWICE, A COINCIDENCE

I open my eyes, and before me I see a ceiling ventilator, tirelessly spinning as it cuts through the air with its blades, making soft noises as it keeps on turning. I feel a soft material pressing me in all the right points in my body. All but my face is covered in this material. I am reluctant to believe it is true, but I realize it now: I have ended in the hospital yet again, lying in a pool of balls.

"Congratulations," I hear So'krang's voice to my left. "You just beat your last record of being comatose."

I want to move my head left to see him, but even a slight movement will ruin the ideal position that I'm in, and I'm way too comfortable to even try to get it back. I move my eyes instead. It isn't enough, as all I can catch is some brown color in my peripheral vision.

"Really?" I ask him, doubting I could stay asleep more than three days, as much as I would love that. "By how much?"

"One week," he tells me simply and directly.

"One week!?" I find it hard to believe. "And you just sat there and waited?"

"Na. I actually managed to go an expedition while you were here. Went back home to Ka'ka'pan afterwards, too. It was really nice."

"I can only imagine," I remark sarcastically. "So you just left me to the orderly? Some friend you are."

"It wouldn't matter to you anyway. You were comatose."

"Hmm. No arguing there."

I hear some snoring to my right. I recognize its Grasshead sleeping.

"He never left your side," So'krang suddenly mentions.

"Who? Grasshead? You haven't seen anything yet." I remark proudly. "He and I are like glue. Or duct tape, depending on how you wanna see it. I mean, me and him are so tight, that sometimes I just forget that he's there besides me. Y'know, as if he's part of my body. Like we're . . . one body. One mind. One everything!"

"Interesting. I don't think that even most Mosak'ga share such a connection with their hiphomoy."

"The Mosak'ga. You mentioned them once. Are they like hiphomoy riders or something?"

"They do more than just ride hiphomoys and fight with them. They form an unbreakable bond. They are Natin who have a natural propensity to bond with hiphomoys, and it best exemplifies itself in combat."

"Oh really?"

"If you had been with me on my last expedition, you would've seen one in action. How he and the hiphomoy dashed at the Airatsmeka and coiled the yang'tirir around his neck and snapped it. His eyes exploded from the pressure. It was just a sight to behold and, if I do say so myself, I don't think I've seen a performance like that in a while."

"Sounds like magic; what can I say?" I reply sarcastically. "What's this yang-thing anyways?"

"It's an elastic rope used by the Mosak'ga to further enhance cooperative combat with the mosak'ga hiphomoy. It's how they fight together."

"I see . . . ."

I remember something else that I'm curious about. So'krang primarily mentions the Mosak'ga as hiphomoy riders. But I think he's missing something.

"There's another clan that rides hiphomoys, right?" I ask him curiously. "I mean, I recall hearing something on our last expedition."

"The only other clan that specializes in fighting with hiphomoys is the clan of Hikama, but they use regular hiphomoy that they customize with weaponized exosuits." He goes on to explain. "You see, the Mosak'ga hiphomoy is the only type of hiphomoy that is naturally designed for combat. That is why I like them so much, because they have a clear purpose from birth. They remind me of myself and the rest of my people. Everyone is predestined for a certain purpose, and the Mosak'ga hiphomoy are a perfect example of that. What the Hikama'ga do is take hiphomoys and give them something to function outside their purpose. This methodology deviates from what we believe in and how we operate on a daily basis, and doing something outside your purpose is not something that the Natin believe in. I might be exaggerating a little, but it's reminiscent of heranga culture. But then again, every clan has a certain purpose and specialty, so I guess the Hikama'ga specialize in turning non-fighting hiphomoys into . . . well . . . fighters."

"Hmm . . . sounds like you really hate them."

"I don't hate them. I don't necessarily have to agree with them, but I, much like the rest of my people, accept the different ways of every clan and embrace the diversity of purposes that we fulfill. After all, it is this philosophy which allows us to create harmony among each other. But just so you know, in essence, the Mosak'ga and Hikama'ga are nothing alike. The techniques which they use are like sky and sea."

"If you say so, then I believe you. After all, you ARE my omniscient tour guide for this place. Heh."

I smile to myself over the joke, although I don't think So'krang enjoyed it as much, seeing as there's no chuckle in the background, and I can't even see if he's smiling or not. But after that, we stop talking, and I find nothing better to talk about.

"Welp," I say while moving my head. "Time to get a mov—"

"Don't move!" So'krang suddenly says, clear and demanding. "You severed your spinal cord. You have at least five more weeks of recovery."

"Five weeks!? That's bullshit! I can't wait that long. I have things to do. And for the record, it wasn't me who severed my own cord. It was her who did this to me!"

"Speaking of which, that was impressive."

"You said that last time too."

"Yes. Keep surprising me like that and it won't be impressive anymore. But still, it wasn't good enough."

"Well what'd you expect? I don't know kung fu."

No response from So'krang. I move my eyes to him to see what's going on. Of course, I can't see anything but some brown color in my peripheral vision.

"You know . . . I don't think I was wrong about you," he says in a calm voice, sounding somewhat intrigued. "You could die a thousand times and still surprise everyone. I do hope that one day everyone will be able to see what you're truly capable of."

"Why the fuck would I want to die a thousand times!?" I remark over his ridiculous construction of words that seemingly make a metaphor. "I'd rather not die at all."

"Well . . . uh . . . ."

"You haven't thought of that, have you?" I stop him short.

He remains silent over my rhetorical question, seeing it as the best response. And although I, too, see it that way, we once again find ourselves in silence.

"What was that thing on her shoulder?" I inquire about her, curious to know. "She had some kind of spikes bulging from her shoulder. Like they were coming from beneath her skin."

"That was a tarmod," So'krang explains. "It's a form of body modification."

"Like piercing and tattoos?"

"Yes. We alter the geometry of the tissue to take certain shapes. Some even add color."

"I recall she had white stripes."

"You mean Am'ka'wi?" an excited voice with a Natin accent comes from my far left, somewhere behind So'krang.

"Is that what her name is?" I ask, unbothered by the random voice attempting to converse with me.

"Akka, she is a kerakka! She destroys everybody!"

I'm curious about his statement as I find it odd that, according to him, she is the best around.

"Wait, aren't you all badasses?" I ask, confused. "I mean, that's what they teach you, right?"

"Well . . . yes," he answers, oblivious to how he wants to phrase his coming sentence. "Others also destroy her, because everybody is good, but I really like her. I remember one time she pierced an Airatsmeka's face with a flying kick. That was the best!"

"If you like her so much, maybe you should do something about it."

"That is an idea to keep in mind."

"I suppose so."

I return back to the silence, seeing as there is no further conversation to create. Then, I wonder.

"What happened to you?" I inquire about his situation while I stare at the ceiling, without any means of knowing how he looks.

"Me?" he asks, sounding he wants to elongate his sentence. "I broke my neck in training. Have another five weeks before I go back."

"Same here."

And then it came to me.

"Wait. Aren't you that guy from that fight with that one girl?" I ask him curiously.

"I fight a lot of girls, but which one are you referring to?" he wittily remarks.

"She stabbed you with three fingers through your throat."

"Ah, you mean Mog'jei. Oh akka, she was really good. I did not expect that move, even with half her ribcage broken."

"Yeah. You were not too shabby yourself."

"Akka, I am the best!"

"You are all the best."

His personal definition of "best" is quite loose, or quite possibly just Natin slang, equivalent of something like "badass" or "awesome" or whatever. Nonetheless, I sense a hell of a lot of pride coming from him, a characteristic I notice in all Natin I have encountered so far.

"So what's your name?" I ask him.

"I am Aam'ka'pa'nik'naam, or Aam'kea ka panar nik'ga naam'marash," he says, giving a full detailing of his name like he's presenting a résumé.

These names just get more complicated the more I know these people. "I think I'll stick with the former." I say while thinking of the complexity of his name. "I'm Neph, by the way."

"The composer!?" He seems surprised. "I should've known."

"Why? Would it change anything?"

"I was not really fond of the idea, but you seem like a nice guy."

"Man, I'm just glad someone's open-minded about this. Y'know, I already get crap because of this whole composer thing."

"Well we're not really fond of the heranga. I hate them the most. Despicable, greedy, selfish scum who would sell their mother for a bread loaf to get what they want."

I think to myself, "That's one serious hyperbole." I remain quiet, knowing that my kind doesn't represent me, although I can't help but feel insulted. After all, I am not a Natin.

"But . . . mother always said: when you meet a person, treat him as an individual, and not as the collective that he belongs to." He continues to give his résumé. "She told me that because she didn't want me to think that all Amroro'ga kill themselves. But I suppose it applies to everyone."

"It does," I reply concretely.

"Yes. I suppose so."

I sigh over the deep conversation we had, and then we return to the silence. A few quiet seconds pass, and I realize there's nothing to do and nothing more to talk about. I hear the blades of the ventilator cutting the air. I hear the snores of Grasshead. I grow bored, and I find that I can no longer tolerate the situation.

"Welp, I've had enough," I say while moving my head. "Getting outta here."

"NA!" So'krang says in a loud voice, seeing as I'm about to leave the pool and seemingly ruin the recovery process.

I pay no attention to his warning as I take my hand, put it on the ledge of the pool and gracefully pull myself out of it. As my feet touch the paved floor, I straighten up on two feet. I can feel the wind all over my body. I look down, and see myself wearing white briefs, just like I did a week ago. Talk about recycling.

So'krang stands up from his chair with a shocked expression on his face. Is he going to say something, or does he just want to stare at my half-naked body all day long?

"It was supposed to be another five weeks," he says, astounded by how quickly I've recovered.

"Yeah, well I can't wait that long," I say cheerfully, eager to start my next mission. "I have a destiny to fulfill, remember?"

Suddenly, I hear someone walking with heels towards us. I look back, and see the nurse approaching, holding a bag of liquids of some sort. I look at her, and she looks at me. She stands still over the shock of seeing me standing upright. I guess nobody saw this coming.

"What am I missing?" Aam'ka'pa'nik'naam suddenly asks curiously over the silence.

Both So'krang and the nurse still remain in their place, still fathoming the magnificence of my fast recovery.

"Only the Samish'ga can heal this fast." So'krang suddenly gives a piece of random trivia, which I, in no way, am supposed to understand.

"Samish'ga what!?" Aam'ka'pa'nik'naam suddenly says, confused as to what's happening and anxious to know. "What's going on!?"

The nurse then turns around and starts walking out of the room. As she turns around, she still stares at me for a few, before completely turning around and leaving out of our sight. As she left, she still seemed confused and shocked about what just happened.

I watch So'krang. He's still trying to figure out what's happening, although some of the shock has left his face, while I am just eager to move on. I look down and think, "I wish I had some slacks right now."

"So what are we doing next?" I ask So'krang with half a smile on my face.

CHAPTER XIV

A SWARM OF BUMBLEBEES . . . OR A CONCERT OF BULLETS?

Grasshead, So'krang and I make our way to the training grounds of the clan of Teseba after making a long trip all the way to the northwestern region of Wotaiga. I have yet to understand why So'krang would take me halfway through the continent just to shoot stuff with a bunch of other people, who could accidentally shoot me in return because they're trigger-happy gunslingers with the thought pattern of "shoot everything that moves and everything that doesn't move" . . . in that order. I heard that just south of here is the clan of Koringbar, otherwise known as the clan of blowing stuff up. I think I would better fit there, but So'krang is the man with the plan, so what say do I have in the matter? I just hope he knows what he's doing, considering the recent events.

"I hear way too many gunshots in this place," I remark, a tad worried, but I remain in the mood. "I've already been twice in the hospital. I really don't want to come a third time."

"Calm down," So'krang replies, certain about my supposed safety. "The Teseba'ga couldn't accidentally hit you even on purpose."

"Accidentally and on purpose. HA! You just made an oxymoron."

"What I meant to say is that they couldn't shoot you even if they wanted to."

"So they suck at their job?" I continue to jokingly provoke So'krang.

"NA!" So'krang yells over his embarrassing wording. He then sighs while rubbing his eyes with his fingers, and then he looks back at me. "Look, you're safe. That's what I meant to say. Just please, stop making me look bad."

"Settle down, man. I'm joking," I cheerfully tell him while patting him on the back.

As we chat, we enter one of the many training grounds of the clan of Teseba, an open field, standing on the foundation of firm grass, with several shooting galleries of different types and styles.

There are galleries for close-range shooting, involving people standing in the middle of it along with dummies, jumping and moving swiftly around the dummies as the trainee shoots at them with near perfection. Aiming is not even a factor as they quickly maneuver their hands to hit targets behind their back and to their sides. The dummies fall to the floor like flies. When they stop moving, I can clearly see that those are in fact just sacks of grain. How they were able to move is not something I can explain, nor do I care to.

Then there are the standard mid-range galleries built for precision; people kneeling down on one knee and shooting stationary targets from about a hundred feet away. Typical rifle training I could find at any military base back when I was in heratrang'ga pan . . . or earth. Nothing diifferent here.

But somewhere in the training grounds, in a dedicated spot on the edge of it, is the most unusual training I've seen yet. People kneeling down on one knee, aligned next to each other, but too close to each other, each holding what appears to be a sniper rifle, aiming at a vast open meadow of nothingness. I can't understand what the hell they are aiming at, as there is nothing for miles that is visible to the naked eye. They do nothing but stand there like statues, and then one of them fires. A large bang is heard, worthy of a sniper rifle, but nothing can be seen on the other side. I keep looking at the meadow, but I still fail to understand what just happened.

The Natin who just shot puts down his rifle on the ground, and proceeds to take off some kind of monocle that's shaped like a scope from his eye. He starts inspecting it, as if something is wrong with it. He turns around, looking at it from every angle, then he flicks it, and then he clicks his tongue, probably because something was wrong with it.

But putting aside his problems with the monocle, I pay attention to the rifle, which, upon closer inspection, has a peculiar design to it. It is black as onyx, has a dough-like lump on its butt, and has no chamber, but instead has a narrow cylinder of glass casing in place, sitting horizontally. Did I mention that the gun has no scope? That's right. They are aiming sniper rifles with no scopes. But I believe that's where the weird monocles come into play.

The same Natin grabs the rifle, with the monocle back on his eye, and then slams the body of the rifle with a thrust of his palm. The cylinder comes jumping out and falls to the ground. As it lies on the ground, bright green light starts to get absorbed into the cylinder through its edges. As it continues to absorb more light, the Natin takes a different cylinder filled with green light, and puts it neatly in the void where the last cylinder was, which continues to refuel itself with green light. The Natin then goes back aiming at the meadow, looking again like a statue.

"They are currently training to hit targets from far away," So'krang explains to me.

"Really?" I respond curiously. "How much is 'far away' exactly?"

"By your measurement techniques, it has to be something like nine miles."

"Nine miles!?"

"Yes. Now come. I didn't bring you here just to stare."

We move along in the training grounds to wherever So'krang wants to take me. I stare back at the snipers one more time before leaving the area.

"Wow. Nine miles," I mumble to myself.

As we move in between and around the various galleries, the sound of hundreds of bullets firing off at the same time forcibly penetrates my ear drums. I feel like I'm in a rock concert called "bullet bonanza." In fact, it is so loud, it sounds like standing in the middle of a bumblebee swarm.

"I BET HALF OF THE CLAN IS HARD OF HEARING!" I jokingly shout to So'krang, resorting to yelling to be heard above all those bangs.

"WHAT?!" he shouts back without even looking at me.

I frown over the feeling that my joke was wasted. I do not feel like saying it again.

We reach a relatively more quiet location in the training grounds. What I see before me is a shooting gallery closed off by a fence made of chicken wire and a surface paved with asphalt. The gallery itself reminds me of a tennis court, only smaller. People there are improperly aligned, standing and shooting at targets with pistols from a hundred feet away, a good way to get shot if you ask me.

"I want you to go in there and start shooting," So'krang says like he ran out of a plan and just decided to improvise.

"What?" I ask, confused over the lack of guidance in this task. "Just like that? Start shooting without any prerequisites?"

"Yes."

"Heh . . . y'know it didn't end well the last time you told me to just 'go in there.'"

"Get in there," he says indifferently. "I know what I'm doing."

"Let's get to the end, and then we can talk about it," I say as I enter the shooting gallery.

I make my way to the gallery. As usual, Grasshead follows me blindly.

"Grasshead, go stand next to So'krang," I tell him as I walk to the gallery. He turns and walks to So'krang.

As I stand at the entrance of the gallery before further moving into it, what I see before me is pretty much what I saw when I was outside the gallery: a bunch of Natin shooting at random targets in front and who may also accidentally shoot each other because they're aligned randomly in the area and there are no safeguards. At the edge of the gallery behind the shooters, where the least chance to get shot at is, stands a long table with various firearms of Natin design. All black as onyx, there are rifles, shotguns, and pistols to choose from. There is no ammo on the table, nor is there anywhere else to get ammo, suggesting that the guns here do not rely on ammo, but function perfectly without it.

I grab myself a pistol. A pistol with a rectangular tube, probably eight inches long, attached to the left side of its body that slopes upwards and backwards towards me. I stare deep into the rectangular hatch of the tube, hoping to see something unusual because of its particular design, curious to know why this tube is even needed. I see nothing, and progress to stand a hundred feet away in front of all the targets, like everyone else.

I follow So'krang's orders, and prepare to shoot. I raise my left hand straight in front of me, and aim. I shoot. I miss. I shoot again. I miss again. On every shot, a green spark appears at the hatch of the gun's tube. I repeat this over and over, and the palm of my hand starts to hurt and turn red from the recoil. I don't understand why I keep missing. Is a hundred feet too much for me, or is shooting harder than they make it look like on TV?

I look to my side, and see all the Natin hitting the targets with near-perfection. Aiming and shooting as if that's the only thing that matters in the world, with their faces holding a stone-like serious expression.

I return to my business and look back at the targets in front of me. I start shooting again. Three shots. The first misses. The second misses too. The third hits, but only at the edge of the target. My hand hurts even more now. I switch the gun to my right hand and look at my left hand. It is red and it burns a little. I shake my left hand in the air to relieve the pain.

Suddenly, I hear laughter to my side over all the gun noises. I look to my side, and what I see is a Natin holding a similar gun to mine, smiling from one side of his ears to the other.

"You're a lousy shot," he tells me cheerfully, still having that stupid smile on his face. "Go grab yourself a shotgun. You should start from there."

Despite his condescending attitude, he's right, and I only find it right to follow his advice, although I'm still annoyed by the way he talked to me.

I head back to the table where all the guns are. I put down the pistol and grab myself a shotgun.

The shotgun has the width of an 8-ball, and so is the barrel. Instead of a tube, the shotgun has four hatches shaped like air vents, two on each side of the gun. It also has the dough-like lump on its butt, similar to that of the sniper rifle I saw earlier.

As I hold the shotgun in both my hands, I aim it down and lean the butt of the gun on my shoulder. It feels so comfortable; kind of feels like a pillow is sitting on my shoulder right now. I look at it, and see the lump adjusting appropriately to suit the structure of my shoulder. I suppose this is what you call an ergonomic butt.

I return my attention back to the targets, aiming down the gun and focusing to deliver the best shot. I wait a little. One second. Two seconds. Three seconds. Four seconds, and then I shoot. A large bang is heard, and the recoil forces me to raise the gun so I don't fall down on my ass.

I lower the gun down and look at the target that I shot. From the hundred feet that I stand away from the target, I barely see the tiny pellet holes in it, but at least I know now that I managed to hit it. Even so, I'm not satisfied. Anyone who's a lousy shot would prefer to use a shotgun because they can't land a precise hit, or at least a meaningful one. I'm not here to learn how to use a gun; I'm here to learn how to shoot.

"Congratulations, you now know how to use a gun. Heh," a familiar voice mockingly tells me from the side.

I look to my side, and I see the same Natin I saw a moment ago, still standing at the same spot he was, with that stupid smile on his face. I look at him, annoyed. His smile slowly starts to wither away into a more neutral expression, probably realizing that he's not funny. After all, everyone is too busy to laugh, or even listen, to his jokes, and I definitely don't find them funny, being the victim and all.

Having enough of this pretend conversation, I turn around and make my way again to the table of weapons. I put the shotgun down and look at the selection in front of me.

One particular gun catches my attention. It is a pistol, twice the size of the pistol I used earlier, but overall it shares the same design. It has a larger and wider circular tube instead of a rectangular one, and a bigger barrel with a silencer attached to it. A bigger barrel means bigger bullets, which means that it should be easier to hit the target. This gun is perfect for beginners!

I grab the oversized pistol in one hand and start to inspect it. The handle barely fitting in my hand, I turn it to look at both its sides, trying to find if there's anything peculiar to it. I grab the silencer with the other hand and I try to remove it. It won't even budge, as if the silencer is built in to the gun itself. Nevertheless, I am satisfied with this gun and return to stand in front of the targets.

Now back in front of the targets, I take a deep breath before trying my marksmanship skills for the third time. I raise the gun in front of me and aim at the target. Again, waiting to find the right angle for the best shot.

"Hey, man," the same jokester from before tries to catch my attention.

I look at him while still aiming the gun at the targets. This time, he looks serious. Hopefully this time he won't have anything stupid to say.

“You don’t wanna use that gun,” he warns me, sounding serious.

“Go to hell,” I tell him, disregarding his warning, still annoyed by his provocative attitude. “I’ll use whatever gun I want.”

Maybe if he had been a bit more helpful to those who don’t know much about marksmanship, instead of laughing at their failures simply because they’re beginners, I would accept what he has to say. So far, all he had done was insult me and give himself a little laugh. Although I wouldn’t expect much from a Natin, the proud race of humanoids that cherish their misanthropy, rather than trying to look above it. Even if they are told to accept only one into their lovable melting pot, some might still find it hard to do so, while others can be a little more tolerant, and I don’t know what category to put him in. Despite this, I can’t help but notice the worried expression on his face.

Regardless, I return my attention back to the targets. I aim down and try to find the perfect angle for the perfect shot. One second. Two seconds. Three seconds. Four seconds, and I have found it. I shoot . . .

A massive bang is heard! The gun flies backwards in the blink of an eye, ripping my hand apart!

“AAAAAAAAAGGGGGHHHHHHH!!!” I shout as I stare horrifyingly at the bloody mess which is my hand.

CHAPTER XV

THRICE, A PHENOMENON

I look at my left hand. I try to close it into a fist, but the fingers can only move so much. I try to close it again, but the fingers can only move halfway into what seems to look like a cat's paw. I try again, and this time I try really hard, but it doesn't even hurt; it just feels like the tendons necessary for the function don't even exist, so I feel nothing.

As I continue to stubbornly try to close my ruptured hand, So'krang enters the room holding two magenta-colored tear-shaped bottles that fit exactly in the palm of a person's hand. The bottles have three prongs protruding outwards from the bottom, placed in a triangular position.

"Tell me," he says while walking, sounding cheerful with a smirk on his face. "How many times are you going to get hospitalized?"

"As many as it takes," I calmly and wittily respond to him while I continue trying to clench my fist. "Although I wouldn't be here if you were paying attention to what I was doing."

"I was talking to somebody. I can't always pay attention to what you're doing. I was assigned the task of a mentor, not a caretaker. Besides, I understood someone already warned you about the man-killer."

"Ever heard of 'the boy who cried wolf?'"

"I can't say that I have."

"Well then, look it up."

I look at my hand worried, tirelessly trying to clench it. I can't help but think: how long will it take for this to heal? Seeing it as it is, I can't help but anxiously feel that it will stay this way forever.

"I can't clench my fist," I tell So'krang, worried.

"Your tendons are currently recuperating," He explains to me, returning to his usual formal voice. "Don't push it. It should take a while before it returns to its original state."

"How long is a while, exactly?"

"The doctors said approximately two months. But seeing you last time, it should probably take two days."

"Two days, huh? The clanmistress could kick me out outta here by then, and I'm not showing any promise. I'm starting to think maybe this salami-brick thing might actually be worth it. It's a guaranteed way of staying here."

"Sima Brak . . . and it's a GUARANTEED way of going back to heratrang'ga pan."

"I want this opportunity!" I slightly raise my voice, mildly agitated. "I don't wanna throw it out the window, and so far I haven't progressed at all. And if this thing is my infallible ticket to stay here, then I'm willing to give it a shot."

"Neph . . . believe me when I tell you this: going after Sima Brak is good way NOT to stay here, dead or alive."

So'krang's eyes suddenly fill up with seriousness and concern as a frown slowly appears on his face, as if this Sima Brak thing is a really big deal. Looking into his eyes under those waves on his forehead, I can't help but heed his warning.

"Then what the fuck are we supposed to do?" I tell him near-despondently as I think about my future . . . or lack thereof.

"Well as a start . . . ," So'krang compassionately replies, "don't rush into mistakes. Know that you won't gain the acknowledgement of the Natin with the completion of a single task. After all, shortcuts will bring you to your destination faster, but to your resolve slower. Even the Tiyot'ga train for ten years before they achieve their fifth form."

"Was I supposed to get that?" I ask him, confused about that last part.

"It's a proverb," So'krang rushes to clarify.

"Oh I get it now. Like 'Rome wasn't built in a day' or some shit."

I think a little about his words. I think to myself: maybe I am rushing to this? Maybe I am just thinking impulsively as a result of failure? After all, who knows better than I the impact of failure? If I truly wish to not fail again, maybe I should bide my time and follow So'krang's directions, even if they're not the greatest.

"Fine. I'll wait with the Sima-thing," I tell him in a more relaxed tone. "I just hope all this shit will pay off . . . for your sake. Heh."

As we talk, I relentlessly try to clench my fist as I look at So'krang, and I still can't form a fist. Bothered by this unfortunate scenario, I stare at my hand to see if it's all right, thinking maybe the doctors missed something. But as I stare at it, I know for a fact that the doctors missed nothing at all, for every piece of my hand is exactly as it was before it got blown off by the massive recoil of the gun known as the man-killer, a gun so powerful that it creates a 120-decibel bang even with a mandatory built-in silencer, or so I was told. Turns out that "man" comes from "manual," as in "hand" and not "person." Not-so-obvious trivia, if you ask me.

The amazement only came to me just now though, mainly because previously I was more concerned whether I would actually be able to punch people again . . . when needed.

"Y'know, I'm amazed," I suddenly tell him. "There's not even a single indication that it got ripped off. It's like it never even happened."

"The doctors rebuilt your hand from what tissue you had left on your hand and what they found on the floor." He explains to me while handing me one of the bottles. "Everything else that couldn't be retrieved was rebuilt with mahakaks."

"Mahakaks?" I say curiously, now holding the bottle from underneath. "What the fuck is that?"

"It's a substance engineered from the cells of hiphomoys and the Samish'ga to artificially create tissue." He says while opening the bottle, and then taking a sip. "Mostly used for casualties after suffering heavy damage in battle."

"Which also explains how you always come back from fights without a single scratch on you. Nice."

As I imitate So'krang, holding the bottle from underneath and drinking it, tasting a juice of an exotic flavor that I'm not at all familiar with, I recall that his wife is missing a finger. If the Natin can recreate any lost body part, then how come she's still lacking one fifth of an entire set of a hand?

"But if you guys can recreate lost body parts," I ask, "how come your wife is missing a finger?

"My wife's a Nok'ga," he starts to explain as his usual self. "They naturally reject the mahakaks because of their ability to adapt. But what they lack in biology, they compensate with combat skills, so they are the least to get injured among the clans."

"I see."

I take a slow and long sip from the juice.

"Don't you have some kind of . . . anti-rejection drug to deal with that?" I ask him.

"Actually there is," He replies. "But the side effects are too strong to ignore. Among the side effects are insatiable hunger, extreme mood swings and . . . some others I can't remember right now. It's a real disaster, I tell you. In fact, the majority of Natin that reject the mahakaks do not take it. My wife took it for two months, then she stopped after all that weight she gained hindered her skills in battle and it nearly ruined our relationship."

"Man. Sounds like a bitch. She did good to get rid of it."

"You're telling me? I was the one to take all the anger attacks."

I take another slow sip from the bottle, but shorter this time.

"Are the uh . . . Nok'ga . . . the only clan that reject the mahakaks?" I ask him

"They aren't," he explains. "But they are the origin of the rejection trait."

"I'm not following ya," I tell him, staring at him in confusion.

"Remember how I explained to you that when a Natin is born they absorb the tiamtsat surrounding them?"

"What about it?"

"Well as I already told you, before komo'kea'ka, each Natin possesses several types of tiamtsat within them. These types are eventually filtered out and make way for a single dominant type of tiamtsat within the Natin's body that will determine what clan they will join. Now, if the baby happens to absorb Nok'ga tiamtsat, then they might suffer from limited rejection, even after having the Nok'ga tiamtsat filtered out of their body."

"Limited rejection? Is there even such a thing?"

"Of course. Why wouldn't there be?"

"Just sounds like something that isn't medically accurate."

"Well, it basically means that certain parts of the body aren't compatible with certain type of mahakaks."

"Oh, so now there are types of mahakaks?"

"Yes. You see, the types of mahakaks are engineered accordingly to recreate certain type of body parts by having it recognize its surroundings, much like how hiphomoys change their appearance based on their location they were raised in. There are types to recreate bone, skin, muscle, nerves, and so forth. You never mix them together, and they come in separate packages. Some Natin, who previously had Nok'ga tiamtsat in them, only reject a certain type of mahakaks on a certain part of their body. So basically, they can recover everything else, except for that specific patch of tissue.

"I see. Y'know, I was asking this cuz I remember that the gloomy girl in our last expedition—"

"YOUR expedition," So'krang jokingly interrupts me.

"Fine." I reluctantly go with his joke. "MY last expedition, the gloomy girl had an eye patch, even though she wasn't a Nok'ga.

So that means that she had Nok'ga tiamtsat in her past, so she rejects the type of mahakaks used to create an eye on the left side of her face. Right?"

"Just because she has an eye patch, so that means she has a missing eye?" So'krang, again, jokes with me, more cheerful than ever.

"Well yeah," I, yet again, am reluctant to accept his joke, now a tad pissed. "What other reason would there be for someone to wear an eye patch?"

"We're a diverse culture. We don't need a missing eye to wear an eye patch. But yes, you're correct about your assumption."

"Well . . . at least we can agree on that."

I take another long and slow sip of the exotically flavored juice. I then look at So'krang with curiosity.

"How did you meet your wife?" I ask him curiously.

"Well . . . ," he starts to say, sitting down on a chair and taking a sip from his juice before continuing his story. "It was hangahang. That's a holiday of ours where we celebrate the beginning of the waraida period. Our domination of the Novaverse and the exile of the Airatsmeka to hanghidobanei. It's not too far from now. Anyway, as I was saying, it was hangahang. I was just leaving the house, and I remembered to wear something that's not black, but forgot to wear a hat to cover my black hair. So I was on the streets, riding Franuk, and a grapefruit hits me in the back, splatting all over and staining my we'jei. I turn around to see a beautiful blonde Nok'ga, wearing a purple we'jei and a white rekarakib as to not get fruits thrown at her. She was laughing at my misfortune and then proceeded on with her life, and so did I. On the last day of hangahang, I went to the local hall to dance with a random girl lucky enough to stand on the side, waiting for someone to dance with, and then have me approach her. So I was looking around. In the center, everyone was moon-dancing. And on the side, there she was, with the same beautiful blonde hair, wearing a purple gown that was just reading 'come and dance with me.' She was staring at the center in hopes that someone will get tired from dancing with the same person and decide to change partners. And then she looked at the sides and saw me. She smiled at me, and in return, I smiled back, but no teeth. I approached her, and upon standing right in front of her, she had nothing to say, but instead just smiled at me, probably seconds away from laughing over our last encounter a few days back. I said to her, 'You owe me a new jacket.' And in response, she said, 'Don't worry. It washes off in the laundry.' I gave her my hand, and she gave me hers, and then we proceeded to moon-dance like the rest. And before we realized it, we were spending the rest of our lives together. Turns out she came back from an expedition before the start of the holiday and decided to stay for it before going back home."

"Who's Franuk?"

"OUT OF ALL THE THINGS THIS IS WHAT YOU HAVE TO ASK!?" he says in a grumpy manner, and then he sighs. "He's my hiphomoy."

"Oh. Well . . . you never talk about him."

"You never asked."

"Hmm . . . fair enough."

"I assume the story didn't captivate you then?"

"It takes something really special to captivate me. Although there's one thing that I'm thinking about."

"What's that?"

"She didn't love you enough to change her name for you," I say jokingly with a smirk on my face.

"Change her name? Why would she do that?"

"Y'know . . . two people get married so the wife changes her last name to that of her husband. Y'know . . . like, your last name is 'krang', right? So she shoulda changed it to 'krang', and then she woulda been called . . . uh . . . what's her name again?"

So'krang then just chuckles a bit. I just stare at him confused while he chuckles, as I have no idea what he's getting at.

"We don't have last names here," he starts to say, somewhat amused with a smile on his face. "So'krang is the didi'kea'nam for Sowi'ga Krang'pegin, which is my full and only name."

"Great . . . ," I reply, somewhat discouraged, anticipating what's coming next. "I suppose you wanna explain to me the naming system of your world."

"Well . . . in short, everyone has one name which consists of a varying number of words, so while I have two words, others can have three. And a 'didi'kea'nam' is a shortening of a name based on the first syllables of each word. SOwi'ga KRANG'pegin, if you get it. And nobody changes their names for anyone."

"I get it now," I say, now mildly interested at this point.

I take another sip from the juice.

"What the fuck is this, anyways!?" I ask impatiently, curious as to know what fruit had been inserted into this bottle.

"It's mangosteen juice," So'krang explains, returning back to his relative calmness.

"Mangosteen?! The fuck is that?"

"Yes. Mangosteen. It's a fruit from heratrang'ga pan. That's where you come from, if you forgot."

"Really? Never heard of it."

"I don't blame you. It's not a popular fruit."

"Yeah. But if the fruit tastes as good as the juice, I can't imagine how it can't be."

"The heranga exist in a society that starts from the end and ends in the start. But I don't need to tell you that because you already know it."

"I know it all too well if, if I may say so." I take another sip from the juice. "Do you steal the fruits from eart . . . uh . . . heratrang'ga pan? Cuz I can't imagine they grow here. Y'know . . . with the creatures being different and all that."

"Actually, the fruit grows here. Unlike the animals, which have changed a lot over the centuries, the plants did not. In fact, the flora doesn't differ much from that of heratrang'ga pan but for maybe . . . ten plants."

"Yeah, I didn't feel much of a difference either . . . when I first got here . . . looking at the trees, y'know. But man, I could really go for more of this juice."

"Well we can't get more if we keep wasting our time here. Do you want to leave already?"

"Well I'm waiting on you."

"Me!? You're the patient here," he replies, assuming a cheerful disposition.

"Well, you're the one who always says what to do," I say as I smirk with more cheerfulness, knowing that our conversation has shifted to a friendly vibe.

"Well then, I say that you are free to leave."

"Fine then. Get your fuckin' ass off the chair and let's go already."

He gets up from the chair while I'm still standing on my feet. Now with both of us standing up, we make our way towards the entrance of the room, and eventually towards the entrance of the hospital.

"By the way, the story with your wife . . . that was nice," I tell him plainly as we leave.

CHAPTER XVI

HE SAYS IT'S A SURPRISE . . . BUT I CAN'T IMAGINE IT'S IMPORTANT

I am currently in the clan of Hetkaba, together with the usual company of So'krang, who is taking me to all the irrelevant places, and Grasshead, my ever-accompanying companion. And now that I know his name, I can also say that Franuk is here with us as well, although mostly just to provide means of transportation for So'krang.

Being in the clan of Hetkaba, this is my first time off of Wotaiga, because this clan is in the eastern region of Dobiya, the continent located just south of Wotaiga, just as long from west to east, but not as big. So'krang says that the continent has a slender appearance when viewed from space, while Wotaiga looks like its fat equivalent, kind of like Laurel and Hardy. The sky here is filled with black clouds and it's kind of breezy; feels like it's going to rain any second now.

We're supposed to embark on an expedition in this region. Which, for me, basically means teaming up with a bunch of random people specializing in different arbitrary fighting styles and going out to kill a bunch of Airatsmeka. It's the killing part that's exciting the most. So'krang says that there's still time, so he wants to show me something in this city. Something associated to me.

Looking around the city, it doesn't bear much difference to any of the previous clans I have visited. More wide buildings, hiphomoy highways, and everything in between. Need I describe any more similarities that this clan shares architecturally with any of the other clans? Because I don't really see much. The same goes for the people: scantily clad with indecent tendencies, sporting the respective tattoo of their clan on their neck. Seeing all the cities are the same, I could say that the united clans are indeed a melting pot.

However, much like every other clan, they have their own battle style that's unique to them. From what I hear, and So'krang managed to tell me a bit on the way, this clan specializes in defense. In fact, So'krang described them as the most defensive of the clans. But even with that, they don't sacrifice all their offense for defense. The methodology that they incorporate in battle is dominantly defense, together with a bit of offense. I don't really understand where the "offense" part falls into the "dominantly defense" part, probably by taking a shield and bashing it into the opponent's face until they bleed to death or something . . . whatever.

Anyways, we ride down a path to an unknown location. Unknown to me, at least, as I'm pretty sure So'krang knows what surprises lie ahead.

"Is there a reason we had to come here?" I ask impatiently. "Kind of a waste of time, if you ask me."

"I have a surprise I want you to see," So'krang says, seemingly excited.

"Will it get me in the hospital again?" I respond wittily, but without a mood. "Cuz three times is enough for me."

"Not unless it falls on you."

"Then you'd better make sure it doesn't."

As we continue to ride, I see a humongous building far ahead of us. I assume this is the official residence of the clanmaster, or clanmistress, of the clan of Hetkaba. I wonder why would we want to visit the clan's most privileged member, who lacks any form of actual authority? Maybe he or she wants my autograph?

Regardless, we get closer to the building. Upon closer inspection, the official residence in this city doesn't look like a mausoleum, like the last one I checked out, but more like Aaron Spelling's house with a giant-ass, metallic, pointy gnome hat, reaching all the way to the black sky, bent a bit backwards and sitting firmly on the middle of the roof. The building was light blue too, and it seemed like the roof was merging with the gnome hat.

We finally reach the entrance of the building. Looking up at the gnome hat, or whatever I should call it, I can't help but think that it looks like some kind of doomsday device. A giant pillar for some angry deity to climb down from and wreak havoc on the land, or for it to fall down and crush everything from here all the way to the city gate. It blends wonderfully with the black sky from this perspective, though.

"I assume we're gonna meet another clanmaster," I say plainly without too much interest.

"You assume correctly," So'krang replies, holding a gentle smile on his face, preparing for the surprise.

"Why? Do they want my autograph?"

"You wish."

As per usual, So'krang "parks" Franuk at the side of the building, and we make our way to the entrance of the building. We walk up the stairs, with So'krang seemingly holding his excitement inside, smiling a bit, and I just want to go on to the mission and get all this over with.

"As you know, after this, we have an expedition close to here," So'krang begins to explain as we walk up the stairs. "Because of this, I thought it would be a good opportunity to show you something. Something special, in fact."

"You've been saying that non-stop now," I respond eerily. "I can't help but feel worried. Y'know, it doesn't happen all the time that someone consecutively ends up in the hospital one incident after the other."

"Don't worry. I'm pretty sure it won't happen this time."

"It'd better not."

"Unless you die, of course. Then you won't get hospitalized."

"I haven't died yet. Don't plan to, any time soon."

We finally reach the front of the giant door leading into the official residence. A giant door worthy of a castle, made of the finest wood and blinging with shiny metal buttons aligned symmetrically on its sides. I couldn't care less about the fanciness of the door, but more about what's inside.

So'krang steps forward in front of the door and opens it.

With him taking the lead, Grasshead and I follow him into the building, and we walk into a large, fancy hall connected to many corridors that lead to wherever, with several employees of the house moving about. Nothing too different from the last official residence I visited.

But right in front of us, right in the center of the hall, stand two men acting as if they own the place. So'krang approaches them, and I do too. Upon closer inspection, one of the men has a tattoo on his forehead similar to the clanmistress of Awari, while the one beside him has a tattoo on his right arm similar to the towering assistant of the clanmistress, although unlike the previous pair, these two are almost the same height and share the same tattoo on their necks. It quickly became very clear to me that these two are the clanmaster of Hetkaba and his assistant.

I wouldn't exactly describe this clanmaster as someone who is prepared for battle, let alone being a competent warrior. He wears a green half-sleeved variant of the we'jei, which is as thin as one but reaches down to his knees. He keeps it loose, showing his bare bosom as he is wearing nothing over or under it. Furthermore, he is wearing what appear to be black square cuts. But the cherry on the cake is his bare feet. The guy looks like a complete slacker, but the square jaw and receding hairline with some grays on the side really compliments him. But for real, this guy's carefree attitude would pretty much allow any hired assassin to stab him in the back, if somehow they managed to get behind him. His assistant, on the other hand, looks like someone who could break knives if anyone tried to stab him in the back.

The assistant looks like Goliath without any weak spots for David's slingshot, minus the gigantism. He wears a silver half-sleeved sidar'jei, shiny as knight's armor, some nasty rekarakib, thicker and blacker than the hide of the blackest rhino, and a pair of wicked boots that would make any hardcore metal fan jealous . . . if it weren't for their off-putting brown color. Additionally, he wears bracelets on his forearms similar to how So'krang does, but he has them in a silver color to suit his jacket, I suppose. Despite all this, the guy is not a metal fan, for his scalp of full brown hair and mildly tan skin says otherwise, and his expression is more serious than depressed, or whatever the expression is called that metal fans like to put on their faces.

I suppose it's important to have someone more responsible protect a leader that feels so privileged that he allows himself to walk around his palace as if he just came out of the shower. His irresponsibility could be his death. But then again, pandas are only cute and seem harmless, but a bear is still a bear.

"Mark'nen Mura'nen Ka Panar," So'krang says, happy to address the clanmaster by his full title. "I am honored to—"

"Please, Yasin'ga," the clanmaster suddenly interrupts him in a Buddhist kind of calmness. "Address me as Mu'ka'pa. As everyone should."

"Very well . . . Mu'ka'pa," So'krang says, dissatisfied and skeptical about addressing the clanmaster as one of his peers. "I assume you already know of Neph Baker?"

"How can I not?" the clanmaster stares at me and smiles a bit.

I walk closer to them. Now all four of us are standing close to each other, trading stares with one another. The assistant stares at me, and I stare back at him. The eye contact lasts for a while; looking at his serious eagle eyes, he seems cautious, frowning slightly to indicate that he's not letting his guard down, even if

I am a friend. I, in return, give him the same kind of stare, only with more frown, as this is my natural expression. All this is a scenario I'm familiar with, as many have already given me a bad gaze.

He moves his head closer to the ear of the clanmaster. "Kata Ai'ga?" he whispers loudly in a deep voice.

"He's one of us now," the clanmaster responds in a calm tone, seemingly unprovoked by his assistant's bold statement. "I suggest you, as well, get used to it."

He stops making eye contact, and then looks back at me, still cautious with a mad look on his face.

The clanmaster and his assistant turn around and make their way to the corridor right in front of us. Naturally, we follow them.

In this long corridor, it soon feels like we've walked forever, and I only wonder when we'll get to the end of it. While Grasshead walks behind all of us, somehow I manage to get behind the clanmaster, even though it is So'krang who initially walked behind him. I guess somehow we got intertwined in our positions without noticing. Regardless, staring at the clanmaster's back, it's kind of hard to ignore that he's in a really vulnerable state right now. I'm not even sure his fortress of an assistant would react in time to save him if something happened. Not that I'm planning anything, of course.

"So . . . Your Majesty, do you usually walk around . . . uh . . . comfortably?" I ask, trying to spark a mood in the quiet atmosphere.

So'krang pokes me with his elbow. I look at him to see what he wants, and he looks at me with an expression that roughly reads "what the hell, man?"

"Only when it's plausible," the clanmaster responds calmly, taking my question lightly, unlike some people. "In fact, I prefer to wear these as much as possible. After all the heavy armor and shields I am equipped with in battle, I need something that makes me feel like I'm walking in water. And you may refer to me as Mu'ka'pa."

"Looks like the kind of 'armor' that could easily be penetrated," I honestly quip. "Someone could easily stab you in the back."

"They'll try," the clanmaster says with the utmost certainty.

I am silent. I have nothing to say about that statement. I believe him. He wouldn't dress like that if he didn't know what he was doing. And, being the leader, I assume he's the strongest of his clan. Then again, I could be wrong.

"You're talking to the leader of the most defensive clan," So'krang suddenly says, sounding serious and insulted for the clanmaster. "It would take more than whatever can opener you have in your pocket to penetrate them. It would be like trying to kill a siderm with a plastic knife."

"Whoa. Someone's pissed," I say defensively, but try to maintain my relatively good mood. "You gonna be like bucket boy over here? Cuz I prefer a more peaceful atmosphere, thank you."

"'Bucket boy' is the royal bodyguard of the mark'nen, and he is the most powerful warrior of the Hetkaba. I suggest you give him the respect that he deserves, starting by referring to him by his real name, Omdroya Ka Bar'tan'i.

The royal bodyguard, formerly known to me as the personal assistant of the clanmaster, doesn't even look backwards to acknowledge the compliment. But standing behind the clanmaster, I can see his profile, and he doesn't even smile. Did he not hear it? Does he even care? If someone was licking my boots I would be more than happy to turn my head just to give them a little smile, maybe even a thumbs up, depending on my mood. He's probably just having a bad day.

"Really?" I wonder, skeptical about what I just heard. "So shouldn't he be the leader if he's the strongest? I mean, usually that's how it works. No?"

"The royal bodyguards are assigned their position solely because of their strength," So'krang points out, still somewhat annoyed. "Their only purpose is to defend their mark'nen and the clan itself. Nothing more nothing less. The mark'nen, on the other hand, are chosen for their leadership and charisma."

"Really? Y'know, for someone who's supposed to swing his sword all day, y'sure know alotta stuff."

"Pfff. Everything I know is basic knowledge," he says, now assuming a more cheerful attitude and a smirk on his face.

"I'm pretty sure your idea of basic knowledge is a Ph.D. in everything. If that's basic knowledge, I can't imagine what the academic guys are learning here. What are they called again? Jackrabbit? Jackhole? Jack-something?"

"Jadak! And I don't think you have the intellectual capacity to keep up with them."

I response with silence. I did not expect that. I look at him. He seems all happy now with a stupid smirk on his face. I go back to staring at the back of the clanmaster while following him, now disgruntled.

"I may be a shitty student," I start to say, feeling at unease. "But I'm not stupid."

"That doesn't feel so good, does it?" So'krang says in a humorous tone.

I look at him again, and he's still wearing that stupid smirk on his face.

"Oh, so suddenly you're OK now?" I say hastily and aggressively, losing my mood.

So'krang too assumes an aggressive position, seemingly unwilling to back down and as if he's preparing for a fight. "You should've shown respec—"

"Quiet, you two." The clanmaster suddenly interrupts our arguments, and he does so with his usual calmness. "I will not tolerate redundant conflicts in my house. We're almost there, so you can either change the conversation to something more friendly or avoid talking. Whichever suits you best."

Considering my mood, I choose silence. If we're almost there, I see no point in talking any further.

Just before reaching our destination, the royal bodyguard turns his head around and looks at me, still holding an angry expression reminiscent of an eagle's face, and then turns it back to look forward. Don't think he really enjoys my company. At least he's discreet about it. It benefits me because I don't have to take shit for being the only heranga among the Natin.

Of course, I couldn't care less what goes through his head, because right now, we are standing in front of the door that contains the mystery surprise that So'krang has been so eager to show me. Although he's probably not as eager anymore after the tension that rose between us just now.

"Here it is," the clanmaster proclaims.

Looking at the door, it doesn't seem so fancy. Just a large door made of wood, supposedly mahogany. I expected more fanciness from the door that holds such a treasure behind it. They should've decorated it with some diamonds or, I don't know, added some glitter so that it would sparkle in the eye.

Nevertheless, the clanmaster opens the door, surprisingly without a key to lock it away from burglars, and we make our way into the room.

Inside, the room is octagonal in shape and completely empty . . . except for one thing.

At the northern edge of the room stands a glass case on a stand containing a spectacular armor. Shining white as a pearl, the entirety of it is smooth and slick like a clean floor. The armor, despite its magnificence, has no prominent features, as it has a plain design with no visible motifs, except for one: its left arm is hideous and the complete opposite of what this armor should represent. Black as tar, the hand looks like a lizard's claw, with sharp nails and a design that looks like deep-cut scars. This interesting design continues on to the forearm and bicep of the arm, with scars of varying lengths and sizes, melding together with another design feature which took the appearance of black round bulges that look like blisters, adding a geometrical element to the design. But all that stops at the shoulder, which has three long spikes that look like devil horns protruding outwards and curving upwards, aligned in a triangular position. What catches my attention the most is the lizard hand, as the other hand, coming from the beautiful side, bears the appearance of a gentle human hand.

I get closer to the glass stand to look better at the armor.

"What's your opinion about it?" So'krang asks.

"It's really unique," I proclaim, mildly fascinated. "But . . . what is it? I mean, it's armor, but what's so special about it?"

"It's the armor of the composer of the calm horizon, designed and crafted by the clan that possesses it."

"Wait. There already was a composer?!" I ask, bewildered at this idea.

"Actually, this was created to showcase what the composer was wearing in the nursery rhyme. It wasn't meant to be worn by anyone. People who want to see it just come in here and observe it."

"It's a public domain, after all," the clanmaster suddenly intervenes.

"I noticed that when you didn't unlock the door," I quip.

"But . . ." he continues from his last sentence, "now that you're here, it might actually come to use."

"Hmm. Nice. I don't think I would refuse to wear that. Although I would have to do some modifications to that left arm."

I raise my hand and reach out to the armor from beyond the glass case, in the way that a child reaches out to the stars on a bright night as if he can catch them in his grasp. I wonder what I will look like when I wear it, and how people will perceive me when I do so.

"So when do I put it on?" I ask eagerly.

"First . . . you will have to gain the acknowledgement of the Natin," the clanmaster explains. "You start wearing it now, and they might become angry."

"So I have to get them to like me first? I'm already at risk staying here, but that is just unnecessary bullshit. I'm not even sure if I'm capable of such an achievement. Mainly cuz of the people here."

"That is why you have a mentor personally assigned to you. You should pay attention to his guidance, because he has a lot to offer. Nobody in the united clans gets that kind of privilege, you know."

"I only got that 'privilege' because everyone hates me here."

"And that is why you can't wear the armor yet," the clanmaster says, and then gives a little chuckle.

"Don't worry," So'krang says while grabbing my shoulder. "The Natin will see what you're capable of, and they will know that you belong here."

"Really? Cuz so far we haven't gotten anywhere," I say impatiently. "Now can we leave? I believe we have an expedition to attend to."

"I suppose so."

We all turn around and make our way back to the entrance of the room, leaving it.

"Y'know, all this is nice, but it's still a waste of time," I tell So'krang wittily as we leave the room. "Shoulda been saved for the end."

CHAPTER XVII

INTRODUCTIONS ARE DEFINITELY MANDATORY!

The gelatinous cube hits the ground. Its shape starts to fall apart while I still breathe through it. As the cube completely melts away, the raindrops fall on my head and gradually soak my hair in water. I get up from the ground and, to my left, So'krang is already here, smirking and waving his hand to me under a tree. I approach him, as I too wish for the trees to provide me with shelter from the rain. I look around and I see only the two of us.

"Where the fuck is everyone?" I ask indifferently after being unpleasantly contained in a gel cube.

"I decided we should come a bit earlier after last time. OUR last time," So'krang explains AND emphasizes. "What kind of a leader would I be if I didn't set an example?"

"I don't think leaders are decided by their punctuality," I quip.

"Still . . . I would be wearing red for nothing."

"What the fuck does red have to do with this?"

"Red is the color of leadership, after all."

"Really? Cuz I'm pretty sure it's blue."

"Na. It's red."

"Blue."

"Red."

"BLUE!"

"RED!"

"Dude, I'm telling you its blue!"

So'krang holds his laughter, and then starts to laugh out loud as he drops hard on the soil, sitting down and leaning against a tree.

"It's red," he tells me calmly while smiling.

I look at him with a bland expression. Silence ensues.

"So when are the others coming?" I ask So'krang after a while.

I look up at the sky, and from where I'm standing, I see a blue spot that gets bigger and bigger as it falls down.

"Speak of the fuckin' devil," I mutter to myself.

The gelatinous cube continues to fall, and eventually lands softly on the grass outside the trees. Naturally, it starts to decompose, eventually allowing whoever's inside to get out.

"WO!!" the person inside yells enthusiastically while quickly getting up from the ground.

As the person stands up, I can clearly see that it's a girl, with a smile that starts and ends at each of her ears. Obviously, someone's hyped to murder some motherfuckers.

She has black hair, slick and combed diagonally to her right with a left portion of her hair shaved clean like those punky hairstyles. She wears a black leather we'jei over a white shirt, tucked in with what appears to be a utility belt at the waist, a pair of blue rekarakib, and, of course, na'sho. She carries five weapons, three on the belt and two on her back. What I see on the belt is a small rolled-up transparent rope, colored magenta which apparently has the head of a snake on its end. Next is a blue triangle thick in its design and seemingly made of metal, with a hilt shaped like triangular crosshairs in the middle of it. The last weapon on the belt is on the other side of it, separate from the other two weapons. It is a small green glaive with four blades. The last two are a green halberd with a smoking blade and a sword that's actually a candlestick with a hilt.

"WO!!" she shouts happily from afar.

She runs to us joyfully, as that huge smile on her face couldn't indicate otherwise. She finally gets to us to look at each of us in turn. But as she continues to smile, we pretend to be more "professional," each in our own way. So'krang shows a serious expression, and I show something that can be sort of interpreted as "Dude, I really could care less about this." Nevertheless, she continues to smile, as our personal bullshit couldn't possibly diffuse her excitement over killing some black-spotted baddies.

"Kata So'krang?" she asks, still ever so joyful.

"That would be me," So'krang responds. "And I have one request for this team: we will speak English. That person over there, he doesn't speak hang'pan'rika."

She then looks at me, with a much smaller smile then what she had when she got here, but a smile no less.

"OK!" she says out loud. She then approaches me.

"Ahh, you must be Neph, right?" she says, still ever so excited. "The composer!"

"That's what they call me." I respond wittily. "I am not anything yet . . . not officially, at least."

"I am Sapin'shik Hika'nan of the Horbarat. We're going to have fun together!"

"Horbarat? Haven't heard of that one yet."

"Horbarat is the Gangra of fancy bloodshed."

"Fancy bloodshed? You ran out of actual titles so you started inventing random stuff?"

"Neph!" So'krang shouts. "Don't be reckless with people's hearts. She's just trying to be nice."

"I'm sorry," I say in a half-assed apologetic tone. "It's just that . . . you know me."

I look at her face after addressing So'krang. She doesn't seem so happy anymore. In fact, she's not smiling anymore and she's looking to the side. Now I feel bad. I hope I didn't hurt her too hard, but I can't help but try to imagine what the hell 'fancy bloodshed' means. Sounds like the brutal genocide of piñatas, or whenever they kill someone, chocolate sprinkles explode everywhere.

As I try to figure this out, she approaches Grasshead, who is just beside me. She crouches to look at him at the same height as she joyfully rubs his face with her hands moving across his grassy fur while he licks her excitedly.

"Hihi!" she exclaims excitedly while she gets her face licked. "He's adorable!"

"You should see him when he's angry. Heh," I jokingly tell her.

I think she's enjoying this more than Grasshead enjoys licking her face. Nice to know someone's having fun.

After a while, everyone finds a spot to lounge while we wait for the others to arrive. So'krang and I lean on some trees, Grasshead takes a nap, and Sa'hi is just outside the forest in visible sight, scouting for any will-be members of our team.

Eleven minutes have passed, and suddenly, footsteps can be heard from the right. We all wait in our spots for whoever's coming. Once again, a big smile can be seen on Sa'hi's face. At least it's nice to know that her mood came back.

Walking slowly to us, a guy appears from beyond the trees, and he looks like he really doesn't have the power to deal with whatever's coming to him.

With uncombed black hair and dark circles around his eyes, the guy looks like he just woke up. He wears a dark green half-sleeved we'jei that looks like it was made from crocodile skin, and he has it loose over a white shirt. He also wears black rekarakib and na'sho, and the most ridiculous paraphernalia I've seen so far. He has three rolls of toilet paper connected by small strings, strong enough to hold them in place without breaking, to a belt he wears over his shoulder, kind of like how So'krang does, and a rake attached to his back.

He slowly but eventually reaches us.

"Kata nen'karat ka So'krang?" He asks in a slightly more eager tone than what his face suggests.

"Yes. This is my team," So'krang says. "We are still waiting for the others, so you can take a nap in the meantime. You look like you didn't sleep enough."

The guy seems a bit surprised, probably because So'krang is talking to him in English. He looks to his right, and sees nothing. He looks to his left, and sees me. Now he doesn't seem so surprised.

"So uh . . . you plan on wiping the enemy to death." I joke.

"What? Why?" he seems confused, unaware of the joke.

"Toilet paper," I tell him while gesturing at his toilet paper.

He then looks at the toilet paper right in front of his chest, and then looks back at me. "This is my weapon." he says indifferently.

"Like I said, 'You plan on wiping the enemy to death?'" I continue to joke, now smirking too.

He's smirking now.

"Just wait and see," he says in an ominous tone.

I wipe the smirk off my face, as I clearly understand that I'm about to witness something big come out of those rolls.

Nine minutes pass, and no more descending gel cubes can be seen in the skyline.

Suddenly, we start to feel the ground rumble. Anyone who is on the ground immediately stands up and Grasshead wakes up from his nap. So'krang and I trade stares. He seemed worried, while I have no idea what to expect.

"I almost forgot!" he shouts to me.

"Forgot what!?" I shout back to him.

And then, all of a sudden, a brown creature bursts out from in between the trees in the woods, toppling them to the ground with massive force. The creature halts between the people of the group.

It is a large creature, probably the length of a rhino, but a tad taller. More so, he has a massive horn on his face. The horn didn't even look like it was sprouting out of his nose, but rather connected to his face. Even more so, the horn looks like it is actually the shape of his skull, seeing as there is no visible spot from where it comes out. But other than the giant horn, the creature also has reptilian legs, like other Novaversian creatures I've seen, and his brown hide looks like iron armor.

The creatures growls quietly. I approach him cautiously as to not startle it and cause a rampage. I touch his face, and the creature seems rather tranquil. Touching his skin, it feels like metal, smooth and just as hard.

I see So'krang looking at the top of the creature.

I look up too, and I see a girl mounting the creature.

"This creature's a long way from home," So'krang says in a friendly tone, although not too satisfied with the situation.

"Bak pilot dropped me a shiandon away from here," the girl says as she jumps off the creature. "And he was the only animal in the vicinity I could ride. And what's with the makis'bak tongue!?"

She then sees me. "Oh," she says, disappointed.

Looking at her better now after she dismounted the creature, she has brown hair, with a portion of it tied into a small ponytail, with the rest flowing down. She wears a brown variant of the popular breast-covering piece—the name of which I have yet to discover—and she has a strap over her shoulder connected to the back of the piece, rather than around the nape; a pair of skinny, hard-looking pants with a net motif to them, and, to no one's surprise, na'sho. As for her weapons, she has a simple dagger attached to the back of her pants, nothing else. Unusually though, she has really long nails, even for a Natin. They were even cut in a way that makes them look more like talons, sharp enough to eviscerate anyone.

"You gonna keep it or take it back home?" I ask her as I look again at the creature.

She gives me an antagonizing look, but says nothing. She approaches the creature, and she places her hand on his face, and then she places her forehead on his horn. The creature growls, and then slowly turns around and walks into the woods, slowly disappearing out of sight.

The girl then looks at me.

"He'll find his way," she tells me with a condescending tone and a stupid smile on her face.

She goes to join the others. So'krang approaches me.

"That was a siderm," he explains to me. "Just so you know."

That interesting tidbit just now clarified to me something that So'krang said a while back at the house of the clanmaster of Hetkaba. Irrelevant to my cause, but interesting no less.

Thirteen minutes pass, and yet another gel cube falls from the sky. This time, it's going to land just outside the woods. We all stare at the cube as it falls. We take a step back to avoid becoming the cushion for its landing, not that it needs one anyway, since it's a cushion by itself.

The gel cube finally hits the ground. Looking through the translucent cube, it's hard to tell who's exactly in it.

Out of the cube bursts a pink figure made of light, splatting pieces of the cube all around us. The figure lands gracefully on the ground with its two legs.

The light making up the figure disperses in different directions, and under it, I witness something I never thought would come true. Something I remember from one of the conjurer's sessions: a girl prettier than a thousand auroras exploding in the night; more beautiful than the most sparkling gem forged under the best conditions of the earth's crust; a girl so beautiful, that if you put her in a field of butterflies, they would all revert back to caterpillars out of shame. Never have I thought that I would ever see her again. Because that girl, THAT girl that is standing right in front, is the same girl from that session, like she was copied and pasted from it.

Contrary to that session, she's wearing something completely different from the gorgeous gown that I remember. She wears a tight, light blue half-sleeved tailcoat, giving her body a refined shape like a corset, zippered up all the way to the breast, showing some cleavage. The tail extends down to her ankles, covering a short-short blue skirt from behind, but not long enough to hide from any angle the na'sho she is wearing, except these are special because they have pointy heels to them. She has no weapons on her whatsoever, and the small gap between her coat and skirt that shows her waistline indicates that she is in no need to tuck her body tight to make herself look skinny, as she is already pretty fine. At least she has the same ocean-blue eyes and black hair flowing down all the way to her lower back.

I open my eyes wide as I gaze upon her beauty. I can't believe she's actually here. I always relied on the conjurer to escape. No threads; no family that doesn't give a shit about me; unbound by the limitations of physics, jumping high and flying simply by waving my arms like the wings of a bird. Above all, I could never feel the anger that resides deep inside me, repressed by my sole determination to keep myself together and continue living in hopes that one day things will change for the better. And they just might, because now the dream has become a reality.

As I continue to awe at her magnificence, everyone else takes her for just another teammate. They stare at her with simplicity as she walks towards us.

She approaches So'krang. She opens her mouth just a tiny bit. She's about to say something.

"Yes, I am So'krang and this is my team," So'krang says impatiently before she can even utter a word. "That guy over there doesn't speak English uh . . . hang'pan'rika. Sorry for any inconvenience."

She gives up on saying anything, and then she looks at me. She waves with her fingers at me with a beautiful smile of white teeth.

I snap out of my awe and approach her. I do so slowly, all the while smirking in the process. I finally stand still in front. I say nothing, still smirking. She says nothing, still smiling. The silence envelops us for a few seconds.

"Are you gonna say something, or are you just gonna keep staring?" she says with a captivating angelic voice.

"Am I supposed to say something?" I respond wittily as my usual self, still smirking.

She giggles with her beautiful smile. And then again we stare at each other silently.

Seeing as there's nothing left to talk about, she retires from the conversation, turning around and showing her back to me as she walks away. She turns her head around to look at me, and once again, she waves her fingers at me before going on to talk to the other teammates. I wave back to her; even though she didn't see, I didn't care.

I feel infatuated. Simply gazing on her beauty invokes a special feeling in my heart I cannot describe. Not a feeling I'm familiar with. Is it because she's the manifestation of that vision in real life that I thought could never happen, or is it simply her magnificent beauty that words cannot describe that pulls me to be around her? Her attractiveness is not merely a physical characteristic, but a power that forces one to acknowledge its existence, as if it's no longer a matter of taste, but a fact. But I feel an attraction to her not only for her looks, but also because I saw her in that session with the conjurer, as if it's a sign that something extraordinary is about to happen. She represents my desire to escape, now brought into reality. Maybe, finally, I won't have to run away any more.

Alas, I find myself alone again. I go back to the tree and wait for the last person to join this team to arrive, much like the others.

An hour passes . . . since the deadline, which means that more time has passed since that pretty girl got here. Looking at So'krang's face, he starts to get pissed. Sa'hi is scouting the vicinity for anyone that might come by. Of course, she won't find anybody walking around here, let alone anybody related to our cause. Lucky for this guy, we're not going to bail on him. Something with Natin regulations, apparently. That's what I assume at least, seeing as we're not actually bailing on him. But clearly everyone has lost their patience. Grasshead needn't dwell on these matters since he just passes the time by taking another nap.

Speaking of naps, toilet-paper guy is snoring LOUD beside me, like "ruptured septums beyond repair" loud. I can't help but look to my side and see him peacefully leaning against a tree, dreaming of whatever while he fills the air with his snores. But suddenly, he violently wakes up, as if he was electrified. He then reaches to his nape, and from there he takes out what appears to be a blue gecko. He holds the gecko in his hand as he stares at the creature, while the gecko stares back at him with the uninterpretable expression of a lizard. He tries to touch it with his finger, but immediately moves back as if he were electrified. He then returns the gecko back to his nape.

I don't know why the hell he has an electric gecko on the back of his neck, but to me it seems like the reason why he hasn't gotten much sleep. But that's hardly the problem, because if this last member doesn't come now, I'm going to have to do something about these snores myself. I mean, I don't know how much of this I can continue to tolerate.

Just as it seemed that he might not be coming, we sight a gel cube falling from the sky. It lands far away from us, and the person who comes out of it starts walking slowly towards, as if he hasn't a care in the world. It's bad enough that he's already an hour late, but this just adds insult to injury. You could throw this guy in a battlefield with a machine gun and have his fellow soldiers blown to bits by the enemy tanks, and he wouldn't even bat an eye. Hope this guy does better in fights than he does with first impressions.

Everyone lines up for the approaching individual as he continues to walk at his leisure.

"Tell him to move faster," I whisper to So'krang, agitated.

"Don't worry," he tells me, also agitated.

Roughly six minutes pass and the guy finally gets close enough for us to get a clear look at his face. And what does he have on it? A stupid smirk and a look in his eyes that show that he's in a fine mood, too fine if I may add. Does he even know the atrocity he has committed?

He finally stands in front of us all. Nobody says a word, and it doesn't seem to bother him that everyone is staring at him with murder in their eyes.

"Kata nik'ron'ga?" he asks.

"By an hour!" So'krang says angrily in a loud voice.

All of a sudden, he wipes that stupid look on his face. His smirk turns upside down and his eyes are wide open.

"Oh," he says, seemingly bewildered.

"This will affect your report and point distribution," So'krang angrily informs him. "You know that, right?"

"I thought it was four."

"Well, then check your clock next time. Don't let it happen again, Mesoyar'ga."

"Someone should tell this guy that it's not daylight saving. Heh," I joke for all to hear.

I then look at So'krang, who doesn't seem so satisfied with the joke and has an unimpressed expression on his face.

"You guys use daylight saving, right?" I ask cautiously, seeing as nobody laughed from the joke.

So'krang says nothing, and instead he maintains his serious leader-esque expression as he goes over to stand in front of the team, gesturing the slacker to join them, and he does.

With all six members standing in front of So'krang as the leader, he crosses his arms and assumes a serious expression.

"All right," he begins, sounding like an army general. "Let us all introduce ourselves. I assume you all know how this goes. I'll start since I'm going to be the leader of this team. My name is Sowi'ga Krang'pegin of the clan of Yasin. Twenty-three years of age. I have been on 167 expeditions, and I have been the leader in thirty-eight of them. My kill count stands at 169."

So'krang looks at everyone one by one. Everyone remains silent, and nobody seems to take the initiative to introduce themselves. The guy with the toilet paper sighs and steps forward to introduce himself as So'krang takes his place in the line. Now he is standing in front of the entire team.

"Ok . . . well . . . ," he starts to say. "I am Kaba'ga Tai Krang of the clan of Noberti. Twenty years. Seventeenth expedition. And fifty-one kills . . . or is it fifty-two? Somewhere in that area. I'll have to check again."

He then moves his eyes around, staring at each and every team member one by one, trying to figure out who might be the next to introduce themselves.

He focuses on Sa'hi, who seems to be rather calm at the moment. They trade smiles, and she replaces him.

Now standing in front of the team, she introduces herself.

"I am Sapin'shik Hika'nan of the clan of Horbarat," she says with a big smile on her face, seemingly excited. "I am eighteen years old and this is my fourteenth expedition. I have killed fifty-three haa'bak. Although I think I should've done more. Hopefully I will get to 100 kills in less than two years."

The girl who came here riding that creature, which if I recall correctly is called a siderm, wastes no time as to walk over there and replace Sa'hi to claim her opportunity to introduce herself.

"I am Kasaika'nan," she says as she turns around to look at everyone. "Nineteen years of age. Sixteenth expedition. And I killed forty-eight haa'bak. Oh, and I'm of the clan of Karastar, but I suppose you already knew that."

She looks at the others curiously, wondering who will step next. Barely a second has passed, and the guy that came late takes her place as she walks back to stand next to the others.

"My name is Sang'smek'hiyan Ka Nik'hoson," he starts. "Of course, nobody actually calls me that. Most Natin just call me Sang'ka'nik, but that's self-explanatory. Heh. Anyways, I hail from the clan of Mesoyar'ga, I've been on eighteen expeditions, not including this one of course, and I killed sixty-one Airatsmeka. And I hope that me coming late won't affect our teamwork, because I plan on giving my best, as every Natin should."

A stupid smirk appears on his face as he looks at everyone and awaits the next person to introduce themselves.

"OK . . . ," I begin, sighing all the while. "Let's get this over with." I step forward to take his place as he returns to stand next to the team. "I am Neph Baker," I continue, already bored by this mandatory introduction routine. "You probably already heard of me. Some of you hate me, and some of you . . . hate me less. Hopefully, things will change in the future, but for now let's try to get along. Anyways, I come from the clan of I-don't-come-from-a-clan. Fifteen. Second expedition aaaaand I actually managed to kill one of the enemies. But only because she was stupid. That's right. I use people's ignorance against them. I mean, if she hadn't put her damn nails in her mouth, she wouldn't be dead now. I mean, who the fuck does that kind of—"

"Neph!" So'krang suddenly shouts, gesturing me to stop. "That's enough."

I guess I let my impatience get the better of me. I finally get to act instead of wait, and I use this to subtly express how dissatisfied I am with these introductions. It just has to burst out, building up after all that time waiting. It was a sweet release, although it is a good thing that So'krang stopped me.

Last but not least, the pretty girl of my dreams is about to give her résumé. Knowing this, and I have been paying attention to whose turn it is, I stare at no one but her. She smiles at me, and I smirk back, because being who I am, I can never get myself to smile, no matter how uplifting the scenario may be.

But as we look at each other, she takes my place, and I take her place next to the team, all while never breaking eye contact.

"I am Yomak Nayan of the clan of Karin," she chimes yet again in her angelic, soft voice. "I am sixteen. This is my fourth expedition, and I have killed eleven Airatsmeka."

She smiles as she finishes her sentence. So'krang steps forward to take her place and proceed with the next step towards killing the enemy. They look at each other, and he nods at her. She returns back to the line as So'krang stands in front of all of us.

I am captivated. Even her name is chocolate to the ears. Of course, I am just speaking for myself here. People don't usually find pleasure in hearing another's name. But her name . . . it was something else. Maybe because it was shorter than all the other names I've heard so far in the Novaversian nomenclature. It sounds like all the letters fall into the right position for the perfect combination of words and pronunciation. I just really love her name so much I might just say it in its entirety, rather than by its abbreviation.

Also, she's rather young compared to everyone else I've fought beside so far. Sixteen? She can barely get her driver's license and she's already prepared for killing. She must be a prodigy or something.

"All right," So'krang says in a serious tone. "I suppose you know the details of this mission. There are six Airatsmeka approximately 180 shiandon from here. The journey should take approximately four days. Also, the mikaryo'ga who discovered the group reports that they are accompanied by a homong. So not only do we have to fight harder, but we also have to be more cautious. Any questions?"

Everyone remains silent as So'krang passes his eyes on us.

"Good," he says. "Let's go."

So'krang turns around and starts walking towards our destination. Everyone follows him, each at their own pace.

"GRASSHEAD!" I yell.

Grasshead wakes up from his nap and runs at me. I run towards So'krang. Grasshead catches up, and as he was just behind me, I jump and mount him with perfect timing. Grasshead rushes to assume So'krang's side.

So'krang looks at me uncomfortably. I just keep looking forward at the sunset, already anticipating who we're going to fight, with hopes this time that I won't be on the verge of death.

"You don't always have to be close to me," So'krang tells me uncomfortably, just as his face suggested.

"What can I say? I've grown attached to ya," I reply in a wittily happy tone. "Besides, I don't know anyone here, so I prefer to be with someone I'm already acquainted with."

"You seem to take a fondness in that Karin'ga. Why not talk to her?"

"I'll bide my time for now. Maybe I'll talk to her after the mission. Everything has to be carefully planned, after all."

"Just don't forget, or she might run away."

"I won't."

We continue to walk towards our mission. We have four more days to go, so who knows what might happen in the meantime. All I know is that we'll be sleeping and eating mostly during this journey, and by the end of it, four days will feel more like four years. Kind of a boring process. At least I have the beautiful sunset to stare at while we walk slowly towards our goal. Too bad it won't last for long.

"Oh, and uh . . . blue," I tell So'krang as I continue to walk and stare at the sunset.

CHAPTER XVIII

MY SECOND BATTLE . . . AND ONE THAT PAYS OFF

For four days, the team has traveled east in Dobiya to reach their destination, a group of Airatsmeka located in a random spot somewhere in the continent, to complete their mission: exterminate the group. They have arrived at their destination and they only wish to go forth with the mission, for they will find enjoyment in using their various powers to dispose of the enemy. After all, every clan has a power of its own, which is why the united clans encourage their members to take pride in their power, because everyone has a talent that they can contribute to making society better, and others must accept those who are different from them. Unless it's a human, in which case they will stay as far away from it as possible as to not contract its selfishness, greed and all the destructive attributes it possesses, because the Natin aspire to be better than that.

But ethics aside, the team is prepared to use their powers to kill the Airatsmeka. After all, that's what they were chosen for.

They organize behind a rock, just out of sight of the Airatsmeka. They stare at the enemy from afar, waiting for the right moment to initiate the battle.

Sitting on top of a small hill, the Airatsmeka, a group composed of four men and two women, feast on some mytrocs they hunted, a rat-like creature twice the size of a rat with bulging vertebrae on his spine and reptilian features, similar to all the creatures in the Novaverse.

One of the male Airatsmeka, bald-headed and ugly with sharp teeth and black rust marks all over, grabs one of the dead mytrocs with his hand, and tears a huge chunk of meat from the carcass. He chews on it joyfully as the dead animal's guts spill out from its ripped stomach.

Ka is infuriated! She can't stand watching the filthy enemy hurt those poor creatures. As she reluctantly watches them feasting, she bares her teeth and growls quietly, holding her anger inside. Unaware of her own actions because of her anger, she starts to stand up. So'krang immediately pushes her back to a crouching position by pressing down on her shoulder. He looks at her, and she looks back at him. His eyes tell her that he is sorry for this unfortunate predicament, but no one could've planned it. Understanding the message, and being a professional, she returns to focus on the mission.

Now with everyone back in the game, the team is organizing their fight plans. Should they start discreetly, or should they just go all-out? Considering the assembly of head-first fighters, the latter seems like the better option.

Like before, and like all missions, the Airatsmeka in the opposing team are assigned numbers instead of their actual names to refer to them in battle and reports, because the actual names of the subjects are irrelevant when they're about to die. Not only that, but there's no actual way to find out what their names are. They are disposable . . . that's all that matters.

Because there are six opponents, they are given the designated numbers: No. 1, No. 2, No. 3, No. 4, No. 5, and No. 6. Additionally, a homong is supposed to be accompanying the enemy, but is nowhere in sight.

"All right," So'krang quietly speaks. "You all know what to do. Considering our organization, I think it would be best to go all-out. Neph . . . what are your plans?"

"I'm fighting too," Neph says with certainty. "Didn't come here for nothing."

"Are you certain?"

"I've never been more certain in my life. I got nothing to lose, after all."

"Very well. I believe in your capabilities."

A subtle smile can be seen on Neph's face.

"Any questions before we start?" So'krang asks.

"Isn't there supposed to be a homong?" Ka'tai'krang asks suspiciously.

"The homong should be in the area. Be aware."

"What does a homong look like?" Neph asks.

"You'll know one when you see one," So'krang responds vaguely.

Neph looks to the side and sighs.

"So much for clarification," Neph mutters to himself.

Now that all the questions have been answered, the team is prepared to fight. Now all they need is to know how they're going to do it.

"Who wants to engage?" So'krang asks the team, now prepared for the upcoming battle.

Everyone remains quiet. Not a word is uttered from anyone's mouth as So'krang slowly passes his eyes on every member of the team. This goes on for a few seconds. No one can find their reasons for starting the fight. If this goes on, So'krang himself will just have to take the initiative.

"I'll start," Sa'hi suddenly says quietly.

All eyes are on Sa'hi as she prepares to start the fight. With all this attention, she just might go back on her word . . . but she doesn't.

She takes a deep, slow breath and then exhales it slowly. She peeks above the stone to see what's going on with the enemy. She then lowers her head back down and then she looks at the ground, thinking. She then looks at her teammates and smiles.

She immediately jumps on top of the rock with excitement, whips out her sisik'tirir, the magenta snake-rope, and throws it at the enemy! The snake-rope bites hard onto one of the Airatsmeka, and with that, Sa'hi pulls herself towards the enemy.

The enemy is startled; they didn't see the attack coming. They barely have any time to react, as Sa'hi flies in the air towards them.

As she prepares to land among them, she takes out the kari'sasasa, the green glaive, from her belt and prepares to plant it in the face of the one she caught in her sisik'tirir. She tries to hit him in the face, but he dodges. Sa'hi hits the ground instead, and an explosion of green light emits from the center of Sa'hi's attack, leaving a huge spiral carving on the soil and dispersing the team of Airatsmeka.

With all the enemies in different locations in the area fighting all the members of So'krang's team, Sa'hi is now facing the same Airatsmeka she tried to kill moments ago with that massive explosion. They look at each other and do nothing as they try to figure out when to attack and how to attack.

Sa'hi puts back the kari'sasasa on the belt, and immediately throws the sisik'tirir at him. The fangs on the snake's head latch tight onto his arm. Sa'hi tries to pull him in, but he resists. He coils the rope around his arm to get better control over it, and he starts to pull her in. They play tug o' war as each one tries to pull the other to their side.

At a moment's notice, with one strong pull from him, No. 1 gains the upper hand in the game as he pulls Sa'hi to him while she flies in the air. Sa'hi quickly adapts by taking out her anim'roo'shin, the green smoking halberd, and as she flies towards him, she spins all the while and slashes at him when she gets close enough. A powerful gust of wind can be felt in the air, blowing away the dirt on the ground and the leaves on the trees.

No. 1 barely dodges the attack. Sa'hi, now standing back on the earth in a combat-ready pose, holding the windy halberd with its blade pointed at No. 1 to intimidate him. She stares at an injured No. 1, holding tight the deep cut on his chest caused by the attack which has exposed his ribcage. As he breathes calmly to prepare himself for the next attack, he notices Sa'hi gesturing at him with her eyes to look to his left. He does so, and what he sees on the ground is a massive cut deep into the earth. He looks back at her, surprised, and she smiles at him with a murderous look on her face.

Furious, No. 1 wastes no thought but to blast Sa'hi into oblivion with a quick swipe of his hand as he launches a condensed ball of blackness at her. The ball moves fast at Sa'hi, leaving barely any time to react as she whips out her raj'or'shin, the candle sword, and swipes at the black ball just as it's about to blow her to bits. At the moment of impact, a massive explosion occurs, consuming both Sa'hi and No. 1 in it and subsequently emitting a black fog that shrouds the entire area.

Did Sa'hi survive the attack? Was No. 1 also blown away by his own attack? Nothing is certain, as the black fog persists, hiding whatever is in it and obscuring them from view. If anyone is around to see, that is.

Suddenly, Sa'hi appears from above the smoke on a fast-rising triangular pole, with just enough room for her legs. The pole stops rising high above the smoke cloud, keeping Sa'hi out of certain danger. She looks down at the smoke cloud and she can't tell what's going on. Is the enemy still alive? Going down there right now without being able to use her eyes is a risk not worth taking. She thinks of waiting until the smoke subsides, but how long will that take? She can't stand on the pole forever, and the enemy could be elsewhere by now.

Suddenly, No. 1 comes shooting out of the smoke straight towards Sa'hi. Once again, Sa'hi reacts at the last second as she dodges the attack, but just barely this time. She falls down from the pole, flips backwards in the air, and lands awkwardly on her feet as they touch the ground, breaking her right leg and maybe even snapping a few tendons.

With the smoke cloud having dispersed already, No. 1 lands to once again face Sa'hi. Seeing her in her unfortunate state, he smiles at her, confident that he's in for the kill, while she's not able to maintain her positive demeanor from a moment ago.

Finished with the trade of confidence, he immediately charges at her, preparing to punch her skull open with a haymaker infused with black sparkling tiamtsat. Sa'hi quickly reacts by taking out her sisik'tirir, blindly throwing to her back and latching it onto a tree. She pulls herself to the tree, and just before landing on the bark of the tree with her feet, she takes out her saka'owora, the blue triangle, and puts it under her feet as she lands on it, hitting hard against the tree. A blue pole elongates rapidly out of the tree, lifting Sa'hi horizontally straight into No. 1's face.

While spinning in the air, she takes out her anim'roo'shin, and as she gets close enough to No. 1, she slashes at his face. Once again, a giant gust of wind can be felt in the air, but this time, she misses.

Using the opportunity to his advantage, No. 1 tries to counter with a punch, but Sa'hi quickly holsters her anim'roo'shin and takes out her raj'or'shin. Without a single thought, she swipes at No. 1's punch, locking it in place with a wall of wax.

No. 1 struggles to free himself from the wax, but Sa'hi wastes no time as she stabs in his direction. A massive jet of flame bursts out of the tip of the candle sword, incinerating everything in its path.

No. 1 barely manages to evade the attack at the last second as his shoulder catches fire. He repeatedly pats his shoulder to extinguish the fire. His skin, burnt away from the fire, leaves only charred muscles for all to see.

She charges at him in an obvious attempt to attack. Seeing this, he quickly acts by stomping on the ground, fracturing the ground with a massive tremor and sending Sa'hi into the air as pebbles and dirt fly in different directions.

Seizing the opportunity as she is rendered airborne without being able to attack, he throws a ball of black tiamtsat at her, trying to blast her out of the air. She barely dodges the attack as the ball keeps flying forward into the sky and she lands poorly on the rubble that was made from the quake. Trying to balance herself from that poor landing, she immediately backs away from No. 1 to prepare herself for what might come next. Before she can even breathe, No. 1 runs at her with another explosion to deliver straight to her face from point-blank range. Alas, he is too slow, as Sa'hi tilts her head to the side while the blast shoots forward.

As the blast continues to travel, it enters the forest behind them, piercing through every tree and scorching the ground. The ball continues to fly forward non-stop, even crossing Sang'ka'nik on the way, who is currently fighting No. 2.

Seeing the ball coming at him, Sang'ka'nik backs away just in time to dodge the attack. But alas, he didn't see No. 2 running at him, getting close enough to deliver a mighty push kick straight to the center of Sang'ka'nik's torso. His torso comes clean off his body, without the limbs, head or any blood spilling, as if he were a mannequin. The limbs and head, on the other hand, fall to the ground right below No. 2's nose.

Seemingly neutralized, Sang'ka'nik is left helpless as No. 2 tries to stomp on his disembodied head that's lying on the grassy soil. Sang'ka'nik rolls his head on the ground to dodge the attack, and immediately counters by kicking No. 2 in the groin with his disembodied leg that is lying right under him. No. 2 folds in pain, as Sang'ka'nik grabs No. 2's face with his disembodied hands, latching hard on his face with thumbs pressing on his eyes to gouge them out. No. 2 struggles to release himself from Sang'ka'nik's hands.

Desperate, No. 2 grabs the hand trying to gouge his right eye with both his hands and throws it away, leaving behind an opening that Sang'ka'nik uses to gouge No. 2's left eye with the hand that is still on his face.

No. 2 staggers backwards, trying to make it hard for the hand to further press the thumb deep into his eye socket. He grabs the hand with both his hands and throws it away.

Holding his eye tight in pain, wincing and writhing, trying to gain back enough strength to get back to the fight, Sang'ka'nik uses this opportunity to call back his torso.

As his head and limbs remain on the ground, his torso comes walking awkwardly on its arm stumps, still in one piece from the kick he got. The hands come walking on their fingers towards the gathering center of the other body parts.

With all the parts in the same place, the hands set the legs upright. The torso then jumps on the legs, reconnecting. The hands crawl on the body all the way to the stumps at the end of the arms. And finally, with the legs and hands in their rightful place, the body crouches to pick up the head and reconnect it to the neck. Now, Sang'ka'nik is in one piece.

Sang'ka'nik cracks his neck at his leisure while No. 2 continues to hold his face. After taking his time, Sang'ka'nik reaches out to his back. A machete materializes in his hand out of nothing, leaving behind only a small purple mist that disperses almost instantly.

From a distance, he slashes at No. 2, stretching his arm like rubber. No. 2 grabs the elongated arm and pulls Sang'ka'nik towards him.

Upon collision, Sang'ka'nik entangles No. 2's body with his own stretchy body, locking him in place and preventing any movements. Sang'ka'nik constricts No. 2 tightly, squeezing his insides and fracturing his ribs, all the while strangling him with his stretchy arms. Sang'ka'nik gets a really tight grip on No. 2's neck, causing blood vessels to pop in his eyes as No. 2 struggles to stay alive and to loosen the grip on his trachea. He grabs Sang'ka'nik's arms and pulls them away from him, with Sang'ka'nik doing the exact opposite by tightening the grip. But No. 2, seeing as he is at a disadvantage, clenches Sang'ka'nik's arms. Alas, his bones will not break, as right now, they are as flexible as rubber.

But these are not No. 2's intentions, as black spiky crystals start to protrude from Sang'ka'nik's arms. Sang'ka'nik endures, desperately trying to break No. 2's neck before he gives in to the crystals. Alas, the crystals are too persistent as they start to spread to the rest of his arms, atrophying him and weakening his grip on the enemy. The pain is too much to bear, and the tide starts to turn for the worse. With this in mind, Sang'ka'nik detaches from his arms and jumps away from No. 2, leaving his arms on the ground, decaying and full of ugly black crystals.

No. 2 turns around and starts to run to Sang'ka'nik. Sang'ka'nik quickly gets up from the ground without the use of his arms and runs away. No. 2 chases him.

The two seem to be equal when it comes to speed, as Sang'ka'nik continues to run away while No. 2 continues to chase. But as they continue to run, No. 2 starts to gain. Seeing this, Sang'ka'nik realizes he needs to resort to other strategies, as he can only run so far from the enemy. So Sang'ka'nik runs straight ahead with little concern to what's ahead. As he runs, he is about to hit a tree, but runs up it vertically like some heratrang'ga pan cartoon character. No. 2, running at full speed, hits his head on the hard bark of the tree, as he could not have anticipated this move.

Sang'ka'nik runs up the tree and stumbles upon a branch, high enough to make life hard for No. 2. Perching high above, Sang'ka'nik stares down on No. 2 and takes his time to regain some energy, just enough time for his next move.

No. 2 looks up and sighs at his unfortunate predicament.

Suddenly, No. 2 sees a grey dot from above getting bigger and bigger. He doesn't understand what it may be, but then it dawns on him. As he opens his eyes wide in realization, he jumps away from the area as a giant rock falls down and lands hard on the ground, nearly crushing him.

Quickly recovering from the dodge, No. 2 gets back up on his feet and stares at Sang'ka'nik. He sees that Sang'ka'nik isn't going anywhere without his arms. With a clear idea that Sang'ka'nik isn't going to move because of his supposed helplessness, No. 2 conjures a black crude-looking spear and throws it at Sang'ka'nik. Sang'ka'nik dodges the spear as it pierces the tree behind him, leaving a gaping hole for him to stare into the sky.

Sang'ka'nik looks down at No. 2. He then looks to his sides, wondering what should be his next plan and wondering how the others are doing.

Ka is currently fighting No. 3, although she is nowhere to be seen as No. 3 calmly and slowly searches for her opponent amidst a bunch of low bushes.

Pushing through the short bushes without a care in the world, No. 3 searches for Ka, hidden somewhere in her vicinity. She knows she's hiding. She knows she's planning. Yet she doesn't seem nervous or stressed. Rather, she's treating the situation with ease, as if she already knows she can easily take on Ka. Yet she can't help but wonder. Where is she hiding? Behind the trees? Under the bushes? She'll find out soon enough.

No. 3 continues to push her way through the tiny bushes; she hears a noise from behind her. She stops in place and turns her back to look and sees nothing. She looks slowly to her sides to check for any weird occurrences, and sees nothing. She then looks straight and remains still, thinking about what may come next. Is it even worth continuing forward, or should she turn around? Maybe her enemy is somewhere behind her.

Suddenly, from beneath the bushes, a creature jumps from behind her and bites her hard on the shoulder, piercing her with its teeth. She reaches out to her back, grabs the creature and throws it forward in an arc over her head.

The creature she can now see in front of her is a thamnicribb. A green wolf, slightly larger than a normal wolf, which grows its fur long and thick to make it look like a bush to blend in with the environment. And when the right moment comes, it ambushes its prey without its prey even knowing that it wasn't a bush, but a thamnicribb.

But alas, the creature flees out of fear, allowing No. 3 to resume her hunt for Ka. But alas for her, another thamnicribb pokes its head from beneath the bushes and bites her in the calf muscle, keeping her in place.

No. 3 struggles with the creature to free herself, but she can't turn around to simply blast the thamnicribb away. She is in an awkward position, as the thamnicribb continues to pull her calf with its teeth, nearly ripping it with every shake of its mouth. Her skin and muscles from her leg loosen with blood pouring freely and she's unable to do anything to defend herself. As she continues to struggle, too preoccupied with the creature biting her leg, she fails to notice what appears before her.

Ka suddenly jumps high out of the small bushes! As she lands, she scratches No. 3's face with her sharp nails, leaving a nasty three-slash wound on her face, ripping apart her cheek.

Out of sheer anger, No. 3 doesn't even think but straight punches Ka right out of the collection of bushes. No. 3 runs straight at her. Ka immediately gets back up on her feet from the punch. Seeing No. 3 approaching her, she thinks quickly, as taking her head on would be a mistake.

Without even looking at it, Ka climbs up a tree to her side just as No. 3 gets to her. She climbs all the way up until she reaches a high enough branch. She jumps from the trunk and immediately swings from a branch. Landing magnificently in front of No. 3, she attempts to once again scratch No. 3 on her face, but this time she'll rip it off. But seeing her coming, No. 3 simply takes a small step back, having Ka land hard on the ground after missing her attack. No. 3 kicks Ka hard in the ribs while she is still recovering from the rough landing, sending her flying in an arc straight into a tree, hitting hard on its trunk. Ka falls down after colliding with the tree, once again landing hard on the ground.

Now in a bad position, a crouching Ka holds her arm tightly in pain and stares at a proud No. 3, smiling with the sure idea that she's going to win. Ka frowns, clenching her fist in anger and grimacing in rage, as she is not going to lose to a filthy Airatsmeka.

"RRRRAAAAAAAAAAAAAAAAAAA!!!" Ka yells from the deepest depths of her lungs.

The roar echoes throughout the forest. No. 3 ignores her menacing attempt to intimidate her, as Ka is obviously in no position to intimidate anyone.

No. 3 slowly walks towards her, all the while smiling with joy and conjuring a black crude-looking saber with her hands.

But before she can even get close enough, a tsekorynch, a grey bird with a big, sharp beak shaped like a pincer, flies down and starts pecking No. 3 with its beak, cutting deep into her flesh.

Out of panic, No. 3 tries to fend off the bird with her hands, but almost immediately she regains her wits and cuts the bird in half with her customized saber. She goes back to her original plan: killing Ka.

Unfortunately for her, before she can even take a step, a flock of tsekorynch flies down from above and proceed to peck the life out of her.

Another peck and another peck, each one stronger than the last, cutting her flesh with those razor sharp beaks.

Overwhelmed by the number of axe-beaks rending her body, No. 3 flings her hands everywhere just to get rid of the birds. She cannot think straight. She is too concerned with getting rid of the birds. But that sword she has in her hand won't be enough to get rid of so many birds at once.

In an act of pure frustration, No. 3 emits a blast of hot air, blowing away all the birds, some getting knocked hard against trees while others disappear out of sight. Visible black particles can be seen in the air, and the scent of ash can be smelled in the atmosphere. Her skin now bleeds from several cuts in her body of various lengths and depths, exposing all the fleshy content beneath it. Despite all this, she can still fight, and her body can still move, for mere paper cuts have no effect on her.

Having dealt with the birds, No. 3 returns back to her original goal. She looks around in search of Ka, but Ka is nowhere to be seen. She is too busy looking to the sides; she fails to see that Ka is right in front of her, already running away on all fours like some kind of beast.

No. 3 frowns over her failure to kill her immediately when she had the chance. She quickly intercepts Ka by tossing her saber in the air. The saber rises high, and then quickly descends right in front of Ka, stopping her in place.

Ka, holding her broken ribs tightly in pain, witnesses a not-so-joyful No. 3 approaching her, angry with every bit of her face showing it, frustrated over Ka's tendency to avoid death at her hands.

But the time has come, as No. 3 starts to walk faster towards her, anxiously expecting her victory, she conjures yet another black crude-looking sword from her hands, and rushes to finish the job once and for all. Ka is doomed.

But as fate would have it, So'krang appears in the air right above her, coming out from behind a tree. He prepares to embed his claymore in the skull of No. 3 with a falling overhead slash. No. 3, bewildered by So'krang's sudden arrival, manages to dodge the attack just in time as So'krang lands. He quickly recovers and attempts to attack again with another slash, only to be dodged once more.

No. 4, too, appears in the air, and shoots a black ball of smoke downwards at So'krang, ignoring the presence of her ally No. 3 in a show of friendly fire. So'krang rolls away just in time before the ball comes into contact with the ground, exploding into a black mist and leaving a small crater on the soil. So'krang runs out of the mist without even guessing which direction he is going; it does not matter, since the only purpose he had was to run away from No. 4.

No. 4, seeing through the black mist, witnesses So'krang running away. She chases after him to continue the fight she had before he interfered in a conflict that was not his, allowing No. 3 to once more focus on Ka. But in all honesty, with friends like those, who needs enemies?

Broken alliances aside, No. 3 goes back to focus on Ka. All the commotion caused her to be distracted, leaving her unable to see that Ka has managed to escape in the meantime.

No. 3 looks around her, and can't see Ka anywhere. She looks up in the trees, and sees Ka climbing in one of them.

Ka climbs all the way up to the highest branch, and jumps to the next tree, effectively escaping No. 3 while maintaining a height advantage. She continues to jump from tree to tree, trying to come up with a plan to kill No. 3 before No. 3 can kill her. No. 3 chases after her before she completely escapes her grasp, and hopefully won't be able to land that trick with the thamnicribbs once more.

As No. 3 continues to chase Ka, others are also fighting the good fight. Like So'krang, who just a moment ago intervened to help out Ka. He continues to defend himself well. But what about the others?

As it would seem, Neph rides on Grasshead in an open meadow, far away from the forest, and as far away as he can from a chasing No. 5.

Grasshead runs fast like a bullet train without its tracks, piercing through the wind without a care to where he's going, as long as he can get away from No. 5.

Alas, No. 5 is just as fast as Grasshead, gaining with each fifth step he takes. He runs fast, as he can be seen from behind, getting closer and closer. Grasshead tries to pick up the pace even more, but can only just barely, as he is near his limit.

No. 5 finally gets close enough, standing side by side with Grasshead. He smiles, mocking their intention to try to get away, for he knows that they can't escape a man of his speed. Grasshead realizes that running away is useless; Neph doesn't even need to command him, as he swiftly turns to the side to catch No. 5 between his massive jaws.

Grasshead is too close and the attack is too fast for No. 5 to realize it in time. Grasshead's massive weight pushes the two away from their path, rolling on the ground as each struggles to gain the upper hand. Neph can't keep his balance anymore and is flung off while the two are rolling.

Grasshead crushes No. 5 with his weight as they continue to roll. Finally managing to stand up on all fours once again, Grasshead attempts to kill No. 5 with a single bite, but is held in place by both his jaws with No. 5's bare hands, as he too now stands upright, with a sunk-in left side of his ribcage and a right shoulder filled with gaping holes spewing blood like a waterfall, courtesy of Grasshead's fangs.

Grasshead pushes himself forward hard to contain No. 5 within his maw of doom, coming ever so close to finishing him off with a single crunch. But as Grasshead exerts all the power he has, No. 5 exerts even more power as he keeps Grasshead's mouth away from him. But even with that blood he's losing, No. 5 proves to be stronger than Grasshead, even though the tides of their struggle keep turning between them.

As they continue to struggle, Neph runs over to aid Grasshead. He jumps onto Grasshead's back and immediately thrusts himself over No. 5, landing right behind him. Neph delivers a flurry of punches to No. 5's back without even thinking. Just punches over and over, each one with the force of breaking the jaw of the most badass of bullies. But even Neph's natural fighting prowess proves insufficient to overcome No. 5, as he doesn't even budge.

No. 5 becomes weary of Neph's redundant attempts at thwarting him, so he delivers a back kick that sends Neph flying backwards.

The struggle between No. 5 and Grasshead starts to favor the former, as No. 5 starts to forcibly open Grasshead's mouth to rip his jaws apart. Grasshead yelps with agony as he now struggles to close his mouth, but finds that his jaw muscles can't keep up with No. 5's arms.

Neph, hearing his beloved Grasshead crying for help, immediately gets back up on his feet, completely ignoring any broken bones he may have suffered after being kicked in the chest.

"NO!!" he yells.

Neph harnesses all his anger as he rushes over there, grabs No. 5 by the legs, turns around, and slams him hard against the ground with all his might. The impact creates a sound that echoes throughout the meadow and a depression shaped just like No. 5 as dirt and dust fly in the air, getting in the eyes of everyone there. Neph brushes away the dust and proceeds to stand right atop No. 5's head. He squints from the dust in his eyes, but it does not stop him, as he raises his foot as high as he can and stomps on No. 5's face like it is the ugliest cockroach he ever saw, driving his head further into the ground.

No. 5 is immobile. Neph stares atop him with anger while Grasshead walks over to Neph's side. Now the two are staring at him as he remains immobile, lying in the dirt like the worm that he is. Neph manages to calm down while he continues to stare at him, still waiting for a response to see if he's dead, and there's no indication that he might be alive, since he's not moving.

Suddenly, No. 5 grips Neph's leg harder than a vise. He squeezes hard, stopping the blood flow and nearly breaking the shin, all with Neph's leg still on his face. Neph immediately backs away, forcibly trying to free himself from No. 5's clutches. But No. 5 lets go as soon as Neph attempts to release himself, for he has no interest in keeping Neph's leg on his face.

Backing away from No. 5, Neph and Grasshead watch as he gets back up on two feet. Exploding with anger over the humiliation he suffered at the hands of a heranga, he collects all the black tiamtsat he can in the center of his palms. His hands absorb the energy faster than an MRI device at full power in an emporium of kitchenware.

But before he can collect all the tiamtast he needs, a war cry is heard in the background, faint at first, but increases in volume as it continues. No. 5 is distracted, for he knows that it means more danger to him.

"aaaaaaaaaaaaaaaaaaaAAAAAAAAAAAAAAAAA," sounds the shout, growing stronger and stronger.

Looking into the distance, Neph and Grasshead see a figure running toward them, dragging something on the ground. At first, it isn't clear who or what it is, but as it gets closer, it becomes obvious:

it is Ka'tai'krang! Raking the dirt off the ground with his rake as he continues to run and yell, leaving behind a trail of scraped-off soil that grows as he continues to drag his rake.

Now a fair distance from No. 5, Ka'tai'krang spins around in a circle and swings his rake from the ground, flinging all that dirt at No. 5. All that massive dirt condenses together and hardens into a giant boulder in midair. The boulder lands hard on the ground, squashing No. 5 into a pancake.

Another Airatsmeka bites the dust, and with that, Ka'tai'krang holsters his rake on his back, takes a deep breath, and walks towards Neph and Grasshead. With his mind at ease, he takes his time to walk over, walking slowly and without a care in the world to what danger might arise in those lonely seconds, even if that means that No. 5 is still alive under that rock, or one of his allies comes to avenge his death. Of course, Neph and Grasshead don't seem to be concerned either, as they simply wait for Ka'tai'krang to come to them, rather than approach him themselves. They bide their time, and Ka'tai'krang finally stands in front of them.

"Already done with your rusty?" Neph asks Ka'tai'krang, subtly happy to see him.

"Yo'na helped me," he explains dully. "It didn't take long."

"Speaking of which, where is she?"

Suddenly, the ground starts to shake. The trembling becomes stronger and stronger as it continues. Cracks start to form on the surface they are standing on. Fissures of varying sizes and depths, they come in large numbers, and more appear the more the ground shakea. In fact, the tremors are unusually long. It's as if the soil itself tried to suspend them for something astonishing coming their way. But then Ka'tai'krang realizes what it is.

Ka'tai'krang thrusts his entire body onto Neph, pushing him away as they both roll on the ground from the force exerted by Ka'tai'krang, just as the ground beneath him erupts in an earthly explosion of rock and dirt, sending Grasshead flying in the air, who is too slow to evade in time. And out of the dirt comes who? None other than No. 5 himself, still alive and kicking, without a scratch from that giant boulder thrown at him by Ka'tai'krang, but pissed as hell, shown by the contorted muscles in his face, frowning with all his might and nearly breaking his teeth from that grimace he's making.

Ka'tai'krang wastes no time and rushes No. 5, raking the ground as he runs. He spins in a circle and throws all that raked dirt straight at No. 5, condensing in midair and hardening into a sharp and pointy rock meant to pierce No. 5's skull, but that proves to have no impact as No. 5 simply slaps the rock into pieces. Ka'tai'krang is nearly close enough to fight No. 5 hand-to-hand. Just before getting close enough, he spins one more time, raking up as much dirt as he can, and throws it all at No. 5 from point-blank range.

The attack merely gets dirt in No. 5's face, as the dirt didn't harden fast enough into a rock to sink his face in. Fortunately, it does blind him. Quickly adapting to these unpredicted circumstances, Ka'tai'krang slashes at No. 5's chest with his rake, leaving twelve deadly cuts, narrow enough to seem pathetic, but deep enough to demand the blood to spill.

Ka'tai'krang slashes again, but No. 5 takes a big leap backwards, just enough to avoid his attacks. No. 5 hastily wipes his eyes and regains his sight. Now with the power of vision once more, he sees Ka'tai'krang predictably rushing at him. Ka'tai'krang swipes his rake at No. 5 just as he gets close enough for another attack. Unfortunately for him, No. 5 sees the attack coming from a mile away; he ducks just as Ka'tai'krang swipes, grabs the body of the rake from the middle, and breaks it in half with a clench of his fist.

Quickly realizing what's happening, a bewildered Ka'tai'krang jumps back to gain some distance over his disadvantage.

With his primary weapon broken, Ka'tai'krang has no choice but to remain helpless unless a better option appears before him. What could he have done? Supposedly he could've done better, but he probably didn't see the enemy regain his sight or forget to rake the ground, for such is the proper use of the weapon. The Natin aren't perfect; they're just the best at what they do, but even that sometimes isn't enough to best the enemy. So a Natin messed up. Probably if he were more experienced, he wouldn't be in this predicament. But he shouldn't feel shame for dying. Death comes to many tak'nen of all ages, for such is their lifestyle, and they accept it; they are proud of it, for every Natin will die for his people. Of course, if he cherishes his life, he can always run away. Then again, No. 5 would easily gain on him, so what use will that bring?

But as Ka'tai'krang laments the supposed last moments of his life and regrets not doing anything else but charge thoughtlessly at the enemy, he disappears in a flash of pink, right before No. 5's dirt-covered eyes. No. 5 yells in rage and frustration.

Elsewhere, Yo'na appears in a flash of pink together with Neph, Grasshead, and Ka'tai'krang. She might look like she's teleporting, but she's in fact moving at high speeds.

Neph and Grasshead seem confused over their new location, although Ka'tai'krang is not too surprised find himself elsewhere. More so, he is relieved to be away from the enemy, with just enough time to pull himself back together. Good thing Yo'na came just as things started to go the wrong way.

"I couldn't find the homong," she declares.

"Aaaaaaaaaaaaaaaaaaaaaaaaaaaaaa!!" a faint yell can suddenly be heard in the distance.

The yelling doesn't stop; as it grows in volume it continues to make itself known, the trio composed of two men and a dog-creature recognize that voice all too well, although Yo'na isn't too familiar with it.

At first, it appears like a little black dot because of the distance. But as it gets closer, it starts to become clearer who it is, even though the only one that needs introduction is Yo'na. Obviously, it is No. 5, charging head-first at full speed towards our heroes, engulfed in a fiery aura of blackness and hatred, his face bleeding from the muscles he exerts, yelling from the deepest depth of his lungs just to make known how much he wants to murder them, and he will do it by simply colliding with them and exploding, with his expectations to leave nothing within the large vicinity but a pitch black mushroom cloud.

He is moving way too fast; there is no time to react. All seems lost just as he gets close enough for the heroes to even do anything. But then, just as he is half of a second away from decimating the four, a giant black cleaver falls down on him, cutting him vertically in half and smashing him to the ground!

The cleaver falls in between the four, leaving them completely untouched. The cleaver rises back up into the air, showing the earthly mess it left behind. A pile of debris made of rocks, sinking into the ground from that massive impact, with a special something in the middle: No. 5, who now looks more like roadkill run over by an SUV with bladed tires.

The four look back to see what is the thing that laid down the massive cleaver and saved their lives. Of course, one half of the group already knows what they are going to look at, while the other half has no idea. But regardless, what they see now is the one thing that concerned them the most, and now will no longer concern them.

The homong! Just coming out of the forest of tall trees that is behind them, Neph and Grasshead finally get to see what this mysterious homong is that everyone is talking about. Neph hadn't been informed of its physical appearance, but rather was given a vague clue as to what it may be. Of course, that same vague clue was more than enough to supply Neph with the information he needed to recognize, since the homong has very distinct characteristics, differentiating it from all of the creatures of the Novaverse.

Roughly the height of a street light, the creature stands as tall as the trees behind him. Looking at his head, it'd be hard to ignore the eye-catching features he possesses. A set of eight eyes like a spider, dark and shiny as black pearls. A big fang-filled mouth shaped like a canoe, with a massive underbite that boasts the longest and narrowest teeth he has ever seen. And above all, the quills he has on his head, long and pointy like that of a porcupine, only much longer and sharp enough to pierce armor.

Once one is done looking at the head, then comes the rest. A body black as the tiamtsat of the Airatsmeka themselves. Skin scaly as a reptile, thick as a tree, tough as armor; it would make crocodiles jealous. He stands on his toes, sporting razor-sharp nails, and his body is thin but muscular, wearing nothing but a black loincloth. And of course, he holds in his hand of sharp nails a black cleaver with a particular design, where the top of the blade further extends and curves backwards, rather than the usual rectangular design, making it look more like the blade of a sword, even though it is still a cleaver.

Everyone looks with awe at this ironically magnificent distortion of nature. It remains silent, untouched by the murder of his supposed ally, if they were allies. He doesn't move. He just stands there. Does he know what to do? Does he recognize the individuals in front of him as enemies? He does not take any action; he just drools like the reptilian ogre that he is. He takes his time, but what is he planning?

The others stare at him, already knowing what they're dealing with. Seeing his current passive behavior, they silently contemplate what will be the right action. Run? Fight? Neither is a good choice without further information. But whatever action our heroes decide to take, they will have to eliminate him eventually.

The homong finally makes his move, as he roars into the sky. The roar sounds like that of a lion with a ruptured larynx, and with that roar, everyone knows exactly what to do next: get the hell out of there!!

Everyone runs as far away as they can from the homong. They all run in the same direction, except for Ka'tai'krang, who runs in a different direction altogether. What are his plans? Nobody knows. But all will find out soon enough.

The homong cares not for just one of the crew, and chases after the many. A stomp and another stomp. Every step the homong takes is like a long distance jump for the greatest of athletes, embedding his hard-hitting footprints into the ground and emitting a boom for everyone to hear.

The three heroes don't even look back. They just run in a straight line away from danger. With Neph riding on Grasshead and Yo'na with her powers, they easily outrun the homong, despite the impressive leaping footsteps he takes. The homong just runs and follows his feeling, a feeling of where his targets may be, even when he can barely see them.

Even after losing sight of his target, the homong continues to run. He can't see his target, but he can feel them. Eventually, he stops feeling them, and stops altogether, far away from the forest from which he emerged. Seemingly without a purpose, he stands still, idle, wondering what will happen next, and what to do next.

Suddenly, the homong is hit hard in the back by a large pink beam of light, moving as fast as the particles that make it. The homong falls forward and onto the ground, dropping the cleaver after the strong hit.

Far behind him, Neph, Grasshead and Yo'na stand and watch the fallen homong. Knowing that the homong had lost sight of them, they quickly and elusively maneuvered behind him without attracting his attention.

Neph looks to his sides and notices something missing.

"Where the fuck is So'krang?" he anxiously asks Yo'na next to him.

"Don't worry," she responds simply, serious, while never losing sight of the homong.

Neph is unsatisfied with her response, but realizes it will have to make do for now, as there are more important matters to take care of.

They both charge at the downed homong without any further thought. As they approach, the homong starts to get up. They've almost reached the homong and the pair are not going to waste another second prolonging his life, as they are going to finish him off immediately.

But before they can get close enough, the homong launches himself back on his feet with a thrust of his arms on the ground, cleaver already in hand. Almost standing back up on two feet, he turns as he rises, cleaver high in the air, and he plunges it down on the ground, splashing dirt and earthy debris everywhere just as our heroes approach him up close. Neph and Grasshead just barely dodge the attack as they continue to charge forward, moving under the homong and between his gigantic legs, while Yo'na jumps back, also avoiding the attack as pebbles fly at her face.

With one opponent in the back and the other in the front, the homong is surrounded. Grasshead bites him hard in the Achilles tendon, pulling it hard with all his might. The homong staggers backwards as Yo'na gracefully jumps in the air, assuming her pink form all the while, and conjures a pink sword of light. The sword glimmers with beauty, radiating with awe, just like its wielder. As she holds the sword in her hand, she wastes no time and slashes at the homong. The homong blocks the attack with his arm but the attack cuts deep into his arm.

Quickly recovering from the attack, the homong flings Neph and Grasshead away from his leg with a simple blind back kick, like a horse would. Neph and Grasshead fly all the way back into a tree. The attack is too much for them, and they both lie down on the grass, trying to recover.

But the homong is distracted by this attack. Yo'na uses this to her advantage and starts spinning around the homong as fast as her pink form of light would suggest. She quickly entangles him in pink strings, thin as hair and bright as the stars in the night. She spins relentlessly, not thinking of anything else but to hold the homong in place. The homong can't even react as she is too fast for him. He stares confused at the bright glow that moves swiftly around him again and again, not knowing what to do.

Feeling the strings around him, he tries to break free. But as he tries, more strings tie him up. He is helpless, as there is nothing he can do for himself right now.

With the homong completely entangled, Yo'na goes back to stand on the ground, but remains in her pink form. Grabbing on to a single string, she pulls down the entangled homong with all her might. The homong resists, pulling himself up in return. A tug of war ensues between them. They continue to struggle against each other, but the homong proves too mighty for Yo'na, even in her empowered form.

The game of pulling the string doesn't last long, as the homong exerts all his strength for one single pull upwards, sending Yo'na back into the air. With her focus off the strings, the homong breaks free as he rips apart the strings that entangle him. He catches Yo'na in the air with his gigantic hand. Firmly holding her in his palm, he immediately smashes her to the ground as if she were a fly, destroying the ground all the while and leaving a depression the shape of his hand. He wastes no time and immediately raises his leg as high as he can, preparing to stomp. Yo'na regains her wits fast enough for her to quickly assume her pink form just as he is about to stomp on her. She tries to get away but she is too late; she mostly makes it out in time but the homong lays down his massive foot on the ground, breaking her legs. The impact it has on her body is too much to bear, forcing her to revert to her regular form.

But even while down and unable to stand up, she continues to fight as she shoots pink balls of light at the homong with one hand while pulling herself away with the other. Alas, her weakened state gets the better of her as the homong can simply brush off her attacks right now.

She struggles desperately, but he can easily get close to her, and with that, he raises his cleaver high in the air above him, holds it in both his hands, and prepares to deliver a massive overhead slash that will send her deep into the earth as a pile of torn viscera.

But far away elsewhere, against that tree, Neph finally recovers. He gets back up on his feet and stares forward at the events that are unfolding. He sees the homong about to crush Yo'na with his cleaver.

"YOMAK NAYAN!" he shouts.

Neph immediately becomes angered, frowning will all his might. Neph doesn't even think as he runs fast to the homong. Just as he gets close, Neph jumps high in the air, leaping over the mighty creature's head, grabs him by the quills and pulls him down to the ground while he's still standing, bending him. Standing atop Yo'na, he swings the giant creature over his head and slams him on the ground! The impact destroys the earth, throwing rubble and dirt as the homong sinks into the ground.

Neph just stands there, watching the downed homong as he takes a deep breath. He feels relieved, knowing that he was able to prevent the creature from killing Yo'na, whom he refers to by her full name for some reason. He doesn't even care how he managed to throw such a massive creature above his head, as his previous feats have shown him that he is capable of more than what his life has taught him. He just continues to stand there, presumably waiting for a response, or maybe he just wants a small break before taking action once more, as all this struggle is starting to annoy him.

Eventually, his waiting pays off, as the homong pushes himself off the ground with his free hand, still holding the cleaver in the other. He slowly rises back up on his feet, recovering from the surprising attack all the while. He turns around and returns his attention back to Neph. Now the homong is back to fight once more, and our heroes have nothing more to attack him with. All hope seems lost.

But elsewhere, Ka'tai'krang stops running, finally assuming the perfect position. He stands and watches the homong from afar, barely seeing Neph because of the distance. He takes a deep breath and prepares. He discharges two rolls of toilet paper he has on the belt he wears over his shoulder. He stands still, holding one roll in each hand. He's nervous, worried that his throw might not be strong enough. He exhales all the air he has and breathes deep once more. With no more time to lose, he throws one roll as hard as he can into the air. He immediately follows up by doing the same with the other roll, throwing it as hard as he can into the air.

The rolls reach high into the sky. They unravel, leaving behind a trail of paper. The paper starts to take the shape of an arc in the sky as it continues to unroll in the air, further extending its tail.

Just as the rolls are about to touch the clouds, they start to morph in midair; distorting and liquidizing into various amorphous shapes, as if they were dough. The tail starts to twist and the rolls start to inflate and deflate over and over.

And then, all of a sudden, they transform into long white dragons! The rolls become the head and the tail becomes the rest of the bodies. Asian dragons, white as marble, with scales that are just as hard. They roar a mighty roar as they fly in the sky, quickly descending towards the homong.

Moving fast with their massive weight as if they were flying trains, they get closer to the homong. One dragon gets ahead of the other; as he reaches the homong, he bites him hard on the side of his ribs, locking his jaws in place. The immense weight of the dragon is too much for the homong to resist, as he forcibly pushes him while the homong struggles to remain on his legs as he scrapes the grass off the ground. The homong slowly manages to halt the dragon in place, as it drops his body to the ground.

Then the second dragon attacks, biting the homong on his legs and holding tight. Much like the first dragon, the weight of it is too much for the homong to bear, as he loses balance and falls to the ground while the dragon keeps on moving, dragging his enormous body across the ground, destroying it all the while and taking the homong with him.

The toilet-paper dragons leave behind ruins of dirt as Neph, Grasshead and Yo'na just stare. Leaving the homong to the toilet-paper dragons, Neph pays attention to Yo'na, who is still lying on the dirty ground with broken legs. He crouches and spreads his arms, preparing to pick her up. He is careful not to hurt her, seeing as every small movement can cause her pain. Nevertheless, pain means nothing for the Natin.

He slowly prepares to pick her up as she looks at him, putting one hand under her head and the other under her knees. He begins to lift her.

"AAAK!" she winces in pain.

"Sorry," he tells her quickly and quietly.

He continues to lift her, slowly and steadily. He rises back up on his feet and proceeds to walk to Grasshead. He mounts Grasshead, all while still holding Yo'na carefully and cautiously. He prepares to ride on Grasshead to the homong. But realizing both his hands are occupied with holding Yo'na, he finds himself in a bit of a hassle. He looks around for a solution, but can't find any. Realizing this, Yo'na helps him by taking her hands and holding Neph by his neck, allowing one hand to let go while the other continues to hold her legs.

Now with one hand free, he grabs Grasshead by the grassy fur on his head and holds tight as Grasshead rides all the way to the homong. Neph needn't even command Grasshead where to go, as the latter's instincts alone guide him.

Riding towards the homong, they follow the trail of destruction to where he might be.

Finally reaching the end, they see the homong from afar, lying on the ground, entangled in the elongated marble bodies of the paper dragons. One still latches on to his ribs, and the other still latches on to his legs. The homong is completely immobilized.

They get close to the homong, standing in front of his face. They have nothing to fear, as the homong right now can't hurt them, let alone fight. Neph stares at the homong as the creature breathes slowly, savoring each of his last breaths. The homong emits a sound of sadness, as if it is crying. He doesn't even seem like he wants to fight back, and seems to have given up.

Neph stares at the now poor creature and starts to feel sad for him, a feeling he didn't exhibit several moments ago when he was determined to kill the creature, who was relentlessly trying to kill his allies. With a burning will to defend them, he didn't even think what kind of life the creature may have for himself, because all he wanted was to kill him. But now, staring at the miserable predicament he's in, Neph can't help but feel bad for any further action he will take on the formerly intimidating monstrosity, as he cannot bring himself to harm a creature that cannot defend itself, regardless of what or who it may be.

As he continues to stare at the creature with sorrowful eyes, the homong starts to breathe even slower than before, reaching his last moments in life. Neph moves his eyes to the ground, contemplating what the right action might be.

"Kill him," Yo'na suddenly says.

Neph stares at her with disbelief, and says nothing.

"You have to kill him," she continues to say.

Neph stares straight and looks at the ground. He sighs, still thinking of what to do. He raises his head, staring at the creature with an answer in mind.

"He's dying," he says in an unusually calm voice. "We should tend to bigger priorities."

Grasshead turns around and starts to walk away from the dying creature. Yo'na, being in no position to take action herself, will have to accept the choice Neph made, whether she is reluctant or not.

They continue to walk away from the homong, leaving him to his last several minutes of breath.

Although they have finished dealing with the biggest threat this expedition had to offer, the others are still fighting the main competitors of the enemy team. Sa'hi, who is still fighting No. 1, remains largely untouched since No. 1's blast nearly pierced Sang'ka'nik's brain. They seem to be nearly equally matched . . . or are they?

As their fight continues, No. 1 delivers a straight punch to Sa'hi. She counters by swiping her raj'or'shin just as he comes punching, conjuring a wall of wax around his arm, locking it in place.

He wastes no time in swiping his other hand at the wall, destroying it with a mighty blow of wind. Sa'hi immediately follows up with a swipe to his legs, conjuring a surface of wax that keeps his feet in place like concrete.

Without a moment to lose, Sa'hi quickly takes action before No. 1 has time to break free and thrusts the raj'or'shin forward at him. No. 1 tilts his body to the side while still locked in place by the wax around his feet and grabs the raj'or'shin by its harmless blade of wax. The sword misses its target as a jet of fire bursts out from the tip of it, nearly burning No. 1's head, but scorching his ear. No. 1 then clenches his fist holding the delicate but powerful raj'or'shin, breaking it.

Sa'hi is shocked over the sight of her candle-sword being snapped. In this split second, she leaves an opening as No. 1 breaks free from the wax holding his legs by raising his knee all the way to her face, sending her flying in the air. She lands on her feet and stands back up. Looking once again at No. 1, he can see that his rising knee was quite effective, as Sa'hi now has a piece of bone jutting from her lower jaw, cutting through the skin.

She spits out a mouthful of blood, just enough to fill a can. She looks back at No. 1 and breathes hard with his mouth wide open. Her red-stained teeth show as she regains her energy. Yet as she prepares herself for her next move, No. 1 stands there, doing nothing, waiting for something. His arrogance will be his demise. The same may go for all Airatsmeka . . . .

But he can only wait so long, so he spontaneously charges at Sa'hi while she's still breathing hard. Sa'hi immediately pulls herself together and grabs her anim'roo'shin and slashes at No. 1 as he gets closer. Seeing the attack at the last second, No. 1 breaks his charge and takes a big jump back. He manages to avoid a fatal attack, but instead takes a deep cut to his arm. The pain is too much for him to handle, as simply lifting his arm proves to be difficult.

Seeing as his now useless arm gets in the way, he grabs the arm's shoulder with his other hand, holds it as tight as he can, and starts to rip it off his body. He screams in pain and shuts his eyes tight as the skin and muscles tear off like fabric. He twitches it in different directions to loosen the bone. Sounds of cracks can be heard as he turns and twists it. Finally, after all that effort, he successfully removes his arm and immediately throws it away.

Sa'hi is shocked over the sight of his excruciating determination. She's never seen an Airatsmeka do anything like this. She knows the Airatsmeka are arrogant, but she didn't realize how committed they are to their agenda. That or they just disregard their own lives as much as they do the Natin, perceiving themselves as nothing but tools for their own cause.

She continues to stare at No. 1 taking care of himself, as he is not finished. As blood continues to spill from the hole in his exposed arm socket, he takes his remaining hand and conjures a black flame in it. With the flame in hand, he presses on the open wound as it burns, cauterizing it. Much like the last time, not a single sensation of pain is missed as he screams in agony. All while still holding his stump, No. 1 extinguishes the flame in his hand. He finally releases his hand, revealing a closed wound.

Now he is ready to fight again, relying completely on the strength of his one remaining arm. Once again, he returns to make eye contact with a shocked Sa'hi, smiling at her, as he is satisfied to once more be able to fight like a born warrior.

Sa'hi shakes her head quickly, leaving the shock and coming back to her senses. She now sees No. 1 and realizes that he is ready to fight once more. Seeing him in his unfortunate position, she realizes this is the ultimate moment to finish him. Even though he may not realize it himself, and even though he is confident in his skills, even if he has just one arm remaining, No. 1 is at a major disadvantage. After all, Sa'hi still has two arms.

Preparing herself for one last stand off, Sa'hi holds tight her anim'roo'shin and assumes a fighting position. No. 1, even though confident with just one arm, maintains discretion.

Sa'hi starts to spin her anim'roo'shin at her side. She spins it slowly, accelerating slowly with each spin. All the while, she walks sideways. Realizing this, No. 1 too walks sideways, only in the opposite direction.

As they both walk sideways as if it were a duel, Sa'hi shifts her anim'roo'shin to her other side, all while spinning it. It continues to accelerate in speed, slowly and carefully, as the wind around the two fighters can be felt getting stronger. She then raises the anim'roo'shin above her head, never stopping its spinning for even a tenth of a second. The halberd spins faster and faster with each second, with the wind getting even stronger as it blows hard on each fighters' hair. Seeing the events unfold, No. 1 foresees a very powerful attack from his opponent. He must plan his next move carefully, for it may be his victory, or just as equally, his demise.

A minute has passed, and Sa'hi still continues to spin her anim'roo'shin. The wind that blows from the halberd as it spins reaches the trees far away and behind the fighters. The leaves fly off the branches. Dust gets in the eyes of all who stand in the zone. Both fighters find it hard to keep their balance on the ground as the wind becomes a gale.

With his arm over his eyes, No. 1 finds it hard to keep an eye on Sa'hi as his vision is partially obscured by the dust in the air. Sa'hi is equally blinded by her own moves; squinting and struggling to not lose sight of her opponent as both her arms are occupied accumulating the strength to land the next blow.

Unable to accurately perceive Sa'hi's fighting stance through the cloud of dust that blinds both fighters, No. 1 believes he sees an opening to attack. With that, No. 1 prepares his next attack, and without a moment to lose, he takes action.

No. 1 charges with all his speed at Sa'hi. He cuts through the screen of dust, squinting his eyes to keep sight of his enemy. He charges faster than ever before, and with one remaining arm, he collects all the power that he has left into that arm and prepares to cut Sa'hi with a swipe of his claws. Reaching her, he is willing to give it all for one last strike.

But alas for him, No. 1 is too slow, as Sa'hi slashes her anim'roo'shin at him just as he nearly kills her. A mighty wind comes out of the halberd, blowing away everything in its path for a long distance. The wind destroys the upper layer of earth, as it reaches all the way to the trees, cutting bark and toppling some. The leaves of the trees can be seen flying in the air from the strength of the attack in a spectacle that looks like an enormous flock of green butterflies. And with all that destruction, the wind obscures the sight of anyone who has been caught in its wake.

Sa'hi closes her eyes tight so that the wind will not destroy them, holding her arm over them to defend them even more while grabbing on to her anim'roo'shin with her other hand as the wind tries to blow it away. She presses one leg hard against the ground to keep her balance, struggling to do so. She nearly falls, but manages to stay upright.

The wind lasts for a while, and Sa'hi cannot open her eyes to see its results, leaving her completely vulnerable for just this moment. Fortunately for her, nobody in the vicinity desires her death right now, as all those individuals are elsewhere fighting her allies.

The awesome wind finally subsides, and Sa'hi is free to use her eyes once more. She removes her arm from her face and opens her eyes. What she sees before her is a meadow in ruins. All the grass is nowhere to be seen; all that is left is a dig site of soil and earth.

She then looks down, and sees what she's been aiming for. No. 1, now nothing but the lower half of his body, still stands upright with a clean cut through the midsection. Where might the upper half be? Nobody knows, and probably never will.

Seconds later, the lower half of No. 1's body falls forward on the ground. Out of sheer exhaustion, Sa'hi drops the anim'roo'shin on the ground and falls hard on her butt. She breathes deeply over and over, slowly regaining her energy. She smiles to herself, knowing that her task in the expedition has been a success.

Sa'hi may have finished her part in the mission, but the others have not, as proven by Ka, who seems to be at a disadvantage with No. 3. Still running away on all three like some kind of animal, with one arm holding her broken ribs, Ka can't find a way to get rid of No. 3, even for just a while, to come up with a plan to turn the tide. No. 3 is merely a touch away from finishing off Ka, as her current condition prevents her from reaching her full speed.

Ka suddenly stops in a nice spot in the forest with a lot of space in the center surrounded by trees. She breathes hard, too hurt and too focused on staying alive as she fails to notice that saliva is dripping from her mouth.

She hears a noise from her back. She quickly looks back since she knows who's coming behind her. It is No. 3, who has finally managed to gain on Ka.

Ka quickly gets back on three limbs, still holding her ribs with the one arm, and starts to back away from No. 3. She continues to back away, without giving a thought to when she has to stop, never removing her eyes from her enemy. No. 3 slowly walks towards Ka, too confident that she already has her prize.

Ka keeps backing away until she eventually hits a tree. Now cornered and with nowhere to run, Ka stares deep into the eyes of her enemy as she is about to take her last breath, for even in defeat, the Natin show neither fear nor cowardice, as facing death is the true warrior's leave.

Nonetheless, No. 3 could care less about her creed. She continues to walk to her slowly, as she has no doubt that she is the victor. She then smiles and laughs a gentle evil laugh. A moment away from killing Ka, she conjures a black saber in her hand, ready to cut her throat or slice her head clean off her body. Getting ever so close to

Ka with each step, with a blade already in hand, all hope seems lost.

And then, Ka smirks. In the face of death, she just decides to smirk. No. 3 is distracted, wondering what her prey may be thinking. She stops in her place and finds herself in disbelief, as her expression silently asks "what's going on?"

Ka then gently points with her nose at the subject of her sudden interest. No. 3 looks back to see what may have gotten Ka so excited. And there, just behind her, sticking firmly to a tree, she sees what it is. Now looking at it, No. 3 finds herself going from a state of disbelief to a state of distress. The tides change in Ka's favor as No. 3 enters a difficult predicament, staring at that one thing that will end her if she does not act fast.

A hive of nexapis! An ugly hive that looks like a small pile of black hay, constructed from the dried-out carcasses of the surrounding animals, sticking crudely like glue onto the tree and containing the deadliest bee-like insects that the Novaverse has to offer.

Twice the size of a normal wasp and black as the hive that they come from, the nexapis looks like a mess of an insect, having spider legs shaped like knives, the wings of a dragonfly, and a long and narrow thorax that moves flexibly like a noodle. Yet with this mixture of characteristics, the head looks no different than that of a regular bee. But the most frightening feature of all is their sting.

The stinger that sits firmly on the edge of the thorax, always outside without ever needing to be unsheathed, slim as the needle of a syringe. A single sting that hurts as much as a salt-coated shard of glass can spread gangrene over an arm in an hour, but many stings in a small period of time and the victim is dead before they even realize it. More so, unlike the bees that heratrang'ga pan has to offer, the nexapis don't die when they sting, making them all the more deadly.

But despite how dangerous they may be, they do produce really delicious honey. Black as tar with a vague taste of marmalade and quince, the honey, which is known as okei'ni, is harvested by the Natin regularly and is a true delicacy among them.

But this particular hive of nexapis that No. 3 faces aren't here to give their honey. Falling under Ka's command, they continue doing as they will, waiting for the right moment to come out.

No. 3 quickly turns her attention back to Ka. Still smirking, Ka stares at No. 3's sorry face one last time before she finishes her off. And with that, she whistles a short whistle.

The nexapis come swarming out of their hive in droves. No. 3 starts to run away, but before she can get far enough, the swarm envelops her.

In a miserable attempt to fend off the nexapis, No. 3 swings her hands thoughtlessly at the air just to free herself, staggering in different directions all the while. She screams as the painful stings find every point of her body. No. 3 continues to helplessly fight the swarm, but all attempts by her are futile as the swarm easily overcomes her with its numbers, and as they continue to kill her slowly, Ka simply watches from the side, knowing that there is no longer any competition, and her job will soon be finished.

With no more energy left and no more power to fight, No. 3 stops staggering and stands still. She drops her arms, no longer waving her hands at the swarm. She just stands there, and slowly leans forward. She then falls to her knees, and remains like this for another while, slowly leaning forward once more. She then finally falls to the ground as the swarm continues to raid her poor body, even when she can no longer retaliate. Laying down on her front helplessly and nearly dead, all she can do is breathe as she slowly awaits death's sweet embrace.

The swarm continues to obscure the sight of the near-dead No. 3, as Ka slowly walks towards her. The swarm clears a path for Ka, splitting in half as she simply walks between the many nexapis as if she were some kind of Moses. Standing right atop No. 3, she looks at her pathetic existence one more time before killing her, thinking how miserable she and her people are.

But her pity doesn't last too long, as Ka mounts her, sitting firmly on her back. She pulls No. 3's hair with one hand, pulling her head back as well, and takes the sharp unattended nail on her index finger of her other hand, inserts it in the far left side of her neck, and forcibly pushes it through her flesh all the way to the other side, slitting her throat. Now made into one of those candy dispensers, Ka lets go of No. 3's hair as her head falls face forward on the grass as blood continues to spill from her open throat, all while the swarm is still there, flying in the air and spectating the final moments of the fight.

Ka gets up and looks to her side. She sighs, exhausted from the fight, wondering what the others are doing. How are they doing? Do they need help? She stands still and relaxes for a bit just before moving on to help her friends, as the fight took a lot from here. Despite this, she can't help but feel concerned about whether they're alive or not.

So'krang is still fighting No. 4. There they stand, facing each other in some random area in the forest, with no knowledge of how close or far their allies stand from them. They continue to fight.

Filled with cuts and bruises all over his body, So'krang sees not a second to relent as he charges at an equally injured No. 4, his claymore at hand, ready to vanquish the enemy. Close enough, he spins around and delivers a mighty slash. No. 4 easily dodges the attack by taking a small jump back, but So'krang continues his assault by spinning again, jumping up half-spin and delivering an overhead chop. So'krang once more misses the attack as No. 4 simply sidesteps to dodge it, embedding his claymore in the ground. He pulls the claymore out of the ground with all his might, holds it high in the air, and swings it forward as fast as he can to sink it deep into the enemy's flesh.

But just before the blow is struck, No. 4 conjures a black shield onto her forearm. Harder than diamond, the shield shatters the claymore as soon as it comes into contact with it, sending shards of metal flying in the air.

"BAK!" So'krang yells angrily, staring with disbelief at his broken sword.

Now distracted, So'krang leaves an opening for attack as no.4 kicks him hard in the chest, sending him flying through the air just above the ground. Landing on his back, So'krang quickly rolls back and stands back up on his feet.

But even when he is still able to stand upright, So'krang no longer has the means to fight, as whatever weapons he had at his disposal are no longer. He quickly realizes that he needs to flee the zone and come up with an effective plan to defeat his enemy or this could very well be his last fight. Then again, he's not so sure that he can escape the enemy, as he is not built for speed, and the Airatsmeka are more than capable of gaining on most Natin. Even at a disadvantage, So'krang tries not to be pessimistic, but he can't see himself winning this fight.

"SO'KRANG!" a voice shouts from behind.

So'krang doesn't even think as to look back to see whose calling him.

Just as luck would have it, there stands Sang'ka'nik, still without his arms and with No. 2 nowhere in sight.

With no better plan, So'krang immediately runs as fast as he can to Sang'ka'nik. Sang'ka'nik crouches, preparing for a fast-approaching So'krang. No. 4 follows up by running even faster to both of them, as she will not allow them to execute whatever they're planning.

Just as So'krang gets close enough to Sang'ka'nik, he leaps forward and flips in the air, just as No. 4 too leaps forward with even greater might, propelling her like a bullet.

They're both airborne just above the ground, as No. 4 quickly closes the gap between them. Nearly colliding above Sang'ka'nik's back, No. 4 is a touch away from killing So'krang, as a sword materializes from nowhere in So'krang's hand, emitting a purple mist. So'krang continues to flip in the air, using the momentum to decapitate a fast-approaching No. 4.

No. 4's body and severed head continue to fly forward in air, fall hard on the ground and roll away until the parts lose speed and stop by themselves.

So'krang, now once more on standing on the ground, looks at the remains of No. 4. He then looks at Sang'ka'nik, minding not his missing arms as he is quite familiar with these kinds of situations.

"Skama," So'krang thanks him, smiling all the while.

"Ba yai," Sang'ka'nik responds back, smiling too.

Their exchange of gratitude does not last long, as a trembling noise can suddenly be heard in the background. They immediately assume a combat-ready position and prepare for what's coming to them.

As the noise gets stronger, it is obvious that it is coming from behind So'krang. And as it gets stronger, so does the danger accompanying it.

Without even looking back, So'krang just jumps to the side as a black beam of smoke flies forward, piercing everything in its path.

So'krang may have been responsive enough to dodge the attack, but Sang'ka'nik is not, as now he has a big gaping hole in his chest that drops no blood, like in the cartoons.

He stands there for a while idly, with a seemingly dead expression. He then falls to his knees, and then on his face.

From out of nowhere, No. 2 suddenly enters the area, walking slowly from where the beam came. He looks at Sang'ka'nik's body lying on the ground. He walks slowly to it, without any concern whatsoever. He crouches, pulls his head by the hair, and stares at his lifeless expression.

Declaring him dead, No. 2 is more than satisfied over his performance and that he finally got the job done. He stands back up, puts a stupid smile on his face, and starts walking away, dragging Sang'ka'nik's by the hair.

As Sang'ka'nik's body leaves a trail on the ground as it is being dragged, No. 2 is almost out of the area. Before he can go any further, he suddenly hears a running sound behind him. A fifth of a second has barely passed, and No. 2 immediately becomes alert, wiping off that grin on his face and quickly turning his head around. Before he can react, a sword pierces his head through his eye.

There stands So'krang, holding the sword he got from Sang'ka'nik's hammerspace as it soaks itself in No. 2's brain matter. Blood dripping from both holes on its head, with the blade still impaled in his skull, So'krang still holds the sword with No. 2 still standing upright. Slowly but surely, No. 2 lets go of Sang'ka'nik's hair. So'krang starts to feel his weight pulling down the blade. Realizing that No. 2 is done for, he lets go the sword as No. 2 falls to the ground, still with the sword in his eye.

Sang'ka'nik then prepares to get up. Having no arms and a perfect circle for a wound in his chest, he balances himself using his head and pushes himself upwards with his legs, staggering while getting up. Standing up once more and still alive, he takes a deep breath, hoping that the expedition is finally over, taking a small break before continuing on to help his friends if needed, but he just hopes that he doesn't have to.

"HEY!" a voice can suddenly be heard from afar.

So'krang and Sang'ka'nik both look in the direction of the voice. There, they can see a figure approaching. A figure of what appears to be a green creature with a rider on top of it. It immediately becomes obvious to them that it could be no other than Neph riding on Grasshead. But what they didn't expect to see is that he is holding Yo'na in his arms.

Eventually, he reaches the two, and upon arriving, everyone starts looking at each other. Neph stares at So'krang; Yo'na looks at Sang'ka'nik; Grasshead gazes at everyone. Everyone acknowledges each other's bad but tolerable condition, and looking at each other's state, they all hope together that it is over, without ever saying a single word. But then Neph goes to look at Sang'ka'nik, who catches his attention with his unusual battle wounds. Neph observes him with disbelief.

"You seem to be in pretty bad shape," Neph tells him in a playful manner.

"Don't worry. I'll just get new ones," Sang'ka'nik responds humorously.

Neph looks around him, trying to estimate the situation, thinking on what to do next. He looks at Yo'na as he still holds her, who remains quiet all the while. He then turns his attention to So'krang.

"We should probably find the others," Neph tells with him mild uncertainty.

"I see no better plan," So'krang responds to him conclusively.

And with that, they leave the area in search of their teammates. They may not know it yet, but the expedition is already over. And with all Airatsmeka dead, all that is left is to group up and leave to the closest clan, concluding yet another day in their tak'nen lives.

CHAPTER XIX

IN THE HOSPITAL OF A GHOST TOWN . . . TRYING TO FIGURE OUT THE FLAVOR OF THIS JUICE

I find myself in the hospital once more, only this time I'm not lying in a pit of supposedly therapeutic balls.

We walked an entire day to reach the clan of Nikma, located somewhere in Dobiya, obviously, since I haven't left the continent.

Upon making our entrance into the city, we escorted ourselves all the way to the hospital, all bloody and bruised with no helping hand to come to our aid. Everyone just stared for a second and moved on with their personal duties. Of course, how many times a day does everyone get to see a bunch of near-dead warriors strolling down the street? All the time, apparently. After all, this is just another end of another random expedition.

But once we finally got to the hospital, everyone registered and then took seats to wait for the doctors to call us to surgery. Approximately two hours later, we're all escorted by staff members to different rooms in the hospital all at once. Weirdly enough, when I entered the surgery room, which looks no different than the surgery rooms I know, the doctors told me that I have no wounds to treat. Apparently, all my wounds disappeared by themselves. This had also been the case when I broke my neck. I was supposed to be in the hospital for six weeks which ended being only one. Guess I have some kind of healing factor, a healing factor that should've manifested when I got these scars, but better late than never, I guess.

Being the only one not in surgery, time didn't fly swiftly for me because I wasn't on anesthetics as I was forced to wait for the others. The doctors said that the surgery should take about sixteen hours. It should be time now.

But while I wait, I have to find something to do in this near-empty hospital. In fact, it's not just the hospital. It's the entire city. The entire place is like a ghost town. You're likely to see one person walking down a single street, but the rest is mostly vacant. I can't imagine how bored the shopkeepers here must be. I mean, the hospital, and by extension the city, is starting to fill up with people just now.

Of course, this was the thing that bothered me when I first laid eyes on this place. So'krang started to explain to me, naturally by using the phrase "you see," that the Nikma'ga are nocturnal warriors. Asleep at day and active at night, they use the darkness to take out the enemy when the enemy's vision is the weakest. Basically, they're ninjas . . . or the closest thing there is to one here, at least.

So'krang also went on to explain that the Nikma'ga are a special type of tak'nen that are referred to as owaika, tak'nen that aren't normally drafted into random expeditions consisting of a seven-man group, but are assigned to special tasks. Turns out that the girl I met back in Withers Woods alongside So'krang and clay-guy are one of those kinds. What was her name again? Shin-something or whatever.

That aside, So'krang finished by saying that the only ones that can fight alongside the Nikma'ga are the Kapen'ga, who can sleep for as much as four days and stay awake for as much as a week.

But with it being eleven p.m. already, the bats are starting to come out of their caves. With that, it's becoming noisier in here. In retrospect, I think I prefer the silence. It was so peaceful.

But right now that is the least of my complaints, as right now I am staring at a series of shelves embedded in a wall that contain bottles of exotic juices that So'krang introduced me to during one of my hospitalizations. Of course, in a society where they don't use money, anyone can just grab a bottle without too many complications, so there's no need for a vending machine.

The bottles came in various colors, supposedly indicating what flavor they are. I'm pretty sure the flavor is inscribed on the bottles, but with the text being in hang'pan'rika, I have no idea what it says.

I stare thoroughly at all the bottles, one after the other. Looking at the multitude of colors of different hues, I try to figure out what the flavors may be. I really don't want to end up drinking papaya juice. Hopefully there isn't one.

I look at one bottle that has the colors blue and light pink merging together like the yin and yang symbol. I assume that it might be litchi and blueberries. I grab that one for So'krang, with the hopes that he won't have a problem with it, since I'm not entirely sure how he likes his juice.

And then came my selection. I look for a juice that will suit my taste. Unfortunately, I don't know what to expect from this variety. I don't want to waste too much time, so I grab a bottle on the lowest shelf. It has the colors green and red also merging like the yin and yang symbol, much like the other bottle I have for So'krang. The colors could mean anything. It could be green apple with cherries or pear with strawberries.

As I try to figure out what the flavor for this juice is, all of a sudden a random patient strolls down the hall on an electric wheelchair. Again, nobody has to pay for anything, so everyone gets to ride on a wheelchair using a joystick, rather than the boring and hand-hurting manual ones.

Rather than continuing to strain my brain on what the inscription says on the bottle, I stop the patient, intending to ask what the hell the bottle says.

"Hey!" I call him.

The man stops in his place. He stares at me with uninterested eyes. Understandably, since he must be on painkillers or something. Nevertheless, he is generous enough to stop in the first place and listen to what I have to say. I approach him.

"What flavor is this?" I ask him nicely while showing him the text on the bottle.

The man on the wheelchair grabs the bottle and adjusts it so that he can see it better.

"Rambutan," he says simply while handing me back the bottle.

I take back the bottle, and the man moves on.

"The fuck's a rambutan?" I mutter to myself.

I imagine it must be some kind of exotic fruit I never heard of, much like the mango-whatever. I decide not to waste time and take the risk in hopes that it will taste good, and continue on my way to So'krang's room.

I approach the elevator. The door to it is wide, probably the width of three regular elevator doors. Of course, I'm not surprised considering all the buildings in the Novaverse are also wide. Basically, everything here is wide architecture.

I call it, and when it finally gets to me it opens up vertically, also understandable considering that it's that wide. There is a lot of space inside it too. Enough to probably hold a hundred people . . . or twenty hiphomoys, depending on your cargo.

Regardless, I enter the elevator. Being in the clan of Nikma, it is mostly empty. There are three other people, distributed randomly in the vast space which is this elevator. One of them has a sash with a neck tattoo like all the other sash wearers, indicating that he's a doctor. Of course, there's no differentiation between functions, so he could also be an orderly or a nurse or . . . something else that works in a hospital. And the other two are . . . well . . . other Natin. The only thing I can tell about them is that they're not from the same clan, judging by their neck tattoos.

I finally reach the floor where So'krang is located. After I witness the magnificent motion which is the elevator door opening up vertically, I leave it and try to figure out where I must go as it closes down.

Being unable to read hang'pan'rika, I have no idea what department this is. Of course, I couldn't care less as I walk down the corridors, looking inside rooms as I pass by them to find So'krang.

And finally, I did. Seeing him, I enter the room.

There he is, shirtless and mostly inside a pool of white balls, but he made sure enough of him was out of it so that everyone can look in awe at his chest hair. His body, clean from wounds, bears no indication that he was in battle. A tube can be seen entering the pool from a sack hanging on a pole, most likely painkillers. To the side of his pool is, of course, my loyal Grasshead, napping.

"Everything all right?" I ask him gently, considering his state.

"Painkillers don't do bak to ease the pain," he says in a drowsy tone, blinking hard for some reason.

"Looking at you, it doesn't seem like it."

Looking at him, I can't help but imagine how tedious it must be undergoing all this after every expedition. Although if he keeps doing this then I guess he doesn't really have a problem with it.

"I brought you some juice," I tell him.

"Thanks," he tells me.

I throw the pink and blue bottle onto the pool of balls. The bottles lands softly right in front of So'krang, with all the balls cushioning its fall.

So'krang lifts his hand beyond the balls and picks up the bottle. He brings it closer to his eyes to look at the text, as he would rather not move in his state.

"This is gum and island punch," he says in a complaining tone.

"That's what it is?" I respond, surprised. "I thought it was litchi and blueberries."

"I would prefer mangosteen. But I guess this will have to suffice."

So'krang opens the bottle and immediately starts drinking.

I grab a chair from the side and sit on it right in front of So'krang's pool. As I stare at him from above, looking at him inside the pool at floor-level, I try to come up with ideas to lighten up his mood.

I find that I don't have anything particular to talk about, although I insist on finding a subject of sorts.

"So what are your plans after this?" I ask him.

"I should be out in approximately four hours or so," he goes on to say, still in pain. "As soon as I'm done with this, the Awari'ga should already have all the information about the expedition. And then I need to get the report done. Then, it's back home to Ka'ka'pan."

"Nice," I tell him indifferently.

"What about you?"

"I'm coming back home with you, as usual. Was I supposed to have any special plans of my own?"

So'krang looks at me with half-closed eyes. Clearly, he's not in the mood for any jokes or sarcastic remarks. I can clearly tell he's in pain.

"Forget I asked," he says, mildly annoyed.

He sinks a little bit deeper into the pool to adjust his comfort.

We remain silent for a while. I didn't know if I should say anything because he didn't look like he was in the mood for further conversation. A friend should still find ways to make things better for another friend, and silence won't help with that.

"If you want, I could get you the flavor you like," I start to tell him. "Mangosteen was it, ri—"

"I want some silence now," he interrupts me crudely.

Apparently, talking isn't a good choice. I suppose I can relate. I also wish for quiet when I'm pissed. He's also in pain so that's another thing. I should've thought this through.

I sigh, get up from the chair I was sitting on, and prepare to leave the room so So'krang can be by himself. Hope he can be a little more cooperative with doctors if not me, even in his mood.

"Take care of Grasshead, will ya?" I ask him as I leave the room.

Just outside the room, I look to my sides, figuring out what to do, what I must do. Looking to the right, doesn't look I have many options.

"Wo," I hear a soft voice to my left. "Neph."

Hearing my name, I turn my head left to see who's calling me.

And there I see Yomak Nayan, beautiful as ever and rolling on an electric wheelchair.

As for hospital attire, she wore a white we'jei, proving that the we'jei is popular even beyond everyday needs. The pants she was wearing look like they are made from the same material, thin as rice paper but wide like the rekarakib, only not thick and heavy. The legs are rolled up to make room for the cast, which is a kind of cast I haven't seen yet. Weird enough as it may sound considering the previous three times I've been in the hospital, but it was either because I wasn't paying attention or there weren't any to look at.

The cast is black and narrow, and isn't even made of plaster, but looks more like plastic or silicone. I can't really figure out the functionality of this special cast, but it doesn't look something that can hold her legs in place and inhibit her movement. Then again, it is the Novaverse. The technology here is pretty advanced, even though they prefer to ride mounts instead of driving cars. There's probably a history to that but if it works for them then there shouldn't be much to complain about.

"Hey," I say as I hide the joy of seeing her, accompanied by a friendly smirk.

She rolls closer to me with her wheelchair. I stand tall in front of her as she sits comfortably in that chair of hers. Looking into her beautiful eyes is like staring at the Caribbean Sea. She's all smiley and positive, never even for a second thinking about removing that smile from her pretty face. Just looking at her you can tell how kind her heart is . . . unless you're fighting her, in which case she won't be so friendly as she turns into a pink goddess of destruction.

Regardless, I think she's quite happy to see me, judging by her smile. Unless of course that's how she greets everyone, in which case I'm not so special.

"Nice cast," I tell her in a friendly way. "How are your legs doing?"

"I should be standing again in a few hours," she says cheerfully, "but if it weren't for you, it would've been my entire body."

"I just did what had to be done," I reply, pretending like my actions back then weren't anything special.

She giggles in response, clearly realizing that modesty isn't well hidden.

"You know, I used to think like all the rest," she adds, "that you were just another filthy heranga that will contaminate us with his hatred. Everyone said that the decision of mark'nan anji akib'satra would bring a plague to this world. But you're more than what I expected. You might actually have a place here."

"Who's anji akib'satra?" I ask, looking to the side, trying to remember. "OH, right it's the . . . um . . . the clanmistress that needs permission to read minds. Haven't heard that one before. Heh."

She giggles even more. She then looks at me quietly for a while with those beautiful eyes that I just can't stop noticing, probably trying to figure out what kind of a person I am. I, too, look back at her with silence, as I assume she prepares to say something.

"I would like to know who you are," she suddenly says. "There's a lot I want to talk to you about."

She then reaches for the pocket in her pants and takes out a thingy that looks like a circular flash drive, kind of like those things that So'krang puts in his TV, only shorter.

As she holds it in her hand, I try to figure out what the hell that thing is. Hopefully it's not another television channel.

Naturally, I take it, as this is what one does when handed something.

"What are you doing?" she says, surprised and giggling into her speech. "Give it back."

"But you gave it to me," I reply defensively, realizing that I'm doing something wrong. "Don't you want me to have it?"

"No. you weren't supposed to take it. Do you even know what this is?"

"Uh . . . a television channel?"

Once again, she giggles, even harder than before, but only loud enough for the two of us to hear. Never have I met a girl that laughs at my behavior so much, nor have I met one that likes to laugh so much. Maybe all this time I was just at the wrong place . . . until now.

"Never mind," she says with a smile ever so big. "Give it back to me."

She reaches out to my open palm to take back her thingy and put it back in her pocket.

"Meet me in the airport of the clan of Karin," she adds. "You'll see me there."

And just like that, she turns her wheelchair around and goes on her way, leaving me with only the desire to talk to her even more.

"Why can't we talk now?" I ask her, realizing the absurdity of the situation.

"I want to rest," she tells me as she keeps moving on. "Then I'm leaving."

"How will I find you?"

"It shouldn't be too hard. Trust me."

I stare at the back of her wheelchair as she leaves, rolling down the corridor, thinking about her vague answer and feeling like the luckiest guy in this world for having such a beautiful girl desire my presence. Even with how complicated she presents the idea of finding her among so many people in an airport of wagon-dragons like some kind of Waldo, I will do what it takes to find her, be it easy or hard, as I, too, wish to know her more. Never have I wanted so badly to be together with a girl, more than any other girl I've met in my life, and judging by her constant smiling, she probably feels the same.

Regardless, even with all her kindness and how sweet she is, smiling all the time and giggling, being able to see the beauty beneath one's anger and look beyond one's flaws, she is no different than any other Natin, as shown by her hatred against the heranga. A hatred shared by all Natin like it is injected into them at a young age, running in their bloodstream like some kind of vaccine, or poison in this case. A poison that not only do they ignore, but also take pride in, much like everything else they do. I don't think she would've treated me as she does if I were any other human, but I'm glad she won't show that side of her too much to me.

While I stand here, thinking about all these things, she's already left my sight. I stand by myself, trying to figure out what I should do next. Go back to So'krang? Take a walk in the streets? Pester the doctors? That last option could be quite satisfying if it weren't unethical.

But while I ponder the options, I catch a figure to my right in my peripheral vision. I look to my side and I see Sang'ka'nik, dressed in casual patient attire, completely "armed" and with no giant hole in his chest like some cartoon character who took a cannonball. I stare at him with surprise, as I thought all the others had already left.

"Late-guy!" I remark jokingly, surprised to see him whole once more. "I see they got you new arms."

"It's Sang'ka'nik," he responds seriously, failing to realize my friendly joke. "And yes, these work just like my original ones."

He then straightens out his right arm, and then bends it backwards with the other arm, stretching it like rubber. He then twists it to further demonstrate his elasticity. Finally, he lets go as the arm immediately reverts to its normal self, with no indication of any kind of stretchiness.

"I just wish I didn't have to replace them," he says with confidence, but with a bit of sadness.

It only goes to show that despite all this advanced technology, it can't bring back what was . . . but only recreate it. I don't blame him. If I had to replace my arms then I would be satisfied that they're fully functional, but I'd have to live with the knowledge and memory that these are not my arms, but prosthetics, and that it just won't be the same again. Then again, in his line of work, it is inevitable. So he knew this might happen. Then what is he complaining about?

"But you got the affection of a karin'ga. Well done, akka," he says excitedly, suddenly raising his mood. "I haven't had one for myself yet. But a karin'ga finding interest in a heranga? That's just preposterous. Guess you are more than what you seem if you managed to do that. Just make sure Sima Brak doesn't get her." He then sighs in a despondent manner, further indicating his jealousy. Nonetheless, he also displayed happiness for me, as he keeps a somewhat happy expression.

"Well, I need to leave to soon," he starts to say. "It was a pleasure knowing you and working with you. Hope we can meet again in the future."

He then pats me on the back and goes on his way. I stare as he leaves, thinking about Yomak Nayan and what to expect from her when I meet her again in her home. Truth is, I don't know what to expect, but judging from the smile on her face every time she sees me, I can only imagine that it'll be good. She's literally the girl of my dreams. And I, for once in my life, finally have something to look forward to. Slowly and surely, I will find a home in this new world, a home that I would actually embrace, rather than run away from.

But hopes aside, what was that he said about Sima Brak? I still have no idea what this thing is, but at least I got one more tidbit as to what it's all about. I need to kill it to gain the approval of the people and it's somehow associated with Yomak Nayan. I think it's time I actually started worrying about this Sima Brak, but for other reasons: to find shortcuts and avoid getting thrown back into the cage. On the other hand, maybe Yomak Nayan can handle herself. She doesn't seem too concerned about it, or anything else for that matter.

I think I'll focus on Yomak Nayan for the time being. She's what's important right now, after all.

CHAPTER XX

NOVAVERSIAN TECHNOLOGY . . . IS WEIRD

I wake up on the couch at So'krang's house since he has no extra bed. It's clearly morning, although I don't know the exact hour seeing as there's no clock next to me.

I move to a sitting position. My eyes barely open since I'm not entirely awake. I look down at the floor beneath, and I see Grasshead sleeping on the carpet.

Due to the relationship between me and Grasshead, So'krang allows him to sleep in the house so he won't feel abandoned. It wouldn't matter much, because even when we're separated, we're always together. If So'krang knew this maybe he would reconsider this decision, but I don't think it's that much of a deal to him. Not even Franuk gets these kinds of privileges, but that's probably just because he's more of an "outside dog."

Moving on, I get up from the couch and make my way to the kitchen quietly to avoid waking up Grasshead. I'm still wearing the same dirty clothes from the last fight, since I don't have anything else. With that in mind, if I want to meet Yomak Nayan, I should get myself new clothes. Torn clothes that serve as both battle gear and casual wear and reeks of sweat won't leave much of an impression, even if that's what the Natin wear on a daily basis.

Looking around, I can't see So'krang anywhere. There wasn't even a cereal bowl or the likes to indicate that he had been here, be it on the table or in the sink. It's rather quiet too, with only Grasshead snoring in the background. I suspect he might be in his room.

I climb up the stairs, seeing as that would be where his room is. Now on the second floor, I look around and see a number of doors; where they lead to I do not know. One possibly leads to the bathroom, while another one probably leads to a laundry room or something. As for the other doors, I have no idea. But I can't imagine one of them leads into a guest room considering that I slept on the couch.

All the doors are closed except for one. If that is So'krang's room, then he probably has nothing to hide. I go over there to see what's inside. As I anticipated, it is So'krang's room, complete with everything one would expect from a couple's room. You got the king-sized bed for the couple, a giant mahogany closet to contain all the clothing and everything between those, although there isn't a TV in front of the bed like how most have in modern times.

Weirdly enough, I find him in an unusual state. I see him at the corner of his room, shirtless with only long pants on, dunking his head in some kind of wide short bucket, big enough for two people to put their heads in it, filled with some kind of opaque metallic liquid. The bucket's exterior design looks like that of a purple computer chip and the liquid is nearly spilling out of it because it's filled entirely. I can't imagine he's trying to drown himself. I can't imagine he's apple bobbing either.

I walk over. I try to understand what he's doing, but I haven't got a clue. Naturally, since Natin technology isn't fully understood to me.

I think whether it would be the right thing to bother him. Maybe he's doing something important, although I can't tell if he's even alive. So'krang isn't the kind of person to rush to kill himself. As I continue to ponder whether he's alive or not, I suddenly see bubbles coming out of the liquid. So'krang definitely isn't dead, and clearly there is no place for worry.

Although I'm still not sure what's going on, I still think whether I should bother him with my matters. Then again, I have a schedule of own to attend to, and there's no way So'krang would be mad at me for something so trivial.

"So'krang?" I call, uncertain about what's going on.

With his ears outside the liquid, he hears my call. He takes his head out of the bucket as the liquid spills from his face. He wipes his eyes and shakes his head a bit, further drying himself. Finally opening his eyes, he looks at me as he holds the rim of the bucket. He says nothing, most likely waiting for whatever I have to say as he stares at me with a face that nearly melts from fatigue. With dark circles around barely open eyes and an inverted smile that looks like it's being pulled down by weights, it's probably not the best time to talk to him, but this won't take much.

"You tryin' t'drown yourself?" I wittily ask him in my usual fashion.

"I'm writing the report for the last expedition," he tells me in a drowsy and uninterested way.

"By drowning yourself?"

"This is the psychopool. This is how we do things. It's our equivalent of what you know as the internet."

"Hmm. So the psychopool is the internet, huh? I heard that word before, but it sounded more like some kind of . . . well . . . something that isn't the Novaversian web."

"I'm not in the mood right now, Neph." His tone changes to sound a bit agitated. "I've been working on this bak for the last half day. I've got to finish this by night."

"Yeah, sorry. Didn't mean to piss you off."

We look at each other as we remain quiet. Looking at his face, I can clearly tell he's not in the mood. The guy hasn't had too much sleep with all this leader commitment, if at all. I, on the other hand, think that a witty trade of words might cheer him up. It's clearly not. I should give him some space, but only once I'm done with the things on my mind.

"Where's Ka'ka'pan?" I ask him, toning down my attitude, considerate of his state.

"She's on an expedition," he tells me plainly and tired.

"I see."

I remain quiet for a small while, thinking about what kind of expedition she's in, even though there isn't much to imagine, but it would it be nice to show that I'm interested, since I know how much he loves and cares about her. Hopefully that made him feel better, even in his current state, but I have to get on with my plans.

"Listen, I plan on going to the clan of Karin," I tell him.

"To meet that Karin'ga," he says, intrigued while a slight smirk appears on his face. "You are a lucky bak'nen."

"Late-guy said something similar."

"You'll understand when you get there."

I think about that statement for a small moment, saying nothing in response.

"Anyways," I continue from where I left, "just thought you should know."

"No problem," he simply responds, showing no interest in my doings.

I prepare to leave his room. But before I even take a step from where I'm standing, I think for a while. I am not whole with this conversation. Like something is missing. Even though I am more than eager to meet Yomak Nayan already, I can't just leave without completing this conversation, even though on So'krang's side there is nothing more to add, nor to receive.

"Am I going to be OK?" I ask, a bit worried. "I mean, I won't get slaughtered out there, will I?"

"You're a part of us now; get used to this already," he responds, tired and grumpy. "The Natin don't just kill whoever they want whenever they feel like it, even if it's a heranga."

"Doesn't seem like it," I jokingly add to the conversation.

He doesn't seem so happy about that statement, let alone show any cooperation whatsoever. Naturally, knowing how tired he is, and he's showing a face that tells that he just wants to get some sleep. I can't help but try to cheer him up with my quips, which is actually a passive-aggressive behavior that serves me as release from that anger I've accumulated all these years. I don't think I should be releasing them on So'krang, even if they only seem to cheer him up, because they're supposed to be funny. I should be releasing them on the heranga. But they're not around, are they?

"You gonna do OK without me?" I jokingly ask him.

"I've been fine without you for twenty-three years," he responds jokingly while popping a smirk. "I think I can take care of myself. Besides, we could use some separate time from each other."

"Yeah . . . I guess you're right."

Once again, I can't help but quip. It's not something deliberate, but just a desire to make friends. I guess collecting all that anger all of those years seems to take an effect on it. Nevertheless, I should keep it more in check. At least he smiled at that one.

"Well . . . ," I go on to say, "I'd best get a move on."

And with that, I leave straight out of the door to the room. So'krang didn't even say a word, preferring to sleep rather than write that damn report, as he prepares to sink his head once more into the psychopool.

"Oh . . . uh . . . ," I am suddenly reminded to say, peeking from the edge of the door.

So'krang couldn't even get back to writing the report, keeping his head dry as he turns around and looks at me, still holding the rim of the bucket.

"Yomak Nayan showed me this . . . thingy," I start to say. "At first I thought she was giving it to me. I guess there was some kind of misunderstanding between us since she took it back."

"What is this thing you're talking about?" So'krang asks, sounding even drowsier than before. "What did it look like?"

"Well uh . . . it looked kinda like those small cylinders you put into your TV. Maybe even smaller."

"Is it the yopak'orim you're perhaps referring to?"

"Is that what it's called?"

"It's how we communicate across long distances. Similar to how the heranga use the telephone."

"How the hell do you use that? Shove it in your ear?"

"In order to use it you need an orim'satra, or a station. These can be found anywhere. You can find one on the streets, and you can even get one for your house. There's mine over there."

So'krang then points at a counter right next to his bed, like everyone has. On the counter, I see a device that bears a strong resemblance to an answering machine, only instead of buttons there's a circular port right in the middle of it. Of course, I couldn't see the station in its original state because this one already had So'krang's whatever-it's-called embedded in it. Seeing as the conversation had continued beyond what I expected, I make my way back into the room

"Doesn't it come with a handle or something?" I ask, mildly disappointed in its design as I walk back to So'krang's side.

"Is it supposed to?" So'krang responds with a passive-aggressive rhetorical question, indicating his growing impatience.

"So anyone could just listen on your private matters?"

"If you don't like people listening to your conversations, then wait until you get home."

"Hmm. I don't know what principles your telephone is based on, but whoever invented it clearly didn't know what privacy is."

So'krang just stares at me, without saying a word, clearly too tired to bother with my complaints about their technology, and also probably because there is no better response.

But I think about this for a second. How the Natin could easily just speak aloud their stuff, having others listen in on whatever they're discussing with the other side. Clearly it doesn't bother them. Do they have nothing to hide? I know I wouldn't want anyone just listening to what I have to say with whomever I'm speaking to on the phone. Just goes to show how different this culture is from the one I grew up in. Don't know if I should see this as awesome, because they don't give a damn that others hear, or flawed, because that just means that they have to be careful if they want to keep things secret, if they have any. Either way, I'm here now and I'm a part of this world, so I'll have to get used to it.

"Where can I get one of these?" I ask peacefully, ignoring the tension from the last subject.

"There are several shops on the street," he explains impatiently. "It shouldn't be too hard to obtain one."

"And I can get one just like that?"

"Would you have it another way?"

I remain silent to that rhetorical question. I almost forgot that the Natin don't use money, so I can just grab one and leave. I just hope the shopkeeper doesn't give me trouble about having one for myself.

"I'll be leaving now," I tell him. "Thanks."

I turn around and make my way toward the door, hopefully without a reason to come back for another conversation.

"Good luck with your report," I tell So'krang as I stand at the door, preparing to leave.

"I'll need skill. Not luck," he tells me angrily, but somewhat relieved too, knowing that he can get back to work.

Just as I'm about to leave the room, and just as So'krang is about to go back to work, I remember that I have one last issue I want to talk about.

"When I get back, can we talk about this Sima Brak thing?" I ask him. "There's a lot I need to know about this."

"Sure. Whatever," So'krang tells me impatiently.

"I mean, I don't even know what the fuck it is, and it seems to get more and more important the more I hear about it. I think it has something to do with Yomak Nayan."

"YES! NOW PLEASE . . . leave." So'krang loses his cool and collects it back at the last second.

"OK, FINE." I rush to sound apologetic. "Jesus . . . no need to lose your shit."

With that, So'krang dips his head back into the psychopool, hopefully never to come out before he's done with the report, while I finally leave the room, go back downstairs and make all the preparations necessary to leave to the clan of Karin and finally meet Yomak Nayan under normal circumstances, which do not include fighting giant bipedal lizards alongside her or seeing her stroll around the hospital with broken legs. Those are probably things that happen to her regularly. But for this time, I get to enjoy her outside her duties. Of course, preparations don't include waking up Grasshead; that comes last. The boy needs his sleep, as it is more important to him than it is to anyone else.

Waiting to meet Yomak Nayan feels like an eternity. I would say I can't wait, but what choice do I have but wait? After all, the time it will take to see her again all depends on how fast I finish with these things and get over there already. But I do wonder how the moment will look like, how will it feel like, when we see each other again. I know for a fact that I'm pretty excited. Hopefully the feeling is mutual.

Speaking of time management, I think I might just add something to my task list that isn't getting me a Novaversian cellphone: get a bouquet of flowers. Hopefully it won't be too time-consuming.

CHAPTER XXI

A CELLPHONE AND SOME CYCLAMENS . . . WHERE CAN I FIND THOSE HERE?

Strolling down the streets with Grasshead. That's what I'm currently doing, trying to find the right stores before heading off to the airport.

This is probably my first time without So'krang in the Novaverse. Actually, it IS my first without So'krang in the Novaverse. Feels unusual being a sock without the other one, but at least I don't look like a dog on a leash to everyone anymore. Then again, it was my choice to stick with him in the first place, mainly because I needed someone to show me around. But because we were always together, at points I just felt embarrassed. Now I can be by myself a little.

So far, it's not helping me. I walk around these streets trying to figure out what is where. People and hiphomoys alike are walking on the road. In fact, I don't think there is a road. The streets are paved with rock like in old days, with no indication as to where the sidewalk is. Someone could easily get rammed by a fast-moving hiphomoy, although their speed remains in check when near people. It's the highway where they really accelerate.

The road connects to the surface streets and starts to rise upwards, standing high above the surface. That's where the riders can get quickly from one place to another, without worrying about having to call an ambulance because they ran over somebody, or in this case, get caught between a hiphomoy's teeth because the mouth was open while running.

But nonsense aside, I still can't find what I'm looking for.

Right now, before going to the airport, there are two things I need to get: a Novaversian cellphone so that I will be able to communicate with the people around here, as well as remember what it's actually called, and a bouquet of flowers, preferably cyclamens.

The search for either isn't going all too well. I can't find a flower shop anywhere and I don't know what kind of store I'm supposed to go in to for a phone, and I've been looking around for five minutes already. I should probably be more patient, but how can I when all I want to do right now is go and see Yomak Nayan. The girl gives meaning to my miserable life.

The stores here are nothing like what I was used to. When it comes to business, there is no competition whatsoever. Looking inside the stores from outside, there is not a single store that is void of customers, although it's probably because there is only a single type of store within several blocks. Right now, I am staring at a store for bathing products, which means that if I'm not satisfied with whatever that store has to offer, be it service of the employees or the products themselves, I'd have to walk several blocks just to get the other store. But to compensate for the scarcity of the store types, each store is frickin' huge, as one would expect from Novaversian contractors. If the Natin did have money, no businessman would be unsatisfied and live his life with regret that he ever wanted to open a shop. But they don't and Natin are pretty satisfied with their lives as is, so it'll have to do.

Must be nice living like this, but I still can't find what I need.

And then, just when I start to lose my temper as well as my patience, I simply look to my left and there it is, as if it popped out of nowhere.

Looking through the window of the phone store, I could see the counter and a nice selection of Novaversian phone-sticks behind it, sitting nicely on a series of shelves. The window stretches along the wall, allowing anyone looking to see what's going on inside the store, although apparently they haven't washed the window recently since I can't really tell what's happening. The window is long, and at the end of it is just a wall, with no store next to it. Either it's vacant space for another shop that will settle here in the future, or it's just more of the store itself, just the parts that you can't see.

Naturally, I go inside. Looking around, I see that the store is far larger than what it seems from outside, as suggested by the long window and the wall that seemingly has no purpose. More so, the store isn't just a series of aisles to walk by and browse for your preferred phone. It's also a factory!

I see a series of people sitting on work benches filled with all kinds of tools, tirelessly crafting these things and dumping them in a basket beside them. Not only that, but to make their job even more comfortable, they are sitting on orthopedic couches with a personal air conditioner blowing cool air at them, so there's no way they can possibly sweat or get any kind of pressure sores. Other than the overprivileged conditions that they work in, this place is still a factory-store. I believe the actual term is factory outlet.

Seeing as there is no clerk to serve me at the counter right beside the entrance, I start to walk around the store, looking around, trying to understand how things work here, what I'm supposed to do exactly and who do I need to speak to.

I walk around in between all the work benches and the labor force. Looking at the necks of the employees that I pass, I can see that they're all from the same clan. A clan of mass labor, or something bigger than that?

I wonder if I should interrupt one for a second and ask questions. Will he or she comply? Is he too busy in his work that he would fail to help me? I'm kind of lost right now, and I could really use some direction. I choose not to interrupt them, deciding instead to keep looking around. Maybe I'll ask someone later if it calls for it, since they are all deep in their jobs. But I can't help but wonder if they're really enjoying this kind of work. Most people doing this stuff back where I come from would only do something so excruciating to put food on the table.

Regardless, I continue moving around until I stumble upon one end of the store. Of course, I don't have a compass, so I can't tell which direction I'm facing, but it's the wall opposite the entrance.

Looking at it, it contains a series of shelves with tons of cellphones sitting nicely on them, much like the display at the entrance. The display stretches all the way to the corner. I walk by the display, quickly moving my eyes on as many phones as I can. They come in a variety of shapes, from simple ones like a triangle or a hexagon, to more intricate ones like a spiral. There are big and small, long and short, but what most differentiates them from each other is the design. One has a cloud design; another one has a jungle design; there is even one with a cobweb design and a little spider-creature figurine on it. This is nice and all, but it still doesn't help me find what I need. Actually, what I need is all around me, I just don't know how to do it.

Reaching the end of the display, I stare away from the wall, only to see more work benches and a door to the left. I don't know where the door leads to, but it's probably what I need.

It is nice seeing everything the store has to offer, but I'm at a loss, and I don't know where to start. Should I go back to the entrance? Maybe there's a clerk now that can help me.

And then, just when I was about to make a decision, a salesman approaches me, dressed in casual Natin wear and not in a uniform like I'm used to, similar to how the doctors here do, but he didn't have a sash. But I know that he's an employee because he is making eye contact with me, the kind of eye contact that tells you that he wants something from you. Also, he has the same tattoo as the labor force, so there has to be some kind of connection.

"Kata dobi'in?" he asks me politely in their language that I don't understand.

Apparently, he failed to notice my lack of neck tattoo. I stare at him with disbelief in response, but I can't blame him since he's probably used to his own kind asking for his help.

"I don't understand," I respond simply.

His expression then indicates that something is amiss. Looking at his face, I smirk, jokingly hinting at what might cause this miscommunication. He then looks at my neck, and realizes that I'm not a Natin. After that, everything becomes clear to him, and his expression said "of course."

"I apologize," he says, sounding a bit worried. "I di—"

"It's OK," I tell him, interrupting his sentence. "You don't need to apologize. I'm not that special, anyways. Heh. But can you help me with something?"

"Of course."

"I'm looking for a phone. Now, I know that they're everywhere, but is there something preferable that I should take? Like something that suits my needs best?"

"Well . . . there is the selection here on the wall."

"Yeah, but . . . y'know . . . something that suits me best?"

He starts stroking his chin, thinking about what I just said.

"There is no such thing." He tells me. "All yopak'orim are the same. They just come in different styles. But if you don't like anything here, we can customize one according to your desires."

"Customize?" I curiously remark.

He then stares at me blankly, realizing that I have no idea what he's talking about.

"Come with me," he tells me.

He then walks by me. I look at the direction he's going, and judging by it, it looks like he's going towards that door I told myself that it'd be no use walking through it. Naturally, I follow him.

Walking through the door, what I see before me are two more work benches, no different than the ones outside this room. One worker is absent from his bench, while the other one is lying down on a sofa at the end of the room like he's some kind of diva, playing some kind of pentagonal handheld console. Looking at what's going on here, I have no idea what's special about this room. Probably some kind of VIP section of the store.

The worker than looks aside from his game to see who just came in. Seeing who it is, he immediately puts aside his console and gets up. He approaches, looking serious as though he's ready to do his job appropriately, unlike the impression I got from him when I walked in here.

"A'jo, yasir'in nen nen'ti'ga yopak'orim," the salesman says.

The guy then looks at me, and, unlike his co-worker, immediately notices my lack of neck tattoo. I suppose he also knows what that means.

"The composer," he remarks, a bit surprised.

I stand corrected, although his expression already spoke for itself.

"What's going on here?" I ask, confused.

"My friend here will make you a yopak'orim according to your desires," the salesman replies.

"Really? Just like that?" I remark, surprised at their generosity.

"This is where everyone comes to get a personally custom-made yopak'orim if they're not satisfied with what we currently have," the other guy explains happily. "It's the best part of the job. All you do is sit here and do whatever you want, unless someone comes in and asks me to build them a yopak'orim. The problem is that it's only once a week per Soparkat'ga."

The salesman just leaves without saying a word as the other guy keeps on smiling, clearly showing how nice he's trying to be. Meanwhile, I try to figure out for myself what kind of yopak'orim I want for myself, if I'm already allowed to design one. Or, more accurately, have someone else design one for me. But what themes suit me best? What represents me?

I'm bent on escaping reality, so maybe I should get something about running away. But what visually represents escape?

Grasshead is my companion for life, so maybe I should get something with grass on it or flowers or whatever. Can they even make these things with grass?

Maybe I should get something with the conjurer? Or maybe a faucet? Maybe something that reminds me of that painful crest she's wearing all the time? Yeah I definitely don't think that would be a sight to behold, let alone an enjoyable one.

Maybe I should get something with the threads after all those years they . . . nah. No way am I getting something with those guys.

Well, I don't have a clear idea of what I want. I kept thinking but I couldn't see a spark in the distance. And then it came to me.

"Could you get me something with an ocean?" I request of him.

"An ocean, you want?" he inquires, somewhat surprised.

"Yeah, y'know . . . a clear blue ocean. Like in the Carribbe . . . a clear blue ocean."

"Like the ocean of Wabang?"

"I have no idea what that means."

"A clear blue ocean it is then. It should about two hours to get it done."

"Two hours!?" I respond in shock. "Man, I don't have that much time."

I think about taking the risk of waiting a little more as opposed to just getting it over with. Clearly, there isn't much a competition between the two choices in my mind.

"Thanks, dude," I decide. "You're really nice, but I'm kinda in a hurry."

"Don't worry about it," he says happily without a care. "It just means I get to relax more."

"Man, is this what your job is about? That's . . . bak!"

The guy then just starts to laugh. I join his laughter in response, although slightly quieter. Much like him, I too find it unusual that I'm rather quickly adjusting to this society. Probably because of my desperation to find a new home and escape the prison from whence I came. One year from now, I'll probably be 90% Natin, even if it's just in heart.

"I'll be leaving now," I tell him.

He just nods to me, turns around and returns to lie down on the sofa. I leave the room, once more staring at the masses of the same clan working their asses off making these things, regardless of whether they enjoy it or not. I would ask them, but I don't want to bother them, nor do I want to waste time.

I return to look at that massive selection over there on the wall, where the salesman came to me for service, only now I can't find him. He's probably somewhere helping someone else, but it doesn't matter.

I once more pass my eyes quickly on all the yopak'orim as I move across the wall to get a look on all of them. Moving my eyes this quickly, all I can see are the colors. Of course, they also come in different shapes, but my eyes focus more on the colors. I think that's actually how everyone works, but whatever.

I find myself nothing that suits me or anything that I like. Until I remember what I want, then I knew what I was looking for, and then almost immediately I found it.

There it was, at the top shelf, out of reach for someone of my height, or anyone's height for that matter, because it was way up there. The one that looks like an ocean. A clear blue ocean like the waters in the Caribbean. From what I've heard at least, since I've never actually been there.

Guess I didn't have to wait two hours to get one like this. It was here all time. Now I just have to figure out how to get it down.

"So what did you tell him to make you?" I hear a familiar voice to my side.

I look to my side and, as expected, I see the same salesman that I interacted with before.

"Huh?" I reply, confused, as it doesn't come to me immediately what he's talking about. "Oh. Uh . . . he's not making anything for me. It would take too long so I decided not to go with that option."

"I see," he replies, intrigued. "Well I hope you find something that you like from here. If it's not that then it's this."

"Actually, yeah. I want the one at the top. The one that looks like an ocean."

The salesman then looks up to see which one I'm referring to. He gets closer to the wall and presses a blue hand-sized button right under the bottom shelf, something that I hadn't noticed. The sound of squeaking wheels can then be heard, and almost immediately I can see a tall ladder on wheels approaching us from the side. The ladder came by itself, as expected from the advanced technology of the Natin. Then again, I think humans also accomplished like this, but I'm not sure, nor do I care.

The ladder stops in front of us. I look at the ladder, figuring out if I'm supposed to climb it or is the salesman supposed to do it for me. I look at him, and turns out he was already staring at me when the ladder got here. Now we just look at each other, each one expecting from the other something that apparently won't happen due to the gap in expectations.

"Are we waiting for something?" I ask him humorously.

"You're supposed to climb it," he tells me directly.

"I know you're supposed to climb a ladder, but isn't that your job?"

"You must be used to different customs. Here we do things ourselves."

"But doesn't that compromise my safety? As a customer, that is."

"This is a society of warriors. We don't get hurt easily just by falling from ladders."

"Hmm. That's an interesting point."

I climb the ladder, as expected by someone who lives in this parallel universe. If I wish to become one of the Natin, and overall be part of this society, than I'd better get used to this kind of stuff.

I climb all the way up to the top, right at the end of the ladder. I heard once that firemen never look down when climbing tall ladders to rescue people from high locations, probably because it would get them dizzy or scare the hell out of them so that they would lose focus. But this ain't no burning building, and I'm no fireman, so I look down anyways. It's not really a big deal, probably something like twenty feet. This barely fazes me; falling down from this height wouldn't be too much of a problem, if it all.

Nonsense aside, I look at the multitudes of options at the top shelf, as I am intrigued by their design. I look at them quickly, and then grab the yopak'orim of my choice.

Grabbing the one that looks like the ocean, I climb down the ladder.

Now once more on the ground, I look at the salesman with the yopak'orim in hand. I smirk at him, as I find myself satisfied with my choice. He in return smirks back at me, glad for my satisfaction and probably his competence as a salesman.

He then walks to the ladder. He grabs it and throws it back from where it came as it rolls on its wheels all the way over there. Guess there was no automated function for that one.

"Are you satisfied?" he asks me, seemingly happy for me.

"Definitely," I tell him with repressed excitement.

"Great. Let's register that with your account."

"My account?" I reply, confused. "Like bank account?"

He, in response, too looks at me with confusion.

"You don't know what an account is?" he then asks.

"I've been here less than a month or something like that." I say, unsure of my own tenure. "So I don't really know what that is."

"Hmm," he simply responds, intrigued about the situation.

He then looks to the side, thinking about the unusual situation, probably trying to come up with a solution.

"No matter," he then says, once more looking at me and seemingly carefree. "You can just take it."

"Just like that?" I reply confused, unsure if that's OK.

"Don't worry. Just make sure next time you have an account. Otherwise I won't be able to make this exception."

"Heh," I smirk at him. "I don't think there'll be a next time."

He smiles back to me in response, and we both make our way to the counter. He takes the lead, and I'm right behind him.

"Shoulda asked So'krang about this," I mutter to myself.

At the entrance, I once more see the life-filled streets of the clan of Yasin, with the beauty of the sun radiating all over. Such a warm feeling I get from her, as I take a deep breath and continue to move on to my next destination.

But before I leave the store, I turn around to see the salesman at the counter, addressing a customer.

"Thank you," I yell to him as I wave goodbye.

He notices me, and waves goodbye in return. I then proceed to leave the store.

"Nice guy," I mutter to myself.

I find myself once more on the streets. I look at my new yopak'orim, if I'm saying it correctly, holding the excitement in me, and then putting it in my pocket. Now, every time I'll look at it, I'll be reminded of Yomak Nayan.

Great. Now all I need is to find me a flower shop. Where exactly can I find a flower shop around here?

I walk around the streets looking for a flower shop, much like how I did before I found the yopak'orim shop. Being in the same situation again is kind of a bummer. I don't have the patience to put up with this. Maybe I should skip the bouquet? But I can't help but feel the necessity to get cyclamens. Despite this feeling that this may or may not be a redundant task, I'm still getting those cyclamens.

I walk around for a while. If I had to guess, I'd say about ten minutes, twelve tops. I'm pretty sure there is no flower shop in the vicinity. I can't believe it took me ten minutes to come to that conclusion.

So instead of turning left or right all the time, I go straight and onto the next area. Walking straight, not even a minute has passed and I already see to my right a flower shop, with a sign made of artificial grass and a giant sunflower, fake or otherwise, at the side of it. It's a pretty fancy sign, I must say; I like it. I guess I already past the flower shop in the last area, and maybe that's why I didn't see it. But it doesn't matter anymore.

I go inside the flower shop, and unlike the previous shop I've been in, the counter is in a different corner. The entrance is pretty much just an entrance here.

I enter the shop. The moment I go in I get this feeling like I'm actually outside, as if the shop has no walls or a ceiling, but is actually located in an oriental jungle. The shop is decorated with a lovely small fountain at the side, statues of different Novaversian animals that looked like sparrows and deer all over and ornamental rocks here and there, the kind that you see in those tai chi places or shiatsu centers or whatever. It is rather quiet too, and the breeze is just so chilling and pleasant. This entire garden-esque atmosphere really contributes to a good feeling, but it would be even better if there were some garden gnomes around here.

Moving through the first aisle, what I see is a pretty normal selection of flowers, the kind that you can find pretty much anywhere. You got roses, violets, tulips, forget-me-nots, those flowers that look like bells. I'm not even sure forget-me-nots are common. I don't even remember where I learned about them. But it's pretty much as So'krang said: the flora here isn't too different from that of heratrang'ga pan. Although I don't know where the "too" serves a function. It's not different at all!

Going deeper into the shop, the flowers that are presented on the aisles start to shift from the normal-looking ones that I'm all too familiar with, to some pretty fancy and unusual plants, as I'm seeing flowers filled with colors that look like they were sprouted on a different world . . . which they were! I don't know if these were artificially created, since So'krang did say that the flora wasn't too different from that of heratrang'ga pan. I can see now what he was referring to.

There was one flower that looked like a pelican's beak filled with water, colored light orange with yellow splats all over it. Another one looked like a bloody trombone with elongated parts. There was another that looked like a mix between a baseball glove and a showerhead, and another one was some kind of cappuccino-colored question mark with an actual halo floating over it. This is how weirdly beautiful these flowers are. But despite how fancy these flowers are, the cyclamens are all I want.

"Hey there," I suddenly hear a soft feminine voice from my right. "Can I help you?"

I look to my side to and I see a woman, obviously, dressed in casual Natin wear who is most likely a saleswoman here who is more than happy to see me judging by that big beautiful smile on her face. Looking at her neck, it is the same as the ones all the employees back at the yopak'orim store have. I thought the people who work here might have the Grasshead tattoo, considering that they are surrounded by plants and that they probably tend to the plants all the time. I guess that tattoo that they have must belong to the clan in charge of businesses, or maybe labor force or the likes or whatever. Speaking of tattoos, she immediately spoke to me in English. Most likely because she didn't see any tattoo on the right side of my neck, which is where the Natin put all their tattoos. Not seeing the tattoo, she probably realized fast who she was looking at.

"Huh? Oh, yeah," I respond indecisively. "Say . . . are these flowers real or fake?"

"They're real, but they're artificially made," she explains in a happy tone. "They're actually extracted from the blood of the Jena'ga, and further engineered to give them a more exotic look."

"Wait . . . ," I ask, confused. "You're telling me these plants are made from the DNA of a single clan?"

"Well . . . yes. That is the case."

"Hmm . . . ," I show some subtle curiosity. "That's nice and all but uh . . . do you have cyclamens maybe?"

"Cyclamens? Yeah, sure. We might have some for you."

"What do you mean 'for me'? Do I get some kind of special treatment here because I'm different?"

Apparently, she didn't hear my joke, since she kept walking on. Maybe it was just a manner of speech, so she probably didn't mean to discriminate. Nevertheless, I follow her.

She takes me all the way back to the section of the normal plants. We walk into the second aisle, which is the one that I didn't enter by myself and just passed by and looked at from afar. Once more, I see the usual-looking plants. You got the orchids, sunflowers, and a bunch of other plants that I probably saw in my life but never bothered to know their names, although I can't imagine who would want to get a bouquet of sunflowers. I mean, they're pretty and all, but just to make a bouquet out of them you'd need to put them in a cement mixer.

And then, at the end of the aisle, or at the beginning depending on where you go through, there sat peacefully the beautiful cyclamens that I have been searching for. They came in a variety of colors. You got the red ones, the white ones, the purple ones. You even got white ones with some purple and vice versa. I needn't even mention how they bow before me. This plant clearly defines itself as something else.

"Hmm. So that's where they were," I subtly remark, pretending not to be excited. "I'd like the white ones with the purple."

She then takes three pots of white cyclamens with some purple at the base, and leaves to a different area in the shop. I contemplate whether I should follow her or look around some more and maybe find something interesting. I mean, what is there to look at? A girl making a bouquet of cyclamens. Pretty much the same as making a bouquet of any other flower. Nothing special there.

I decide to look around the shop.

Going back and forth around the shop, I find myself in pretty much the same areas as I was before: normal-looking flowers; weird flowers; statues of Novaversian creatures that I haven't seen before. Basically nothing new. Probably should've just stared at the girl making the bouquet. At least that would be something new to look at.

But standing near the statues, I find myself suddenly intrigued by one particular statue, since I have nothing better to do. Looking at the statue closely, it looked like some kind of deer. A deer with round horns that look like balls and reptilian legs, a feature which persists on all creatures of the Novaverse, and something that I have to figure out the reason behind . . . when I find the interest to do so. I don't know why I find this particular statue more interesting than the others. Probably because I have nothing better to do while I wait for the bouquet to get ready. Speaking of which, I should probably check what's up with that.

I go over to the place where they make bouquets, wherever that's supposed to be. Moving past all the aisles, I see on one corner the counter where people check out, and on the other corner an all-purpose section or something, which is where I see the girl just finishing making the bouquet. Looks like I came just in time.

I walk over there. The girl is just picking up the beautifully arranged bouquet, wrapped in a plastic white paper decorated with golden sparkles, and handing it over to me with a big smile on her face. Apparently, she's happier about this than I am. I, in return, only respond with a smirk, as usual, and take the bouquet from her hands.

We both then walk to the counter so that I can check out. Not surprisingly, the counter didn't have a register or a computer, but instead that thing that looks like a wide bucket, just like how So'krang has in his room.

She puts her hand in the wide bucket, and besides her appears a holographic detailing of something, projected from underneath a camera-like device embedded in the counter. I couldn't possibly understand what is written since it's in their language.

I am then suddenly reminded that I need some kind of special account to register this bouquet with, something that I still don't have.

"I don't have an account yet," I tell her in an apologetic tone. "That's not supposed to be a problem, is it?"

She then seems surprised and wipes the smile off her face, shifting her eyes to me while her face was still pointing at the hologram, with an expression that makes her look like she heard some bad news.

"Oh," she says, clearly surprised in an unexpected predicament. "Well . . . ."

She sighs, trying to figure out how to properly deal with this situation. She seems indecisive. I don't blame her, considering that it doesn't happen every day that someone without an account comes by and asks to buy something. Kind of an unusual predicament.

"I'll just have to register it to my account then." She says, putting on a smile once more.

"You would do that?" I ask skeptically.

"For you, anything. But it's only because you don't have an account yet. Don't think I give this kind of treatment to just anyone."

"Doesn't seem that way," I sarcastically remark.

She then waves her hand gently inside the bucket. The hologram changes dynamically as the numbers and words that make it disappear and appear anew.

Putting aside how they do things and what the hell is going on right now, this just shows how advanced their technology is, which contradicts their need to do certain things the old way, like riding creatures instead of just driving cars. I guess they just prefer to do certain things with means that should naturally be obsolete already. Then again, who am I to judge? I come from an impulsive consumerist culture that constantly renews itself without even considering the harm. I guess the Natin just have the collective awareness of differentiating between what's good for them on the long-term from what might cause more damage than revolution. Regardless of whether I agree with this style of thinking or not, I'll just have to get used to it.

"Can't you just . . . lemme have it without doing anything?" I ask her. "I mean, that's what the last guy did for me. I mean, in the last shop I visited."

"I could do that," she says, still maintaining her happy tone. "But it could lead to all kinds of problems. You wouldn't want me to get in trouble, would you?"

She then leans on her elbow and stares at me as if I'm the stars in the sky, all while still holding on to that smile. Looking at her as she looks at me, I now notice how well-groomed her eye lashes are, black as a shadow and beautiful as a meadow soaked in the finest ink. Whether they are natural or she wears too much mascara, I find them unusually beautiful, as I smile at her to return her kindness. Looking at those eyes, realizing her good nature and the way she treats me, which seems to go against what most Natin believe in, I can't help but feel a comfort in my heart. Nevertheless, my heart belongs to Yomak Nayan. Also, brown eyes aren't really my thing.

"I would NEVER want you to get in trouble," I say in a nice-guy kind of fashion with half a smirk.

She returns back to finish waving her hand inside the bucket. Since she was already halfway through it, it didn't take too much before she finished with it and finally handed me the bouquet, without ever letting go of that smiling. I guess she was really happy to serve me.

I take the bouquet and then I make my way towards the entrance of the shop, or in my case right now, exit. Before leaving the shop for good, I turn back one more time to look at the saleswoman.

There she was, still standing behind the counter and still smiling, probably staring at my back as I make my leave. She sees me looking at her, and she winks and waves goodbye to me as how a cute girl would do to a guy. I smirk at her back, and simply gesture her goodbye by raising my hand, or basically just the goodbye wave without the wave.

At last, I leave the shop, with all the things I need in hand and no more stations to pass by other than the station which is Yomak Nayan's house, or wherever she wants to meet me.

I find myself once more at the streets of the clan of Yasin. Now I just need to know where the airport is, since I'm done with all the preparations, and get on to the real part. The problem is I don't know where it is.

A Natin passes by me, dressed in Natin casual wear and who's probably a Yasin'ga, since he shares the tattoo with So'krang, if I remember it correctly since I never paid too much attention to that. He didn't look like he was going to battle, but he sure dressed like it. Then again, everyone here dresses like they're prepared to kick some ass.

"Hey uh . . . excuse me," I address the man. "Which way is the airport?"

The man doesn't say a word, but instead just points in a direction. Clearly he isn't in the mood. That or he's not really fond of the composer.

"Thanks," I simply tell him.

The man just continues on his way, still without saying a word.

I couldn't care less, as I mount Grasshead and prepare to ride to the airport and after that . . . Yomak Nayan!

I find myself eager for this meeting, something that doesn't usually happen to me. Usually I find myself pissed over everything, never wanting to feel something different. But with my new home I might be able to loosen up a little. Even with different feelings, the anger still resides somewhere, stubbornly clinging to my soul. An anger which I do not understand why it persists. But I don't plan on letting this anger affect what I'm feeling now. I'm excited, and I want Yomak Nayan to feel that too. But even with this change of mood, the eternal frown still won't go away.

Nevertheless, I maintain a good mood and finally give the order to Grasshead to dash. Grasshead starts to run, and as he accelerates, he enters the hiphomoy highway. I can feel the steepness as we go up the highway, and feel it leveling off as we get higher.

Standing at the highest altitude these streets have to offer, I tell Grasshead to stop for one moment. He stops in his place, and I look around as I stand high above the streets, feeling like I'm touching the sky without a fear in my heart, witnessing all the buildings in this magnificent panorama as I feel the breeze in my face. I find this sight to be very beautiful.

But as beautiful as it may be, I have something even more beautiful waiting for me somewhere in a different part of this world. As I am reminded of my goal, I tell Grasshead once more to dash forward on the highway. Without too many restrictions, Grasshead just runs forward as fast as he can without looking back, but still cautious as to not crash into other hiphomoys as we make our way to the start of our next adventure.

CHAPTER XXII

I WAS NOT EXPECTING THIS . . . IN MORE WAYS THAN ONE

It's already sunset, and I'm just about to land in the airport of the clan of Karin. As expected, it's crowded in the wagon tied to the wagon-dragon, not in the sense that people here don't have space to breathe, but in the sense that everyone here is sitting on the floor without any means of comfort. This again begs the question as to why the Natin prefer to do things the old way. I mean, it's like being in the cargo trailer of an eighteen-wheeler smuggling a bunch of fugitives from some third-world country. At least put a sofa here; make it nice while it lasts. But I guess they'll just go with whatever works for them, and I'll have to be the victim. Regardless, I'll just have to get used to it.

But enough complaining. The wagon-dragon has finally landed. Unlike how we do it with expeditions, when you're going to a clan, the wagon-dragon takes you there directly. Would've been fun sky-diving, but I guess the normal way will have to make do for now.

As everyone jumps in an unruly manner out of the wagon from whatever edge they were closest to, some with children in hand and some not, I follow the lot and do the same. The fall was longer than I expected. I thought it was something like five feet, turns out it was double that. I thought my tendons were going to explode from that jump and I accidentally dropped the bouquet on the floor, although Grasshead seemed to handle the jump better than I did. I pick up bouquet from the floor and check that the cyclamens didn't get to filthy. They didn't.

Now that I'm out, I just have to figure out where the hell Yomak Nayan waits. I think she told me she'd wait for me, if I recall correctly.

I walk around randomly in the massive open area which is this airport. There is no indication as to where I'm supposed to go. No terminals or anything for that matter, just one huge roofless area. It's as if the people here instinctively know where they are supposed to go around here. If that's the case, I don't have that instinct.

As I continue to walk randomly without any idea where I'm going, I suddenly catch in my eye a bunch of people standing in a line; some hold signs and some don't. I have no idea what the signs say since . . . well . . . hang'pan'rika. It's natural to assume that that's where all the people waiting for their associates to get off the planes and meet them. If that's the case, maybe Yomak Nayan is there.

I go over there. Looking at it closely, one particular feature about the crowd that I cannot ignore is the amount of beautiful girls standing there, among other types of individuals. It is hard for me to tell if they belong to the same clan since everyone is moving too much and distance kind of makes it hard to look at their tattoos. Whether they are or not is trivial, since I have a beautiful girl of my own waiting for me here . . . somewhere.

With all the people over there, I can't for the love of me guess where the hell Yomak Nayan is supposed to be. I don't even know if she's there. For all I know there could be another thing like this going on in a different section of the airport. At least they aren't shoving and pushing each other like a bunch of barbarians. If this was Earth, it would be a mosh pit.

Nevertheless, I search among the crowd for Yomak Nayan. I run sideways left and right, looking above everyone's head to see if I can find her, making sure I look above the heads where there isn't a giant sign behind them.

I grow tired of this nonsense. I move all the way to the side of the crowd to look from the side if I see her. I look everywhere among the crowd. I can't find her, and I find myself lost without knowing what to do.

"NEPH!!" I hear a beautiful voice shouting my name.

I immediately recognize the voice, and there is no doubt about it. I look to where it came from, and I see Yomak Nayan from afar, smiling as always and waving to me. I, being who I am, just smirk to her in return, repressing my excitement but I am still very much glad to see her, even though the eternal frown still won't go away.

Nevertheless, I run to her, and she runs to me, until we finally get close to each other. She greets me with a hug. I'm startled, as I'm not used to people embracing me. I can't tell if I just skipped a beat as I feel her arms around me, since the anger still lingers within me, refusing to subside. I want to let go and experience other things as they materialize as feelings within me, but the anger refuses to make room for emotions other than itself. Nevertheless, her arms are warm and welcoming, and it's nice to feel desired for a change. I guess I have skipped a beat.

"Aren't you going to hug me back?" she asks optimistically as ever.

"Sorry," I say with uncertainty. "You caught me off guard."

"I guess someone needs a little more hugs in his life."

"Yeah . . . I guess so," I say calmly with a bit of hidden sadness.

"Ooooo . . . ," she utters, seemingly intrigued about something. "And you came to me smelling like blood and battle."

"What?" I reply, confused.

I sniff myself, quickly moving my nose from left to right as I smell my clothes.

"FUCK!" I shout. "I knew I forgot something!"

"Don't worry," she tells me happily and unconcerned. "It's very manly . . . and sexy!"

"Really?" I ask her, confused but also mildly intrigued. "Is this the Natin's definition of sexy? Then maybe I next time I should drench myself in a bucket of blood before coming here. Heh."

I don't know how impressed she was with the joke, as she didn't laugh, but just smiled.

But as I look at her and she looks at me, Grasshead steps in to get some attention too. He raises his head to look at Yomak Nayan, and she looks at him and pets him on his head.

"Oh hey there!" she says. "What's his name?"

"Grasshead," I tell her simply.

She then ducks to look at him eye to eye. She holds his head with both her arms. As she continues to look at him, he licks her face like how a dog would do to show his affection. Yomak Nayan seems to appreciate the love but backs away a little so she doesn't get too much saliva on her. She eventually stands back up and turns her attention back to me.

"Pretty sure I already told you his name." I tell her. "But I could be wrong."

"If you did, I would remember," she says.

"Hmm. I guess you're right."

I almost forgot due to the excitement. I hand her the bouquet of cyclamens.

"Oh wow," she exclaims. "What flowers are these?"

"They're cyclamens," I tell her. "It's my favorite flower."

"Wow. They're really . . . special," she says indecisively. "I don't remember ever seeing a flower that curves like this."

"That's what so special about them. See, unlike ordinary flowers, cyclamens have the power to recognize one's worth and look up to them. That's why they bow before those they revere as kings and queens.

She giggles over my perception on the flower.

"Wow!" she says in laughter. "That's an interesting perception."

"It's not interesting. It's the truth!"

She continues to giggle, and then she calms down a bit.

"You're funnier than I thought," she says calmly.

"Meh. I try to be," I quip in response, as usual. "Anyways, are we leaving this place any time soon?"

"Whenever you're ready."

"I AM ready. Are you?"

Once again, she giggles at whatever I have to say. At this point, I can't tell if I'm that funny or she's just easy to get a laugh from. Regardless, I feel something different, something besides anger, but I can't tell what it is yet. But still, never have I felt the need for someone's company this much before. Things are changing, both on the outside and the inside.

"Then let's go," she says.

She then mounts a hiphomoy that is standing right beside her. I look at him with surprise, as I didn't even know it was there because I was too busy paying all my attention to Yomak Nayan.

The hiphomoy pretty much has the physique of any other hiphomoy, like Grasshead or Franuk. He's colored bright pink and has no fur of any kind. And, like all hiphomoy, the main differentiating feature about him is his head: other than the large head and teeth, his face is full of folds, kind of like a shar pei, starting from the back and all the way to the front. His eyes are also pink and seemingly angry, although I can't say that's indicative of what emotion he's trying to convey, being a dog-like creature and all.

But her hiphomoy's appearance is the least peculiar thing right now, as Yomak Nayan spontaneously starts moving on without even giving me a heads up. I stare at her surprised and in disbelief as I see her venturing off further away from me, turning around all the while winking at me, and then laughing a happy laugh.

I'm not mad, as I realize this is just her way of being playful. I smirk as I realize this, but even with my feelings for her, and even though I WANT her, I take my time feeling comfortable around people. Then again, it never happened, so I'm not too sure about it, but that's what I feel about myself.

But before she gets too far away from me, I mount Grasshead and we dash to chase her. Soon, we catch up to her. I don't think she was even going too fast, while we were kind of worried that she'd get away. Nevertheless, I find myself right now riding alongside her.

We ride all the way out of the airport, zigzagging through people and wagon-dragons so that we won't crash and have an unnecessary accident. We keep galloping without breaking the speed limit, whatever it is, until we finally leave the airport.

Stopping for just a short moment, I look back to see the airport from behind. I see wagon-dragons from afar with a lot of people randomly located throughout the airport, standing under wagon-dragons and whatnot. It really looks beautiful from here.

I turn back around to continue my journey to wherever Yomak Nayan is taking me. I see her and her hiphomoy standing still from afar. Apparently it took her a while to realize that I stopped for a second. She waves to me, probably trying to figure out what went wrong that I had to stop. Of course, nothing went wrong. More so, everything went right, as I just wanted to look back at the airport one more time before I leave.

I continue riding forward, eventually coming back to stand by Yomak Nayan, and then we ride together once more.

We continue to ride until we reach a highway, already far away from the airport. On it, we ride without worrying about crashing into anyone, but still maintaining caution so that we won't crash into other hiphomoys or accidentally fall off the road, since it is pretty high up here. We run so fast we can't even converse while we are riding. I can't even count how long it's taking me just to get to the end of it, and before I even realize it, I'm already off the highway and back to the roads shared by riders and pedestrians alike.

Now, in the commercial area of the clan of Karin, we just ride at low speed towards wherever Yomak Nayan wants to take me. The city here isn't much different from any other city I've been to culture-wise. You got people walking about together with their hiphomoys, all kinds of stores and restaurants, and multiple writings in hang'pan'rika which I should remind myself that I need to learn if I plan on staying here forever.

But one particular feature I find in this clan that is pretty hard to ignore is the abundance of beautiful girls. I mean, for the love of God, this clan is like the world's biggest beauty pageant. Sure, there are some guys here and there and Natin from other clans, but this clan is dominated by angels. I now understand why everyone is excited for me about Yomak Nayan. Then again, that just means she's not special, but one of many. She's still special to me, and I feel like I won the lottery of awesomeness.

As we continue to ride, I look around endlessly, constantly moving my head left and right to catch all the beautiful girls in sight. I try to hold my excitement in as I feel it circulating through my shoulders, gathering up as if it's preparing to explode. I can't help myself, as I would never find myself in such a scenario where a single city is dominated with the most beautiful girls. In all honesty, I feel like I'm in a safari of beautiful girls. That's what I feel like, at least.

But as I constantly turn my head left and right, I also look at Yomak Nayan, predictably since she's right beside me. On one glance, I don't see her smiling, which is unusual considering that she is so smiley. During that moment, I give her my full attention, putting aside my sightseeing of all the beautiful girls. With a better look, she definitely doesn't seem too happy with what I'm doing, but she doesn't seem mad, as her expression is just bland without a smile. I respond to this by wiping off the stupid smirk on my face.

"Is something the matter?" I respond, worried, but pretending that nothing's wrong.

She responds with silence, and then she looks down and shakes her head.

"No," she responds quietly, sounding kind of sad. "It's just that . . . this is the bane of every Karin'ga. It's a gender-exclusive clan, and we are revered for our beauty, which is exactly why men like to come here and look at us, maybe even do more than that. It's just that . . . sometimes everyone makes me feel like's it's my only asset. As if that's what I was made for."

"I am your asset," I suddenly tell her, "and you are mine. You have more assets than you know. Besides, you're a fuckin' warrior, and everyone knows it, even if they don't tell you directly."

I then look at her as I am talking while looking at what's in front of me. Looking at her, she has a relieved expression, and I suppose that also lifted her mood.

"I mean, that is the case, right?" I ask her with uncertainty. "Isn't that what Natin is all about? Pride. Not only for themselves but also for each other. Everyone here looks out for each other and looks up to each other. And this is coming from a guy who doesn't know shit about the Natin."

She then giggles. That giggle I like so much. It's what shows me that she's OK and she's the Yomak Nayan that attracted me in the first place.

"You know . . . ," she starts to say happily. "The Karin'ga are also common lovers of adulterers."

That statement of hers right now came to me as a complete surprise, as I once again wipe the smirk off my face. It wouldn't be that surprising either. Who wouldn't want a Karin'ga for a lover? But cheating on your wife with one is just insult to injury.

"Hmm. If that's what you're worried about than I SWEAR ON MY FUCKIN' GRAVE that I will NEVER cheat on you!" I tell her humorously and with clear certainty. "Hell, I don't even know what's it like to have a girlfriend."

Hearing that, she puts a gentle smile on her face, realizing my iron-hard commitment for her, and knowing that I would stand by my word.

"Until you die, of course," I tell her jokingly.

She then laughs outright, not more of the cute and modest giggle I have heard from her. And as much as I enjoy her laughter, I wonder if there is anything that could get her upset. Actually, it doesn't matter.

"We're here," she says.

I put a surprised expression on my face. I was so caught up in the conversation that I didn't even feel us moving. I find it hard to imagine that we're already in the living quarters of this clan, since last time I checked I was surrounded by beautiful girls in the active part of the city. Were we riding too fast, or were we talking too much?

Nevertheless, we're already here, and it's time to focus on what we're going to do next. And it starts by knowing what I'm entering.

Before me is a giant apartment building, no different than any other apartment building as one would expect, except for the wideness typical of Natin architecture. I find it unusual that they live in apartments here, considering that So'krang lives in a house. I guess each clan has their own style.

I see Yomak Nayan getting off her hiphomoy, whose name I still have to learn. I do the same by getting off Grasshead. We both enter the building with our respective hiphomoys following us, naturally. As we continue to walk inside the building, we eventually make it to the elevator, which to no one's surprise is really wide and opens up vertically, much like the one I saw in the hospital. We get inside the elevator, Yomak Nayan presses a button, and the elevator closes and takes us to our desired floor. A little waiting and the door opens up on floor eight.

What I see is not two different paths that lead to different doors like what I know and expected, but one door right in front of us, suggesting that the entire floor belongs to Yomak Nayan, similar to those penthouses of rich people, or so I think at least.

We walk to the door and we just open it, no locks or anything, similar to how So'krang does with his house. I guess this is an actual thing in the Novaverse. Regardless, Yomak Nayan's house is pretty fancy, kind of like the pictures you see in catalogs for penthouses.

To the immediate right of the apartment upon entering is the living room, filled with a sofa and couch and the Novaversian TV which, of course, looks like a metallic cube, and a fancy age-old table right in the middle of the room. Right behind the living room, and on a slightly higher level than it, is the kitchen, sparkly and squeaky clean as if it came straight out of a catalog for kitchen interior design. As for what's on the left? A corridor leading somewhere. What's beyond it is something that I have yet to find out.

"Nice house," I compliment her. "Way better than what I have, because I don't have a house. Heh, I'm practically homeless. Most of the time I just freeload at So'krang's house."

"Well, then what do you say you start living with me?" she tells me flirtatiously.

"That's a thought," I reply ambiguously.

Yomak Nayan goes over to the kitchen and grabs a tall glass from one of the cabinets. She then proceeds to fill it with tap water from the kitchen sink and drink it slowly and elegantly without stopping once. I just stare as everything happens. Apparently there isn't much to say that moment. But looking at her, I guess she is really thirsty, as she didn't notice that one drop of water escaped from her; I watch as it slowly slides off her lips to her chin and then falls off. Such a sexy performance from a simple drink. I clearly enjoy watching that, although she ruins it with typical Natin food manners by wiping her lips with the back of her hand. Should've seen that coming, but in no way do I think less of her for this, as she is still Yomak Nayan.

She then walks up to me, but not before gently putting the bouquet of cyclamens on the marble table in the kitchen, and holds my hand with both of hers. Such a firm and gentle touch. The feeling of her skin is like a silky pillow wrapping itself around my hand. To think that these hands are the hands of a warrior. A warrior that stains her body with blood day after day. With all that enemy's blood soaked into the cracks on her, I can't imagine how she manages to keep them soft and so nice to touch. They should be sturdy and hard as rocks, unless it's actually the blood that makes her skin smooth, and if that's the case then it's just disturbing. Regardless, I can already see that she has plans for us. Can't wait to see what kind of plans she's made.

"Come," she says softly.

She pulls me gently as she moves away. I follow her, holding her soft hand all the way. She takes me through the corridor. As I move by, I see a closed door to my right. Clearly not important as we move past it. And then I see door to the left. Yomak Nayan is preparing to enter that room. I can tell she is by the way she moves.

Upon opening the door, smoke slowly comes out of it as the smell of fire fills my nostrils and gets in my eyes. I try to look inside, but there is too much smoke to be able to see what is in it, although I could make out a sofa at the far end straight ahead of me.

Looking at where the smoke is rising from, I can see that it's coming from a grill that's sitting in the middle of the room, already lit with burning coals. Its heat can be felt across the entire room as the crackling sound of fire can be heard and the sight of the coals that sparkle with it are the only things that can be seen brightly in the room full of thick smoke.

But the coals weren't all too visible, as on top on the grill is the most peculiar object present in the room: it's some kind of purple bag, and it has a rather weird appearance. It has five tentacle-like extensions, each ending in what appears to be a hose, kind of like a water pipe. The middle of it has some kind of soft filling in it. From afar, one can say it looks like a purple octopus.

"Dora ronon!" I hear a manly voice from the side.

I look to the side, and I see three individuals there lounging on the sofas. They are two girls and one guy, and I am disappointed upon seeing them, as I now realize that Yomak

Nayan and I are not going to get some alone time. I don't know what she has in mind, but clearly we aren't in sync.

The two girls aren't so much for decency, with one wearing an open we'jei over nothing, with the jacket barely obscuring the sight of her rack, while the other one is wearing that breast-piece that I still don't know the name of. They aren't as pretty as Yomak Nayan, if I might say, but are still somewhat attractive, but not up to the standards of a Karin'ga, that's for sure. They do have notable features which are not simply beauty. One of them has an additional tattoo on her pinky that is shaped like a ring. And the other one has a square-shaped scar on the lower portion of the left side of her rib cage. The scar was red, and shows that the upper layer of her skin was removed. It was so geometrically precise that it looked like it was surgically removed from her, and definitely not a combat scar.

As for the guy, I look at him and I think to myself: who the hell does this guy think he is? This guy looks like a hobo, with an ugly five o'clock shadow, eyes barely open and unattended shaggy hair that looks like if he lays down on a pillow one more time he's going to wake up with big ugly-ass dreadlocks. More so, the guy is shirtless, as if he owns the place. Way to start a first impression right there. Then again, he probably doesn't give a damn. I can tell by his face.

"Kata domae nen tate'in iteka?" the guy says in a disparaging manner while pointing at me.

"Yes," Yomak Nayan replies. "And if you come here you can see who it is."

"English!?" he remarks, surprised and confused.

Everyone then just walks towards the grill and sits around it like this is some kind of campfire.

"Everyone, I suppose you already know Neph?" Yomak Nayan introduces me.

"The composer?!" shouts the guy in a carefree manner like some kind of stoner. "You didn't say you were bringing the composer here! I didn't even know you knew him."

"Well . . . now you do," I wittily reply.

"You know . . . ," he goes on to say in a patronizing tone. "When I saw you standing next to the mark'nan, I could've sworn to Gangra they were going to kill you. Hehe. As some kind of ceremonial sacrifice or something."

"Good thing they didn't," I say in an equally patronizing tone, dissatisfied with his attitude. "Otherwise you wouldn't have any gods to pray to. Heh."

"Only stupid people believe in gods. You don't expect me to join your league. Do you? Hehe. Na, I'm just joking!"

I can't really tell what's up with that guy. Is he trying to be antagonistic or friendly in a provocative kind of way? Regardless, I stare at him with disbelief, as he does anything but impress me.

"Who is this asshole?" I whisper to Yomak Nayan.

Yomak Nayan seems somewhat embarrassed, as she moves her eyes swiftly between all the participants inside the room. She seems at a loss, trying to figure out how to address this situation, as I can bet she too feels the animosity created in this company.

"Neph, this is Do'ba," Yomak Nayan says in a hesitant tone.

"I am from the Shanga," he says, continuing with his carefree manner of speech. "Did they tell you about Shanga already? Or do you still need to fill that void?"

I continue to stare at him with disbelief.

"How the fuck do you expect me to respond to that?" I rhetorically ask him, mildly agitated as I try to keep the friction to a minimum.

A quiet envelops the atmosphere, as all that I can see on his face is a stupid smirk. I think Yomak Nayan is still a bit tense, but I can't actually tell what she's feeling from this conversation.

"And these are O'or, she's a Kaberati'ga, and Er'sang, a Santian'ga," Yomak Nayan continues to introduce her friends.

The girls just gesture to me, each with their own style. O'or, the one with the square scar, waves her fingers at me, while Er'sang simply holds her hand up. It's a much more decent greeting than the flamboyant attitude that the other guy displays. Although the names of the clans don't really mean much to me right now, I guess it's important for Yomak Nayan that I know more about their culture. What interests me more though is what's up with those additional assets. The scar and the finger tattoo that is.

"So what exactly are we doing here?" I suddenly ask.

"Just wait and see," Yomak Nayan mysteriously tells me with a slight smile on her face, seemingly excited.

With everyone sitting around the grill with the purple octopus bag over it, everyone grabs a tentacle and prepares for something. I'm only the one who didn't grab a tentacle, as I have no idea what's going on, let alone what I'm supposed to do.

While everyone else is biding their time, Do'ba went off alone and started inhaling the hose in his hand like a water pipe. After removing the hose from his mouth, he exhales calmly and slowly as purple smoke comes out of his mouth and nostrils.

"You ever smoked woldi, composer?" Do'ba asks me calmly.

"I don't even know what that is," I respond wittily, somewhat confused.

"Well . . . it's about time you tried some. Heh."

Yomak Nayan hands me the hose that is closest to me, since apparently I didn't notice it, that and also because I have no idea what to do with it. I just hold it in my hand, not knowing how to do this. I look at everyone else who had already started smoking this crap, and from the looks of it it's pretty simple. They simply inhale from the hose, exactly like a water pipe.

I'm not too whole about this thing. I look at Yomak Nayan, and seeing her smoke, I can understand that there's more to her than just beauty and charisma. This is definitely not charismatic behavior.

Eventually, I'm like, "fuck it." I smoke the hose that I had been given. I can feel thick air running through my throat and going into my lungs. I hold it inside for just two seconds before releasing it back out.

Everyone just sits quietly and smokes, like this is some kind of sacred ritual. I look around, staring at all the others, thinking maybe I should say something, but instead realize that doing what all the others do is the better choice right now.

And then, the sensation comes. The sensation of this substance called woldi comes rushing to my brain. It's different than any other drug that can be found on the black market. Not that I've tried, but the effects of woldi definitely don't match what I've been taught about drugs. Of course, this is the Novaverse, and I have many things to learn about it.

The sensation of woldi just gets stronger as I sit in my place, thinking and waiting for something to happen. Suddenly, the concepts of good and evil get intertwined, as I can't tell the difference between them. The matters of teen-hood suddenly become irrelevant, as I feel like raging hormones suddenly disappear and my desire for alcohol suddenly seems like a sin. I feel the need to run around aimlessly and play and have fun. I look at the others, and they all suddenly look like adults to me. I feel innocent. I feel . . . like a child.

I find myself spontaneously next to O'or. I don't even know how I got to her. We get close to each other, rubbing our arms together. I suddenly put my head on her lap. It feels nice.

"How did you get your scar?" I ask her hazily.

"They cut me," she says, also hazily, "adapting to new techniques all the time is such a pain. Sometimes I wish I was a kriya'ga, you know. Freezing haa'bak all the time would be yai'pa."

"Yai'pa. What does that mean?"

"It means banana."

"Banana huh? I think I'll marry you."

I go over to be next to Er'sang. I didn't even tell O'or, but I don't think she cared. I put my head on Er'sang's lap. It feels nice too, maybe even more than O'or. I want to stay like this forever. I take her finger with the tattoo to look at it better. Her skin is so soft and nice. I think I like her better than O'or.

"Why do you have a tattoo on your finger?" I ask her hazily. "You're supposed to have only one."

"It's what I do," she says, also hazily. "I fuse with others to form a big monster so we can become stronger. I really just want to stay home. I don't want to do this."

"You're nice. Let's be friends."

"OK."

I'm becoming sleepy. I want to sleep. I feel happy, but why? I don't know why I'm so happy. I just want to go to sleep. But everything is so nice. Do'ba is so mean. I'm never going to be friends with him. And Yomak Nayan is a naughty girl. Good girls don't smoke. Smoking is bad. I will never smoke when I grow up, and I'm going to find me the best wife in the world.

I'm sleepy. My eyes close by themselves . . .

. . . This is nice.

CHAPTER XXIII

A SPLITTING HEADACHE WITH A TOUCH OF DISAPPOINTMENT

I wake up, but I take my time getting up as I prefer to keep my eyes closed and head down for the time being. Speaking of head, I have a really serious migraine that is splitting my brain apart. The surface I'm sleeping on is hard and I find myself drenched in sweat as my clothes stick to my body. As if it isn't bad enough that I've been wearing the same clothes for some days now.

Man, what a night. From what I can remember, we were smoking this thing and then I remember feeling like a kid, as if the world that I saw at that moment was from the eyes of a kid. It's definitely no substance that's similar to anything I have knowledge of, although I can't remember what its name was. Something with a W.

I remember clearly everything before that massive rainbow session. The two girls were kind of quiet and the guy was rather talkative, and that's an understatement. What I remember during the session is a little hazy. They were talking to me about their clans or something. I had my head on their legs too, if I can recall correctly. Don't think I'm going to smoke that stuff again.

But staying for too long lying down, I figure it's time to get up. I do so, and the migraine gets a tad stronger. The next thing that comes to my head is where is Yomak Nayan, and the next thing after that is where the hell can I get an aspirin.

I open my eyes, and I find that I'm in the same room where I smoked that stuff with all the others, except that none of them are here. Grasshead is sleeping on the sofa over there, and I can't see the grill or that octopus bag anywhere. They probably put those things back where they belong.

Nevertheless, I get up from the floor, slowly and achingly, and make my way out of the room, letting Grasshead sleep a little longer. I go all the way to the kitchen, and I can't find Yomak Nayan there. With my eyes half open and a splitting headache to boot, I nonchalantly look around to see if maybe I missed her. I look to the right; I look to the left. I can't find her. In all honesty, I just want an aspirin right now. Also, I wonder what else happened that I don't remember. Probably the stuff that I wish I did remember.

"Ai'ga miyan," I hear a familiar voice say from behind me.

I turn around, and to no one's surprise I see Yomak Nayan. Need I even say how pretty she is? I don't, because I already know that, and it's a fact, because apparently it's part of her clan's theme to look that good. She even looks like she had a really nice beauty sleep, as I don't know anyone who looks that good after waking up, unless she woke hours ago. In all honesty, right now all I care about is getting rid of this friggin' headache.

"Hmm?" I respond ambivalently and oblivious to her statement.

"It means good morning," she explains to me.

"And I'm supposed to know that?" I respond passive-aggressively.

She puts a bewildered expression on her face, presumably because she isn't used to the not-so-friendly "me." Then again, it isn't her fault either, as I woke up in a pretty shitty condition.

"I thought . . . it would be nice," she says hesitantly.

I respond with silence, since the migraine I have puts too much of strain on my mind to come up with a proper response.

"T'fuck is everyone?" I spontaneously ask her.

"They went home," she tells me.

"By themselves?"

"Um . . . yes. Are they supposed to go with somebody?"

"Well, I just didn't expect them to go home in the condition we were in."

"Oh, don't worry. It doesn't last long. Although first-timers might experience the effects a bit stronger than . . . people who use it regularly, which is why you fell asleep."

"So it's an acquired taste? I mean, is that thing even legal?"

"It is. Just don't use it outside your house."

"Why? Will they shoot me?"

She then looks at me in discomfort. Her face says that she isn't satisfied, and her eyes are looking at me weird, like she's trying to figure out what's wrong with me. Now that I think of it, there is something else bothering me other than the headache. I thought we were going to be alone, and I was kind of disappointed to find out that her friends are waiting for us. I guess that's what also is affecting my mood.

"Why are you looking at me weird?" I ask her, trying to figure out what's wrong.

"Why are you acting so weird?" she asks innocently.

"Me? Weird?" I respond passive-aggressively. "I think I'm acting quite fine, thank you."

"It doesn't seem like it."

"Trust me . . . I'm A-O-fuckin'-K! Thanks for asking, though."

She continues to look at me like something's wrong, clearly realizing I'm not telling her the truth. And she's right, although I don't really know how to convey my feelings of dissatisfaction to someone else. Not a thing I'm familiar with, but I'm going to have to make a change if I'm going to live in this world, and open my head for new experiences, even if it's the kind that I don't know yet how to deal with.

"Are you angry at something?" she persistently tries to find out.

"Angry?" I say, after calming down a bit. "I'm not angry, just disappointed."

"Why?"

"Well . . . I thought you wanted some alone time together. Y'know, to talk and stuff. I didn't expect your friends to be here. And especially that asshole friend of yours. I'm not really fond of him."

"Is this what this is about? I thought it would be nice if I introduced you to my friends. You know, you get to know more people and we can do stuff together. You even got to learn more about how the clans work."

"I don't give a shit about the clans. For all I care the clans are like pizza toppings: different flavors but it's still pizza. Same thing, different techniques, but all you do is fight. I can learn about the clans by myself."

A small smile can suddenly be seen on her face. A face I'm more than familiar with and the face that I like to see. I guess I said something that changed her mood, although I'm not too happy myself . . . still.

"Pizza toppings?" she says. "Is that what we are for you?"

"Well, no. it's just that . . . why do you need so many military clans?" I say in confusion. "I mean, where I come from, one is enough, ten at best."

"There's a reason for that."

"I don't give a shit about the reason. I didn't come here to get lectured on the backstory of ridiculous militant techniques. For fuck's sake, a guy that uses toilet paper as a weapon. Where have you heard of that one before? Oh right, you live here, so you already know."

"You're still angry."

"NO SHIT!" I roar at her.

The vibrating anger-filled sound wave that emitted from my throat sent her into complete silence. Not because she is intimidated, since someone of her power needn't be frightened from the likes of the cruelest warmonger, but because she realizes how disappointed I am over the events of yesterday, and therefore feeling sorry for me and that things did not unfold the way she thought they would.

"I'm sorry." I say apologetically, realizing my mistake. "It's not your fault. I have a migraine the size of a mountain and the people here either hate me or . . . have ambiguous feelings for me. I came here because everyone hates me back where I come from. They told me I have a calling here, and I thought I could start anew here, make new friends and forget whatever puddle of shit it was that I came from. And so far it hasn't gone my way. I mean, I feel like it's everyone's life's goal here to persecute me cuz I don't have tiny horns on my face or something. It's almost as bad as what I had before I came here."

"Well, if you have a headache then you should've told me. I would've given you something to relieve it," she says.

I don't respond. I just think about me coming here, whether it was the right thing or not. It's not like the previous world I lived in had anything better to offer me. Then again, I wonder if this world does either. I just hope, and I really believe, that this so-called calling will reveal itself eventually . . . hopefully sooner than later. But the people here . . . I don't know what to make of them. I'm supposed to be a part of them, yet instead what I do is tolerate them. I don't really feel like things have changed since I came here. I still feel . . . lonely.

"Y'know, you're really nice to me," I say gently, after calming down some more. "I don't usually receive this kind of attention in my life. And it means even more when everyone here doesn't really like me. Y'know, it's nice to have this kind of feeling that . . . that someone respects me."

I remain quiet for a while with my palm on my face, continuously thinking about my situation, where I am and where do I want to go from here.

"Y'know, I just left the only guy that kept me safe here," I pick up from where I left, removing my palm from my face. "Don't forget I'm only fifteen. Not easy doing things by yourself."

"For someone who's fifteen, I think you're quite independent," she tells me sincerely.

"You think so? Well . . . I guess so. I didn't have anyone to guide me in my life so . . . I guess I had to figure out things for myself all the time."

"Don't forget that fifteen here is the age that everyone becomes completely independent."

"Yeah. I remember having a conversation about this with So'krang. What was that thing called? That bar mitzvah thing."

"Komo'kea'ka."

"Yeah, that."

She then giggles, catching my attention as I look at her again. I smirk, and have a little laugh with her together. Things are starting to get back on track between us, and hopefully we can get this thing going and make it even better.

"Look, I'm sorry about having my friends being here," she tells me, changing to a more light-hearted tone. "If I knew . . . ."

"You didn't know . . . ," I interrupt her, but gently. "It's OK. At least now we can be together. Whaddya say we go out somewhere? Maybe to a fancy restaurant or something."

"I have a better idea. Besides, if I wanted to take you to a fancy restaurant I'd have to work even harder in battle."

"You were quite badass in battle the last time I saw you."

"Really? That's not what the report said."

"Fuck the report. You were bitchin' back there!"

"Still won't get me into a fancy restaurant."

"Fine. Then surprise me."

"I'll try my best."

Eventually, things just settled out themselves and went back to being all right. I'm quite excited to see what adventures await us both, and hopefully it won't include any of her friends, or anything that could get me disappointed for that matter. The future looks bright again. But despite all this, I could REALLY use an aspirin right now . . . and a shower . . . and some new clothes.

CHAPTER XXIV

THE BEAUTY HUNTER

We're far away from any clan there is in the relative vicinity. I can't see any giant walls around me. All I see is me, Yomak Nayan, Grasshead and her hiphomoy, whose name I still have to find out, running on the meadow as fast as the wind takes us. Must be some special place Yomak Nayan is taking me to. I expected something more casual, but then again, who better connects to nature than me?

We continue riding, caring not about where we're going, but just about what's happening at this very moment. Riding randomly on a terrain filled with grass and flowers. Going nowhere but only towards our joy.

I ride alongside her, looking at her, gazing at her beauty while feeling the strong wind on my face. She looks straight, focused on the thrill of the ride. Then, she turns her head to look at me. She smiles at me, and I smirk back because that's the closest I can come to show my joy.

I then give Grasshead the signal to gallop faster as I hold tight to the grassy fur on his head. Grasshead picks up the pace. I can feel the wind now striking at my face like small balls of ice from a hailstorm. I'm gaining on Yomak Nayan and her hiphomoy. I now find myself riding by myself.

Quickly enough, Yomak Nayan gains on me, and I once more find her by my side. Although this doesn't last long, as she returns the favor by going ahead without me, I realize at this moment that we're in a race.

Grasshead goes full speed ahead as I hold his fur even tighter, without a care in the world but to get to first place. Yomak Nayan is now far ahead of me, as she now appears as a small dot in my vision. The wind now throws itself at my face over the speed at which I'm going. At least the goggles protect my eyes from being destroyed.

I gain on Yomak Nayan, and as I get closer to her, she starts to appear less like a dot and more like herself. I now see her beside me once more, and she looks at me and smiles, and then immediately picks up the speed to stay ahead. I refuse to give up the race, as I pick up the speed even more; every mile per hour that Grasshead gains feels like he's one step away from reaching his breaking point, although I don't see that happening any time soon.

Now with both of us at full speed, we just charge forward, as the hiphomoys stomp on the flowers in the field in front of us, scraping the dirt with their claws, knowing not where they're going. We just ride wherever it will lead us. But if someone were to know where we're going, it would be Yomak Nayan, since she's the girl with the plan. I'm just here for the surprise.

We ride relentlessly, jumping over small rocks and dodging trees by moving sideways. I'm not even paying attention to where we are right now as I'm too caught up in this race. She thinks she can gain on me, but little does she know of Grasshead's superior speed, or so I think since I myself am not fully aware of what he's capable of.

And then, all of a sudden, I notice her slowing down, taking down the speed one step at a time. I'm surprised, as I was sure that she wanted to win this race just like me, although I wouldn't want to win a race unless it was fair, otherwise it would just be childish to claim a victory without a challenge, and it wouldn't prove anything but how childish one is.

I, too, slow down, as I wish to figure out what's going on. Now, as we slow down, we just ride now, slower than a moment ago, and as we continue we keep slowing down, one step at a time.

I look at her with an expression that says "what the hell?" and she just looks at me with those mesmerizing blue eyes and a small smile on her face. I am quickly captivated by her charm, as usual, as I put on a stupid smirk quite immediately, accompanied by my eternal frown, never to give up the unrelenting repressed anger.

"We're here," she says.

I look around. What I see before me are a bunch of trees. Clearly, this is a forest.

"A forest, eh?" I state the obvious. "I expected something a bit more casual. But a forest . . . that might just work."

"What's wrong with a forest?" she asks me innocently.

"Nothing really. I mean, who's better to hang out in a forest than me? Grasshead and I used to walk in the forest near our house all the time, but I think for a date something like a restaurant would be good."

"Restaurants are for eating. This is how the Natin spend mutual time together."

"Riding out to forests?"

"Nature. Besides, there's something very interesting I want to show you here in this forest."

"It HAS to be if you brought me here."

We get off our hiphomoys, and we start walking to the forest with our hiphomoys walking behind us.

Inside the forest, it seems like it's just a plain forest. Nothing out of the ordinary that I can find here. I can't even hear or see any animals anywhere. I bet this is the most interesting part about it.

"So, you said that Natin like to date in nature, right?" I start to say. "So that means we coulda went to a beach, or maybe a jungle. Heck . . . maybe even a swamp. We could catch us one of those bunyip creatures and make us a rug out of it. That'd be a fuckin' adventure."

"I chose a forest," she starts to say. "Maybe we can go to a beach next time, but I chose to come here for a particular reason.

Besides, catching a bunye isn't simple, and we don't kill the creatures of the Novaverse, not even for sport."

"Is the particular reason that there is no reason? Heh."

"AAH!" she says despondently while shoving me gently. "You can be such a dumbass sometimes."

"I'm ALWAYS a dumbass. Why do you think I ended up here?"

A small giggle can be heard from her as a gentle smile can be seen on her face, clearly showing that she remains unperturbed by my shenanigans.

"Come," she says. "Let's go for a walk. I'll show you around here."

And so, we just start walking, slowly going deeper into the forest, and hopefully leading up to what's so special about it. What I see is nothing but simplicity, and what I hear is nothing but pleasant silence. Definitely the things I'm familiar with about forests. I just hope this gets more interesting as we go deeper.

"I was intrigued by you," she suddenly says.

"How?" I inquire.

"How you spared the homong."

"What's a homong again?"

"The giant we fought in our last expedition."

"Oh yeah. I'm still trying to get used to all the names. Y'know, some I remember better than others."

"We don't spare the lives of our enemies, and neither do they. Nobody takes hostages here; everyone dies in the battlefield. I'm sure you're the first to do such a thing."

"He couldn't protect himself. I couldn't bring myself to end him."

"He had a giant cleaver that he used to nearly kill us."

"I meant after he got caught up in the toilet-paper dragons. Seeing him lying on the ground helpless, all tied up, and he was already dying too. It woulda been an injustice to kill a creature who couldn't protect himself."

"What are you talking about? We do it all the time. You don't need to take shame in that. And besides, he could very well protect himself."

"Not in his last moments," I start to sound more empathetic.

"Either way, he would've died. What's the difference?"

I sigh, trying to figure out a way to explain to her. I am dissatisfied that she fails to understand why I chose to spare the homong as I saw him helpless and dying. Then again, I can't blame her. She comes from a militant culture filled with warriors that base their lifestyle on justified murder. And I . . . come from my own world, taught by the hardships of life and the trials that I endured in my existence. But over time, she will learn where I come from.

"I base my life on three principles," I start to tell her. "One, never abandon a friend. Two, never hurt those that can't defend themselves. And three . . ."

I pause for a moment, thinking about the crucialness of the third principle.

"Three . . . the most crucial principle of all . . . ," I pause for another moment, thinking further about the third principle.

"Deliver justice to those who deserve it."

I remove what little signs of happiness or joy I had from my face as I put on a disgruntled one. The third principle reminds me why I am alive and what I must do so that I may be complete. I just stare straight into the forest, thinking about my life.

"Neph?" Yomak Nayan tries to address me, a tad frightened.

I look at her, and I see her worried face. I am reminded that I am currently enjoying a date with Yomak Nayan, and that I do not want to ruin it. I, too, put on a worried face, realizing the wrong that I have done.

"Oh," I proclaim. "Sorry. Got a little carried away with that. But yeah, that's pretty much what I live by."

"It's OK," she gently says. "It's just that for a moment you seemed . . . tense."

"Na. Don't let it bother ya," I say while putting on an somewhat cheerful face.

I return to my normal state, as I resume walking and talking with Yomak Nayan in this seemingly special forest; according to her words, that is, even though what I see is just a regular forest. But I'm here for Yomak Nayan, not the trees. Although I think if she insists on showing me how special this forest is, she's not really succeeding in that.

"You didn't show that kind of compassion at first," Yomak Nayan says, returning to her casual self.

"That's because he tried to split you in half," I explain to her in a wisecracking manner. "Besides, first principle. Remember?"

"But doesn't that mean that the principles contradict each other?"

"Huh? Whaddya mean?"

"Well, first he attacks us, I'm about to die and you attack him. Then he's about to die, and you leave him be. You applied two principles to the same subject."

"Jesus, it's not that complicated. It's like this, really simple: he was going to kill you; I jump in to help you. First principle. Everything clear until now? Good. He lies on the ground wrapped in toilet-paper dragons, near-dead, therefore he can't defend himself. SECOND PRINCIPLE. The principles don't have to overlap or contradict each other to work. They work separately based on the situation. I felt a pinch in my heart when I saw him like that. Cut me some slack. I'm sorry not everyone can be as brutal and merciless in war as your people. Christ, why the hell can't a guy live by his own rules without other people giving him crap for it?"

I put on a more appropriate expression according to the tension I feel inside me, that is, putting on an angry face. I'm a tad irritated, feeling mocked because to me the principles sound like an intelligent creed to live by, but to her it just seems like a contradiction. But I should've probably detailed further about what else I felt about the giant creature.

"He was an animal," I tell her after calming down a bit. "I couldn't get myself to kill a helpless animal. Were it a human then the situation would likely be otherwise."

She looks at me, worried that she might have said something out of place, but I continue looking forward. I know that Yomak Nayan has no ill intentions toward me, but her lifestyle and the way her people go is very linear, as in "just get the job done," without any alternatives, and there don't seem to be any alternatives. That and sometimes people just say things without realizing what they said.

"I didn't mean to mock your way of life," she says softly and apologetically.

"You didn't," I tell her clearly. "It's not easy trying to understand others. Also, maybe I should've been less sensitive about it."

Maybe I didn't explain it too well. She said I contradicted myself; that's what got to me. I didn't expect that, but I stay true to those principles.

"But hey, at least you know it now," I say with a cheerful tone. "Hopefully next time you won't have any complaints when I do something."

"Gotcha," she says happily. "It's okay to attack the enemy, unless they're lying on the floor slowly dying."

I look at her, stupidly smirking once more, showing her that everything is OK and back to normal. She smiles at me in return, naturally. She giggles like her usual self, and I let out a small laugh.

She then suddenly grabs my hand, and pulls me towards a tree. She sits down, leaning on the tree and pulling me down all the while, implying that she wants me too to lean on the tree.

We now both lean on the tree, sitting side by side, looking at the forest around us.

"You know what else was amazing?" she says teasingly.

"My humor?" I wittily respond.

She giggles, as usual.

"Maybe that too." she says cheerfully. "BUT THE WAY YOU THREW HIM!" she suddenly bursts in excitement. "YOU'RE NOT SUPPOSED TO DO THAT!"

"Apparently I am," I wittily respond.

"No. I meant that it's something expected of a Natin, but I would never imagine you could do something like that."

"Well I guess that makes me a Natin, Right? Nah, I'm just kidding. I could never be like you."

And then, we both just started laughing. I try to contain the volume of my laughter, trying to hide it as it is part of my demeanor to remain tough. But her, she just giggles, never shy or afraid of letting others know her laughter. I wouldn't expect otherwise from her.

"But tell me . . . ," she asks, "how did you manage to do it?"

"Truth is there's no proper explanation," I tell her. "I just saw you there, lying on the ground with your broken legs; seconds away from being sliced in half, and then something just burned in me, y'know. Guess I just wanted so badly to save the girl of my dreams."

"Well . . . it's nice to know I can give someone that kind of power. That and someone calls me the girl of his dreams."

"You actually came to me in my dreams, y'know that?"

"Really? You saw me in your dreams?"

"Yeah. It's also the reason I want to be so close to you. I think it means something. A prophecy or maybe a foreshadowing of some shit."

She then grabs my hand firmly and gently, and holds my arm with her other hand and she softly tells me . . .

"It means love."

"WHOA!" I let out a yell as I pull my arm from her.

I stand up, frightened. I look at her and what I see is a bewildered expression, desperately trying to figure out what went wrong. I didn't mean to scare her, but the sound of that word, in that sole instant, ignited a tiny rage within me that I could not hold back. I could not ever stand hearing that word, as it feels like a knife in my flesh.

"Love is . . . ," I start to say, holding the rage from coming out. "Bullshit!"

All of a sudden, she seems frightened and confused, as her expression from a lovable beauty to a hopeless wanderer in an endless valley of despair. She continues to stare at my angry face, with no answer to the situation, as she remains quiet while trying to figure out what went wrong.

Realizing the wrongs I have committed just now, I slowly calm down, taking deep breaths one after the other, with each one being shorter than the last. Soon, I come back to my usual senses.

"Sorry," I tell her calmly.

"I didn't mean t—"

"It's not your fault," I cut her short, but still calmly.

"I don't understand. Your parents must have given you love," she says as if she's sure about it.

"All my father ever gave me was shit!" I tell her with a bit of anger. "Most of the time I was alone."

"And what about your mother?"

I sigh, as the answer to that hurts even more when I think about it.

"I don't know . . . ," I start to tell her with sorrow. "I never met her."

"I'm sorry to hear that."

"Don't be. It's not your fault. It's also the reason why I have nothing with my dad." I slowly raise my voice as I continue. "Motherfucker thinks I killed her at childbirth."

I then exhale, and I become quiet. I put my palm on my face as I try to relax. I can't even hear a whisper from Yomak Nayan. I assume she prefers to be quiet too considering the tense atmosphere. But she should know that's it's not her fault. She didn't know, and she has the right to ask.

"I'm sorry, Neph," Yomak Nayan says in a careful tone. "I didn't mean for things to happen like this."

"It's OK." I try to comfort her as I look in her eyes. "I guess it was just meant to happen. Let's try and enjoy the rest of this trip, whaddya say? Can I see a smile?"

And then, just like that, a small smile can be seen on her face as her beautiful blue eyes catch all the beauty of her regaining happiness. The mood slowly returns back to normal, as I too put on a stupid smirk to show that, since that's the most I'm willing to do.

Suddenly, just as we are continuing from where we left off, I can hear the branches of the trees swinging strong. I look over toward the sound, and it doesn't seem like the wind to me. The branches swing up and down like some kind of physical force is causing it. I get the feeling we're being watched, as I put on a worried and unsatisfied expression on my face. What a way to bring back the good atmosphere.

I look at Yomak Nayan, and she doesn't seem worried at all. More so, she's still smiling, with an even bigger smile than before. I get the idea that she planned this. Maybe this was the special thing about this forest that she so much wanted to show me.

And then, from the top of the trees, a creature with the color of mustard appears from beyond the leaves. Looking at it from the bottom, I couldn't possibly tell what kind of creature this is.

How convenient for me that the creature decided to come down to us. The creature scales down the trunk of the tree, and then finally stands upright on the ground. The creature now faces us, and I have a clear view of him.

He looks like a lizard with the morphology of monkey, about half of my height. Sharp claws on all four limbs, a bulky physique with a fat tail, and a fancy crest to boot. And much like a gorilla, his front legs are on his knuckles, but his hind legs are on his toes. And his head didn't look like that of monkey at all, but more like a land lizard or something. The creature, being right in front us now, slowly approaches us.

"What the fuck is this creature?" I ask Yomak Nayan, a tad worried that we might be monkey chow.

"Don't worry," she tells me. "They're called blibbite."

"The names don't mean much to me right now. I just wanna know if this concerns our safety."

And then, I hear two thuds on the ground next to me, one after the other. I look to my side and I see more of these blibbite. I take a step back, cautious of these creatures and what they may do.

The creatures come even closer to us, and I have no idea what they're going to do and what's going to happen next. Then again, why should I be frightened? We're four and we all have the necessary strength to handle this fight, if there will be one. I don't like hurting animals, so we'll likely just escape.

Then again, Yomak Nayan isn't worried, and she knows better than I, so why should I be worried?

"Is this the special thing you wanted to show me?" I say as I calm down, lowering my defenses. "What's so special about these . . . reptilian chimpanzees?"

"Just watch," she mysteriously tells me.

The creatures come even closer. With them being close enough, Yomak Nayan ducks to look them in the eye. They move their heads around, inspecting her. Then, weirdly enough, one of them hands out his palm and opens it in front of Yomak Nayan, as if he's asking for money.

Yomak Nayan just smiles, as she seems to really enjoy this interaction. I just stare with confusion, trying to figure out the niche of these creatures.

As the creature continues to keep his palm open, Yomak Nayan reaches in to her pocket to take something out. She keeps her palm closed until she holds it atop the creature's palm. Then she opens it as she drops crumbs of something. Something yellow. Something familiar . . . tirasartan.

Now that the creature has his food, he runs away as he keeps it closed in his fist. He runs away, climbing the trees and eventually out of our sight.

And then step in the other two, as it is apparently their turn now. They both approach Yomak Nayan carefully, and after they determine that it is okay, open their palms in front of her to beg for some food. Yomak Nayan does the same as she did with the last one; she takes out crumbs of tirasartan from her pocket and hands it to them, enjoying every moment of it as if she were feeding monkeys at the zoo.

The two remaining creatures, much like the one before them, just run away with their newfound treasure, which will only last until they decide to chomp it down. I just look at them as they disappear before us, trying to wonder what is so special about this.

"So we came here to feed monkeys, huh?" I tell her, dissatisfied. "Not just any monkeys. Monkeys that behave like homeless people. Couldn't we just do that at the zoo?"

"Maybe next time," she says cheerfully. "But this is better."

"If you say so," I respond sarcastically.

I suppose this is some kind of fad of the Natin. Going out to these kinds of forests and feeding these blibbites. I don't mind feeding the monkeys, but I expected something a lot more spectacular when she said interesting, like some kind of giant heavenly fountain that shoots orange juice and attracts fireflies. Feeding beggar monkeys is fine and it's interesting to see that they know how to beg, but we could've done the same at the zoo. Then again, I don't even know if the clans have any zoos. I just hope that there is something deeper than these beggar monkeys.

And then, just as my hopes got up that things will get more interesting, the exact opposite happens and some more blibbites jump down from the top of the trees, landing firmly on all four of their feet. Clearly, they came to beg for food. What else would they want?

Yomak Nayan is so cheerfully excited about this. She just laughs and rushes to feed them, but not before they beg for it. I, mildly disgruntled, just walk over there slowly, spectating from the side as Yomak Nayan enjoys this. At least she's happy; I can enjoy that.

As expected, they hand out their palms and open them, begging for whatever Yomak Nayan has for them, which in this case is probably only limited to tirasartan. She gives them food one after the other. I just stand tall over all of them and watch as the interaction unfolds. One of them even tries to beg from Grasshead, showing that they can't tell who can give them food and who can't. Grasshead just smells the creature's hand in response, as he has no idea what the hell he wants from him.

"Come!" Yomak Nayan yells excitedly. "Join me."

She pulls me down with force, and she has force. I barely balance myself as I finally manage to squat. She takes my hand and gently puts crumbs of tirasartan on it before she returns to feeding the blibbites herself. I love the thing so much that I just want to eat it myself, but crumbs won't do me much, and the monkeys are better off with it.

I look one in the eyes. I look at him disgruntled, with an expression that says "look what you're making me do." The creature in return just stares at me, tilting his head a bit from side to side, with an expression that can't be read, because it's a reptile, and I'm quite sure that reptiles don't communicate via expressions.

"Are you gonna ask for food or something?" I ask the creature impatiently.

Eventually, the blibbite hands out his palm and opens it, asking for whatever I have to offer him. I smirk a bit, as I'm quite curious to see how this unfolds. I slowly lift my hand, eventually having it above his.

I release the crumbs from my hand so that they can fall into his hand, because he begged for it, and what does the bastard do? Drop his hand, with the crumbs falling on the ground.

I stare at the crumbs as they hit the dirt. I'm shocked, as this was not the reaction I expected, nor was it the reaction Yomak Nayan got every time she gave those creatures some of her crumbs. I lift my head to stare back at the creature.

"What the fuck!?" I remark angrily.

The creature backs off a bit, probably intimidated by my mood. I stand up as I now understand that this is no longer fun. But standing upright, I have a better view of all of them, and weirdly enough, they all seem frightened. I didn't think my anger would get to all of them.

They continue to back away, slowly. I can't possibly understand what's gotten into them. I stare at Yomak Nayan, and she too seems worried. She clearly understands that there's something wrong, and I too assume a cautious position, as I have no idea what's going on.

And then, all of a sudden, some kind of rumble, as if it's coming from someone's throat. It is loud, distorted and so painfully unpleasant, as if whoever is making it is bleeding from his throat, continuously coughing up blood. And as it continues to sound, it feels almost like doom is filling the atmosphere.

At the first hint of the noise, all the blibbites just scrammed. And now as I look around us, the only ones I see are me, Yomak Nayan and our hiphomoys.

"Bak!" Yomak Nayan exclaims, awfully worried.

I continue to look around us. All I see are the trees and bushes surrounding us, but the rumble is still sounding in the air.

"You mind telling me what the fuck's going on?" I ask her, also worried.

Yomak Nayan doesn't answer. I can understand she's deep in this situation. She might also be frightened, and I feel powerless to help her, as I have no idea what we're dealing with. But if the Airatsmeka don't scare her, who are complete powerhouses, then what the hell are we dealing with?

Grasshead too catches the wrong of this atmosphere, as he growls violently, assuming a defensive position.

"What's the matter, boy?" I ask him as he continues to growl.

But his attention seems to going towards one direction, as if he already knows where the trouble might be. Looking at him, I notice that he's paying attention to a bush, and staring together with him at that specific bush, I can understand what has set everyone off.

Behind that bush stands something purple. I can't tell what it is, but it is humanoid, and clearly no work of nature. And just as I caught my eyes on it, the rumbling stopped.

I carefully tap twice on Yomak Nayan's shoulder, as I wish to show her this thing.

"Yomak Nayan. Baby?" I whisper to her.

Despite the tension and how focused she currently is, I manage to catch her attention. She looks at me, and I look at her. I gesture with my eyes towards that bush with that peculiar figure.

And then, without a moment's notice, Yomak Nayan just opens her eyes wide, frightened as hell. She turns around fast to quickly get the hell out of there, but before she can even move, something throws itself at her with amazing speed. The speed causes both of them hit hard against a tree, and I can see things clearly.

The humanoid is atop Yomak Nayan, pushing her hard against the ground. She struggles to release herself as she tries to push him away with her hands, but he grabs her head and continuously slams it on the ground. Yomak Nayan is screaming in agony and fear, which is unsuitable for a warrior such as herself. I didn't even pay attention to this creature and what he is, as the only thing I see is my helpless Yomak Nayan.

"NO!" I yell from the deepest depths of my lungs.

I charge over there without even a thought; Grasshead beside me moves even faster. I prepare to punch the humanoid so hard it will break his head, as I am raging with anger. But just before we get close enough. Yomak Nayan lets out a screeching scream as she explodes into a pink mist, flinging the creature through a tree, breaking it, only to hit hard against a tree behind it.

Once the pink mist disperses, I see the glorious and magnificent form that Yomak Nayan assumed during the last time we fought together. A being made of pink bright light with the exterior of a goddess, with an aura of beauty surrounding her. Her power can be felt from far away as she simply stands there on two bare feet, with her pink bright hair floating in the air, defying gravity, and nothing on her face but blank eyes. It is as if she forced all forest and its creatures to embrace her awe, as I now know that things just got real.

She leaps into the air with all her power as a gust of wind can be felt from her force. She is about to go all the way to fight the beast, but out of nowhere, the humanoid came and they clash in midair. The force of the impact sends them both flying high in the air. I now watch high above the trees, as they struggle and fly in random directions, hitting the trees and the ground. They move so fast I can't tell who's winning and who's losing. I can't even see them land any moves because of their speed.

Eventually, they both land fast like a meteor. I see them hurling themselves fast at me. I realize that I'm seconds away from becoming a pancake as I jump to my side to avoid them. The impact breaks the ground as it releases a huge pounding noise, and they immediately bounce off straight into a tree, halting their dynamic fight as they fall to the ground.

Now both on the ground, I see that Yomak Nayan has lost, as she reverts to her normal self. He holds her with both his arms as if he's holding the dead body of his loved one, as she just lays in his arms seemingly motionless. Without any warning, he just bites the left side of her neck as if he's some kind of vampire, but he is not sucking any blood. He is taking a big meaty chunk from her neck like a lion. Yomak Nayan screams in agony as he starts to tear her skin apart with his teeth. A pink glitter can be seen coming from under Yomak Nayan's torn skin, but I had no time for pink blood or whatever it is, as the girl of my dreams is becoming some freak's dinner.

My blood is boiling like water in a cauldron over an open fire as I rush over in the blink of an eye, literally. I can't explain this nor do I have the time to do so, but I find myself instantly grasping the humanoid's neck without even thinking about it, as it just happens by itself. I clench my fist so hard in an attempt to crush the thing's muscles and tendons. The veins in my forehead gorge with blood as my teeth nearly break from locking my jaw so hard. I stare straight at his face, but pay no attention to the details, as these are the least of my interests right now.

As I continue to choke this thing with all my might, he kicks me away and I fly backwards. I immediately get up and I see that Grasshead is a second away from fighting that humanoid.

The humanoid is still lying there on the ground, as Grasshead just goes over there and closes his enormous mouth on half of its body. The humanoid lets out a very loud rumbling screech, as it can feel the puncturing sharpness of Grasshead's fangs protruding into its flesh. But it didn't last long, as the humanoid simply grabs Grasshead by his upper jaw and just throws him away like he is some kind of toy. Grasshead lands beside me, hitting hard on the ground, and I need to tend to him before I go back to dealing with this thing.

Lucky for me, the impact isn't too hard, as Grasshead easily stands back up, although the landing might've caused some minor fractures in the ribs, but nothing that Grasshead can't handle.

My next course of action will be killing this monster. But I am so caught up in the heat of the situation that I almost forget that Yomak Nayan is lying there on the ground with a rip in her neck, seemingly helpless. I am blinded by rage and I can't even tell if she's still conscious. Whatever that thing is, it's stronger than an Airatsmeka, as not even Yomak Nayan could handle it.

Speaking of that thing, I stare at him, and he is back on two feet. I now have a clear view of what he looks like, and he's extremely ugly.

The humanoid has purple skin shiny as a soap bubble. He wears nothing but pitch black pants, torn all over and stained with years of dirt. His right arm is degenerated and underdeveloped, as if it didn't make it properly through gestation, while on the other side of his body he has seven arms, nicely positioned in a line one after the other, with the two front ones dwarfing all the rest by another arm length, and all of his limbs have sharp crystal-like nails. The right side of his face has one eye, while the other side of his face had seven eyes. One where it should be, one on the forehead, one on the chin, one on the side of the jaw, one on the temple, one on the cheek, and one on the side of the cheek. He has crude-looking crystals on his head instead of hair, and his mouth is filled with sharp narrow teeth.

I look at him, and he looks at me. His eyes move rapidly like the eyes of a chameleon, looking everywhere with no direction as to where to look at. I can't expect this thing's next move, as I can't tell what he's focusing on. He just stands there, without an indication of what he's planning. Is he going to attack me? Or is he going to attack Yomak Nayan?

And then, without a warning, he just lets out a rumbling scream. The scream echoes through the forest, as I can feel it pounding into my heart, invoking fear. I don't know what will be the outcome of this situation, but I have to stay strong.

But just as the creature finishes his massive cry, he instantly turns around and runs away very quickly, disappearing from behind the bushes and out of our sight.

I don't know what this means. I don't if we're safe now. But the creature ran away, probably because he realized something. Maybe I proved too strong for him? Maybe he realized that he won't get a piece of Yomak Nayan as long as I'm around? Safe or not, we have to get out of here, because this creature might come back and if that happens, I won't be able to promise anything. One way or another, I need to take Yomak Nayan to a hospital.

With seemingly no danger in sight, I tend to the next biggest priority: I rush over to Yomak Nayan, still lying there on the ground, with Grasshead right behind me. With a better look at her, I can see that the bite in her neck is really deep. Her skin is torn and the flesh beneath it is cut, but the chunk that he tried to rip is still intact. Blood continuously flows out of it as purple sparkles can be seen from under the skin flaps. I wonder what it is, but I can wonder that later. Right now, I need to take Yomak Nayan to a hospital.

I pick her up with both of my hands and I immediately mount Grasshead. Her wound continues to drip blood as it stains my clothing and my hands. I can feel her almost slipping out of my hands. I put her lower body on Grasshead while holding her upper body with my arm and pushing it against my body so that she won't fall, while the other arm holds Grasshead by his hair, as I do whenever I ride him.

"Grasshead, GO!" I yell.

Grasshead immediately dashes. I'll have to maintain the speed so that she won't fall, but have to make sure that we move fast enough before she bleeds to death, even though there's no way a warrior of Yomak Nayan's caliber would die from a puny neck wound, definitely not in a world where all the warriors fight even with their legs and arms ripped off. I sincerely have no doubt that she's going to survive this, but regardless, I can't shake this feeling of fear and pressure, as if something bad is going to happen if I don't rush her to a hospital. Maybe it's just my anger that's guiding me right now, but even so I know that she's going to live, as such a death would be unsuited and disgraceful for a Natin. That's the kind of pride they showed me about them.

Due to all the pressure I'm feeling right now, I failed to check if Yomak Nayan's hiphomoy was following us or if he's okay, since I know the hiphomoys here are trained to act docile, even in the face of danger. I have no idea what he's doing right now, but right now I have to tend to Yomak Nayan. Worst case scenario I'll come back for him later. For now, I suppose he can enjoy the company of the blibbites.

But I care not for anything and everything right now, as the only thing that my mind tells me right now is to get Yomak Nayan to safety and bring back her health. I have no idea what that thing is, and I don't know what the purple sparkles under Yomak Nayan's skin are. All these trivial questions will come after Yomak Nayan is back to herself.

Grasshead will shortly make it out of the forest, and once he does he will go full speed to the first clan we set our sights on, since we have no idea which one is the closest to us. But I just want to say, that despite my initial expectations for this date, and despite the pressure I'm feeling right now . . . this experience truly was interesting.

CHAPTER XXV

A MAN WHO NEVER SETTLED FOR LITTLE

I am currently sitting here by myself in the lobby of another hospital in the clan of Saodin, with Grasshead sleeping peacefully by my side. It's midnight; Yomak Nayan should be coming out of the ER any moment now, and all the patients are either sleeping in their rooms, with or without visitors, or taking a walk somewhere else. From time to time I see someone strolling down here, but they don't bother stopping by to give me company or watch whatever's on the TV here. It's understandable, considering that nobody likes me here, and the few that tolerate me aren't here. All this makes for some boring-ass waiting time. There's no way the TV here can catch my interest. All I see is some kind of talk show with two men facing each other, sitting comfortably on couches and talking about stuff in hang'pan'rika. Maybe if there were a bit of visual context then I'd have something to entertain me while I sit here like an idiot. This is so excruciating every minute feels more like a year. I wish we had never gotten ourselves into this predicament.

I remember it; how I saw the first city I could put my eyes on. How I yelled behind the walls and knocked on the door with all my might until my palms turned red and swollen. The doors opened up, and Grasshead immediately started dashing in random directions, not knowing where is where but only to find the first hospital I can set my eyes on. And as I moved, people nearly got toppled by Grasshead as I was less than cautious this time, since a torn neck is more crucial to fix than falling on one's ass. I was helpless, and I didn't know where to turn, until a nice-enough stranger realized my emergency, and pointed me in a certain direction, uttering only one word: "rononban'pani." I have no idea what he said, but I said "thank you" in response while nodding my head, as I ordered Grasshead to go over there, whatever it may be.

But I also remember during all the chaos that I experienced how I was almost distracted by the aromatic perfection that captivated my nose. The smells of soups and steaks enveloped the atmosphere and redirected my trail of thoughts for a split second to food, and the smell of authentic pizza . . . I was nearly conquered by the joy of smelling it alone, as I wanted to stuff my face silly with pizza. So much fine food around me, and it seemed like a perfect place to enjoy a buffet.

But alas, I had no time to enjoy a fine meal, as I am immediately remindeded what I must do; how I am holding in my hands an injured Yomak Nayan and I must rush her to a hospital.

And there it was. As I got closer to wherever that Natin pointed me, I could see the hospital. I got closer to it, and as I got closer to the entrance, I told Grasshead to slow down, and at the right speed, I jumped off him straight into the hospital and nearly fell forward due to the momentum.

"HELP!!" I shouted repeatedly and helplessly, not knowing what to do. But, of course, with it being a hospital and doctors and nurses everywhere, it didn't take long before I was addressed, as they just took Yomak Nayan off of my hands and straight into wherever, supposedly into the ER. I was later informed that this was indeed the case. Now with my heart at rest, I went to sit somewhere and wait for whatever needs to happen.

And now I'm here, sitting in the middle of the night, or very early morning depending on how you want to see it, waiting for Yomak Nayan while trying to make the best out of these talk shows.

I hear someone walking to my side. I assume it's probably just another everyman, but I can't help but look over there after all this boredom.

It is Yomak Nayan! Walking on her two feet wearing hospital clothes and that weird black plastic cast wrapped around her neck. Seeing this, I can't help but smirk, as this is the maximum I can display when it comes to cheerfulness. However, in complete contrast to me, she just smiles like the magnificence that she is. She walks closer as the sound of her footsteps echo in the emptiness that is the lobby of this hospital.

"They have some nice smells here," I randomly say.

She doesn't say anything, but instead just walks close to me, and sits on the chair beside me.

"This is the clan of Saodin," she tells me. "This is where all food makers come from."

"All of them?" I ask curiously. "Or just the best ones? Cuz I almost dropped you on the side of the road for some pizza."

"You wouldn't really do that, would you?"

"FUCK NO!" I yell out of excitement.

"Ssssshhhh!" she immediately lets out a hush without a thought. "People are sleeping," she then says quietly.

I immediately shut up, looking to my sides out of embarrassment to see if I disturbed anyone, as I didn't realize the volume of my voice. I am just so glad to see that Yomak Nayan is OK.

"Sorry," I say quietly. "But for real, what do these guys do? Surely the bakers must have their own clan. I mean, making bread and making a filet mignon is not the same."

"They make everything. Whether it's the bread or tirasartan or that . . . uh . . . filet?"

"Filet mignon."

"Yeah, that; they make all the food. It's just expected that the veterans do all the fancy things."

"Kinda like the doctors here. It's just 'expected.'"

I think to myself about the wonders of coming here. All the good restaurants concentrated in a single city. Unless all the smells come from the houses, then you can just pay a visit to a Saodin'ga's house for a delicious bowl of soup, or maybe a fine steak.

"So this is where you come to blow up your stomach?" I remark randomly. "What a way to invest your time. Do you think they have an entire restaurant for potato chips?"

"I don't know," she tells me, "but you're welcome to check."

I smirk at that reaction, as I can tell she meant that humorously, with a slight implication that there might not be an entire restaurant for potato chips. Then again, it doesn't matter to me, as it was a joke to begin with.

And the conversation about the guys who bake the bread and serve you fancy food altogether is really nice and all, and I'm glad that everything is back to the way it was, but that doesn't take away from the real subject at hand: what the hell was that thing back in the forest? When the question comes to my mind, I let go of the joy I'm having in this talk and I am reminded of what really bothers me. The concern can be seen on my face by my worried expression.

"You mind telling me what the fuck that thing back there was?" I tell her quietly and with concern.

The happiness in Yomak Nayan's beautiful face can then be seen sliding away, as fear can be seen taking over. Slowly, her expression shows signs of hesitation and sadness, as she knows what that thing was, yet it's clear that she doesn't want to talk about it. Together with her fear of the subject, not a word about it comes out of her mouth but a sigh of despair.

I give her time to think about it, whether she wants to talk about it or not. I know she'll talk about it, as Yomak Nayan is not one to back down from death, or even the thought of it. No Natin does, and that it something I've learned during my stay here.

"His name is Sima Brak," she tells me fearfully.

"That's Sima Brak!?" I say, surprised at the discovery. "Up until now I've only heard about him, but nobody said he was that ugly. Heh. But seriously, what the fuck is he?"

"He's a murderer." She suddenly explodes in grief without breaking her voice or raising it. "He's been killing Karin'ga for more than seventy years now."

"Seventy years?" I remark, surprised at yet another notion. "How hard is it to catch one fucker?"

"He hides. And whenever a Karin'ga walks by him he just jumps out and kills her, and then he proceeds to absorb her kalocytes. He never stays in one place and he can teleport, which makes it impossible to track him with retrocognition. We tried escorting Karin'ga to protect them, but he proved too strong for whatever escorts we had, and we don't even know what the extent of his power is. They always say . . . look out for yourselves when walking outside the cities. I don't know how much this helps, but it doesn't look like it works."

And then, she just stops talking. Her expression gives away the implication that something deep caught her mind. I don't know what could be so strong as to suddenly sway her from the conversation like that, but it does seem like the subject is a bit hard for her.

Her face becomes even more stone-like and lifeless as she becomes harder to interpret with every second that passes.

I move her hair aside like a curtain so I can get a better look at her, but alas, it does nothing to show what she's feeling.

"Yomak Nayan?" I try to address her gently, holding her hair as I try to look at her. "Is everything all right?"

"HE KILLED MY MOTHER!" she suddenly says in anger and a raised voice, very much unlike her.

And with that, I could finally see her face again, and this time, I did not find pleasantness in looking at her. She was clearly filled with hate, as her eyebrows bent with anger, giving away a nasty frown as the beautiful blue eyes that stood beneath them were filled with murder. I could never imagine that the ever-lovable and jolly Yomak Nayan that I know would be able to give in like this to rage. But everyone has their fuse which varies in length, and hers just burnt down.

"Sucked the life out of her," she says hatefully towards that wretched being. "Sucked the kalocytes out of her!"

And then, in an act of comfort-seeking, she just stops talking and slowly calms down as all the muscles in her face relax, and she slowly reverts to what she was before. She then leans on my shoulder. With the quiet enveloping us, we both stare aimlessly at the empty corridor right in front of us. I can feel her calm once more.

"Don't worry," I whisper gently to comfort her. "I can't imagine that there is anything I can say to compensate for your loss. But . . ."

I look to the side for a slight moment. I really don't know what to say. I guess the confrontation caused her to deal with these circumstances once more. The same circumstances that she wishes to avoid in order to stay strong and collected. But sometimes life just pushes us in the wrong direction, forcing us to cope with certain situations and deal with the pain. I guess the least I can give right now is part of me.

"My mother's also dead," I continue to attempt to comfort her with some of my humor. "At least now we know that we have something in common."

I lash out a small smirk to indicate that I only mean humor. Of course, she can't see it, as she is still staring at the empty corridor. She seems deep in thought once more, but I just hope I didn't make it worse with my joke, since it might've been inappropriate.

And then, she raises her head. I finally get a look at her face again, and I don't really enjoy seeing her like this. Her face becomes once more hard like stone and I can't make out what she's feeling or thinking. She clearly holds sadness within her, but she holds it back. It's as if it naturally happens that she can overcome it without breaking. But even so, the subject is strong enough to make her lose her character and sink deep into thoughts of whatever that traps her soul at this moment.

"I don't get it," she vaguely remarks, disappointed in something. "Is everything a joke to you?"

"What?! No!" I reply quickly to defend myself, surprised at the accusation. "I was just trying to make you feel better."

I felt embarrassed, as I realize the mistake that I just made, and it was indeed inappropriate. I'm now silent as a sign of my regret, but I continue to look at her. She too remains silent, as her expression loosens up and it seems as though she's reverting to the Yomak Nayan I know, no more a stoneface filled with tormenting thoughts.

Then she just spontaneously lets out a small laugh, clearly indicating that she is back to her usual self. It only goes to show that, despite the hardships, she easily gets over them to not let herself become a victim, although I still wonder what made her laugh.

"You're so sweet," she says in a calm, soft voice.

"First principle. Remember?" I tell her in good humor.

Like always, she realizes my humor as she just laughs.

"And don't call me sweet," I tell her, changing my tone to be a bit more aggressive. "Sweet is for the weak."

I look away, wiping the smirk off my face, thinking about what I just said, about my way of life, and how I must remind myself of who I am and where I want to go. She too, out of confusion, stops laughing and smiling, trying to understand where the hell that statement came from.

"Being good-hearted doesn't necessarily mean that you are weak," she tells me softly in a hesitant tone.

I exhale from the nose, as I don't know how to say this right now, especially not after that aggressive statement. I meant it to come out in a different way, but sometimes I just can't help myself but be unaware of my behavior.

"I'm sorry," I tell her regretfully, looking to the side. "It's just that . . . ."

I exhale air from my nose once more, indicating the dilemma I'm confronted with. Not much of a big deal, just a mistake, but I prefer to let go of it. This is pretty much what I do regularly and the thing that I must overcome: the desire to escape.

"I still don't understand what this guy is," I ask her in a quick attempt to change the subject, looking at her once more.

She looks down for a second, as she apparently did not expect the sudden change in the subject.

"He used to be a Natin," she goes on to explain after calming down. "But now he's nothing but a distortion of nature."

"That . . . that doesn't really help me understand what he is."

She sighs, realizing that she has to reluctantly elaborate on the history that is Sima Brak.

"Sima Brak was born a Natin, like any of us," she says as she starts to tell the story. "But he was special: he was the first male to become a Karin'ga."

"He was the first one seventy years ago?" I add some of myself to the conversation. "How long have you guys been around?"

She looks at me critically, as if my comment is inappropriate, yet she says nothing. I should stop trying to be witty all the time and better realize that certain situations call for tact.

"The reason that no males exist in the clan of Karin is because the Karin'ga tiamtsat does not respond well to large amounts of testosterone, and they are naturally repelled by it," she continues. "But Sima Brak defied that when he entered the clan of Karin. I heard everyone was shocked at his komo'kea'ka, but I wasn't there so I couldn't know. Nobody saw it coming, and they couldn't even imagine what would become of him. Of course, it didn't take them too long to find out. At first, he showed promising results, utilizing the kalocytes in ways that not even the females could. He could teleport, something that no Karin'ga had been capable of."

"There's a first for everything," I comment wisely, or at least trying to sound wise. "And you'd be surprised what surprises life holds."

"He seemed to be stronger than any other Karin'ga; I suppose that's logical considering that he was a man. But even for him, his potential seemed way out of the borders of normal capabilities. He went on his first expedition only eight months after his komo'kea'ka, which is even less than what I managed."

"Is that a good thing?"

"It's a great thing! It means that you're an accomplished Natin. More so, in most of his expeditions, he got most of the kills. That's what they say at least. The stories about him vary, whether it's about his origin or his accomplishments or whatever."

"And what version of his origin did ya hear?"

"Something ridiculous. That the Gangra were drunk and wanted to mess with the tiamtsat in the air so they shoved all the Karin'ga tiamtsat into a baby. But there's one thing that everyone is certain about him."

"And that is . . . ?"

She sighs, realizing that the story gets deeper and more intense. I'm already eager to find out where things go downhill for this Sima Brak.

"In one of his expeditions . . . ," she explains, "he deliberately stabbed an Airatsmeka through one of his teammates with a spear he had forged. It was no mistake, and everyone knew he did it on purpose. I heard that he didn't even deny it, saying that he got in the way or something."

"Oh shit," I reply, as I'm shocked to hear this. "That is just . . . fucked up."

"I wouldn't be surprised about it because despite his accomplishments, there were signs foreshadowing that something like this could happen. They say he was unusually aggressive towards his peers and was quite unruly, and as he kept on battling his skin would turn pinker with every expedition. Of course, no one expected that he would betray his own kind, as we Natin always stand by each other. It is part of our creed and our nature."

"So what did they do about it?"

"He was suspended from going on expeditions and was . . . house-arrested. Even so, he disobeyed those orders. They punished him by adding even more days to his sentence, but he didn't seem to mind, until the day that he was threatened that if he kept this on, he would be banished from the Novaverse, the greatest punishment one can get."

"Worse than death?"

"Death?" she says with a smirk. "Death is a compliment here. I'm pretty sure you noticed by now that we live to die."

"Hmm. Yeah . . . ."

"But during that day, he already looked like a monster. His skin was pinker than that of a gonglik, like he was producing more kalocytes than usual and that they completely filled his skin, and all of his teeth looked like fangs. But that was just the beginning of his deformation into a filthy animal."

"And how did he react to the threat?"

"He just sat there in his house. Nobody heard from him for days and nobody knew what was going on with him. Some even believed that he was dead, and they were more than glad to believe that was the case. But one day, he just killed a Karin'ga. Left her thrown in a random alley as if she were trash, with the kalocytes sucked out of her. Nobody saw who killed her, but everyone knew it was him. And on that moment, they decided to banish him, and he didn't take it lightly. He killed the messengers right in front of his door and then he proceeded to make his way out of the clan, killing several Karin'ga on the way, taking their corpses with him only to suck out their kalocytes."

She sighs, as she apparently had grown tired of the misery that he had left in his wake, yet it seems like she isn't done talking.

"At first he would be no concern," she adds. "But as the death toll grew with each year, we knew that we needed to hunt him down, but we could never find him. As we struggled to find him, he would become even more elusive and continue the killing, further deforming into what he is today."

"Wow that's . . . quite a story," I remark half-mindedly. "But there is something that I still need to understand: these kalocytes . . . are they tiamtsat or what? I'm sorry; usually I don't ask about this stuff but it seems like an important factor here."

"Kalocytes are cells that exist in the subcutaneous tissue of the Karin'ga. They are a product of Karin'ga tiamtsat together with the body, and it's where the beauty and power of the Karin'ga come from."

"I suppose that's the pink stuff I saw when he tore your neck?"

"Yes. Whenever I use my powers, I harness the kalocytes in my body. I can condense them to a single place and release them to form a blast, or I can raise them above my skin to take on the form that you saw. That way, I can control them more easily. I can use them in more ways than one, and that's the same for every Karin'ga, except for him. I think it has something to do with the kalocytes reacting differently to his body. The kalocytes are supposed to cause beauty, yet they made him ugly and hateful. A glutton seeking to fill himself with even more kalocytes. Who the bak even does that?"

"Hey. Even the prettiest garden has weeds, even if it's just one. The garden I come from . . . it's full of weeds."

She laughs gently in response, but not as happily as she often does, still indicating that the sadness still lingers in her. At least now I know that it's slowly leaving her, little by little.

"And who better to know that than you," I finish my sentence with a compliment.

And at that moment when I look at her, I see something that's out of place. She's already calmed down, as all her face muscles relax and she reverts to the lovable Yomak Nayan I know that always loves to smile. But there was just one thing that didn't quite fit the picture: a gentle tear sliding down her beautiful eye, leaving behind a narrow trail of water across her face.

"Are you . . . crying?" I say, confused, as I think that the tear came a tad too late.

"What? No!" she says, somewhat embarrassed.

She immediately wipes the tear from her face, never letting go of that quirky smile, as if the sadness doesn't really affect her, and the tear just decided to come out by itself, and there is completely no connection between what she's feeling and what her body discharges.

"I'm sorry," she says, still somewhat embarrassed. "The Natin don't cry over the dead. But sometimes it just . . . happens, I guess. It's unusual. I shouldn't be doing this."

"Don't feel bad, OK." I tell her in an uplifted tone, trying to comfort her. "Just try not let it happen again. OK?"

"I'll try," she says as she giggles.

Suddenly and out of the blue, a bewildered expression catches her face, as if she is reminded of something.

"It's getting late," she suddenly remarks. "I have an expedition tomorrow!"

"Oh, really?" I reply with surprise.

"Do you want to join me?" she asks me excitedly "We can duo."

"Duo?"

"Every Natin is allowed to bring one person with them to an expedition, but not without their consent."

"So THAT'S how So'krang managed to get me in all of his jobs," I comment. "But he never mentioned anything about duo."

"So do you want to or not?"

"Wait a minute; I don't get this. Aren't they cutting you any slack for being in the hospital or whatever?"

"I'm getting released tomorrow morning, and the expedition starts like ten hours after that. So, no. Now do you want to or not!?" she says optimistically, returning even more to herself.

"Sign me up, baby. I wouldn't want you to die without me."

She laughs once more, returning ever so close to her usual personality of happiness and a cheerful demeanor.

"Great," she says. "You've been on a capture expedition already?"

"No," I reply clearly. "What's that?"

"You'll find out," she tells me vaguely. "Now shall we get some sleep? We have an adventure waiting for us."

"Most definitely. I think I'm also kinda tired."

And with that, she gets up from the chair and makes her way towards her room. I watch her back as I see her walking away from me, only to see each other again the day after.

"Yomak Nayan!" I call.

She turns around in response, but she says nothing, as she awaits whatever I have to say to her.

I'm about to tell her whatever I have to say, but I am skeptical about it. I just want her to feel better.

"We will find him," I tell her with clear certainty, but secretly with doubt. "And we will kill him."

She just lets out a small smile as she looks me in the eyes, accepting my answer and believing in it, and she knows that if I can't bring it forth, than at least I am true to her.

"I know," she says somewhat ominously, "because I plan to kill him myself."

That makes the second time this night I've seen her with murder in her eyes, but this time it isn't out of anger, but determination. I am a bit freaked out, as she didn't seem like the bubbly Yomak Nayan I know, but a bloodthirsty warrior who will stop at nothing to dispose of the enemy. That's the last thing I saw of her just before she turned back and walked towards her room, leaving me only with that thought.

Of course, all this is just a bad happening, as I know for sure that Yomak Nayan is still Yomak Nayan, and that she will completely return to herself by the end of the night. As the night comes to a close, I try to find a comfortable position on this not-so-comfortable chair as I listen to the unintelligible nonsense coming from the TV as Grasshead peacefully sleeps in the background.

And as I slowly enter the dream world, as hard as it may be sitting on a chair and all, I am suddenly reminded of something that I saw just moments ago. An intriguing sight, but definitely not something that's going to ease my sleep: that one tear that came out of Yomak Nayan's eye. It didn't even seem in the slightest that she was holding herself from crying, but rather that she is naturally more resistant to crying, as if it is some sort of natural strength, which I assume all Natin share. A strength that could almost be felt as it radiates all over the atmosphere. But alas, the sorrow was too much for her, and she had to let it out. If it means anything, she handled it pretty well. If she was a human, she would've released a waterfall of tears that would have drowned the entire hospital.

The Natin don't cry over the dead, huh? I guess this is just another example of how badass these people are. But if they don't cry over the dead, then what do they cry about? Actually, it doesn't matter. I have bigger problems on my mind right now, and one that's currently bothering me the most . . .

When the hell am I going to fall asleep?

CHAPTER XXVI

INTRODUCTIONS ARE NOT MANDATORY!

The blue jello cube never gets old, as I fall through the sky while inside it, seeing the ground come closer and closer to me through a filter of blue gel. I couldn't even tell the textures of the ground we're landing on, but Yomak Nayan mentioned that it's in Raboja near the clan of Tarik, not that it means much to me but good to know. But this cube thing they constantly use to ease their landing . . . it beats parachutes by miles.

As I fall, I think about last night's conversation I had with Yomak Nayan, mainly the part about Sima Brak, and even more about the part where she said she plans to kill him herself. I wouldn't want something to get in the way between me and Yomak Nayan, but now that I know who this Sima Brak is and what he is all about, I really want to kill to him to guarantee my stay here, even though So'krang told me that I don't stand a chance against him, but I just realized something: I'd rather be dead then go back to the cage, so I might as well take the risk. I just hope it's not as important to her as she makes it look so I can take Sima Brak's head as a trophy. But before I figure out how to start this manhunt, I first have to get this expedition over with. I'd better put aside any and all thoughts about a grotesque purple octo-man, because I need to focus hard on this mission, and then I can think about whatever I want.

The cube lands on the hard ground and slowly dissipates into nothingness as I find myself once more able to move freely without any resistance. My hands touch the hot hard ground beneath, as if I'm on a grill, and the warm beams of the sun strike my back, slowly getting hotter as the remains of the cube evaporate from my shoulders.

I stand up on my legs and I feel a strong wind hitting me in the face, as if I'm seconds from suffering a nasty defenestration. I look around me, and I see red rocks of varying sizes aligned next to one another, with the spaces between them differing in size as well. The area is rather sandy and seems to be filled with cracks. I soon realize I'm in a canyon.

As I continue to stare at the hot scenery, I hear a splat to my side. One piece of the cube manages to splash into my hair, but it didn't take too long for it to dissipate. I look to my side, and I see that it's already dissipated halfway through its short life cycle into a pile of blue ooze. And out of that pile comes Yomak Nayan, as she had been falling together with me. Of course, there's always Grasshead. But he's an integral part of my being, and he came landing with his own cube. We always look out for each other, so I'm not really worried about him, even though right now I can't see him, nor do I know where he is.

I feel a body behind me and I hear a short quiet growl of a hiphomoy behind me. Of course, I have no doubt who it is. I look back behind me and I see Grasshead.

"Hey, boy," I tell him. "What're you doin' behind me?"

I do find it weird, as Grasshead always takes my side.

I look to my side to see if anything's wrong with it. What I see before me is a fall to my death, as apparently I am standing at the edge of a cliff.

"Whoa!" I let out as soon as I realize where I'm standing. I freeze in my place, as I realize that any further step may or may not lead me to my end. I believe that I'd prefer the latter. After standing still like a statue and assessing the situation properly, I slowly and carefully take a step back, without even looking behind me.

Now, with danger out of the way, I can once more return to what I'm supposed to be doing. I look to my side, and I see Yomak Nayan standing on two feet. She looks at me and smiles gently, although a bit hesitantly and not in her joyful kind of way. I guess the contents of last night's conversation still runs in her head. I have no doubt that she will get over it sooner than later.

"WO!!" a voice shouts from far away, echoing through the canyon. "Kata am'in ik na?"

I look over to where the voice is coming from, and I see a group slightly away from us. Of course, it can't be any other than the group we are assigned to, but why the hell does that voice sound familiar? I just can't quite put my finger on it.

Nevertheless, we three go over there. The closer we get to the group, the better I catch the appearance of all of them. It suddenly becomes apparent that a woman is standing in front of a bunch of people, obviously making her the leader. But in addition to that, something slowly comes to my mind about that woman, and as I get closer, that thing slowly becomes more and more apparent, but is still not obvious.

Eventually, we reach the group, and I have a very clear view of the leader. For a second, I get a quick look at all the other members of this team, but then I focus all my energy in trying to figure out what the hell's wrong with this woman. That black hair, that stupid face. If I'm using these words to describe her then my instincts tell me that we didn't get along much, yet I still can't figure out who she is. She, too, looks at me intriguingly, as if I'm some kind of alien . . . which is true, by the way.

"Yoooou?" I say confused, trying to figure this out. "Have we met before?"

"To'shin, remember?" she tells me like she's some kind of badass. "From your first day."

I take a moment to think, looking to the ground and further focusing to remember who the hell she is, as I'm not sure what she meant by that vague sentence. First day of what exactly? First day of my life? First day of my tenure as the president? I've met a lot of Natin during my short stay here, relatively speaking. I suppose someone might've waved me hello when I got here but . . . wait . . . .

"Oh!" I exclaim. "You!"

I let out a fake half a smirk as I want to be as diplomatic as possible and not mess this up for everyone, especially not for myself and Yomak Nayan. She in return does nothing but hold some kind of disappointed expression.

She was never really fond of me; I could tell that much even with what little she said when we first met. I, on the other hand, am dismayed by her lack of empathy, even before I had a clear first impression of her. I don't think we'll see eye to eye much on this trip, but I can imagine that we'll find a compromise between our decisions. She has to accept me by now, as I am part of this world, and I don't care how tough she pretends to be.

"How's your stomach?" I ask her indifferently, still holding a fake smile.

She says nothing, but instead continues to hold that disappointed expression.

I guess the impression she left on me was so bad that I just wanted to forget her. Not really a fond memory when someone tries to choke you to death, or kick dust in your eyes when you're completely helpless to do anything. That and all the adventures I had up until now kind of distracted me.

"So what, you're a leader now?" I ask her cynically.

"First time," she tells me somewhat antagonistically. "Although I never thought it would be with you."

"Yeah. What a fucking coincidence. If I'm seeing you here I musta crossed a black cat on my way here. Or . . . whatever you guys have here."

The animosity increases as she continues to hold onto that disappointed expression, which changes to look like more of a disgruntled expression now. I think her bitterness towards me just stems from the fact that a heranga was able to fight on par with her, if not better. That thought alone probably pisses her off, but she has to stay diplomatic for the sake of the team and her leadership, even if she struggles to do so, which is quite apparent to me.

But seeing her now like this, I think she lightened up a bit. As more people become familiar with me, so does their tolerance with me. She can't be xenophobic by herself, although she has the privilege of holding a personal grudge. We're not friends, and we probably never will be, but we're definitely not enemies. Does that make us frenemies? I'll just have to give this relationship time and see where it goes.

"Go stand in line," she says coldly.

With no better option, I do as she says, even though I would prefer it be my own initiative. On my way to stand in line, which is not too far from her as she is standing right in front of everyone, I have a clear view of all the teammates I will be fighting alongside in the forthcoming battle, the details of which I still have to learn.

The members didn't look too different from any other Natin. They didn't look different at all from any Natin, really, although I don't think they're from clans I know of yet. I see one girl and three guys in front of me, which altogether makes it four guys and three girls, the usual composition of any team. Nothing to expect otherwise.

One of the guys wears a beige we'jei, rekarakib and na'sho. Parallel to his hip is a sickle and a long knife that, upon closer inspection, is actually a wakizashi. His tattoo is similar to some other tattoo I've seen before, but I can't quite remember. The last time I saw someone carry this many sharp objects at once was that smoker on my first expedition. Maybe they come from the same clan?

Another guy also wears rekarakib and na'sho, but his we'jei has an intricate tribal motif of sorts over a black color, rather than just a simple color. He has no weapons whatsoever. It's probably just part of his style.

The last guy on the team also wears the same as the other two men, only his we'jei is colored a pinkish bright red. Like that other guy, he too has no paraphernalia of any sorts. I wonder what he's planning.

The only other girl wears a tight orange vest tucked tight by a belt around her stomach, which is unlike all the other members who just wear we'jeis, although it does go well with her orange hair. In addition to that, she wears short rekarakib down to her knees and na'sho. She has some kind of giant water gun floating behind her back, and some kind of thick knife with a canister attached to the end of its hilt sticking to her hip, just beside something that looks like a censer. Her weapons look the most interesting, but I'll just have to wait and see what she has in store.

After assessing all the information I can simply by looking at them, I go over to stand by the girl's side. I get a feeling that she would be friendlier, or at least more tolerant, if I stand next to her. Don't know why, but I get the feeling that girls respond with more tolerance than guys, although To'shin contradicts this, but she's a special case.

Yomak Nayan soon catches my side, and with all the team members finally taking their places, everyone can prepare for the mission to start whenever the leader gives the word.

But with all this just waiting to happen, I'm more concerned about Yomak Nayan, as the events of last night still sit in my head. I look over to her, but she doesn't make eye contact with me, nor do I think she even notices I'm looking at her. She bears a neutral expression on her face indicating that she might be focusing on the mission at hand, which proves her professionalism. That or she's just blocking it, but I can't tell.

"Naidi'jek'in, nen'pen," To'shin says seriously.

As she calls out in a loud voice, whatever she might've said there, everyone pays attention to her.

"Imas jek'in, etiki an hidotat tidrai. Imas kata etoki jek'in oho'in?" she says in hang'pan'rika, almost deliberately out of spite. "Etiki eti'in—"

"ENGLISH, PLEASE! God!" I interrupt her, irritated.

She sighs, as if a mountain of terrible things has befallen her.

"This is a capture mission," she continues reluctantly in English. "As you know, we have a high-profile torpadon not too far from here responsible for the deaths of approximately one hundred Natin. It's uncommon for a farma to kill this many of us, but if it happened then it was probably our fault to some extent that we allowed him to achieve this. In cases like these where a low tier haa'bak becomes high-profile, the captain is a shakten'ga, which is where I come into play. This is my first time as captain, so don't make this hard for me."

I look at her with disbelief, since she seems more interested in herself and her ego rather than the wellbeing of her teammates. Her speech wasn't even very professional or leader-like, and some of it was dedicated to her. Then again, it is her first time, and she's only doing her best, even if it doesn't go too well for her.

"Any questions?" she asks as if she wants to get it over with.

"Capture? Torpadon? Farma? Explain . . . in that order," I say impatiently with a humorous touch.

She looks at me, clearly unamused by my attempt at a joke. She blinks hard once, and then a second later, clearly displaying her impatience and maybe even intolerance towards me. She then rubs her eyes, further indicating at her strife over a trivial matter. And finally, she sighs, as if the examples of her nonsense before that weren't enough. It is her call, after all. I mean, she asked if there were any questions.

"Capture missions are when a haa'bak kills a lot of our people," she explains impatiently. "Then, instead of killing it, we capture it and bring it home for execution. Torpadon is a type of haa'bak that belongs to the third tier of haa'bak power classification known as the farma, which also answers the third question. Anything else?"

"Maybe later," I respond wittily.

She just stares at me, without saying anything. Her eyes and the silent anger that she displays show a complete lack of will to accept me. She can't understand me; she refuses to acknowledge me; she rejects the idea that my place is here. She is the perfect example of a conservative Natin; one who loathes the heranga with every cell in their body. But even among those that stubbornly cling to their collective hatred of humans, they can't deny that I'm here for a reason, whether they like that reason or not.

"The subject is a distance away from here," she says seriously to everyone, trying to look professional. "As common, we will walk to him. He should be together with at least two other haa'bak according to reports. I suppose you all know how to do your job, so I won't have to guide you much."

Hearing that, I'm saying to myself in my head, "Bitch, you won't be able to guide them at all." Once more, I find myself in disbelief as to why she's the leader. Clearly there must have been some factors that whoever evaluated her must've missed. Factors that should've been taken into account and obvious ones no less. What about personality? I mean, she seems kind of desperate here. I hope for her that this whole leadership thing is going too hard on her. More so, she doesn't seem like she knows what she's doing. So'krang would've handled this situation so much better, but comparing her to So'krang is like comparing a whale to an elephant.

And that's the thing, because she doesn't know what she's doing. It's her first time, and eventually she'll get the hang of it the more she does it. What's more troubling is why am I feeling sympathy for her?

"Let's go," she says impatiently, already desiring to move on.

"Wait," I call her out.

She is already facing our destination, and then she turns her attention back to me. Looking at her face, I can see that she's completely displeased with having to further delay what she may or may not want to get over with, with an expression that says "what the hell do you want?" I thought Natin liked killing stuff.

The silence emitted from her as she stares at me with those reluctant eyes puts me in a bit of an uncomfortable spot. I take my time with what I have to say, as I ask myself why I keep up with this nonsense.

"Don't we do introductions?" I ask.

"It's not mandatory," she says in her impatient way that I'm quite familiar with now. "Now let's go." She turns to her left to face our destination once more, already prepared to get a move on.

"Then let's do it," I call before she can move on.

And once again, she turns her attention back to me, facing all of us and away from our destination. She looks at all of us, and not just me this time. I, too, look at everyone, something I hadn't done before because I was too preoccupied with To'shin's leadership-in-the-making, which wasn't so pleasant to the eyes and ears. Some look like they are already preparing to leave; others take their time. I can't tell by their expression what they think of To'shin's performance as a leader so far, although I don't think it matters to them as much as it does to me. Probably because I have some personal history with her, and also maybe because they don't doubt their leaders. But I still have much to learn.

I look back at her. She's still looking at everyone, and then she looks at me. She stares deep into my eyes, and I stare back at her. The eye contact between us this time is strong, and isn't accompanied by impatience or a lack of desire to tolerate the other.

"All right," she says, looking back at everyone. "Let's introduce ourselves. Name and clan."

She didn't even sigh at that moment. It's probably for her peers more than it is for me, as it would probably seem disrespectful if her teammates didn't seem important to her.

"And kill count and maybe what you like to eat," I suggest as something friendly.

"No, just name and clan. Make it short," she shuts me down.

And once more, I see the typical To'shin that I have quickly become familiar with over the last several minutes. In addition to knowing her before this, of course.

"Who wants to start?" she asks seriously.

At first, everyone is silent, as no one knows who will be the first to introduce themselves, nor does anyone want to take the initiative. But it will happen eventually.

Of course, it didn't take too long before it happened, as the guy with the intricate tribal motif on his we'jei indecisively raises his hand, indicating that he wants to start, as he apparently realizes that if he won't start, then no one will.

"I am Yai'war Shin'stak from the clan of Bibira," he says.

Afterwards, there is complete silence, as once more everyone is afraid to take the initiative. Nobody knows where to go next as everyone looks at each other, waiting for a response from anyone.

"I am Sosom'bawit Dong of the Isopera," suddenly says the girl.

With all the remaining members who haven't introduced themselves, it shouldn't be too difficult now for anyone to take the initiative, as everyone now knows where this is going.

The girl isn't patient enough to wait for a voice to be heard volunteering an introduction, as she looks to her left and right to see if anyone wants to take the next turn. Looking right, she focuses her sight on me, as if she wants me to introduce myself next. I stare at her with a feeling that this might be out of spite, but do not rule out the option that it might not. I quickly decide to take it lightheartedly.

She still looks at me, apparently insistent that it will be me who introduces himself next. With no other volunteers, I give in to the pressure applied by her eyes and prepare to introduce myself.

"Neph Baker," I say seriously, still staring at her. "Not from any clan."

Now with my turn over, it's up to the next person to introduce themselves, and in the same manner that that girl did to me, I stare straight into Yomak Nayan's eyes, but with a smirk to show her that I mean no harm, even though she already knows that. She smirks back, but does it much more elegantly in a way that I can never achieve. I could never get tired of looking at those ocean-blue eyes.

"My name is Yomak Nayan of the clan of Karin," she says while looking straight at To'shin.

"Sahit'em Rarik'nen. Sonoka'ga," the guy on the other end says without a moment to waste.

That was quite fast of him. I guess that as the choices narrow down, it's getting obvious who takes the next turn.

And with one participant left, it shouldn't be too hard to figure out who will introduce themselves this time. But out of curiosity or whatever other reason, the remaining guy that didn't introduce himself yet looks to both his sides, staring at everyone, probably trying to find if there's anyone else other than him, as he's probably in denial that he's the last one. At least that's how I see it.

The guy shrugs to himself, realizing that he is the only one left, and prepares to make his name known.

"I am Shin'ga Gari'shin Tijak'kaya of the Sokokit," he says calmly.

And with that settled, I now know the names and the clans of all those that I'm going to work with, although I still have to learn the purpose of each clan.

"Well . . . everyone ready?" To'shin asks everyone in a loud, supposedly leader-like voice.

Everyone just stands still and upright. Not a word is spoken, but their bodies tell that they are ready for some ass-kicking, and they are more than eager to do it.

"It's settled," she concludes. "Let's move!"

And with that, To'shin turns to her left, hopefully for the last time since I don't think she has any more patience reserved for delays, and gestures everyone to keep moving.

Everyone then turns to their right and starts walking, close to the edge of the cliff, without any fear of falling. Naturally, we walk slowly, as commonplace for expeditions.

But as everyone moves at their own pace, with some ahead of others, and some behind the rest of the group, I discreetly take To'shin's side as she walks straight without caring who might come to her sides.

Standing by her, I take my time before telling her what I want, since I don't know how to approach her properly, nor do I know how she will react. I find myself in an uncomfortable situation. She, on the other hand, doesn't even bother to look at me. I wonder if she even knows who's standing next to her. If so, she would probably have me die.

As I continue to contemplate which words I will use, I find myself in a place where I can't find the right words to tell her what I want. By the end of it, I think to myself, "To hell with it."

"Whether you like me or not," I tell her quietly in a disgruntled voice, "I'm staying here. So you'd better get used to it."

And with that, I walk faster to stand by Yomak Nayan's side, who is further ahead of To'shin. As I continue to walk, I take a look back to see how To'shin is doing. Her expression seems neutral in a careless way, as if what I said didn't faze her much. It doesn't matter, because I don't need her acknowledgement. She's just one of many who will soon feel the truth as it hits them hard in their face as I prove my place here.

Because I know . . . I KNOW that things will change with this. I will find my place here and this is where I belong, because all the people that I left behind in my previous world didn't give me any reason to think I belong with them. Soon, everyone here will accept me as . . . one of them.

That is, of course, if I manage to satisfy the clanmistress and not give her a reason to send me back to the cage. Luckily, nobody knows of the conditions by which I am allowed to stay in this world. But it doesn't change the fact that I need to work hard to stay in this new home that I'm in, because I really don't want to go back to a place where I had nothing and nobody. I've been given a chance to make a new home here, and even if I find some imperfections, it's still better than the shit I used to live in.

I keep talking about how I'm part of this world already, when I can't even get that one thought out of my head. The thought that there might still be a chance that I won't get to live the rest of my life here. This is how important it is for me to stay here, because as far as I'm concerned, this is my last chance for a better life. Legendary superhero or otherwise, I just want a place where I can feel at home. And that's why I know that I will find the guts and conviction to pass any and all trials that these people throw at me, for I AM part of this world. There is no other purpose for me, let alone a purpose in the shit from where I came.

But enough worries for now. I want to walk by Yomak Nayan's side . . . maybe even hold hands while doing so. Whatever comes first.

CHAPTER XXVII

CAPTURE THE MASTODON OF A MAN WHICH IS THE TORPADON

The hot sun scorches their skin as they walk through the barren and dry canyon. Not even for a second did she stop heating them with her mighty rays of light; the only time she gives reprieve is at night. Nevertheless, they go unfazed by the heat, as the unpleasantness of this means little to them, for what they are about to face is far worse, and even then . . . it's only part of their job.

Only after nineteen hours of walking tirelessly through the canyon do they finally reach the point where they should see their targets. It's not every day that expedition teams take little time to reach their destination. But when it does happen, it's probably either due to luck, when the team isn't too far away from the enemies when they first land, or due to the competence of the leader, such as if he or she knew which direction to go to shorten the journey. In this case, it's more likely to be the former.

And there they are, at a random spot in the vast canyon, walking away from the team, showing their backs to them. Three Airatsmeka stand by one another, unaware of the fight they will soon find themselves in. Two are just normal pawns, no different than any other pawn, escorting the fearsome beast that stands in between them, and which is the subject of this mission.

A torpadon. A massive specimen of an Airatsmeka, standing nearly eight feet tall, hunching over his own weight that he can barely handle. Wearing a crude, torn trenchcoat similar to a we'jei, stylized for an Airatsmeka, tucked tight onto his massive body, along with rekarakib-esque armored pants, but tighter, and a pair of armored boots that look more like they were made for a rhino, which is exactly the case with this particular villain. Aside from the usual black marks on his face and his pitch-black eyes of nothingness that can be seen on certain individuals of his kind, the torpadon has a biomechanical horn that covers most of his forehead, roughly two feet in length. The horn is black all over, but white at the tip, and that's where it gets interesting, because the tip of the horn is not pointed and sharp as one would expect, but appears more like the barrel of a Gatling gun, with six holes around a gap in the middle that contains the outer surface of the torpadon's forehead, but is too dark to see, and each of the cannon-like holes holds inside a blade-tipped missile, waiting to be lunged deep into the enemy's flesh.

The torpadon might seem like a behemoth among Airatsmeka with his intimidating size and horrendous exterior. In truth, he is but a low-tier fighter, belonging to a lower tier among all the tiers, but still higher than the tier in which the pawns belong.

It is rare for a torpadon,an Airatsmeka of the third tier of power categorization known as the farma, to be the subject of a capture expedition, where a team of Natin are tasked with bringing to the clans a live Airatsmeka that killed several of their brethren, usually somewhere in the hundreds. Normally, the strength of the Natin would never allow such a scenario to exist, but alas, sometimes certain circumstances happen that allow such a weakling to fall into the high-profile targets of capture expeditions.

Because the Shakten specialize in dealing with enemies much stronger than they, it is the least of desires to send them to deal with such a case. But since this already happened, an alternative solution is available, where a Shakten'ga takes the role of a leader, responsible for taking care of Natin with scores lower than theirs. This way, the clans actually have an excuse to task the Shakten'ga with something they aren't supposed to deal with. It's unfortunate, but sometimes things like this happen. Hopefully, they won't happen to the same person twice.

Nevertheless, the team is already burdened with such a scenario, so they might as well enjoy it. Or—depending on who they might be—get it over with. Most of the team might enjoy this, seeing as they have no problem with the circumstances, and that they just see it as an opportunity to fight and display their skills, and that is about to unfold.

The team stands behind a giant boulder, waiting for the right moment, coordinating actions and validating that everything is in the right place. They just wait there as the enemy just keeps on walking away from them, unaware that their adversaries are hiding only a walking distance away. But soon, the waiting will end and the fight will commence.

"You all know what to do," To'shin says without a single doubt. "Incapacitate the big one, and then I will neutralize him. The other two can die."

It's as simple as that. No need for guidance; no need for instructions; no need for directions. Unless a member of the team had a special task, everyone goes all out on the enemy. Same goes for every expedition. The only thing important here to remember is not to kill the capture target, as it is imperative to the mission.

"Should I know something about the target?" Neph asks indiscreetly. "I mean, last time I was nearly poisoned to death. So if there's anything I can know to help me here that would be nice."

Everyone looks at him, aware of the volume of his voice and bothered by it. Nobody gives him a concrete answer, as they are more concerned right now whether they were heard all over the canyon or not. Everyone trades looks with each other, making certain that everything is all right and in place.

Sa'ra, the Sonoka'ga, gestures to Neph to lower his voice. Neph doesn't respond, but quietly in his heart realizes Sa'ra's desires. Nonetheless, Sa'ra walks up to Neph in order to properly explain the situation to Neph, and even answer his question. But just as he is about to quietly talk to avoid alerting the enemy so the team can have the first strike when everyone is in place, fate has other plans.

As Shin'ga'ti, the Sokokit'ga, hides by the edge of the boulder keeping an eye on the enemy, he witnesses a movement by the enemy that he wished hadn't happened, as the enemy turns around to catch the suspicious noise they heard.

The torpadon raises his body high to see all that he can see, hurting his back over the bent spine that plagues him. He moves his head left and right as he can't tell if he's seeing clearly. The two beside him just stare in confusion.

Shin'ga'ti realizes that they are one step away from finding out where the Natin are hiding. He hides completely behind the boulder, not even peeking to see if the enemy is lowering its suspicion. He holds his breath over the chill that crawls through his nerves. In that moment, his impulses get the better of him in hopes that he can still save the situation. He stands completely, like a statue of ice, as he cannot think of anything else. Others just stare at him in confusion.

But it didn't take them too long to realize what is going on. So'dong, the Isopera'ga, peeks from the boulder to see how the situation with the enemy is going. Apparently, the enemy is still trying to figure out what is going on with that particular boulder. It is not surprising, as the torpadon is not renowned for its intelligence. The pawns aren't that bright either, and nothing at all is expected from them.

So'dong, seeing there is no place for worry, goes back behind the boulder. She responds more calmly than Shin'ga'ti, and she is sure that the team has everything under control. Although from the sight of it, everyone in the team either prepares themselves for an imminent battle or tries to prevent it in an attempt to gain control of the situation. As evident from this scenario, the members are not in sync. Such performance does not help the team to succeed in the mission, and could possibly be the result of poor leadership, as the leader needs to coordinate everyone for victory.

But such contemplation over tactics and the way the situation should be addressed will not last long as a rumbling can suddenly be heard. Nobody wants to believe it, but they can't lie to themselves and only hope that it isn't real, as it sounds more like a . . . stampede.

Shin'ga'ti, who is standing by the side of the boulder, peeks once more from behind it. Much to his misfortune, and the team by extension, it is true, as the torpadon charges at them, pounding the ground as he moves on all fours like an actual rhino, horn first straight into the boulder.

The team knows exactly what to do: they all disperse in random directions, getting out of the way of the incoming threat.

As everyone flees, the torpadon shatters the boulder with his mighty horn as pieces of it fly in the air and dust covers the field. The torpadon immediately turns around. Without a clear view of his opponents over the dust that gets in his pitch-black eyes, he lets out a roar of anger and hate as he shoots out all of the six missiles from his intricately designed horn. The missiles fly in different directions, swirling and zigzagging as they move and gather momentum, misguided like a moth around a lantern as they have no target.

The missiles eventually stop flying and find something to stick their bladed heads into. Mostly rocks, since there isn't much else around. They embed themselves in the surface with their sharp blades, and after a brief delay, explode. All but two hit rocks.

One missile had incidentally made its way towards the side of Shin'ga'ti's head. The missile is too slow, as Shin'ga'ti's awareness and quick reflexes allow him to respond fast enough just as he looked to the side to see it, dodging it with a fast tilt of his head. The missile moves forward past Shin'ga'ti, eventually hitting a rock, and exploding seconds later.

But just beside Shin'ga'ti, only a short distance away, stands Yai'shin, the Bibira'ga. He is not blessed with the reflexes of his peer, as he fails to notice in time a missile, still in flight, moving quickly towards him. Just as he turns his head to see where the noise is coming from, the missile is already right in front of his face, flying downwards, and a tenth of a second later lodges itself in the right side of his stomach, just below his lowest rib.

Yai'shin gets pushed back immensely by the force of the missile. He drops to the ground and rolls back, all with the missile still in him. Without a second to waste, Yai'shin gets back up and attempts to remove the missile from his body, as he only has seconds left before he is nothing but a jigsaw puzzle of a messy pile of gibs.

Yai'shin holds the missile with both his hands and pulls, screaming in pain as the bladed tip continues to cut his flesh even more. Alas, the missile is stuck too hard, and Yai'shin alone cannot bear to remove it himself. Knowing that he's doomed doesn't condition him to give up trying, as he continues to pull, even when he knows that he is done for. But alas . . . there is no hope for him.

Shin'ga'ti, hearing his ally in pain, immediately notices him in distress, surprised that he is just beside him. He quickly realizes the situation he's in, and sees the missile embedded in his stomach. Shin'ga'ti wastes no time as to thrust himself with a push of his legs against the ground, moving so fast it seems like he disappeared, only to reappear right by Yai'shin's side, a common technique among Sokokit'ga and other notable clans alike.

With only seconds left, Shin'ga'ti holds the missile over Yai'shin's hands, and with the two now holding the missile, they both pull with all their might. With their combined force, they easily extract the missile out of Yai'shin, only for him to immediately throw it away. The missile explodes in midair as the two are blinded by the light of the explosion, but save Yai'shin from certain death.

They soon regain their sight, as the explosion happened a safe distance from them and did no harm to them. Yai'shin writhes over his newly acquired wound all while clutching it, but collects himself in no time to return to a battle-ready attitude. Now standing straight once more and letting go of the wound, he and Shin'ga'ti stare at each other. They say nothing, as the stare alone and the friendly smirk on each of their faces is message enough of each other's appreciation. They then share a manly handshake, grabbing each other by the bicep and pressing tight, reminding each other that they stand by one another, as is their way, and the way of every Natin.

But in that moment they have forgotten that the enemy is right in front of them, charging at them at full speed, horn first without any missiles left. They quickly get themselves back into the fight as they look at him in shock, reminded that he is still there as he gets closer to them, ready to impale them on his horn. They jump high and away from the oncoming beast, each in a different direction.

As expected, the torpadon misses and immediately turns around, clutching the ground with his fingers to halt his speed, scraping off the sand from it as the momentum that he gathered pushes him forward. Like the monster that he is, primitive and reliant on sheer strength, he lets out a roar to intimidate his opponents. Little does he know that doesn't work on the Natin, especially not from the likes of him.

Yo'na then suddenly drops down from the sky faster than a diving falcon, already in her magnificent pink form. A shockwave is emitted upon her hard landing as dust fills the air around her. She pays no attention to the cloud of dust as she puts both her hands together and aims them at the torpadon. He doesn't see it coming as a big beam of pink light shoots at him, dispersing all the dust.

The light is too bright for his eyes as he blocks it with his right arm, blinded. His arm burns from the heat of the beam as the pink photons condense on his skin, scorching it, and slowly leaving nothing but a crispy tissue. His sleeve has already dissipated as tiny fires dance on the edges of his burnt clothing.

Yo'na continues to release that beam relentlessly onto the torpadon. The force of the beam becomes stronger and stronger as it continues to flow with more energy, gaining mass, and pushes the torpadon backwards as he tries to resist the oncoming weight while his hands continue to burn. But even the beam has its limit, as no matter how hot it burns, the torpadon simply takes it. Slowly but surely, it will penetrate through his arm and roast his heart.

One of the torpadon's compatriots, a simple pawn that for the sake of the mission shall be referred to as No. 1, jumps onto Yo'na's back from out of nowhere. He tries to strangle her by locking his arms around her neck. He refuses to let go as Yo'na tries to shake him off. She refuses to yield as she maintains her pink form.

The clutches of his arms that lock tight around her neck seem too much to free herself from him. She realizes that he won't let go so easily. In a spontaneous attempt to free herself, she flies into the sky, all while he still holds onto her. She flies straight up so fast that she disappears into the sky, leaving the torpadon to fight someone else.

The torpadon quickly recovers from Yo'na's attack, but Shin'ga'ti won't let him make any more moves; he quickly appears above the torpadon's head in a flash, just about to cut his head off with his sickle. Alas, as quickly as he acts, the torpadon's other ally, yet another pawn who will ever only be known as No. 2 of this mission, jumps at Shin'ga'ti, pushing him away in midair away from the kill.

The torpadon looks up to see what has happened above him, to slow to catch what it is. Still with his head in the sky, he fails to notice sharp icicles lodging themselves in his chest. He doesn't budge as he looks at his chest, impaled with icicles, and then he looks forward. He sees Yai'shin standing in front of him, swiping his hands at him as fast as he can, with each swipe ending with more icicles sticking in his chest. He doesn't even move backwards as Yai'shin relentlessly continues to conjure more icicles which materialize halfway, moving and sharp, right into the torpadon's torso.

Now with most of his front covered in icicles, the torpadon has had enough; he breaks all the icicles off his chest with a simple swipe of his hand downwards. His body now shows the exposed holes caused by the attack as the remains of the icicles pile up below him, slowly melting from the heat. Yai'shin looks in shock as he realizes that his attacks are for naught.

But things are about to get even worse as the torpadon grimaces, his head shaking and his eyes closing hard. Suddenly, a thick black liquid comes out of the missile sockets. The liquid moves and shakes as it slowly assumes a form. It stops shaking and finally forms into black arrowheads like those of the missiles he had launched. Now the torpadon has six missiles once more sitting firmly inside it, waiting to be plunged into flesh and subsequently blow that flesh to bits.

The team knows that the torpadon can grow back the missiles, as they are biomechanical in nature, utilizing synthetic cells discharged by an augmented brain. But they did not expect this particular individual to grow them back so soon, as it usually takes a lot more time for the missiles to grow back. Maybe this explains how he became a high-profile capture target. Though surprising, mutations do happen, and situations like these should be often considered.

Nevertheless, Yai'shin won't let him shoot those missiles a second time, as he holds both his hands together parallel to his body, collects all the energy he can in one second, and then shoots out a fireball with an outward motion of his hands straight at the torpadon's head. Unfortunately, Yai'shin might've hit him too high, as he hit the durable horn instead, with the torpadon going unfazed by the attack.

Immediately afterwards, the torpadon falls on all four limbs and aims his horn at the poor victim in front of him. All six missiles shoot out of the horn once again, flying in random directions as they twirl towards the obvious target right in front of them. Yai'shin conjures a gust of wind right in front of him that spreads outwards, just as missiles nearly embed themselves in his body, dispersing the missiles away from him. The missiles spread out and away from Yai'shin, hitting the rocks and sand of the barren landscape, only to explode seconds later, saving Yai'shin from certain death once more.

But while Yai'shin is dealing with the missiles, he fails to notice the torpadon charging at him. Luckily, the torpadon is still further away, and there is enough time to act. But attacks won't do much in this situation as the torpadon is already on the move and a single attack definitely won't halt him.

Realizing that he must take a more tactical action, Yai'shin runs straight away from the torpadon, all the while conjuring walls of earth in a series like a trail of dominos. The torpadon ignores the walls, breaking through them with his horn as if they were ceramic. Nevertheless, Yai'shin continues to conjure more walls, trying even so to tire the torpadon, but he just breaks wall after wall. Finally, the torpadon is too fast for Yai'shin, as he breaks through all the walls and reaches Yai'shin. With shards of earth flying everywhere, Yai'shin notices the oddly-shaped edge of the horn about to crush his trachea with extreme blunt force. He is so sure of his death that for a moment he perceives everything in a fraction of a second, as it seems like all the flying shards stand still in place and the horn will never reach his throat. He cannot react in time as his movements cannot match his mind. He thinks about his life as a tak'nen and how they die for their people . . . and accepts it.

But in that blink of a moment, Yai'shin simply disappears from the torpadon's line of attack, as the torpadon continues charging into empty air.

Yai'shin finds himself away from the torpadon and To'shin beside him, who has saved him. Much like the Sokokit'ga, the Shakten'ga specialize in instantaneous movements. Yai'shin lies on the ground, as To'shin had to push him away. She gives him a hand, and he takes it as she pulls him back on his legs.

The torpadon stops charging and like before, turns around instantly, grabs the ground with his nails as he scrapes trying to halt his momentum. Now standing in place, he looks around and sees nothing. No corpses, no blood, no carnage. All he sees is the debris he caused from breaking the walls of earth made by Yai'shin.

Suddenly, liquids splash at the side of the torpadon's face. The liquid corrodes the torpadon's cheeks as vapor comes out and his skin slowly melts. In a quick reaction, he blocks it with his right arm that blocked Yo'na's beam of light and it takes the damage instead, as if that arm isn't burnt enough from all the heat.

He sees So'dong, holding her acid gun against him as she continues to shoot acid at him. The jet of acid fires nicely onto his wrist, corroding his skin as it starts to fall off, exposing the tendons.

His arm may be melted away and burnt, but he keeps it strong and tough, as he shows by kicking sand into her eyes, blinding her as the sand gets inside her mouth and all over her face. He grabs her with that same arm she nearly turned into a meaty fondue. He holds her with one gigantic arm, strong enough to hold a lightweight person by itself and throw that person away.

Just before he can fling away So'dong like a rock, Sa'ra comes running up front, right in his face. Sa'ra immediately pushes his right arm in front of the torpadon as a blue spark comes out of it; out of the blue spark appears a blue gecko-like construct of blue shining energy onto the torpadon's face. The construct crawls around the torpadon's face, much like a gecko, as it goes through his cheek to just above his ugly lips. The torpadon catches the construct with his tongue with a lick of his lips, swallowing it. A muffled explosion can be heard coming from his mouth as blue smoke comes out of his nostrils. The torpadon then smiles viciously at Sa'ra as blue smoke comes out from in between his teeth.

"Bak!" Sa'ra mutters as he stares at the torpadon in terror.

Sa'ra runs straight away from the torpadon. The torpadon tries to run after him, but is quickly intercepted by Grasshead, mounted by who other than Neph, as he bites him hard on that right arm, messing it up even more as Grasshead's sharp teeth puncture his flesh. The torpadon is forced to release So'dong and she falls to the floor, for the damage is too much for him. Grasshead continues to lock his jaws even harder on the torpadon's arm, already touching the bone with the edge of his teeth, coming even closer to crushing it. But the torpadon punches Grasshead in his ironwood-sturdy head. Grasshead struggles to maintain his grip as his teeth slide off the arm, cutting it. The torpadon punches him a second time and Grasshead finally lets go. He then kicks Grasshead away, all while Neph is still mounted on him.

So'dong, lying just beside the torpadon's leg, takes out a kas chik'shin, a long knife with a thick blade that can't cut, but is pointed at the edge. With three rows of holes on it, aligned like that of a flute, at the end of the hilt sits a metallic canister, containing some sort of gas. But all of its technical complexity is overshadowed by its finely decorated and well-invested golden crossguard, shaped like the symbol of the clan of Isopera. Whatever this weapon is capable of, none should desire falling victim to it, as will be the unfortunate torpadon.

So'dong jams the knife deep into the torpadon's leg, just above the ankle. The torpadon staggers forward and nearly trips. He minds not what hurt his leg, as it feels to him like a mere sting of an insect. He attempts to walk, but feels an agony when he presses his hurting leg against the ground. Looking at his leg, he watches as it inflates as he struggles to balance himself over the ever-growing pain coming from it. No longer just the sting of an insect as the knife continues to fill his leg with gas that expands inside his leg, now giving it the shape of a tumorous appendage filled with body liquids. Of course, the leg can only hold so much gas . . . .

It finally explodes! The gas erupts from a bloody mess of exposed tendons and dangling skin. Torn muscles and a cracked shin bone can be seen from beyond a thick yellowish cloud of gas as the torpadon falls to one knee, spilling blood from his leg as it soaks into the sand and stains his clothes. The torpadon is unrelenting as he gets back up on his legs, waving the flesh wound he suffered just now. This only proves his might.

Alas, To'shin appears fast behind him. He can't react; he can't even see her as she moves too fast for him. She grabs him by one arm, ties a black rope around his wrist, and quickly moves to his other arm. She ties the wrist of that arm too, all with the same rope and behind his back. Pulling the rope, his hands are tied together behind his back as To'shin spins fast in the air around his hands like a windmill, further constricting his hands together until the rope becomes so tight he can't break it.

As she finishes with his hands, To'shin quickly jumps high above his head, falling gracefully as she mounts him on the shoulders and immediately puts on a black lid ergonomically designed just for his horn, covering it and preventing him from using it.

She then jumps off him, looking around to see what's happening, thinking about what else they have left to do. Neph and Grasshead come to closer to her.

"Let's kill the other ones and get this over with," she says impatiently.

Suddenly, they hear a ripping sound. Their eyes become wide open as they try to figure out what it could be. They know what it is and they wish it were not true as they stare at the torpadon. On his knees, he starts to rumble and shake, as his arms spread out behind his back, slowly moving apart from one another.

"rrrrrrrrrrrrRRRRRRROOOOOOOOAAAAAAAAAAHH!!!" he roars as he violently breaks the ropes that confine his hands.

Hairs of the ropes can be seen gently floating in the air, as it is all that remains from them. With his arms free, he grabs the lid on his horn with both his hands, each holding tight to one side of it. He starts to break it apart as he shakes, showing the power that he exerts over the sturdy lid. It starts to crack as fissures show and pieces start to fall off, until finally it breaks. The torpadon's arms spread out over the momentum he gathered and the force that he exerts, as the two halves of the lid are thrown in the air, far apart from each other, disappearing out of sight with only broken pieces left on the ground. Now, the torpadon is free once more, and all havoc is about to break loose.

Realizing the danger, To'shin, Neph and Grasshead run away from him. He stands still, as he starts to shake in a familiar motion. An ugly grimace shows on his face and a familiar one, no less. Black liquids start to come out of the holes of the missile sockets on his horn, shaking and squirming, slowly assuming a form. It becomes all too obvious now what it's going to be.

Realizing the danger, To'shin jumps away from the line of fire, disappearing in a flash. Neph rides Grasshead away from the torpadon.

Now with all the missiles finally formed and in place, the torpadon assumes the right position as he gets down on all fours, balancing himself on his knuckles, and aims the missiles placed in his horns right at Neph and Grasshead.

But in a swift thought, Neph realizes that running away is futile, as he orders Grasshead to turn around and run towards the torpadon, seconds away from firing.

The torpadon takes too long to get in the right position, as Grasshead closes his mouth on the horn the instance he arrives close enough to him.

Grasshead locks tight on the horn as the torpadon rises to his legs. Grasshead continues to bite down on the horn as he tries hard to break it. Cracks can be heard coming from in between his powerful jaws as pieces fall out of his mouth and into his throat. And as Grasshead exerts all his might into this bite, the horn shatters!

The remains of the horn lie in Grasshead's mouth and he just spits them out. All that is left on the torpadon's forehead is a mechanical stump, broken and brittle and full of shame. Now, the torpadon's trump is no more, as the only thing that will help him now is his brute strength . . . if that will help him.

Suddenly, Shin'ga'ti slams hard on the torpadon's face out of nowhere as if he had been thrown at him by a catapult. Shin'ga'ti immediately falls to the ground, but the torpadon reacts not, as he is too startled at having a Natin hit hard against his face.

A black figure can be seen rising to the air, and quickly comes down in an arc to where all the commotion is happening, quickly growing bigger and landing hard on the ground as a strong thud can be heard, now making it obvious that it is the torpadon's compatriot No. 2.

He rushes to a fallen Shin'ga'ti to finish the job. But just as he gets right above his body, Sa'ra notices from afar and acts quickly: he quickly straightens his left arm directed at No. 2, with nothing at hand, in a gesture like he's holding an invisible gun. Instantly an orange gun with a long narrow barrel materializes in his hand out of an orange spark. Sa'ra immediately shoots at No. 2 without a thought, as an orange laser beam shoots fast in the blink of an eye. The beam hits No. 2, sending an electrical surge throughout his body, accompanied by a beautiful display of orange electric bolts. The pawn then stands still, seemingly losing control over his movements, as his eyes turn a transparent orange, quickly increasing in opacity.

And then a burst of orange laser beams explode out of his eyes! The torpadon immediately moves out of the way. Shin'ga'ti, who is just recovering, notices what's happening and quickly plans to use it to his advantage. With a thrust of his leg, Shin'ga'ti instantly appears behind No. 2 and grabs his head with both his arms, aiming the unruly beams straight at the torpadon's arm as it burns the flesh all the way down to the bone. The torpadon tries to move out of the way, but Shin'ga'ti just redirects the lasers straight back to his near torn-off arm, as it keeps hitting it in the bone, since there is no flesh left to burn.

All of a sudden, the lasers stop, seemingly having exhausted themselves. Shin'ga'ti throws the near-fainted No. 2 to the ground. He now stares at the torpadon, who is staggering and grieving over his arm that has been punished over and over, as it hangs by a broken humerus, swinging back and forth as the wind blows at the open fractures and nearly falling off.

The torpadon continues to stagger, slowly turning around as he can't hold himself for too much longer, as he too has his limits. As he turns around, he faces Yai'shin, who is still struggling to keep himself together from the serious wound he suffered earlier, but refuses to relent.

Yai'shin puts both his hands together, just above his open wound. Blood starts to siphon into his hand, slowly forming a blob. Finally, when the blob of blood is just big enough, Yai'shin swings his left arm upwards over his shoulder, as all the gathered blood quickly transmutates into a javelin, colored crimson from all the blood, but solid as steel. Yai'shin throws the javelin at the torpadon and it pierces through the air.

The javelin hits the torpadon right at the side of neck, just missing the windpipe, piercing the flesh so hard that one half of it comes out the other side and makes itself not so easily removable.

The torpadon grabs both of the halves of the javelin with each of his hands, still staggering as he realizes that he can't go on. He pulls hard on each half with whatever might he has left, as the javelin's sturdy material bends gently, only to subsequently break. But even so, a piece of the javelin still rests within the torpadon's throat, and it's no ordinary piece of a javelin, but a javelin made of blood.

Suddenly, black marks start to appear just at the area of attack, as they spread like a rapidly developing necrosis. They spread so fast over the entirety of the torpadon's neck all the way to his shoulder and down to his biceps, and there's nothing that he can do as he holds his neck in pain, deluding himself that he can stop the magical poison, but there's nothing he can do, and the indescribable pain makes it a whole lot worse.

The torpadon falls on one knee, and his friend is just about to wake up. As he does, he quickly gets up and pulls himself together, as he needs to act fast on the battlefield. But just as he gets up, in comes So'dong for a final touch to end the battle once and for all, holding in her hand an intricate gas canister that contains one of the clan of Isopera's favorite weapon: artichoke gas!

Potentially lethal for non-lethal purposes, artichoke gas is one of the best neutralizing weapons that the Novaverse has to offer, as long as the user is outside the area of effect and upwind.

So'dong throws the canister right between the torpadon and his compatriot. Now everything will take care of itself.

"Everyone, DISPERSE!" So'dong yells in the air.

Everyone from the team moves as fast as they can away from the canister, taking all the precautions to stay outside the area of effect. Now, all that are left around the canister are the torpadon and No. 2, and they aren't fast enough to react to what's about to happen next.

The canister releases the artichoke gas and the gas quickly fills the air around in a wide field. The cloud of gas grows thicker and thicker until all that are inside can barely be seen. Once a single breath is taken within that cloud, it is too late.

The torpadon and No. 2 feel a movement in their stomach, going all the way up their esophagus. It feels like nausea, as they both gag, but nothing comes out. A second time, and a waterfall of vomit upchucks out of their mouths. They can't stop, as they continue to puke whatever they had in the last several hours. They can't resist, as chemicals trigger the response from their stomach, and they continue to regurgitate violently as tears come out of their eyes. In the end, they puke so much that nothing is left in their stomachs. But even so, they still puke, but all they release is air, since they can't resist the feeling of nausea triggered by the artichoke gas.

With that, the torpadon and No. 2 fall face flat on the ground, near-dead and dehydrated from all the liquids that have left their bodies. But with all that thick gas obscuring whatever happened, So'dong figures that enough time has passed and it's time to clear the cloud.

So'dong takes out a hep'gogo, a grey ball, and throws it right at the gas cloud. The ball enters the cloud and disappears into it. Seconds later, the gas cloud implodes, immediately absorbed by the grey ball and clearing the area from any danger of exposure to the gas, as not even a puff of has is left in the air. Now it is safe to go in, and the team is almost ready to finish the mission.

What they see before them is exactly what they expect: fallen enemies lying down near-dead with their faces to the ground. After all, nobody can resist the artichoke gas . . . not many, at least.

The team walks closer to the fallen Airatsmeka, each at his or her own pace. Grasshead, mounted by Neph, moves towards No. 2. Standing above him, Neph needn't even tell Grasshead what to do, as Grasshead puts No. 2's head in between his teeth and starts pressing. Bits of crunching sounds can be heard as Grasshead only uses a minimal amount of his strength; he slowly breaks No. 2's skull fracture by fracture. Finally, a big crunching sound can be heard over the sound of exploding viscera, as Grasshead spits out a bloody mess of brains and bones, finishing the job.

Simultaneously, To'shin quickly ties the torpadon's arms and legs in a thick black rope, and she did it as quickly as she did when she first met Neph. Alas, tying the arms is a bit of a problem, as the right is too loose from all the damage, as it is nearly falling apart. Creatively, she decides to get rid of the arm, pulling the arm as she holds it with both her arms and pushes her leg against his body. A weak groan can be heard coming from the torpadon as he has no power left to even make a sound. But the arm eventually comes off, and To'shin proceeds to quickly tie his arm to his body with some more thick black ropes. To finalize it all, she puts a lid on the stump of his broken horn, like she did earlier . . . just in case anything happens, and hopefully this one won't break.

"Keika omain'in nihir'ke'in na," To'shin says as she looks at the torpadon, worried that he might die before he faces judgment.

The team then gathers up. Everything seems in place, and it is time to go home.

"Where's Yomak Nayan?" Neph mentions.

Everyone seemed surprised, as they were so into the battle that they failed to notice that one of them is missing. They look around them and over their shoulders, but Yomak Nayan is nowhere to be seen. Definitely not in the close vicinity.

"YOMAK NAYAN!!" Neph shouts.

Alas, no answer, only an echo of Neph's words.

To'shin sighs, as she realizes that the current predicament delays her arrival home for a nice hot shower, as she has finished the mission, and she wants to get it over with.

"We don't have time for this," she mutters impatiently. "But it's a good thing we have a hiphomoy."

"What do you mean?" Neph asks curiously.

"They have a superior sense of smell. Now if only we had something from her."

Neph is slightly worried, as he realizes that they have yet another barrier to overcome, as neither he, nor does anyone from the team have something from Yo'na for Grasshead to smell. But then, he has a hunch . . . .

"Maybe . . . ," he says indecisively, stopping short over the thought of the possibility.

Everyone just stares at him, as they can't figure out what he has in mind, wondering what he will do.

"What?" To'shin says in confusion.

Neph crouches to look Grasshead in the eye. Looking into his eyes at the same altitude as Grasshead's big head dwarfs that of Neph, he puts his hand on his head, to remind him that they will always be together forever, and they will always be there for each other, both in mind . . . and in heart.

"Grasshead," Neph addresses him. "Yomak Nayan."

Grasshead calmly looks to the sides as Neph rises back on his feet. Grasshead can't find what he is looking for, so he turns around. But after realizing that she is nowhere in sight, he raises his head and smells the air. A sniff and another sniff, and then he quietly stands still, thinking of whatever a hiphomoy might think when he smells the air looking for someone.

And then, just like that without a sign, Grasshead runs straight, passing through the team members, seemingly go nowhere, but everyone knows that he's going somewhere.

"Neph, So'dong, Sa'ra Shin'ga'ti, go find Yo'na," To'shin orders

them seriously. "Yai'shin, you come with me. As soon as you guys find Yo'na, go to the nearest clan and contact me immediately. Fill me in on any additional information."

With that order, So'dong, Sa'ra, and Shin'ga'ti run after Grasshead, with Neph staying behind. Just as Neph prepares to leave, he stares at To'shin and smirks at her, and she smirks at him back, as this is the first exchange of respect the two have, leaving the future between the two hopeful.

And with that, Neph runs on to follow his teammates, who are in turn following Grasshead, as To'shin and Yai'shin stand there, seemingly waiting, standing by a mutilated corpse and a neutralized torpadon. As they wait, they see their teammates continuing with the mission, while they can finally retire.

CHAPTER XXVIII

MEANWHILE . . .

The fight is over, yet another expedition among hundreds of thousands that happen every Novaversian year has been completed, and everyone is at a different place. To'shin is taking the torpadon into custody together with Yai'shin who is badly injured at the liver. The rest of the team searches for a missing teammate. What's up with Yomak Nayan? She's the missing teammate, obviously. She's doing just fine. But that is yet to be discovered.

Sitting on a random rock in a canyon somewhere in Raboja, Yomak Nayan rests, breathing deeply and slowly, gradually regaining her energy as she stares at the corpse of her opponent, yet another Airatsmeka pawn who had accompanied a high-profile torpadon.

She wonders how the others are doing. She worries not for them as she has confidence in their skills, or more appropriately, the prowess of the Natin. But even with their might, the Natin die, and they die in the many, as do all tak'nen. Yomak Nayan can't help but ask herself whether they are alive or not, even if they have triumphed over the enemy.

As she sits there quietly by herself, with the stench of blood filling her nose and the atmosphere around her, she takes the time to calm down and enjoy the silence. Just like that, a grip clutches tight on her shoulder, hurting her severely! She writhes loudly over how tightly it squeezes her, as she grabs at whatever is clutching her and throws it to the sky.

Whatever she threw explodes into a purple dimensional rift before her and instantaneously disappears. In the slight second that comes, she wonders what it was, but she immediately realizes what it is as something throws itself on her back, launching her forward as if she had been hit by a large rock.

As she flies through the air, she descends quickly to the ground, sliding on the sand over the momentum built as the thing lays down its weight on her back. She finally halts, lying face down on the ground with the thing on her back. She immediately transforms into her pink form of power in a burst of pink light, sending the thing flying high above her in the air as she quickly gets back up on her feet.

The thing falls quickly. Yo'na gracefully spins in the air just as the thing hits the ground, and she kicks it hard with her shin as it gets launched into the ground beside her, sliding on the hard surface, slowly coming to a stop. As it stays there on the ground, its appearance becomes clear.

A sight of seven arms and a toned purple body can be seen from Yo'na's perspective. It gets up, pushing itself off the ground with the single arm on the other side of its body. Back on its feet, it staggers a bit, only to turn immediately to face Yo'na. As if it weren't already obvious who it is, then it just made itself apparent.

Sima Brak, with his ugly face showing to Yo'na, with every one of his eight eyes rotating randomly like the eyes of a chameleon, and his mouth open, drooling excessively as the saliva spills from between his razor sharp teeth. A being that can teleport, he can appear at any given moment at any given place, seeking prey that just might be there. But his powers aren't just limited to teleportation, as he can also smell his prey from miles and miles away, lashing out his tongue as he collects the molecules in the air and tastes them. That's how he always finds his prey just in the rare case that he loses them, which is exactly the case with Yo'na. Now, he can finally finish what he had barely started.

"Itoke nayan. Marang nayan'in," he remarks curiously in a broken decrepit voice. "Eteki waranon'in Karin'ga itiki ronon'an amken'in. Kata jek'in iteki?"

Yo'na answers not to his question. She stands there, saying nothing, staring at him, watching his movements and waiting for the right time to act. She is horrified to hear once more of her mother's death at the hands of Sima Brak, yet she is relieved to know that he knows not of their connection. Despite looking into her eyes, and seeing eyes that remind him of the Karin'ga he devoured, he knows not nor can he figure out that she is that woman's daughter.

Sima Brak is baffled at her choice of silence, refusing to answer him. However, he is not moved, as it does not matter to him, for he sees her as nothing more than a meal.

As the wind continues to blow at their faces, one a face of beauty and the other a face of disgust, they stand quietly, one expecting an answer he'll never receive, and the other planning her next set of actions.

"Kata taiin? Kata rarik'in itoki nihir?" he provocatively asks her. "Harsayan'in na. Dora Natin bak'tes! Dora Natin makis'pes! Didi'in! Dora Natin ma heranga!"

Hearing his words, Yo'na finds herself in a state of anger and rage. She finds a desire to respond to his monologue, yet she holds herself as she knows that he provokes her. Who the hell does he think he is? Who is he to patronize the Natin? He has no right to compare the Natin to the heranga! Those are the thoughts that run through her head right now, for she and all Natin know the truth about Sima Brak: a promising warrior, wasted on arrogance and a desire for reckless bloodshed. Yet even so, as the anger flows through her veins, she keeps herself from acting recklessly; she needs to assess the situation properly, as she is against one of the toughest adversaries of the Natin who is not an Airatsmeka.

But then she realizes that Sima Brak is swept away by his own emotion, talking about his hatred of the Natin and feelings of betrayal that he brought upon himself. He is not attempting to provoke her, but he fell into his own pit of angst and frustration as the memories of his struggles with his own people back in his prime fill his spirit. A feeling that he so much wants to erase, but as he can't let go he fails to realize everything around him and a small, momentary opening is shown.

Now is the time to attack as Yo'na dashes forward in the speed of light, appearing before Sima Brak in a blink. Energy collects around her soft hand, sharpening itself to be able to penetrate through the hardest of material as she straightens all her fingers and holds them together. She pierces Sima Brak's shoulder with a poke of her straightened hand, as it comes out of the other side. The blood doesn't even have time to spill as it happens so fast. He immediately retaliates by putting his palm from one of his seven left arms on her ribs and thrusts it hard, shattering her ribs from the inside.

As Yo'na bends over in pain, she immediately regains herself and grabs that same arm by the elbow and pulls it to her, bending it and breaking it beyond use. Still holding on, she spins around as Sima Brak is lifted off the ground, only to be thrown away like a ball. Far away, he disappears in the purple dimensional rift and instantly reappears before Yo'na. She dashes back in the speed of light, but he again teleports to her in his dimensional fashion. Trying to find an escape, she jumps high into the air. He once more appears before her in a flash of purple dimensional rift, and slashes at her face with the claws from his many arms.

To finalize this aerial clash, she conjures a pink ball in her hand that flashes bright and thrusts it onto Sima Brak's chest. The ball glues itself to him as Yo'na puts her foot onto the ball and thrusts hard.

A pink explosion appears brightly in midair, and a smoke screen obscures all within. A body can be seen falling from within the smoke downwards in an arc, landing hard on the ground. The smoke slowly disperses, and Yo'na slowly descends to stand on the soil.

She is ready for yet another confrontation with the beast, and hopes that every subsequent clash will be shorter than the previous. Until the monster gets up, she has time to think of her actions and maybe concoct a plan, because she knows that by herself she doesn't stand much of a chance, as there is no escape.

Right now, her best chances at victory would be a miracle . . . .

CHAPTER XXIX

THANK YOU. THOSE WERE HIS LAST WORDS

We wander in the canyon endlessly. Grasshead takes us to Yomak Nayan or where he believes that she might be, according to his sense of smell. I can't tell how much time has passed since we started searching, and the scorching heat is killing me, squeezing a bucketload of sweat through my skin. For all I know, Yomak Nayan's power could take her anywhere, and everyone just seems like they want to give up already.

Suddenly, a boom is heard in the air, and a bright pink cloud of smoke can be seen high above us, not too far from us either. Something falls from that cloud, but that doesn't really matter to me. I knew who made the cloud, but I don't know what the others recognized. They probably do since they know more about the Karin'ga than I do, and by extension their own people.

Naturally, we rush over there. Everyone assumes their own speed, but the closer we get we can see more of what is going on over there. What I see before me in the distance is a pink glowing figure. My assumptions are absolutely correct and there isn't a single doubt of who it can be. But seeing her like this means that she's in a fight. To think that her opponent is strong enough to keep her fighting until now is just ludicrous, but all together we can end it fast.

"Yomak Nayan!" I yell to her.

Yomak Nayan turns her head to look at us. Seeing her expressionless face in that form as we get closer to her, I can't tell what emotional state she's in. Not that it matters, as we have to kill her adversary right now and get her out of here so we can end this. I'm getting sick of this mission.

As we finally reach her, we surround her, ensuring her safety from all sides and preparing for what may come next.

"Is everything OK?!" I ask her excitedly.

Yomak Nayan says nothing, nor does she change back into her regular form. I have no idea if she can even talk in this form, but if she's not reverting that probably suggests that there is still work to be done.

"Oooo bak," So'dong mutters frighteningly.

Hearing So'dong say those words like that, I realize something is wrong. The fear that came out of her throat, I could feel it, but could not have guessed what it is, as I can't imagine what possible danger we might be up against. This is no typical pawn we're dealing with I guess, but all together we can take him.

I look in the direction everyone is facing, and I see our enemy slowly getting back up on his feet. My eyes open wide; I fall into despair as I see what's before me. I really thought that I would have to go to the ends of the Novaverse just to see him again, and I never imagined that he would prefer to come to me instead. But I'm glad he did . . . because this is the moment where I finally get my Novaversian green card.

Sima Brak! Now standing back on his two feet, still wearing the same pants and ass-ugly mug since I saw him last time. His entire chest has been removed, showing his broken ribcage with several fractures as shards fall off of it. I have to give kudos to Yomak Nayan for being able to do such a thing, although too bad it didn't finish the job.

He seems to be lightheaded right about now, as he is just standing there, taking his time. He probably sees all of us and realizes that getting to Yomak Nayan won't be as simple as it was a moment ago. That or Yomak Nayan's attack gave him a concussion and he's dizzy, but I can't tell what's really going on with him. Out of all the places that he teleports to, did it have to be here? Never mind. While an unlucky coincidence it might be, we're going to have to end this now. But why is everyone not attacking and standing still just like that monster over there? I assume that the shock really got to them. That or they're just devising a plan, but without talking to each other?

Without warning, Sa'ra shoots himself in the stomach with that orange gun. An orange surge can be seen flowing through his body as it quickly concentrates in his head. Orange lasers explode out of his eyes straight to Sima Brak, disintegrating the sand and air around them.

The bright light emitted from the lasers makes it hard to see the results, but Sima Brak doesn't seem to be there. Not even a piece of him. I guess the lasers were too much for him to handle. Good job, Sa'ra.

Sima Brak suddenly appears before us out of thin air. Being right between Sa'ra and So'dong, he grabs both of them by their throats and tears them out. A waterfall of blood gushes out of the holes that were their tracheas, spilling onto the sand and soaking their clothes as Sima Brak drops the chunks of meat he held in his hands, filled with their skin and muscles as all the tissues separate and slide away from each other upon landing, showing all the gruesome details.

Sa'ra and So'dong fall to their knees, their heads falling backwards, connected to their bodies only by the bones of their necks, as they subsequently fall to the ground, lying flat and dead.

I am shocked by the sight of Sima Brak being so fast, and so deadly too. I thought all of us had it, but in an instant he just killed these two, and I couldn't do anything to save them.

Shin'ga'ti doesn't even waste time and immediately attacks with his sickle. He cuts Sima Brak on the shoulder, embedding the sickle into his flesh. But Sima Brak doesn't even budge as he simply grabs Shin'ga'ti's wrist. He closes tight on his wrist with his bare hand, quickly squeezing the bone together as it starts to snap. Shin'ga'ti lets out a grunt of pain only to instantly follow up by quickly drawing out his long knife from behind his back and stabbing Sima Brak in the neck, just behind the windpipe. Sima Brak attempts to grab that arm too with one of his many left arms, but before he could even touch another wrist, Shin'ga'ti dashes backwards, nearly cutting Sima Brak's throat from inside his flesh, but he quickly tilted his head just in time, avoiding death, but leaving him with a deep cut behind his throat.

As Sima Brak bleeds profusely from his neck, he tries to pull himself together from that attack. He staggers forward, but immediately regains balance. He looks at Shin'ga'ti, who looks scared and frightened to near-death. After all, nobody expects to fight one of the greatest adversaries of the Natin right here in nowhere. Nobody is prepared for this, and Shin'ga'ti has it written all over his face.

As he stares straight at Sima Brak with those eyes filled with fear, Sima Brak stares at him straight back with eyes filled with murder, and he has eight of those, four times as many as Shin'ga'ti. Sima Brak is just about to make a move as he takes a step forward and prepares to run straight at Shin'ga'ti, planning on doing who-knows-what. But Shin'ga'ti can't handle the pressure, and jabs his long knife straight into his stomach, performing seppuku.

As if I wasn't already surprised, I was surprised even more that a mighty warrior would prefer the easy way out. Not that he stood a chance against the beast anyways, seeing as how he easily dispatched the other in a jiffy. I guess he wanted to save himself the humiliation; better that than even try. I can't tell what Sima Brak is even thinking, as I am standing behind him and I can't see his face, but he stands still so I suppose he's also kind of surprised. But the worst thing of all is that I couldn't even save Shin'ga'ti from death, and all this happens while I'm still shocked, powerless to do anything.

And as I stand there like an idiot, I hear Sima Brak let out a rugged grunt as he slowly turns around.

"Sang'nen," he utters in disappointment, looking at Shin'ga'ti's fallen body as he slowly turns away.

Of course, I couldn't possibly tell what he was saying, but his tone and attitude suggested that he expected more of a fight, seemingly disappointed in Shin'ga'ti's actions, as if he were calling him a coward.

I barely knew him, but I don't see Shin'ga'ti's actions as an act of cowardice, but out of knowledge. The knowledge of realizing a stronger opponent and avoiding it, and if you can't avoid it, then there's only one way out. The one way to avoid humiliation at the hands of an adversary you never stood a chance against. I, too, would wish to avoid humiliation, but I always fight, like I've done all my life. And yet a naturally born warrior chose to kill himself. I'm confused, maybe he was a coward. It pisses me off just admitting that it's the truth, because I can't stand the idea that the enemy is right. But what pisses me off even more is that I let another ally fall, and that's my responsibility.

As the rage boils beneath my skin, I see Sima Brak turning to me. As he faces me with his ugly face, I leave him no time to react as I deliver a straight punch to his nose with all my rage and anger so he can feel it at the fullest. I can feel my fist sinking into his face just before sending him flying backwards. And as he rolls on the ground backwards, he gets back up on his feet, loses balance and falls again, only to get back up once more.

What I see from afar is a flattened nose and blood all around his mouth. But I couldn't care less what injuries I inflict on him, as I'm not going to even give him time to react.

I run over there with Grasshead by my side. He stands still for whatever reason, be it dizziness or arrogance, I don't care. I feel my speed increasing by itself. I can feel my anger pushing my body beyond its capabilities as it flows through my legs, thrusting me forward with each step I take, pushing the air around me and getting me closer to him before he can retaliate.

Just before the moment of impact, Grasshead opens his mouth and prepares to chomp down on his body. Sima Brak grabs Grasshead's mouth by both his jaws, the lonely right arm holding the lower jaw and the other seven holding the upper one together. I jump on Grasshead's back and subsequently thrust myself upwards in the air, and as I come falling down I deliver an overhead diving punch straight to Sima Brak's skull.

The punch is so hard I swear I hear a crack and is strong enough to force Sima Brak to let go of Grasshead. Immediately, I see something swiftly move past Sima Brak's back in a pink flash. A cutting sound is heard as a splash of blood erupts from his shoulders. It's obvious to me who has come to my aid.

It seems like Sima Brak is about to break as he falls to his knees. We might've been able to push him this far, but he's not done yet.

I go behind him, grab him by the head with both my arms and attempt to break his neck, but he pulls himself back together just in time to save his own ass, as he holds my right arm with his right arm, while I can feel three hands holding tight onto my left arm.

As I struggle to twist his head, he resists, holding onto my arms, squeezing hard to force me to release them. I continue to push against his resistance, and as much as it hurts me, I won't let go, as I am determined to murder him, putting an end to this bloodshed and his vendetta.

As I continue to push against the odds, a glimmer of hope appears in front of me in the form of Yomak Nayan, or better yet, her pink form of awesomeness. I am relieved to know that she will deliver the final blow, as she swiftly gets closer to Sima Brak's heart, ready to puncture it with her gentle fingers as she holds them together, pointed straight at him. I can see it all from where I am right now.

Her straightened-out fingers, infused with her pink glow and powers, are just about to finish the job and pierce his heart. But her hand stops short just an inch from his chest, as he grabs her hand with one of his unoccupied left arms.

I can tell Yomak Nayan is shocked from beneath that layer of pink power, as she stands motionless. I, too, am surprised at his speed, but to think that he is fast enough to stop her attack, which is even faster than her whole body. The shock is more than effective, as Sima Brak uses the opening to grip tight on her arm with his remaining unoccupied left arms. One arm holding the hand; one arm holding the forearm; one arm holding the elbow; one arm holding the bicep. Four arms holding on to four different portions of her arm, and in an instant he squeezes all his hands as hard as he can. A large cracking noise can be heard as I witness Yomak Nayan's arm being crushed. I can almost feel it as I witness her reverting into her normal self, accompanied by a scream of pain as she falls on one knee.

I can't keep on watching, as I let go of Sima Brak's head and rush over to his many arms to release Yomak Nayan from them. It might seem stupid, forcing the mighty arms off her one by one, but I haven't a better idea.

And with Sima Brak free from my clutches, he gets back up on his feet, lets go of Yomak Nayan's arm and swings all of his left arms at me, sending me flying and knocking me against a rock. As I lean on the rock, dizzy and in pain, I see from beyond the stars in my eyes Sima Brak grabbing Yomak Nayan by the neck and throwing her away so strongly that she disappears from my sight. Then I see Grasshead biting on Sima Brak from the side. It seems like Sima Brak is trying to release himself from Grasshead, but that doesn't seem to work for him. Now they seem to be spinning around, and Grasshead is hovering in the air. Looks like Grasshead's in danger.

GRASSHEAD'S IN DANGER!?!

At the last moment, I pull myself together, snap out of this dizziness, immediately jump back on my feet and run over there. But Grasshead is already flying towards me, slamming me against the same rock and anchoring me there with his weight.

With 1300 pounds sitting on me, there's no way I can get out of this situation. Nevertheless, I try to push Grasshead aside and get back to the fight . . . but I can't.

For a second under pressure, I forget that Grasshead can move by himself.

"Hey boy, get up!" I nervously tell him. "Get up!"

Grasshead isn't responding, and I hope for the world that he's still alive; otherwise I'm going to destroy it. I look at him and everything seems to be intact, until I look at his head and I notice blood coming out of it, and a lot of blood too. I panic and hope that everything is all right, but on closer inspection, it turns out that it's actually Sima Brak's degenerated right arm in his mouth, torn right from his body. I am relieved . . . and proud.

But feelings aside, I know now that Grasshead won't respond, regardless of why.

As I continue to push Grasshead so I can get back up, I see a shadow covering me. I look up to see who it is, and as much as I hoped it wouldn't be him, it was him.

Sima Brak stands tall above me with his degenerated right arm torn from the socket, now nothing but a bleeding hole. I sit against a rock while a massive tiger-lizard keeps me nailed to the ground with his weight. I relentlessly push Grasshead, but he doesn't even budge. He's too heavy, and I'm stuck here, reluctantly waiting for my doom.

For a moment, I raise my head. I look at Sima Brak, and he seems rather pissed. The muscles in his forehead nearly explode with anger as he frowns really hard. His hairless brows curve diagonally, nearly touching his nose from all that power he exerts. That ugly-ass grimace he's showing right now, full of his razor-sharp narrow teeth and every bit of his face shows fury and rage. A wrath waiting to relieve itself, and I am the victim.

As I keep staring at that grimace, waiting for what might happen, which is most likely my death, Sima Brak slightly twitches, with random spasms all over his body. His arms and face twitch in different directions. He seems to be losing control, as probably his anger got the better of him. He desperately collects himself, holding tight his body to remain in control. And then, just like that . . .

"RRRRRRRRRRRRRRRRRRRAAAAAAAAAAAAA!!" he lets out with all his fury.

The roar punctures my ear drums as it continues. It seems like it's taking forever as I await my death. My hearing grows weaker as it is replaced with tinnitus, and all I see is his open mouth as his saliva sprays me in the face. He roars endlessly, and I am helpless.

I guess this is the end of the line. Maybe I wasn't meant to be here after all. I should've stayed at home with my piece of shit family. Who knows, maybe I could've gotten somewhere if I stayed. Meh, it's not like I would get far there anyways. I guess either way I was doomed. At least in death I can find salvation. Yes . . . everything's over . . . and I can start anew in a different life . . . .

But as he roars, something happens: something swift moves through his neck.

Silence suddenly envelops the air. Sima Brak stops roaring, and his face assumes a dead expression. I still sit there, anchored by my own animal companion, trying to wonder what the hell just happened. And while I wonder, Sima Brak slowly falls.

His knees touch the ground, and his face suddenly starts to move. His face gradually assumes an expression. A smile slowly forms on his face, and he slowly closes his eyes. Weirdly enough, he seems happy, like he never had happiness his entire life . . . until now.

"Skama," he says in a relieved tone, almost happy.

Sima Brak stops falling; he stays on his knees. And as he stays like this, kneeling, I still try to figure out what happened. He completely stops moving, not even a single twitch, as if his body has been infused with liquid serenity, and he almost looks like a statue.

And then, all of a sudden, his body starts to evaporate, provoking my curiosity even more. Individual particles start to rise from his body. His body evaporates faster, as more and more particles further rise. As more particles rise, they no longer fill the air by themselves, as a purple mist evaporates from his body. The mist grows bigger and bigger, flowing in the air and rising to the sky, obscuring the sun and the clouds. It disperses in many directions, spreading even further until there is nothing left to see but the mist itself. And as the mist grows even bigger, Sima Brak's motionless body is consumed by it, hiding within it, and he didn't even move a single inch.

The mist is now very large, and I can't see anything but it. Weirdly enough, the mist starts to disperse, quickly so. The mist quickly disappears from my sight as it dissipates. I can once more see the skies from beyond a transparent wall of purple mist that is losing its opacity. Soon, the mist disappears completely and everything that was behind it is once more cleared. But still, I haven't a single clue what just happened.

And now, with the purple mist gone, I can look around once more. Exactly where Sima Brak stood before he turned into the fine mist was his head, seemingly decapitated with a clean cut at the neck, sitting upright on the ground, still with his eyes closed, but the smile gone. There is no blood or anything, but the clue to what caused this is just behind, and even more surprising than what happened to him.

Shin'ga'ti! Still alive, but barely standing. I watch him as he breathes hard and struggles to stand. He has a serious wound right at the side of his stomach from which he bleeds profusely.

"Holy shit, you're still alive!" I remark, surprised and shocked.

I look at him, and he seems like he's in dire need of assistance, but I can't imagine he'd die so easily, definitely not from a self-inflicted wound. I guess he isn't a coward after all.

But compliments aside, I realize what I must do. In a futile effort, I once again try to push an unconscious Grasshead off of me. As I expected, I can't. I just hope my legs are still receiving blood circulation.

Realizing my struggle, a wounded Shin'ga'ti limps over to me. He trips on the way, but quickly gets back up. As he gets closer to me, he grabs Grasshead and starts to pull. While I was just about to give up, I realize that in a joint effort, we might just be able to solve this situation. I push, and he pulls.

Luckily and surprisingly, Grasshead budges a bit, and I just might be able to get out. But in a second's notice, Shin'ga'ti bends forward over his agonizing wound. Regardless, he refuses to give in to the pain and continues to pull. Unfortunately, the pain only allows him to pull so much, as he screams in pain, pushing himself to the limit to free me. As he tries hard, screaming and pulling, I too push with all my might. Grasshead moves a bit, but not enough to completely get him off me. And as I realize that, I try to squeeze my way out of this mess. I move my legs, trying to slide under Grasshead's massive body. With each pull, I can feel my legs getting looser and looser. A final pull, and one leg is out. With one free leg, I use it to push myself against the ground while I push with one hand against Grasshead as I pull my trapped leg. Finally, as I exert all the might I have left, my trapped leg comes loose from under Grasshead, as the momentum I gathered sends me rolling backwards, but I get up immediately.

And with that, I rush over to Shin'ga'ti. I give him a shoulder to lean on, as he seems like he's about to fall to the ground. I just hope for him that he won't die.

"Man, you're gonna need some serious blood transfusion," I tell him cheerfully. "Unless your blood type is A, I can't really help ya."

Despite the mood I try to bring to the atmosphere, seeing as how all danger has been dealt with, Shin'ga'ti doesn't really seem to care for my jokes. It's understandable, considering the hole he has in his stomach. I guess the joke was out of place, but I'm in a good mood right now.

But as Shin'ga'ti leans on my shoulder, he starts to drop, pulling me down with his weight. I steadily let go of him, as he drops on one knee, resting, taking deep hard breaths. Besides, it's not like I am going to drag him across the canyon somewhere. I, as an outsider to this world, have no idea where I am, and he could die by the time we get somewhere. He is better off resting right now. Besides, we're missing some people. Where is . . . ?

"NEPH!!" I hear a soft voice in the distance yelling my name. "NEPH!!"

Just as I was about to think, "Where the hell she could be?" there she is, calling out my name.

I look over and I see Yomak Nayan in the distance, running towards me.

And as she continues to run, I start to walk to her. I gradually increase my speed, as I go from walking to running. And as she gets closer to me, I get a better view of her. Overall, she's fine and healthy, except for a loose right arm flapping in the air like a noodle, although no blood is coming out of it. She can't even lift it over the broken bones she has there, but I know she'll be fine . . . eventually.

As I reach her, I quickly embrace her, as nothing else comes to my mind but the satisfaction of seeing her all right.

"Aak," A slight and quick noise of pain comes from Yomak Nayan.

I quickly let go of her, seeing as she's quite in pain, and I'm only making it worse, even when it's against my intentions.

"Your arm!" I exclaim worriedly.

"It's OK, Neph," she tells me.

I think about how it can possibly be OK. It looks like the situation is pretty dire. Then again, they already discovered the formula to repair any injury. I guess it's only a matter of time until we get to a hospital before she dies, I guess. Not that it'll happen, but I think we'd best hurry. And then, after processing those thoughts of safety, I am reminded of what we just accomplished. And by extension, what the united clans have accomplished.

"It's over," I tell her, relieved.

She, in response, looks at me with those beautiful eyes I can't get enough of, which right now seem confused over my vague sentence.

"What is, Neph?" she asks me confused and curious.

"It's finally over," I continue, again in a vague way.

And yet, she still looks confused. I can't blame her, so instead I resort to showing her what I mean.

I move to the side, and I reveal before her what lies upright on the sand. Of course, it couldn't be anything else but Sima Brak's head.

I already knew it, but when she saw it, her eyes opened wide in surprise, as if she had already considered us dead by his hands.

"In all honesty, I thought we were done for," I tell her with some surprise. "But we actually managed to kill him."

I inhale deeply, and then I sigh, reminded of what I didn't manage to achieve. Or plainly put, what I've lost.

"I just wish it didn't have to come at the expense of those two," I say in sadness.

"Neph, we talked about this. It's part of the Natin way of life," she tells me in a gentle tone in an attempt to comfort me. "It's not your fault. The loss of life on the battlefield is inevitable."

I can understand what she tells me. But despite this, I can't wave away the feeling of failure I have and the responsibility I feel for their deaths. Like somehow I could've prevented it, but at the same time I couldn't have prevented it. I could've attempted to save them, but I couldn't because I was not strong enough to do so. Regardless, I think I should learn to accept the fact that I can't save everyone. Not even the greatest heroes can save everyone, but I should take this as a sign that I should become stronger, so that I can at least save someone from certain death. And once I do, I might find my place here, and I will be . . . accepted.

I try to cheer up from this feeling, so I can go from having a sad face to putting on a not-so-sad face. I haven't forgotten that Sima Brak's head is still sitting upright on the ground behind me, and that he can't stay like this forever. Someone will have to do something about it sooner or later.

I walk to it, and I pick it up by the solid spiky crystal stuff he has instead of hair. Holding it in one hand, I walk back to Yomak Nayan, and I present the head to her.

"Here, take it," I tell her.

She, at first, looks at me with confused eyes.

"Why?" she asks.

"This was your life's goal," I tell her. "He might not have died at your hands, but you helped the fight in killing him, and at least you can claim his head. I think it's only fair that you have it. If that's OK with you, bro?"

I turn my head around to look at Shin'ga'ti as I address him, and he looks like all he wants to do right now is take a really long nap. Out of sheer exhaustion, all he does is slowly nod his head as a gesture of approval. I guess being a big player doesn't really mean much to him. Go figure.

"I bet you'll be revered as a goddess when you get back home," I jokingly tell Yomak Nayan, paying attention to her once more. "I mean, it doesn't really mean much, cuz I already do it for you. Heh."

She didn't really seem to care much for the joke, as she seems to be deep in her thoughts as she stares at the disembodied head of the purple monster. I can't tell what she's thinking, or whether the subject is of sadness or of worry.

But regardless of what might have come through her mind, she just unexpectedly hands me the head, and all I do is stare into those beautiful ocean-blue eyes of hers while trying to understand what might have prompted her to give me back the head.

"I want you to take it," she tells me.

As she stills holds the head with her one hand that isn't broken, I still try to understand this.

"Aaaaand that is . . . why exactly?" I ask her wittily.

"You can use this to gain the trust of the Natin," she explains to me. "Everyone will think you killed him, and they will never see you as they did once, regardless of how tolerant they are to you."

The moment I heard her explanation and idea of how I should gain the acceptance of the Natin, I just smirked. I understand her good will, which most likely stems from her kind yet fierce personality, but that idea itself just sounds ludicrous.

"What's so funny?" she asks, confused, as she stares at me smirking.

"I can't take it," I tell her simply as I push the head back to her while she's still holding it. "You need to take it."

"Why?"

I put on a serious face, and I tell her with all seriousness, "The head might be used to fool the Natin, but I would also be fooling myself. What I've learned is that I'm far from where I want to be, and the achievement of killing Sima Brak wouldn't be able to bring me there faster. I need to work hard to get there and not search for shortcuts. It's like a friend once told me: shortcuts will bring you to your destination faster, but to your resolve slower. I just hope it's not too late."

"Wow . . . ," she exclaims, seemingly amazed while maintaining calmness. "That friend of yours must be really smart."

"He has a lot to offer. But we don't see each other anymore," I say with half a smirk.

Upon delivering this speech, I can see Yomak Nayan slightly smiling with a sparkle of admiration in her eyes, probably seeing me as more than just a goofball for the first time.

"I understand," she tells me gently. "I will keep the head."

And with that, she no longer holds the head in front of me, but instead keeps it to herself as she holds it by the spiky stuff with one hand.

But then, once again, she presents it to me.

"But I need you to hold this for a second," she tells me as I stare at the head.

I am confused, and it is quite apparent on my face. But . . . seeing as how it's just for "a second," I have no problem complying, as I take the head with both my hands from her, and hopefully I won't have to hold it for too long.

But after having taken the head off her hands, what she does next is reach into her pocket and take out her yopak'orim. She grabs the butt end of it with her teeth and then she twists it. After that, she presses the butt end twice.

A purple dimensional rift instantly appears and disappears before me.

"OH SHIT!!" I yell out in panic.

But what appears out of the rift was a Natin, no different than any other Natin, with a we'jei and whatnot and the tattoo that says what clan is he from, one which I have yet to learn the purpose of.

What a relief! For a second, I thought Sima Brak was still alive somehow.

"Kata nihikban?" he says, whatever that means.

But then, he looks at me, and he recognizes me as Neph Baker, the one seemingly referred to as the composer, and the only human currently in the Novaverse.

He seems confused, but then he looks around, and he sees Yomak Nayan. He then looks at what she might be holding, and he sees Sima Brak's decapitated head. He doesn't move, as he just stares at the head for a while. He's probably in shock, but on the exterior he seems to be holding himself together, as he stands still just looking at the head.

He then quickly turns his head around, and he sees my unconscious Grasshead lying against a rock, and Shin'ga'ti who is just sitting on the ground, as he can't stand up anymore over the pain.

Once more, he just stares, probably in shock and curious as to what the hell is going on, without any exterior signs that that is indeed the case. And as much as I respect his confusion, sooner or later, he will have to do his job.

"Hey!" I call his attention.

He looks at me.

"We are four injured. One hiphomoy and one in serious condition," I inform him. "Can you help us? Also, we have two dead."

He remains quiet in response. He seems to be assessing the situation in his head, staring at the ground. I guess this isn't the typical situation these guys have to deal with.

"Yes," he tells us after a while. "I will come back with reinforcements. This will be short."

And with that, he disappears into the purple dimensional rift, leaving us alone once more.

I'm just glad to know that this is all over, and that soon, we will be back at a safe location, away for a while from the scene of battle, until the next time we have to fight.

But until we wait for him to come back with his friends, I get closer to Yomak Nayan, and she gets closer to me. She leans on me, as the damage she sustained during the fight seems to be taking a toll on her right now, but not enough to make her fall. I embrace her, keeping her safe, and keeping her from falling. It's . . . nice to have someone to hold onto. It gives me a feeling of safety. A feeling that there is someone for me, as much as I am for them.

But the important thing is that everyone's going home now, and everything will be fine. Everyone . . . except two. And those two . . . I just can't get them out of my head.

CHAPTER XXX

A THOUSAND KNIVES . . . AND AN UNCERTAIN FUTURE

It's been two days since we killed Sima Brak. Everyone went their own way after we all came to the clan of Tarik, since it was the closest clan to where we were, according to Yomak Nayan. Everyone was hospitalized immediately after we arrived, except for Sa'ra and So'dong, who will eventually be cremated, much to my understanding. Unfortunately, I won't be able to pay my respects and attend the cremation. It would be nice to see how a Novaversian cremation works. I was also told that the Natin don't hold funerals, just cremations. Haven't been told the reason though. I'm sure I'll find that out in the future.

I also came to the hospital the first moment I arrived here. Stayed there for a day, then left. Turns out the only problem I had was a few broken ribs and a minor fracture on the vertebrae. No need for any patches or anything since my body took care of that by itself. But it was Grasshead who required more attention, whose entire left side of his ribcage was broken when he slammed against that rock. Luckily, all the doctors needed to do was to realign his ribs, and from there they should rebuild themselves. He currently has a cast around his chest which I will remove as soon as possible.

As for Yomak Nayan, she needed to stay there a little longer, as a completely destroyed arm is not something that can be taken care of in one day. More like two days, according to Novaversian standards. She should be coming out any time soon. She's still holding onto Sima Brak's head. She had it wrapped in her we'jei to hide it, saying something about wanting to keep it as a surprise when she gets back home and to reveal it when the right time comes. I hope she's not conspiring to have me take credit for his murder. I already told her she needs to do it herself, and I have no doubt she'll respect that.

As for the others, I saw some of them in the hospital, some walking and some still in the bed. Whether they've already left back home is beyond my knowledge; for all I care they can still be in the hospital. I mean, they're all OK, but I'm more concerned with myself right now and the people I know on a more personal level.

Speaking of which, So'krang came to visit me. He heard I was in the hospital, and took some time off to see how I was doing. It's a good thing too because I wouldn't know what in the hell to do once I was released from the hospital.

So turns out there's this kind of hotel called ronon'pani. These ronon'pani, roughly translated to "temporary house," is a kind of lodging where people check into after they're done with a mission. It provides a nice place to sleep while making preparations to go back home, and this is a REALLY nice place. The place here is kind of reminiscent to a five-star hotel. I was really surprised when I came into the room I am in now: this fancy king-sized bed, this really cooling AC, this huge tub. All this and I didn't even have to pay for it. The downside is that it only includes this much. Catering, recreation and the likes are not provided, since people only stay here long enough to relax after a mission and go home. But it's a good thing that So'krang came along and took care of everything. I don't think they would have allowed me to check in by myself since I don't have an official profile or whatever I'm supposed to have.

As for the torpadon that we captured in the last mission, he's currently in custody, kept somewhere in this clan in a safe and secure location. He's supposed to be put on the execution stage later today to be . . . well, executed. After all, the subject is delivered to the closest clan to where he was captured, and the execution method, as I was told, is pretty interesting: the condemned is placed in the center of the stage. Then, one by one, one member of the each of the families of the victims sticks a knife in the condemned's back. And once there's no place left for knives on the back, they start sticking them on the front. And once there's no place there, they start doing the same on the rest of the body. What happens when there's no place left on the body? I have no idea. But that's only the first part, since after everyone's done with the stabbing, the condemned is hung in the air by his arms as they are stretched out and is left to bleed to death. They call this form of execution . . . sianshin.

What really gets to me about this is that they call all the families of the fallen just to have them line up and stab that piece of crap. What if one of the families didn't want to participate? Actually, it doesn't really matter. The Natin get an A for creativity on this part.

As for me? I'm sitting here in my room in this ronon'pani, waiting for the execution to unfold so I can watch how it goes. Afterwards, I don't really know. Do what I always did since the moment I got here: stay in someone's house, and then go on a mission, trying to prove I'm this composer guy. The title doesn't really mean much to me, although the respect that comes with it does. But in truth, I just want a home where I have a purpose and for people to acknowledge me as one of their own, or at the very least to not ostracize me. Although I'm not sure how plausible that is anymore considering how things have gone up until now. I guess I'll just have to hope for the best.

As I continue to lie on the bed and ponder about the future with anxious thoughts, So'krang comes back to the room with our tirasartan.

I move from lying down on the bed to sitting on it, and as he sees me doing so, he throws me my tirasartan. Flawlessly, I catch it with one hand. I peel the paper wrapper at the top and I immediately start munching down on this Novaversian equivalent of the hamburger.

"Make haste," So'krang tells me seriously as he too munches down on his tirasartan. "The execution is imminent. You wouldn't want to miss it, would you?"

"Fuck no," I tell him clearly. "But I need to eat first. Wouldn't want to walk there with tirasartan all over my face."

"Dorn't worrry about irt. Your'll clean irt laterr," he says with his mouth full, typical of a Natin.

"What about Yomak Nayan?"

He swallows before answering, but I can see how he's eager to talk already.

"Don't worry, she'll meet us there," he says.

"You sure?" I ask.

He takes another bite from the tirasartan before answering.

"Absorlutelry. I made sure orf thart," he tells me, once again with his mouth full.

And I just stare at his stupid face and how he stuffs it full of tirasartan, talking with his mouth full like a child.

"Y'know . . . ," I say. "You might wanna try talking with your mouth EMPTY."

So'krang swallows before answering.

"I'll take your advice to consideration," he responds sarcastically.

And I just stare at him with disbelief at how it's not something to even consider. It's funny to think how badass he is during missions, but regresses to an eight-year-old when he allows himself. Then again, the Natin don't give a crap about table manners. From what I've seen, they've adopted a more libertine way of life, at least when it comes to food and itching, I guess. Everything else I have yet to learn.

But putting aside the Natin's crappy primitive behavior traits, I look around me and I keep thinking to myself what a nice room I have here. Would be a shame to leave it so fast, but I guess it'll have to come to end eventually, and I'll have to go to the way of life I've had from the moment I stepped foot in this world. At least I can come to a place like this again after a mission, but most likely it would be a different ronon'pani. I just hope they all have rooms as nice as these. I'm surprised I didn't get a chance to visit these places after all the previous missions I've been on. Then again, I was too busy making my presence in hospitals. I'll be sure to adjust that in the future.

"Y'know . . . ," I tell So'krang, "they coulda given us more than four days."

"Those are the rules, and they apply to everyone. Deal with it," So'krang tells me, just before taking another bite from his tirasartan. "Now do you warnt to reave? The execution is abourt to starrt any morment."

"Sure. Just . . . do me a favor: don't talk with your mouth full. K?"

So'krang swallows before answering.

"No promises," he tells me jokingly.

With that, we start to make our way to the area where the execution will take place, each with a tirasartan in hand. So'krang makes his way to the entrance of the building; as I reach the front door, I do one last thing before leaving.

"GRASSHEAD!" I call.

And from beyond the other side of the bed, where my sight cannot reach, Grasshead walks slowly to me, all patched up at the chest with that black cast. I'm reminded to refrain from riding him for a while, according to what the doctor said. Hopefully he will heal in no time, but right now I just hope he can move fast enough before the execution ends.

Ten minutes later, we finally arrive at the center of the forum where the execution will take place. This seems like a really big deal since there are a lot of people here. A lot of Tarik'ga especially, naturally since this is their clan, but there are also members from other clans.

I didn't notice this before, but the Tarik'ga seem to carry a lot of hair with them. But not just one strand of hair, but multiple strands of hair. There are strands of different colors, ranging from blonde to black to red, varying in length from very short to very long. There are strands that are tied together into a rope, and strands that are tied to throwing knives, and strands that are attached to all kinds of different materials and weaponry. I suppose this is how they like to fight, even though I have no idea where the hair comes in. I suppose I'll learn in the future, but right now, I want to see what happens to the torpadon.

Speaking of which, he's right there on the elevated stage in front of us all, on his knees, chained by his arm as it is stretched out so we can see all of him, while the other chain is embedded deep inside his arm socket, since that arm got torn off. If that isn't bad enough, not to mention what's going to happen to him next, his mouth and eyes are stitched shut with metal. It's agonizing just to look at, but I suppose that's what you get for messing with the Natin. He's struggling to free himself, pulling his arms in a constantly failing attempt to break loose from the chains, but the poles that are connected to the chains barely budge. He's also grunting a lot, but in all honesty he should use his remaining time to think of how he's going to die, rather than try the impossible and escape. After all, his death will be justice well served.

Everything seems like it's in place. There's a lot of people, the bad guy is chained up, so what are we waiting for? I know what I'm waiting for, and it's not for the execution to start.

"Where the fuck is Yomak Nayan?" I ask So'krang, who is just beside me. "Thought you said she's coming."

"She's probably just searching for us among the crowd," So'krang tells me calmly, not worried a single bit. "Don't worry, she'll come."

That's what he thinks, but I'm not so sure.

"NEPH!" I hear a soft voice calling me from the side.

I look to my side, and of course, it's Yomak Nayan, waving to me with the arm that isn't broken, while the other is completely wrapped in black cast as she runs to stand by my side.

"Speak of the devil," I jokingly say with a smirk as soon as she gets close.

Without even a single warning, she hugs me as she wraps her one loose arm around my neck. I just stare at the air in confusion with my arms down, as I don't know how to respond. I can't tell what her expression says as it is currently over my shoulder.

But eventually, she lets go, and I get to stare at her face once more. As usual, she's all smiles. Of course, I wouldn't want her to stop smiling. It brightens my day, even amidst the horror that will happen shortly.

"You're awfully gleeful today," I jokingly tell her.

"When am I not?" she responds with equal humor.

"Yeah . . . I guess you're right."

I look back to the stage to see if things are starting to unfold, but there's still no one there but the torpadon. I turn my attention back to Yomak Nayan.

"I'm just glad to see you're all right," I tell her calmly.

"Come on," she cheerfully replies. "Did you have any doubt?"

"No . . . not really."

Just then, I notice the crowd gradually become quiet. I wonder what the change is all about. I look at the stage, and there's finally someone standing there. I can't tell what his purpose on stage is, but his presence is a clear indication that the execution will start shortly.

Everybody looks ahead, paying full attention to the man at the stage. I see So'krang and Yomak Nayan doing the same as everyone, staring straight at where the stage is, putting aside our conversation as if I never existed. I do the same, seeing as how things are going to start.

Slowly and surely, the volume of the crowd reaches zero, and everyone is silent and still. The silence is only interrupted by the constant grunts of the torpadon and the clanking sounds of the chains whenever he tries to free himself.

But now, it looks like the guy on the stage is about to say something.

"Taiin Natin." His voice is loud and echoes through the crowd. "Itike dobi satra'nam'in sa nihir'satra mark'nen ka Tarik: Ojak'ga shin ka masak."

And with that, that man walks off the stage, walking to his left and going down a small staircase. I would expect some applause at this moment, but the crowd is weirdly quiet. To me, it's another display of their discipline and obedience, as no one lets out even a single word. I find it out of place and lacking of a rebellious spirit. Yet another thing I learned about the Natin. Then again, I'm just used to different customs.

Putting that aside, as the man leaves the stage, another man, apparently more important than the first one, walks up the same small staircase and right into the center of the stage.

This man didn't dress in any fancy manner to indicate that he was more important than the other. And in all honesty, he didn't need to, as a very familiar tattoo on his forehead pretty much gives his identity away. He didn't dress too differently from any other Natin, having a yellow we'jei and the casual rekarakib accompanied by the usual na'sho. Clearly he isn't much for fashion. But if he's a Tarik'ga like everyone else, then I can't see any hairs on him of any kind, although he does have two pouches on each side of his belt. Maybe that means something.

Additionally, I notice on the side of the stage a man leaning against a wall. He has his head down, staring at the floor. I can't tell from the distance, but I think he has his eyes closed, partially sleeping or something. His clothing didn't differ from a regular Natin, having a yellow we'jei and the casual black rekarakib. The more interesting feature about him are the strands of hair tied into bracelets around his right arm, which is covered in a very familiar tribal tattoo.

I think I know who these guys are.

But now the supposedly important man is about to give a speech or whatever. And judging by how serious he looks right now, it seems like it's going to be a dramatic speech.

"Taiin Natin," he says in a deep voice. "Itike dobi rononban'in terek sianshin ka Airatsmeka. marang Hidoban ka toma Natin an iteke hars, wen toma kin'karat pasaita'in. rang'ora, etiki prak'kea'in tang'ga, wen asaian'in eteke nihir, ikiya imra to nihir nen rang'ronon'ga, ikiya etiki ronon'rang'in na. rang'ora, keika terek anpa'in nota rang'wair tate'in an Airatsmeka. Dora etiki waraida, wen eteki seda. Dora sianshin hang'in!"

All of a sudden, the crowd cheers! Jumping and shaking their fists in the air. The combined voice of the massive crowd fills the void around it, as everyone can hear the excitement that unfolds right now.

But as the noise slowly subsides, a bunch of people line up near the staircase of the stage, each holding a knife in their hands. A lot of people actually. Seeing the events unfold, plus what I know of the execution, those people have to be the families of the fallen. Additionally, a man walks past all the families, walking up the stage and standing next to the torpadon. He wears a white we'jei and a black rekarakib. I have no idea who this guy is. Judging by the white we'jei, I suppose he could be a medic.

But now, everything is in place, and the execution officially starts.

A man first walks up on the stage. He approaches the back of the torpadon, and violently jabs a knife in his back. The torpadon grunts loudly beyond his stitched mouth. The man then walks off the stage.

Next, another man walks up on the stage. Same as the last one, he approaches the back of the torpadon and jabs a knife in his back. Yet again, the torpadon violently grunts beyond his stitched mouth. The man then walks off the stage.

This time, a woman walks up on the stage. She approaches the back of the torpadon and jabs a knife in his back. Again, the torpadon grunts in pain beyond his stitched mouth, but it seems like he's already getting used to it. The woman then walks off the stage.

This cycle repeats itself several times: someone walks up, stabs the torpadon, then leaves. In between the sequences, I stare around me. Everyone is so quiet and focused on the execution; no cheers, no nothing. Yomak Nayan and So'krang are also really into this thing. I'm thinking of talking to them during the execution, but they look like they don't want to be disturbed. I supposed I can try later.

Twenty minutes into the execution and the crowd is still huge, although I can't tell if anyone has left. When the next person to stab the torpadon approaches, he is suddenly halted by the man in white, who gestures him to wait. He then looks at the torpadon's back, and apparently he does some things to him. I can't really see what's going on because he's obscured by the torpadon, but I can see some green light emanating from there.

"The Okati'ga is now healing the Airatsmeka's wounds so he can withstand the entire process without dying," So'krang suddenly whispers to me.

I stare at So'krang, but he is still focused on the execution.

"Sheesh, that's . . . harsh," I sarcastically comment, almost out of empathy.

The Okati'ga, as he is referred to, finishes healing the wounds and returns to the sides, and the execution continues.

Thirty minutes into the execution, and it still goes on. More people stabbing over and over. I wonder when we get to the part where they stab him in the chest.

"How long do these things take?" I whisper to So'krang.

"Well it really depends on how many families are involved," So'krang whispers back to me.

"Is there an average?"

"Families or time?"

"Time."

"I guess . . . ninety minutes or something."

I understand that we're going to stay here for a while. I wonder if we have to stick around to the end of this.

Thirty-five minutes or so into the execution, and I notice that the crowd has become smaller, making it apparent that some don't have the patience to stay to the end of the execution.

"Well . . . ," Yomak Nayan suddenly says, "I'll be leaving now."

"That's it?" I ask her. "We plan on staying here a little longer. Sure you don't wanna stay with us?"

"I'm certain about it," she says in her bubbly way. "Besides, I'd rather spend time with you . . . alone."

"Quiet. People are listening."

"Nobody is listening."

She then puts both her hands on my chest, and without a single warning, swiftly kisses me on the lips. I'm shocked, and find myself oblivious as how to respond as I stare blankly into the air.

She then starts to move backwards as she still maintains eye contact with me. I can still see her smiling, but then she turns around and starts to move out of the crowd. But before she disappears from my sight, she turns back one more time to look at me, and waves goodbye like the good girl she is. Still recovering from the shock of that surprise kiss, I respond by waving back to her nonchalantly.

And with that, she leaves the crowd. Of course, this isn't the end of the relationship.

But suddenly, I feel a strong pat on my back.

"You got yourself a Karin'ga," So'krang says cheerfully. "You lucky son of a bitch."

"Christ, everyone keeps saying that," I say, mildly annoyed.

"Yes. And you should know why by now."

"Yes I do."

"Just make sure you don't forget where she lives."

"Don't worry. I'll never forget . . . ," I sigh for a moment, "unfortunately."

And with that, we return to focusing on the execution.

At this point, I've completely lost count, but I have to say we're like fifty minutes into this thing. The crowd has become even smaller, and we haven't even reached the part where they start stabbing the torpadon on the chest, let alone where they hang him in the air. The process just keeps repeating itself: people come in and stab the torpadon one after the other. Occasionally, the Okati'ga heals the wounds to prolong the torture, but that's it. I'm not one to stay so long for something so repetitive. Others might show more dedication, but not me. It's understandable since many Natin are patriots, so they are willing to stick with tradition until the end.

"So uh . . . ," I say indecisively, "you wanna leave already? This thing is really nice and all but . . . they're kinda overextending it."

"Well . . . ," So'krang replies, "I don't have a problem leaving. I've seen many executions, but wouldn't you want to stay and watch the end? There's still another phase to this."

"Nah. You already told me how it goes. Just the information is enough for now. Maybe another time I'll find the patience to stick to the end."

"Well in that case . . . ," he sighs for a moment. "Let's go."

I look at him, and he looks at me. A slight pause in our conversation.

"OK," I say calmly.

And with that, we turn around and start to leave the crowd, walking away from the stage as the grunts of the chained torpadon become weaker and weaker.

"You know . . . ," So'krang says as we continue to walk away from the scene of the execution. "Yo'na . . . she has a very strong identity."

"What does that mean?" I ask So'krang, confused about his comment.

"She is determined, ruthless in combat, unwilling to leave anyone alive, and that is the way that every warrior should behave. Yet she doesn't let her dedication to her role in society play a part in her everyday life; she presents herself as friendly and kind."

"I kinda figured that out myself. Is there something specific you're referring to? Cuz I'm not catchin' it."

"What I'm saying is that her personality played a crucial role during her komo'kea'ka. You see, if it wasn't for her strong attitude, then she might've been something else."

"I thought what determines which clan you go to only depends on your skills."

"I don't know how you got that idea; there's more than just skills that determines your future. Strength, personality, and uh . . . well . . . other stuff, I guess."

"Well, you didn't mention that the first time we talked about it."

"I can't always remember something exactly when you want me to."

We remain quiet for a while. I think for a bit about what So'krang told me about Yomak Nayan's personality being part of her power.

"Yomak Nayan . . . she . . . ," I sigh before continuing with my sentence, "she was pretty determined to avenge her mother. I saw it in her eyes. You shoulda been there. She was like a fuckin' psycho murderer or some shit."

"Like I said, it was her strong desire to avenge her mother that made her a Karin'ga. That's what I was referring to about her determination. I just hope she can find peace after you killed Sima Brak."

"Yeah, well . . . wait . . . she told you about that!?" I ask him, shocked that he knows.

"Well, of course," he says proudly. "After I presented myself as the composer's mentor, she was more than happy to share with me the details."

"Don't fancy yourself too much. You only got that role by default."

"Still the mentor."

I chuckle over that comment.

"But," I add, "in all honesty . . . I don't think I would want anyone else. Hell, who knows how it would end up with anyone else. Could be better, could be worse . . . but I think it's best not to find out."

"Well that's . . . ," he says, "nice to hear. Especially from you."

It's also nice to hear that from him. I didn't think I could actually compliment someone out of sincerity. Of course, right now . . . it's an exception. But I hope to make it more common and adjust my attitude the more I stay here . . . assuming I will stay here, that is. After everything that happened, all options should be taken with a grain of salt, especially since I feel like I've given the clanmistress all the reasons to send me back to the cage. In all honesty, I don't want that, because as far as I'm concerned, I have nowhere else to be but here, and that is what I want.

These thoughts induce worry in me over my uncertain future. I don't know what to expect now.

"So . . . ," I begin, trying to hide my anxiety, "how do you think the clanmistress is gonna respond? I feel like some random shithead you confused for the composer."

"You needn't worry about the clanmistress," So'krang assures me, seemingly unaware of my concern for the future. "She might've unintentionally led you to believe that you have little to no opportunity to prove yourself, but you're not even close to leaving here. Besides, you avoided death many times now, and that is indication enough that you have a purpose here. Maybe the Gangra are trying to tell us something."

"Yeah, but . . . y'know . . . I'm not up to par with your level. Your strength, I mean; the Natin are fucking strong. I'm pretty certain a Natin could easily beat the shit out of three gangsters in a random alleyway. But me . . . you guys are way above my league, and I don't know if I have what it takes to keep up with you guys."

"What did I just say?"

"Yeah but . . . ," I halt in my place, and I stare at So'krang, who halts too. "Sima Brak nearly killed me!"

"And you survived!

"And I nearly died before that too!"

"And you survived!"

"I WAS NEARLY POISONED TO DEATH!"

"AND YOU SURVIVED!"

And then we just remain quiet, standing still and staring at each other blankly. So'krang made his point very clearly, yet why do I still have a hard time having faith in myself? It's a question that I have no answer to.

I sigh.

"Don't you see!?" So'krang tells me tensely, while putting his hands on my shoulders and looking me deep in the eye. "You survived because you're something special. A mere heranga wouldn't be able take all that damage and survive. You punched the Airatsmeka into oblivion, and you fought valiantly. Need I remind you how you healed a torn spinal cord in one week? Something that would've taken anyone else six weeks!"

I don't say anything. I just heed his words. So'krang also becomes silent after that speech. Apparently, he has nothing more to say. He doesn't need to. He already made his point clear, but I still have doubt in myself for some reason.

"Neph," he tells me after calming down. "Have faith in yourself. You are here right now, and you're not going anywhere whether you're the composer or not. Because the only place you're going after here is the afterlife."

"The clanmistress would beg to differ."

"An'a isn't going to kick you out so fast. So while you're still here, I suggest you work hard to stay this way . . . so that you may never have to go back to the cage."

Again, silence. I just listen to him. His words seem deep and caring, as if he's the only person in this world that actually thinks I have a purpose here.

"Afterlife, huh?" I say with a smirk on my face. "Well then, I hope it's not coming any time soon."

Then I start to laugh. Then So'krang starts to laugh, and before we know it, we both laugh out loud with our heads in the sky and for all to hear. Cheerfully and gleefully as if we have been friends since the age of zero.

"I can see you're still in a good mood," So'krang says in between his laughter.

"I'm NEVER in a good mood," I respond in between my laughter.

And with that, we continue to laugh. It feels like the laughter is never going to stop.

But eventually, we calm down, and we return to a calm, casual mood.

"Do you want to go home now?" So'krang says as he starts to walk. "Ka'ka'pan made morsh for the first time. Can't wait to taste it."

"This morsh thing . . . ," I ask as I walk beside him. "Is it good?"

"It's a murdermouth!"

"Is that a good thing?"

"Yes!"

And with that, we continue to walk. I care not for where we are going, even though I know for a fact that we're going to So'krang's house.

I am concerned no more with what awaits me in this world. What future waits for me as I continue to discover more about my purpose here? I still have doubts that I might be the composer, but So'krang's got a point. No mere human would have been able to pull all that off. Maybe I do have a place here, even if I'm not the composer. I always believed that the stork got the wrong address, and I might just find out in the end that that is indeed the case.

I have so much to discover; I have so much to find out. I need to stay here and work hard to know what these things are. To find those answers that I seek. But when . . . when will the moment come that I am truly, fully satisfied with my life and my new home?

Only time will tell.

About the Author

Al Romano studied philosophy, video game design and screenwriting from various academies. He always strives to discover new things, but never manages to find them, which is what led him to write his debut novel. due to his experience with video games, he believes he can present works of fiction from a different perspective that people are not familiar with.

Made in the USA
Middletown, DE
10 September 2019